The
Foreigner

Early Canadian Literature Series

The Early Canadian Literature Series returns to print rare texts deserving restoration to the canon of Canadian texts in English. Including novels, periodical pieces, memoirs, and creative non-fiction, the series showcases texts by Indigenous peoples and immigrants from a range of ancestral, language, and religious origins. Each volume includes an afterword by a prominent scholar providing new interpretations for all readers.

Series Editor: Benjamin Lefebvre

Series Advisory Board:
Andrea Cabajsky, Département d'anglais, Université de Moncton
Carole Gerson, Department of English, Simon Fraser University
Cynthia Sugars, Department of English, University of Ottawa

For more information please contact:

Lisa Quinn
Acquisitions Editor
Wilfrid Laurier University Press
75 University Avenue West
Waterloo, ON N2L 3C5
Canada

Phone: 519.884.0710 ext. 2843
Fax: 519.725.1399
Email: quinn@press.wlu.ca

The Foreigner

A Tale of Saskatchewan

Ralph Connor

Afterword by Daniel Coleman

Early Canadian Literature

Wilfrid Laurier University Press acknowledges the financial support of the Government of Canada through its Book Publishing Industry Development Program for our publishing activities.

Library and Archives Canada Cataloguing in Publication

Connor, Ralph, author
    The foreigner : a tale of Saskatchewan / Ralph Connor.

(Early Canadian literature series)
Reprint. Originally published in 1909.
Issued in print and electronic formats.
ISBN 978-1-55458-944-9 (pbk.).—ISBN 978-1-55458-945-6 (pdf).—
ISBN 978-1-55458-946-3 (epub).

    I. Title. II. Series: Early Canadian literature series

| PS8463.O58F6 2014 | C813'.52 | C2014-900849-X | C2014-900850-3 |

Cover design and text design by Blakeley Words+Pictures. Cover image: *Rev. Dr. Wilson and "Ralph Connor" [pseudonym for Rev. Charles William Gordon, Canadian clergyman and novelist], author and lecturer* (detail), 1917. Photo by Stuart Thomson, from Stuart Thomson fonds, City of Vancouver Archives; item CVA 99-578.

Every reasonable effort has been made to acquire permission for copyright material used in this text, and to acknowledge all such indebtedness accurately. Any errors and omissions called to the publisher's attention will be corrected in future printings.

This book is printed on FSC recycled paper and is certified Ecologo. It is made from 100% post-consumer fibre, processed chlorine free, and manufactured using biogas energy.

Printed in Canada.

Contents

Series Editor's Preface

Charles W. Gordon was born in Glengarry County, Canada West (now Ontario), on 13 September 1860, the son of Scottish immigrants. Educated at the University of Toronto, Knox College, and the University of Edinburgh, he was ordained as a Presbyterian minister in 1890 and became Doctor of Divinity in 1906. He worked as a missionary in mining villages and lumber camps in Banff, Alberta, before becoming the minister of St. Stephen's Presbyterian Church in Winnipeg in 1894. He also served as a chaplain overseas during the First World War. As Presbyterian moderator, a post to which he was elected in 1921, he moved his own congregation toward the union of Presbyterian, Methodist, and Congregationalist churches that formed, in 1925, the United Church of Canada. Married to Helen Skinner King in 1899, with whom he had one son and six daughters, he died in Winnipeg on 31 October 1937. His memoir, *Postscript to Adventure*, appeared posthumously in 1938.

As Ralph Connor, he began writing fictional sketches to raise funds for his missionary work in Western Canada, collected as *Black Rock: A Tale of the Selkirks* (1898), which was an immediate success in Canada and the United States. It marked the first of more than thirty books that made him an internationally bestselling author, including *The Sky Pilot: A Tale of the Foothills* (1899), *The Man from Glengarry: A Tale*

vii

of the Ottawa (1901), and *Glengarry School Days: A Story of Early Days in Glengarry* (1902). He was one of the most widely read Canadian authors of his generation—his first three books alone sold "well over five million" copies (Roper, Beharriell, and Schieder 336)—and as the entry on Connor in *Encyclopedia of Literature in Canada* notes, "His enthusiasts admired his fast pacing, melodramatic plots, happy resolutions, and espousal of conventional gender roles: good men are heroic, the West is a cauldron of social testing, and successful men are those whose 'muscular Christianity' reforms the wicked both by counsel and by example" (231). But his popularity started to wane in the period immediately following the First World War, and few of his books have continued to be reprinted since his death. As Judith Skelton Grant observes in *The Oxford Companion to Canadian Literature* (1983), "his characters now seem one-sided, his plots melodramatic, and his Christianity oversimplified" (307).

First published in 1909, *The Foreigner: A Tale of Saskatchewan* contains many of the elements of a typical Connor novel: an action-packed plot, lively characterization, explicit links between physical courage and moral courage, and an adherence to Christian uplift. Through the story of young Eastern European immigrant Kalman Kalmar, the novel also tells a larger story about a particular form of male maturation and cultural assimilation that recurs in his popular tales about the Canadian west. Although scholars have referred to this novel as likely "the first fiction to be really concerned with the relation of the land and the people who come into it," one that "dramatized the problems of immigration" (Roper, Schieder, and Beharriell 311), Ruth McKenzie noted in 1961 that the novel's "attempt to penetrate the problems of the immigrant" is "only partially successful," given that Connor, approaching fiction as a missionary, "wishes to convert the immigrant, not to accept him as he is" (24). In fact, when *The Foreigner* was considered for inclusion in the Social History of Canada series published by University of Toronto Press in the 1970s, the text was deemed worthy of reissue not because of its literary quality but because it fit the series mandate of "reprinting important texts from Canada's past that had significance for the bourgeoning field of Canadian social history" (Marshall 202). The project was abandoned because Connor's son objected to an introduction that interpreted Connor as having "an 'imperialist, middle class, Anglo-Saxon approach to social problems in the West'" (qtd. in Marshall 202). Plans to include *The Foreigner* in McClelland and Stewart's prestigious New Canadian Library were also abandoned (Friskney 207). The novel's vision of a culturally assimilated Canada seem even more troubling today, but as Daniel Coleman notes in his afterword to this edition, Connor's story still has much to offer twenty-first-century readers: as Coleman suggests, the novel urges us to "read *for* difference," and the way it raises and solves the "problem" of immigration continues to circulate under new guises.

This Early Canadian Literature edition of *The Foreigner* contains the complete text of Connor's novel, originally published by the Westminster Company of Toronto in 1909; it was also serialized in the Montreal farm paper *The Family Herald and Weekly Star*. An American edition, using the same plates, was published in New York by the George H. Doran Company, which sublicensed a cheaper reprint edition to Grosset and Dunlap. A British edition, minus Connor's preface, appeared as *The Settler: A Tale of Saskatchewan* from London publisher Hodder and Stoughton. This edition silently corrects obvious typographical errors but retains outdated conventions of spelling, hyphenation, capitalization, and syntax. As a product of an earlier time, this novel contains terminology and attitudes that are incompatible with the ways in which Canada is imagined in the twenty-first century. The reprinting of this novel does not signal an endorsement of those views but suggests that there is much to learn about a vision of Canada and its future that proved so appealing to readers of a century ago.

BENJAMIN LEFEBVRE

Works Cited

Connor, Ralph. "The Foreigner." *Family Herald and Weekly Star* 9 Mar. 1910: 5; 16 Mar. 1910: 5; 23 Mar. 1910: 5; 30 Mar. 1910: 4; 6 Apr. 1910: 4; 13 Apr. 1910: 4; 20 Apr. 1910: 4–5; 27 Apr. 1910: 4–5; 4 May 1910: 4–5. Print.

"Connor, Ralph (Charles William Gordon)." *Encyclopedia of Literature in Canada*. Ed. William H. New. Toronto: U of Toronto P, 2002. 231. Print.

Friskney, Janet B. *New Canadian Library: The Ross–McClelland Years 1952–1978*. Toronto: U of Toronto P, 2007. Print.

Grant, Judith Skelton. "Gordon, Charles William." *The Oxford Companion to Canadian Literature*. Ed. William Toye. Toronto: Oxford UP, 1983. 306–08. Print.

Klinck, Carl F., ed. *Literary History of Canada: Canadian Literature in English*. 2nd ed. Vol. 1. 1976. Toronto: U of Toronto P, 1977. Print.

Lennox, John. "Charles W. Gordon ['Ralph Connor'] and His Works." *Canadian Writers and Their Works: Fiction Series*. Vol. 3. Ed. Robert Lecker, Jack David, and Ellen Quigley. Toronto: ECW, 1988. 103–59. Print.

Marshall, David B. "'I Thank God . . . That I Am Proud of My Boy': Fatherhood and Religion in the Gordon Family." *Essays in Honour of Michael Bliss: Figuring the Social*. Ed. E.A. Heaman, Alison Li, and Shelly McKellar. Toronto: U of Toronto P, 2008. 177–210. Print.

McKenzie, Ruth. "Life in a New Land: Notes on the Immigrant Theme in Canadian Fiction." *Canadian Literature* 7 (1961): 24–33. Print.

Roper, Gordon, S. Ross Beharriell, and Rupert Schieder. "Writers of Fiction 1880–1920." Klinck 327–53.

Roper, Gordon, Rupert Schieder, and S. Ross Beharriell. "The Kinds of Fiction 1880–1920." Klinck 298–326.

The
Foreigner

Contents

Preface

In Western Canada there is to be seen to-day that most fascinating of all human phenomena, the making of a nation. Out of breeds diverse in traditions, in ideals, in speech, and in manner of life, Saxon and Slav, Teuton, Celt and Gaul, one people is being made. The blood strains of great races will mingle in the blood of a race greater than the greatest of them all.

It would be our wisdom to grip these peoples to us with living hooks of justice and charity till all lines of national cleavage disappear, and in the Entity of our Canadian national life, and in the Unity of our world-wide Empire, we fuse into a people whose strength will endure the slow shock of time for the honour of our name, for the good of mankind, and for the glory of Almighty God.

C.W.G.
Winnipeg, Canada, 1909.

Chapter I

The City on the Plain

Not far from the centre of the American Continent, midway between the oceans east and west, midway between the Gulf and the Arctic Sea, on the rim of a plain, snow swept in winter, flower decked in summer, but, whether in winter or in summer, beautiful in its sunlit glory, stands Winnipeg, the cosmopolitan capital of the last of the Anglo-Saxon Empires,— Winnipeg, City of the Plain, which from the eyes of the world cannot be hid. Miles away, secure in her sea-girt isle, is old London, port of all seas; miles away, breasting the beat of the Atlantic, sits New York, capital of the New World, and mart of the world, Old and New; far away to the west lie the mighty cities of the Orient, Peking and Hong Kong, Tokio and Yokohama; and fair across the highway of the world's commerce sits Winnipeg, Empress of the Prairies. Her Trans-Continental railways thrust themselves in every direction,—south into the American Republic, east to the ports of the Atlantic, west to the Pacific, and north to the Great Inland Sea.

To her gates and to her deep-soiled tributary prairies she draws from all lands peoples of all tribes and tongues, smitten with two great race passions, the lust for liberty, and the lust for land.

By hundreds and tens of hundreds they stream in and through this hospitable city, Saxon and Celt and Slav, each eager on his own quest, each paying his toll to the new land as he comes and goes, for good or for ill, but whether more for good than for ill only God knows.

A hundred years ago, where now stands the thronging city, stood the lonely trading-post of The Honourable, The Hudson's Bay Company. To this post in their birch bark canoes came the half-breed trapper and the Indian hunter, with their priceless bales of furs to be bartered for blankets and beads, for pemmican and bacon, for powder and ball, and for the thousand and one articles of commerce that piled the store shelves from cellar to roof.

Fifty years ago, about the lonely post a little settlement had gathered—a band of sturdy Scots. Those dour and doughty pioneers of peoples had planted on the Red River their homes upon their little "strip" farms—a rampart of civilization against the wide, wild prairie, the home of the buffalo, and camp ground of the hunters of the plain.

Twenty-five years ago, in the early eighties, a little city had fairly dug its roots into the black soil, refusing to be swept away by that cyclone of financial frenzy known over the Continent as the "boom of '81," and holding on with abundant courage and invincible hope, had gathered to itself what of strength it could, until by 1884 it had come to assume an appearance of enduring solidity. Hitherto accessible from the world by the river and the railroad from the south, in this year the city began to cast eager eyes eastward, and to listen for the rumble of the first trans-continental train, which was to bind the Provinces of Canada into a Dominion, and make Winnipeg into one of the cities of the world. Trade by the river died, but meantime the railway from the south kept pouring in a steady stream of immigration, which distributed itself according to its character and in obedience to the laws of affinity, the French Canadian finding a congenial home across the Red River in old St. Boniface, while his English-speaking fellow-citizen, careless of the limits of nationality, ranged whither his fancy called him. With these, at first in small and then in larger groups, from Central and South Eastern Europe, came people strange in costume and in speech; and holding close by one another as if in terror of the perils and the loneliness of the unknown land, they segregated into colonies tight knit by ties of blood and common tongue.

Already, close to the railway tracks and in the more unfashionable northern section of the little city, a huddling cluster of little black shacks gave such a colony shelter. With a sprinkling of Germans, Italians and Swiss, it was almost solidly Slav. Slavs of all varieties from all provinces and speaking all dialects were there to be found: Slavs from Little Russia and from Great Russia, the alert Polak, the heavy Croatian, the haughty Magyar, and occasionally the stalwart Dalmatian from the Adriatic, in speech mostly Ruthenian, in religion orthodox Greek Catholic or Uniat and Roman Catholic. By their non-discriminating Anglo-Saxon fellow-citizens they are called Galicians, or by the unlearned, with an echo of Paul's Epistle in their minds, "Galatians." There they pack together in their little shacks of boards and tar-paper, with pent roofs of old tobacco tins or of slabs or of that same useful but unsightly tar-paper, crowding each other in close irregular groups as if the whole wide prairie were not there inviting them. From the number of their huts they seem a colony of no great size, but the census taker, counting ten or twenty to a hut, is surprised to find them run up into hundreds. During the summer months they are found far away in the colonies of their kinsfolk, here and there planted upon the prairie, or out in gangs where new lines of railway are in construction, the joy of the contractor's heart, glad to exchange their steady, uncomplaining toil for the uncertain, spasmodic labour of their English-speaking rivals. But winter finds them once more crowding back into the little black shacks in the foreign quarter of the city, drawn thither by their traditionary social instincts, or driven by economic necessities. All they ask is bed space on the floor or, for a higher price, on the home-made bunks that line the walls, and a woman to cook the food they bring to her; or, failing such a happy arrangement, a stove on which they may boil their varied stews of beans or barley, beets or rice or cabbage, with such scraps of pork or beef from the neck or flank as they can beg or buy at low price from the slaughter houses, but ever with the inevitable seasoning of garlic, lacking which no Galician dish is palatable. Fortunate indeed is the owner of a shack, who, devoid of hygienic scruples and disdainful of city sanitary laws, reaps a rich harvest from his fellow-countrymen, who herd together under his pent roof. Here and there a house surrendered by its former Anglo-Saxon owner to the "Polak" invasion, falls into the hands of an enterprising foreigner, and becomes to the happy possessor a veritable gold mine.

Such a house had come into the possession of Paulina Koval. Three years ago, with two children she had come to the city, and to the surprise of her neighbours who had travelled with her from Hungary, had purchased this house, which the owner was only too glad to sell. How the slow-witted Paulina had managed so clever a transaction no one quite understood, but every one knew that in the deal Rosenblatt, financial agent to the foreign colony, had lent his shrewd assistance. Rosenblatt had known Paulina in the home land, and on her arrival in the new country had hastened to proffer his good offices, arranging the purchase of her house and guiding her, not only in financial matters, but in things domestic as well. It was due to Rosenblatt that the little cottage became the most populous dwelling in the colony. It was his genius that had turned the cellar, with its mud floor, into a dormitory capable of giving bed space to twenty or twenty-five Galicians, and still left room for the tin stove on which to cook their stews. Upon his advice, too, the partitions by which the cottage had been divided into kitchen, parlour, and bed rooms, were with one exception removed as unnecessary and interfering unduly with the most economic use of valuable floor space. Upon the floor of the main room, some sixteen feet by twelve, under Rosenblatt's manipulation, twenty boarders regularly spread their blankets, and were it not for the space demanded by the stove and the door, whose presence he deeply regretted, this ingenious manipulator could have provided for some fifteen additional beds. Beyond the partition, which as a concession to Rosenblatt's finer sensibilities was allowed to remain, was Paulina's boudoir, eight feet by twelve, where she and her two children occupied a roomy bed in one corner. In the original plan of the cottage four feet had been taken from this boudoir for closet purposes, which closet now served as a store room for Paulina's superfluous and altogether wonderful wardrobe.

After a few weeks' experiment, Rosenblatt, under pressure of an exuberant hospitality, sought to persuade Paulina that, at the sacrifice of some comfort and at the expense of a certain degree of privacy, the unoccupied floor space of her boudoir might be placed at the disposal of a selected number of her countrymen, who for the additional comfort thus secured, this room being less exposed to the biting wind from the door, would not object to pay a higher price. Against this arrangement poor Paulina made feeble protest, not so much on her own account as for the sake of the children.

"Children!" cried Rosenblatt. "What are they to you? They are not your children."

"No, they are not my children, but they are my man's, and I must keep them for him. He would not like men to sleep in the same room with us."

"What can harm them here? I will come myself and be their protector," cried the chivalrous Rosenblatt. "And see, here is the very thing! We will make for them a bed in this snug little closet. It is most fortunate, and they will be quite comfortable."

Still in Paulina's slow-moving mind lingered some doubt as to the propriety of the suggested arrangement. "But why should men come in here? I do not need the money. My man will send money every month."

"Ah!" cried the alert and startled Rosenblatt, "every month! Ah! very good! But this house, you will remember, is not all paid for, and those English people are terrible with their laws. Oh, truly terrible!"

continued the solicitous agent. "They would turn you and your children out into the snow. Ah, what a struggle I had only last month with them!"

The mere memory of that experience sent a shudder of horror through Rosenblatt's substantial frame, so that Paulina hastened to surrender, and soon Rosenblatt with three of his patrons, selected for their more gentle manners and for their ability to pay, were installed as night lodgers in the inner room at the rate of five dollars per month. This rate he considered as extremely reasonable, considering that those of the outer room paid three dollars, while for the luxury of the cellar accommodation two dollars was the rate.

Chapter II

Where East Meets West

The considerate thoughtfulness of Rosenblatt relieved Paulina of the necessity of collecting these monthly dues, to her great joy, for it was far beyond her mental capacity to compute, first in Galician and then in Canadian money, the amount that each should pay; and besides, as Rosenblatt was careful to point out, how could she deal with defaulters, who, after accumulating a serious indebtedness, might roll up their blankets and without a word of warning fade away into the winter night? Indeed, with all her agent's care, it not unfrequently happened that a lodger, securing a job in one of the cordwood camps, would disappear, leaving behind him only his empty space upon the floor and his debt upon the books, which Rosenblatt kept with scrupulous care. Occasionally it happened, however, that, as in all bookkeeping, a mistake would creep in. This was unfortunately the case with young Jacob Wassyl's account, of whose perfidy Paulina made loud complaints to his friends, who straightway remonstrated with Jacob upon his return from the camp. It was then that Jacob's indignant protestations caused an examination of Rosenblatt's books, whereupon that gentleman laboured with great diligence to make abundantly clear to all how the obliteration of a single letter had led to the mistake. It was a striking testimony to his fine sense of honour that Rosenblatt insisted that Jacob, Paulina, and indeed the whole company, should make the fullest investigation of his books and satisfy themselves of his unimpeachable integrity. In a private interview with Paulina, however, his rage passed all bounds, and it was only Paulina's tearful entreaties that induced him to continue to act as her agent, and not even her tears had moved him had not Paulina solemnly sworn that never again would she allow her blundering crudity to insert itself into the delicate finesse of Rosenblatt's financial operations. Thenceforward all went harmoniously enough, Paulina toiling with unremitting diligence at her daily tasks, so that she might make the monthly payments upon her house, and meet the rapacious demands of those terrible English people, with their taxes and interest and legal exactions, which Rosenblatt, with meritorious meekness, sought to satisfy. So engrossed, indeed, was that excellent gentleman in this service that he could hardly find time to give suitable over-sight to his own building operations, in which, by the erection of shack after shack, he sought to meet the ever growing demands of the foreign colony.

Before a year had gone it caused Rosenblatt no small annoyance that while he was thus struggling to keep pace with the demands upon his time and energy, Paulina, with lamentable lack of consideration, should find it necessary to pause in her scrubbing, washing, and baking, long enough to give birth to a fine healthy boy. Paulina's need brought her help and a friend in the person of Mrs. Fitzpatrick, who lived a few doors away in the only house that had been able to resist the Galician invasion. It had not escaped Mrs. Fitzpatrick's eye nor her kindly heart, as Paulina moved in and out about her duties, that she would ere long pass into that mysterious valley of life and death where a woman needs a woman's help; and so when the hour came, Mrs. Fitzpatrick, with fine contempt of "haythen" skill and efficiency, came upon the scene and took command. It took her only a few moments to clear from the house the men who with stolid indifference to the sacred rights of privacy due to the event were lounging about. Swinging the broom which she had brought with her, she almost literally swept them forth, flinging their belongings out into the snow. Not even Rosenblatt, who lingered about, did she suffer to remain.

"Y're wife will not be nadin' ye, I'm thinkin', for a while. Ye can just wait till I can bring ye wurrd av y're babby," she said, pushing him, not unkindly, from the room.

Rosenblatt, whose knowledge of English was sufficient to enable him to catch her meaning, began a vigorous protest:

"Eet ees not my woman," he exclaimed.

"Eat, is it!" replied Mrs. Fitzpatrick, taking him up sharply. "Indade ye can eat where ye can get it. Faith, it's a man ye are, sure enough, that can niver forget y're stomach! An' y're wife comin' till her sorrow!"

"Eet ees not my—" stormily began Rosenblatt.

"Out wid ye," cried Mrs. Fitzpatrick, impatiently waving her big red hands before his face. "Howly Mother! It's the wurrld's wonder how a dacent woman cud put up wid ye!"

And leaving him in sputtering rage, she turned to her duty, aiding, with gentle touch and tender though meaningless words, her sister woman through her hour of anguish.

In three days Paulina was again in her place and at her work, and within a week her household was re-established in its normal condition. The baby, rolled up in an old quilt and laid upon her bed, received little attention except when the pangs of hunger wrung lusty protests from his vigorous lungs, and had it not been for Mrs. Fitzpatrick's frequent visits, the unwelcome little human atom would have fared badly enough. For the first two weeks of its life the motherly-hearted Irish woman gave an hour every day to the bathing and dressing of the babe, while Irma, the little girl of Paulina's household, watched in wide-eyed wonder and delight; watched to such purpose, indeed, that before the two weeks had gone Mrs. Fitzpatrick felt that to the little girl's eager and capable hands the baby might safely be entrusted.

"It's the ould-fashioned little thing she is," she confided to her husband, Timothy. "Tin years, an' she has more sinse in the hair outside av her head than that woman has in the brains inside av hers. It's aisy seen she's no mother of hers—ye can niver get canary burrds from owls' eggs. And the strength of her," she continued, to the admiring and sympathetic Timothy, "wid her white face and her burnin' brown eyes!"

And so it came that every day, no matter to what depths the thermometer might fall, the little white-faced, white-haired Russian girl with the "burnin'" brown eyes brought Paulina's baby to be inspected by Mrs. Fitzpatrick's critical eye. Before a year had passed Irma had won an assured place in the admiration and affection of not only Mrs. Fitzpatrick, but of her husband, Timothy, as well.

But of Paulina the same could not be said, for with the passing months she steadily descended in the scale of Mrs. Fitzpatrick's regard. Paulina was undoubtedly slovenly. Her attempts at housekeeping—if housekeeping it could be called—were utterly contemptible in the eyes of Mrs. Fitzpatrick. These defects, however, might have been pardoned, and with patience and perseverance might have been removed, but there were conditions in Paulina's domestic relations that Mrs. Fitzpatrick could not forgive. The economic arrangements which turned Paulina's room into a public dormitory were abhorrent to the Irish woman's sense of decency. Often had she turned the full tide of her voluble invective upon Paulina, who, though conscious that all was not well—for no one could mistake the flash of Mrs. Fitzpatrick's eye nor the stridency of her voice—received Mrs. Fitzpatrick's indignant criticism with a patient smile. Mrs. Fitzpatrick, despairing of success in her efforts with Paulina, called in the aid of Anka Kusmuk, who, as domestic in the New West Hotel where Mrs. Fitzpatrick served as charwoman two days in the week, had become more or less expert in the colloquial English of her environment. Together they laboured with Paulina, but with little effect. She was quite unmoved, because quite unconscious, of moral shock. It disturbed Mrs. Fitzpatrick not a little to discover during the progress of her missionary labours that even Anka, of whose goodness she was thoroughly assured, did not appear to share her horror of Paulina's moral condition. It was the East meeting the West, the Slav facing the Anglo-Saxon. Between their points of view stretched generations of moral development. It was not a question of absolute moral character so much as a question of moral standards. The vastness of this distinction in standards was beginning to dawn upon Mrs. Fitzpatrick, and she was prepared to view Paulina's insensibility to moral distinctions in a more lenient light, when a new idea suddenly struck her:

"But y're man; how does he stand it? Tell me that."

The two Galician women gazed at each other in silence. At length Anka replied with manifest reluctance:

"She got no man here. Her man in Russia."

"What!" exclaimed Mrs. Fitzpatrick in a terrible voice. "An' do ye mane to say! An' that Rosenblatt—is he not her husband? Howly Mother of God," she continued in an awed tone of voice, "an' is this the woman I've been havin' to do wid!"

The wrath, the scorn, the repulsion in her eyes, her face, her whole attitude, revealed to the unhappy Paulina what no words could have conveyed. Under her sallow skin the red blood of shame slowly mounted. At that moment she saw herself and her life as never before. The wrathful scorn of this indignant woman pierced like a lightning bolt to the depths of her sluggish moral sense and awakened it to new vitality. For a few moments she stood silent and with face aflame, and then, turning slowly, passed into her house. It was the beginning of Paulina's redemption.

Chapter III

The Marriage of Anka

T he withdrawing of Mrs. Fitzpatrick from Paulina's life meant a serious diminution in interest for the unhappy Paulina, but with the characteristic uncomplaining patience of her race she plodded on with the daily routine at washing, baking, cleaning, mending, that filled up her days. There was no break in the unvarying monotony of her existence. She gave what care she could to the two children that had been entrusted to her keeping, and to her baby. It was well for her that Irma, whose devotion to the infant became an absorbing passion, developed a rare skill in the care of the child, and it was well for them all that the ban placed by Mrs. Fitzpatrick upon Paulina's house was withdrawn as far as Irma and the baby were concerned, for every day the little maid presented her charge to the wise and watchful scrutiny of Mrs. Fitzpatrick.

The last days of 1884, however, brought an event that cast a glow of colour over the life of Paulina and the whole foreign colony. This event was none other than the marriage of Anka Kusmuk and Jacob Wassyl, Paulina's most popular lodger. A wedding is a great human event. To the principals the event becomes the pivot of existence; to the relatives and friends it is at once the consummation of a series of happenings that have absorbed their anxious and amused attention, and the point of departure for a new phase of existence offering infinite possibilities in the way of speculation. But even for the casual onlooker a wedding furnishes a pleasant arrest of the ordinary course of life, and lets in upon the dull grey of the commonplace certain gleams of glory from the golden days of glowing youth, or from beyond the mysterious planes of experience yet to be.

All this and more Anka's wedding was to Paulina and her people. It added greatly to Paulina's joy and to her sense of importance that her house was selected to be the scene of the momentous event. For long weeks Paulina's house became the life centre of the colony, and as the day drew nigh every boarder was conscious of a certain reflected glory. It is no wonder that the selecting of Paulina's house for the wedding feast gave offence to Anka's tried friend and patron, Mrs. Fitzpatrick. To that lady it seemed that in selecting Paulina's house for her wedding Anka was accepting Paulina's standard of morals and condoning her offences, and it only added to her grief that Anka took the matter so lightly.

"I'm just affronted at ye, Anka," she complained, "that ye can step inside the woman's dure."

"Ah, cut it out!" cried Anka, rejoicing in her command of the vernacular. "Sure, Paulina is no good, you bet; but see, look at her house—dere is no Rutenian house like dat, so beeg. Ah!" she continued rapturously, "you come an' see me and Jacob dance de 'czardas,' wit Arnud on de cymbal. Dat Arnud he's come from de old country, an' he's de whole show, de whole brass band on de park."

To Anka it seemed an unnecessary and foolish sacrifice to the demands of decency that she should forego the joy of a real czardas to the music of Arnud accompanying the usual violins.

"Ye can have it," sniffed Mrs. Fitzpatrick with emphatic disdain; all the more emphatic that she was conscious, distinctly conscious, of a strong desire to witness this special feature of the festivities. "I've nothing agin you, Anka, for it's a good gurrl ye are, but me and me family is respectable, an' that Father Mulligan can tell ye, for his own mother's cousin was married till the brother of me father's uncle, an' niver a fut of me will go beyant the dure of that scut, Paulina." And Mrs. Fitzpatrick, resting her hands upon her hips, stood the living embodiment of hostility to any suggested compromise with sin.

But while determined to maintain at all costs this attitude toward Paulina and her doings, her warm-hearted interest in Anka's wedding made her very ready with offers of assistance in preparing for the feast.

"It's not much I know about y're Polak atin'," she said, "but I can make a batch of pork pies that wud tempt the heart of the Howly Moses himsilf, an' I can give ye a bilin' of pitaties that Timothy can fetch to the house for ye."

This generous offer Anka gladly accepted, for Mrs. Fitzpatrick's pork pies, she knew from experience, were such as might indeed have tempted so respectable a patriarch as Moses himself to mortal sin. The "bilin' of pitaties," which Anka knew would be prepared in no ordinary pot, but in Mrs. Fitzpatrick's ample wash boiler, was none the less acceptable, for Anka could easily imagine how effective such a contribution would be in the early stages of the feast in dulling the keen edge of the Galician appetite.

The preparation for the wedding feast, which might be prolonged for the greater part of three days, was in itself an undertaking requiring careful planning and no small degree of executive ability; for the popularity of both bride and groom would be sufficient to insure the presence of the whole colony, but especially the reputed wealth of the bride, who, it was well known, had been saving with careful economy her wages at the New West Hotel for the past three years, would most certainly create a demand for a feast upon a scale of more than ordinary magnificence, and Anka was determined that in providing for the feast this demand should be fully satisfied.

For a long time she was torn between two conflicting desires: on the one hand she longed to appear garbed in all the glory of the Western girl's most modern bridal attire; on the other she coveted the honour of providing a feast that would live for years in the memory of all who might be privileged to be present. Both she could not accomplish, and she wisely chose the latter; for she shrewdly reasoned that, while the Western bridal garb would certainly set forth her charms in a new and ravishing style, the glory of that triumph would be short-lived at best, and it would excite the envy of the younger members of her own sex and the criticism of the older and more conservative of her compatriots.

She was further moved to this decision by the thought that inasmuch as Jacob and she had it in mind to open a restaurant and hotel as soon as sufficient money was in hand, it was important that they should stand well with the community, and nothing would so insure popularity as abundant and good eating and drinking. So to the preparation of a feast that would at once bring her immediate glory and future profit, Anka set her shrewd wits. The providing of the raw materials for the feast was to her an easy matter, for her experience in the New West Hotel had taught her how to expend to the best advantage her carefully hoarded wages. The difficulty was with the cooking. Clearly Paulina could not be expected to attend to this, for although her skill with certain soups and stews was undoubted, for the finer achievements of the culinary art Paulina was totally unfitted. To overcome this difficulty, Anka hit upon the simple but very effective expedient of entrusting to her neighbours, who would later be her guests, the preparing of certain dishes according to their various abilities and inclinations, keeping close account in her own shrewd mind of what each one might be supposed to produce from the materials furnished, and stimulating in her assistants the laudable ambition to achieve the very best results. Hence, in generous quantities she distributed flour for bread and cakes in many varieties, rice and beans and barley, which were to form the staple portion of the stews, cabbage and beets and onions in smaller measure—for at this season of the year the price was high—sides of pork, ropes of sausages, and roasts of beef from neck and flank. Through the good offices of the butcher boy that supplied the New West Hotel, purchased with Anka's shyest smile and glance, were secured a considerable accumulation of shank bones and ham bones, pork ribs and ribs of beef, and other scraps too often despised by the Anglo-Saxon housekeeper, all of which would prove of the greatest value in the enrichment of the soups. For puddings there were apples and prunes, raisins and cranberries. The cook of the New West Hotel, catching something of Anka's generous enthusiasm, offered pies by the dozen, and even the proprietor himself, learning of the preparations and progress, could think of nothing so appropriate to the occasion as a case of Irish whiskey. This, however, Anka, after some deliberation, declined, suggesting beer instead, and giving as a reason her experience, namely, that "whiskey make too quick fight, you bet." A fight was inevitable, but it would be a sad misfortune if this necessary part of the festivities should occur too early in the programme.

Gradually, during the days of the week immediately preceding the ceremony, there began to accumulate in the shacks about, viands of great diversity, which were stored in shelves, in cupboards,—where there were any,—under beds, and indeed in any and every available receptacle. The puddings, soups and stews, which, after all, were to form the main portion of the eating, were deposited in empty beer kegs, of which every shack could readily furnish a few, and set out to freeze, in which condition they would preserve their perfect flavour. Such diligence and such prudence did Anka show in the supervision of all these arrangements, that when the day before the feast arrived, on making her final round of inspection, everything was discovered to be in readiness for the morrow, with the single exception that the beer had not arrived. But this was no over-sight on the part of Jacob, to whom this portion of the feast had been entrusted. It was rather due to a prudence born of experience that the beer should be ordered to be delivered at the latest possible hour. A single beer keg is an object of consuming interest to the Galician and subjects his sense of honour to a very considerable strain; the known presence of a dray load of beer kegs in the neighbourhood would almost certainly intensify the strain beyond the breaking point. But as the shadows of evening began to gather, the great brewery dray with its splendid horses and its load of kegs piled high, drew up to Paulina's door. Without loss of time, and under the supervision of Rosenblatt and Jacob himself, the beer kegs were carried by the willing hands of Paulina's boarders down to the cellar, piled high against the walls, and carefully counted. There they were safe enough, for every man, not only among the boarders but in the whole colony, who expected to be present at the feast, having contributed his dollar toward the purchase of the beer, constituted himself a guardian against the possible depredations of his neighbours. Not a beer keg from this common store was to be touched until after the ceremony, when every man should have a fair start. For the preliminary celebrations during the evening and night preceding the wedding day the beer furnished by the proprietor of the New West Hotel would prove sufficient.

It was considered a most fortunate circumstance both by the bride and groom-elect, that there should have appeared in the city, the week before, a priest of the Greek Catholic faith, for though in case of need they could have secured the offices of a Roman priest from St. Boniface, across the river, the ceremonial would thereby have been shorn of much of its picturesqueness and efficacy. Anka and her people had little regard for the services of a Church to which they owed only nominal allegiance.

The wedding day dawned clear, bright, and not too cold to forbid a great gathering of the people outside Paulina's house, who stood reverently joining with those who had been fortunate enough to secure a place in Paulina's main room, which had been cleared of all beds and furniture, and transformed for the time being into a chapel. The Slav is a religious man, intensely, and if need be, fiercely, religious; hence these people, having been deprived for long months of the services of their Church, joined with eager and devout reverence in the responses to the prayers of the priest, kneeling in the snow unmoved by and apparently unconscious of the somewhat scornful levity of the curious crowd of onlookers that speedily gathered about them. For more than two hours the religious part of the ceremony continued, but there was no sign of abating interest or of waning devotion; rather did the religious feeling appear to deepen as the service advanced. At length there floated through the open window the weirdly beautiful and stately marriage chant, in which the people joined in deep-toned guttural fervour, then the benediction, and the ceremony was over. Immediately there was a movement toward the cellar, where Rosenblatt, assisted by a score of helpers, began to knock in the heads of the beer kegs and to hand about tin cups of beer for the first drinking of the bride's health. Beautiful indeed, in her husband's eyes and the eyes of all who beheld her, appeared Anka as she stood with Jacob in the doorway, radiant in the semi-barbaric splendour of her Slavonic ancestry.

This first formal health-drinking ceremony over, from within Paulina's house and from shacks roundabout, women appeared with pots and pails, from which, without undue haste, but without undue delay, men filled tin cups and tin pans with stews rich, luscious, and garlic flavoured. The feast was on; the Slav's hour of rapture had come. From pot to keg and from keg to pot the happy crowd would continue to pass in alternating moods of joy, until the acme of bliss would be attained when Jacob, leading forth and up and down his lace-decked bride, would fling the proud challenge to one and all that his bride was the fairest and dearest of all brides ever known.

Thus with full ceremonial, with abundance of good eating, and with multitudinous libations, Anka was wed.

Chapter IV

The Unbidden Guest

The northbound train on the Northern Pacific Line was running away behind her time. A Dakota blizzard had held her up for five hours, and there was little chance of making time against a heavy wind and a drifted rail. The train was crowded with passengers, all impatient at the delay, as is usual with passengers. The most restless, if not the most impatient, of those in the first-class car was a foreign-looking gentleman, tall, dark, and with military carriage. A grizzled moustache with ends waxed to a needle point and an imperial accentuated his foreign military appearance. At every pause the train made at the little wayside stations, this gentleman became visibly more impatient, pulling out his watch, consulting his time table, and cursing the delay.

Occasionally he glanced out through the window across the white plain that stretched level to the horizon, specked here and there by infrequent little black shacks and by huge stacks of straw half buried in snow. Suddenly his attention was arrested by a trim line of small buildings cosily ensconced behind a plantation of poplars and Manitoba maples.

"What are those structures?" he enquired of his neighbour in careful book English, and with slightly foreign accent.

"What? That bunch of buildings. That is a Mennonite village," was the reply.

"Mennonite! Ah!"

"Yes," replied his neighbour. "Dutch, or Russian, or something."

"Yes, Russian," answered the stranger quickly. "That is Russian, surely," he continued, pointing eagerly to the trim and cosy group of buildings. "These Mennonites, are they prosperous—ah—citizens—ah—settlers?"

"You bet! They make money where other folks would starve. They know what they're doing. They picked out this land that everybody else was passing over—the very best in the country—and they are making money hand over fist. Mighty poor spenders, though. They won't buy nothing; eat what they can't sell off the farm."

"Aha," ejaculated the stranger, with a smile.

"Yes, they sell everything, grain, hogs, eggs, butter, and live on cabbages, cheese, bread."

"Aha," repeated the stranger, again with evident approval.

"They are honest, though," continued his neighbour judicially; "we sell them implements."

"Ah, implements?" enquired the stranger.

"Yes, ploughs, drills, binders, you know."

"Ah, so, implements," said the stranger, evidently making a mental note of the word. "And they pay you?"

"Yes, they are good pay, mighty good pay. They are good settlers, too."

"Not good for soldiers, eh?" laughed the stranger.

"Soldiers? No, I guess not. But we don't want soldiers."

"What? You have no soldiers? No garrisons?"

"No, what do we want soldiers for in this country? We want farmers and lots of them."

The stranger was apparently much struck with this remark. He pursued the subject with keen interest. If there were no soldiers, how was order preserved? What happened in the case of riots? What about the collecting of taxes?

"Riots? There ain't no riots in this country. What would we riot for? We're too busy. And taxes? There ain't no taxes except for schools."

"Not for churches?" enquired the foreigner.

"No, every man supports his own church or no church at all if he likes it better."

The foreigner was deeply impressed. What a country it was, to be sure! No soldiers, no riots, no taxes, and churches only for those who wanted them! He made diligent enquiry as to the Mennonite settlements, where they were placed, their size, the character of the people and all things pertaining to them. But when questioned in regard to himself or his own affairs, he at once became reticent. He was a citizen of many countries. He was travelling for pleasure and to gather knowledge. Yes, he might one day settle in the country, but not now. He relapsed into silence, sitting with his head fallen forward upon his breast, and so sat till the brakeman passing through shouted, "Winnipeg! All change!" Then he rose, thanked with stiff and formal politeness his seatmate for his courtesy, put on his long overcoat lined with lambskin and adorned with braid, placed his lambskin cap upon his head, and so stood looking more than ever like a military man.

The station platform at Winnipeg was the scene of uproar and confusion. Railway baggagemen and porters, with warning cries, pushed their trucks through the crowd. Hotel runners shouted the rates and names of their hotels. Express men and cab drivers vociferously solicited custom. Citizens, heedless of every one, pushed their eager way through the crowd to welcome friends and relatives. It was a busy, bustling, confusing scene. But the stranger stood unembarrassed, as if quite accustomed to move amid jostling crowds, casting quick, sharp glances hither and thither.

Gradually the platform cleared. The hotel runners marched off in triumph with their victims, and express drivers and cab men drove off with their fares, and only a scattering few were left behind. At one end of the platform stood two men in sheepskin coats and caps. The stranger slowly moved toward them. As he drew near, the men glanced at first carelessly, then more earnestly at him. For a few moments he stood gazing down the street, then said, as if to himself, in the Russian tongue, "The wind blows from the north to-night."

Instantly the men came to rigid attention.

"And the snow lies deep," replied one, raising his hand in salute.

"But spring will come, brother," replied the stranger.

One of the men came quickly toward him, took his hand and kissed it.

"Fool!" said the stranger, drawing away his hand, and sweeping his sharp glance round the platform. "The bear that hunts in the open is himself soon hunted."

"Ha, ha," laughed the other man loudly, "in this country there is no hunting, brother."

"Fool!" said the stranger again in a low, stern voice. "Where game is, there is always hunting."

"How can we serve? What does my brother wish?" replied the man.

"I wish the house of Paulina Koval. Do you know where it is?"

"Yes, we know, but—" the men hesitated, looking at each other.

"There is no place for our brother in Paulina Koval's house," said the one who had spoken first. "Paulina has no room. Her house is full with her children and with many boarders."

"Indeed," said the stranger, "and how many?"

"Well," replied the other, counting upon his fingers, "there is Paulina and her three children, and—"

"Two children," corrected the stranger sharply.

"No, three children. Yes, three." He paused in his enumeration as if struck by a belated thought. "It is three children, Joseph?" he proceeded, turning to his friend.

Joseph confirmed his memory. "Yes, Simon, three; the girl, the boy and the baby."

The stranger was clearly perplexed and disturbed.

"Go on," he said curtly.

"There is Paulina and the three children, and Rosenblatt, and—"

"Rosenblatt!" The word shot from the stranger's lips with the vehemence of a bullet from a rifle. "Rosenblatt in her house! S-s-s-o-o-o!" He thrust his face forward into the speaker's with a long hissing sound, so fiercely venomous that the man fell back a pace. Quickly the stranger recovered himself. "Look you, brothers, I need a room for a few days, anywhere, a small room, and I can pay well."

"My house," said the man named Joseph, "is yours, but there are six men with me."

Quickly the other took it up. "My poor house is small, two children, but if the Elder brother would accept?"

"I will accept, my friend," said the stranger. "You shall lose nothing by it." He took up the bag that he had placed beside him on the platform, saying briefly, "Lead the way."

"Your pardon, brother," said Simon, taking the bag from him, "this is the way."

Northward across the railway tracks and up the street for two blocks, then westward they turned, toward the open prairie. After walking some minutes, Simon pointed to a huddling group of shacks startlingly black against the dazzling snow.

"There," he cried with a laugh, "there is little Russia."

"Not Russia," said Joseph, "Galicia."

The stranger stood still, gazing at the little shacks, and letting his eye wander across the dazzling plain, tinted now with crimson and with gold from the setting sun, to the horizon. Then pointing to the shacks he said, "That is Canada. Yonder," sweeping his hand toward the plain, "is Siberia. But," turning suddenly upon the men, "what are you?"

"We are free men," said Joseph. "We are Canadians."

"We are Canadians," answered Simon more slowly. "But here," laying his hand over his heart, "here is always Russia and our brothers of Russia."

The stranger turned a keen glance upon him. "I believe you," he said. "No Russian can forget his fatherland. No Russian can forget his brother." His eyes were lit with a dreamy light, as he gazed far beyond the plain and the glowing horizon.

At the door of the little black shack Simon halted the party.

"Pardon, I will prepare for my brother," he said.

As he opened the door a cloud of steaming odours rushed forth to meet them. The stranger drew back and turned his face again to the horizon, drawing deep breaths of the crisp air, purified by its sweep of a thousand miles over snow clad prairie.

"Ah," he said, "wonderful! wonderful! Yes, that is Russia, that air, that sky, that plain."

After some minutes Simon returned.

"Enter," he said, bowing low. "This is your house, brother; we are your slaves."

It was a familiar Russian salutation.

"No," said the stranger, quickly stretching out his hand. "No slaves in this land, thank God! but brothers all."

"Your brothers truly," said Simon, dropping on his knee and kissing the outstretched hand. "Lena," he called to his wife, who stood modestly at the other side of the room, "this is the Elder of our Brotherhood."

Lena came forward, dropped on her knees and kissed the outstretched hand.

"Come, Margaret," she cried, drawing her little girl of six toward the stranger, "come and salute the master."

Little Margaret came forward and offered her hand, looking up with brave shyness into the stranger's face.

"Shame! shame!" said Lena, horrified. "Kneel down! Kneel down!"

"She does not understand how to salute," said her father with an apologetic smile.

"Aha, so," cried the stranger, looking curiously at the little girl. "Where did you learn to shake hands?"

"In school," said the child in English.

"In school?" replied the stranger in the same language. "You go to school. What school?"

"The public school, sir."

"And do they not teach you to kneel when you salute in the public school?"

"No, sir, we never kneel."

"What then do you learn there?"

"We sing, and read, and write, and march, and sew."

"Aha!" cried the stranger delighted. "You learn many things. And what do you pay for all this?" he said in Russian to the father.

"Nothing."

"Wonderful!" cried the stranger. "And who taught her English?"

"No one. She just learned it from the children."

"Aha, that is good."

The father and mother stood struggling with their pride in their little girl. A sound of shouting and of singing made the stranger turn toward the window.

"What is that?" he cried.

"A wedding," replied Simon. "There is a great wedding at Paulina's. Every one is there."

"At Paulina's?" said the stranger. "And you, why are you not there?"

"We are no friends of Rosenblatt."

"Rosenblatt? And what has he to do with it?"

"Rosenblatt," said Joseph sullenly, "is master in Paulina's home."

"Aha! He is master, and you are no friends of his," returned the stranger. "Tell me why this is so?"

31

"We are Russian, he is Bukowinian; he hires men to the railroad, we hire ourselves; he has a store, we buy in the Canadian stores, therefore, he hates us."

The stranger nodded his head, comprehending the situation.

"And so you are not invited to the wedding."

"No, we are not invited to the wedding," said Joseph in a tone of regret.

"And they are your friends who are being married?"

"Yes."

"And there is good eating and drinking?"

"Yes," cried Joseph eagerly. "Such a feast! Such a load of beer! And such a dance!"

"It is a pity," said the stranger, "to miss it all. You fear this Rosenblatt," he continued, with a hardly perceptible sneer.

"Fear!" cried Simon. "No! But one does not enter a shut door."

"Aha, but think of it," said the stranger, "the feasting and the dancing, and the beer! I would go to this wedding feast myself, were I not a stranger. I would go if I knew the bride."

"We will take our brother," cried Joseph eagerly. "Our friends will welcome him."

Simon hesitated.

"I like not Rosenblatt."

"But Rosenblatt will be too drunk by this time," suggested the stranger.

"Not he," replied Simon. "He never gets drunk where there is a chance to gather a dollar."

"But the feast is free?"

"Yes, the feast is free, but there is always money going. There is betting and there is the music for the dancing, which is Rosenblatt's. He has hired Arnud and his cymbal and the violins, and the dancers must pay."

"Aha, very clever," replied the stranger. "This Rosenblatt is a shrewd man. He will be a great man in this city. He will be your lord some day."

The eyes of both men gleamed at his jibes. "Aha," the stranger continued, "he will make you serve him by his money. Canada is, indeed, a free country, but there will be master and slaves here, too."

It was a sore spot to the men, for the mastery of Rosenblatt was no imagination, but a grim reality. It was with difficulty that any man could get a good job unless by Rosenblatt's agency. It was Rosenblatt who contracted for the Galician labour. One might hate Rosenblatt, or despise him, but it was impossible to ignore him.

"What say you, my brothers," said the stranger, "shall we attend this feast?"

The men were eager to go. Why should Rosenblatt stand in their way? Were they not good friends of Jacob and Anka? Was not every home in the colony open to a stranger, and especially a stranger of rank? Simon swallowed his pride and led the way to Paulina's house.

There was no need of a guide to the house where the feasting was in progress. The shouting and singing of the revellers hailed them from afar, and as they drew near, the crowd about the door indicated the house of mirth. Joseph and Simon were welcomed with overflowing hospitality and mugs of beer. But when they turned to introduce the stranger, they found that he had disappeared, nor could they discover him anywhere in the crowd. In their search for him, they came upon Rosenblatt, who at once assailed them.

"How come you Slovaks here?" he cried contemptuously.

"Where the trough is, there the pigs will come," laughed one of his satellites.

"I come to do honour to my friend, Jacob Wassyl," said Simon in a loud voice.

"Of course," cried a number of friendly voices. "And why not? That is quite right."

"Jacob Wassyl wants none of you here," shouted Rosenblatt over the crowd.

"Who speaks for Jacob Wassyl?" cried a voice. It was Jacob himself, standing in the door, wet with sweat, flushed with dancing and exhilarated with the beer and with all the ardours of his wedding day. For that day at least, Jacob owned the world. "What?" he cried, "is it my friend Simon Ketzel and my friend Joseph Pinkas?"

"We were not invited to come to your wedding, Jacob Wassyl," replied Simon, "but we desired to honour your bride and yourself."

"Aye, and so you shall. You are welcome, Simon Ketzel. You are welcome, Joseph Pinkas. Who says you are not?" he continued, turning defiantly to Rosenblatt.

Rosenblatt hesitated, and then grunted out something that sounded like "Slovak swine!"

"Slovak!" cried Jacob with generous enthusiasm. "We are all Slovak. We are all Polak. We are all Galician. We are all brothers. Any man who says no, is no friend of Jacob Wassyl."

Shouts of approval rose from the excited crowd.

"Come, brothers," shouted Jacob to Simon and Joseph, "come in. There is abundant eating. Make way for my friends!" He crowded back through the door, taking especial delight in honouring the men despised of Rosenblatt.

The room was packed with steaming, swaying, roaring dancers, both men and women, all reeking with sweat and garlic. Upon a platform in a corner between two violins, sat Arnud before his cymbal, resplendent in frilled shirt and embroidered vest, thundering on his instrument the favourite songs of the dancers, shouting now and then in unison with the melody that pattered out in metallic rain from the instrument before him. For four hours and more, with intervals sufficient only to quench their thirst, the players had kept up their interminable accompaniment to dance and song. It was clearly no place for hungry men. Jacob pushed his way toward the inner room.

"Ho! Paulina!" he shouted, "two plates for men who have not eaten."

"Have not eaten!" The startling statement quickened Paulina's slow movements almost to a run. "Here, here," she said, "bring them to the window at the back."

Another struggle and Jacob with his guests were receiving through the window two basins filled with luscious steaming stew.

As they turned away with their generous host, a man with a heavy black beard appeared at the window.

"Another hungry man, Paulina," he said quietly in the Galician tongue.

"Holy Virgin! Where have these hungry men been?" cried Paulina, hurrying with another basin to the window.

The man fumbled and hesitated as he took the dish.

"I have been far away," he said, speaking now in the Russian tongue, in a low and tense voice.

Paulina started. The man caught her by the wrist.

"Quiet!" he said. "Speak no word, Paulina."

The woman paled beneath the dirt and tan upon her face.

"Who is it?" she whispered with parched lips.

"You know it is Michael Kalmar, your husband. Come forth. I wait behind yon hut. No word to any man."

"You mean to kill me," she said, her fat body shaking as if with palsy.

"Bah! You sow! Who would kill a sow? Come forth, I say. Delay not."

He disappeared at once behind the neighbouring shack. Paulina, trembling so that her fingers could hardly pin the shawl she put over her head, made her way through the crowd. A few moments she stood before her door, as if uncertain which way to turn, her limbs trembling, her breath coming like sobs. In this plight Rosenblatt came upon her.

"What is the matter with you, Paulina?" he cried. "What is your business here?"

A swift change came over her.

"I am no dog of yours," she said, her sullen face flaming with passion.

"What do you mean?" cried Rosenblatt. "Get into your house, cat!"

"Yes! cat!" cried the woman, rushing at him with fingers extended.

One swift swoop she made at his face, bringing skin and hair on her nails. Rosenblatt turned, and crying, "She is mad! She is mad!" made for the shelter of the cellar, followed by the shouts and jeers of the men standing about.

Raging, at the door Paulina sought entrance, crying, "I was a good woman. He made me bad." Then turning away, she walked slowly to the back of her house and passed behind the neighbouring shack where the man stood waiting her.

With dragging steps she approached, till within touch of him, when, falling down upon her knees in the snow, she put her head upon his feet.

"Get up, fool," he cried harshly.

She rose and stood with her chin upon her breast.

"My children!" said the man. "Where are my children?"

She pointed towards the house of her neighbour, Mrs. Fitzpatrick. "With a neighbour woman," she said, and turned herself toward him again with head bowed down.

"And yours?" he hissed.

She shuddered violently.

"Speak," he said in a voice low, calm and terrible. "Do you wish me to kill you where you stand?"

"Yes," she said, throwing her shawl over her face, "kill me! Kill me now! It will be good to die!"

With a curse, his hand went to his side. He stood looking at her quietly for a few moments as if deliberating.

"No," he said at length, "it is not worth while. You are no wife of mine. Do you hear?"

She gave no sign.

"You are Rosenblatt's swine. Let him use you."

Another shudder shook her.

"Oh, my lord!" she moaned, "kill me. Let me die!"

"Bah!" He spat on the snow. "Die, when I have done with-you, perhaps. Take me where we can be alone. Go."

She glanced about at the shacks standing black and without sign of life.

"Come," she said, leading the way.

He followed her to a shack which stood on the outskirts of the colony. She pushed open the door and stood back.

"Go in," he said savagely. "Now a light."

He struck a match. Paulina found a candle which he lit and placed on a box that stood in the corner.

"Cover that window," he commanded.

She took a quilt from the bed and pinned it up. For a long time he stood motionless in the centre of the room, while she knelt at his feet. Then he spoke with some deliberation.

"It is possible I shall kill you to-night, so speak truly to me in the name of God and of the Holy Virgin. I ask you of my children. My girl is eleven years old. Have you protected her? Or is she—like you?"

She threw off her shawl, pulled up her sleeves.

"See," she cried, "my back is like that. Your daughter is safe."

Livid bars of purple striped her arms. The man gazed down at her.

"You swear this by the Holy Cross?" he said solemnly.

She pulled a little iron cross from her breast and kissed it, then looked up at him with dog's eyes of entreaty.

"Oh, my lord!" she began. "I could not save myself. I was a stranger. He took my money. We had no home."

"Stop, liar," he thundered, "I gave you money when you left Galicia."

"Yes, I paid it for the house, and still there was more to pay."

"Liar again!" he hissed; "I sent you money every month. I have your receipts for it."

"I had no money from you," she said humbly. "He forced me to have men sleep in my house and in my room, or lose my home. And the children, what could I do? They could not go out into the snow."

"You got no money from me?" he enquired.

Again she kissed the little cross. "I swear it. And what could I do?"

"Do!" cried the man, his voice choked with rage. "Do! You could die!"

"And the children?"

He was silent, looking down upon her. He began to realize the helplessness of her plight. In a strange land, she found herself without friends, and charged with the support of two children. The money he had given her she had invested in a house, through Rosenblatt, who insisted that payments were still due. No wonder he had terrified her into submission to his plans.

While his contempt remained, her husband's rage grew less. After a long silence he said, "Listen. This feast will last two days?"

"Yes, there is food and drink for two days."

"In two days my work here will be done. Then I go back. I must go back. My children! my children! what of my children? My dead Olga's children!" He began to pace the room. He forgot the woman on the floor. "Oh, fatherland! My fatherland!" he cried in a voice broken with passionate grief, "must I sacrifice these too for thee? God in heaven! Father, mother, brother, home, wife, all I have given. Must I give my children, too?" His strong dark face was working fiercely. His voice came harsh and broken. "No, no! By all the saints, no! I will keep my children for Olga's sake. I will let my wretched country go. What matter to me? I will make a new home in this free land and forget. Ah, God! Forget? I can never forget! These plains!" He tore aside the quilt from the window and stooping looked out upon the prairie. "These plains say Russia! This gleaming snow, Russia! Ah! Ah! Ah! I cannot forget, while I live, my people, my fatherland. I have suffered too much to forget. God forget me, if I forget!" He fell on his knees before the window, dry sobs shaking his powerful frame. He rose and began again to stride up and down, his hands locked before him. Suddenly he stood quite still, making mighty efforts to regain command of himself. For some moments he stood thus rigid.

The woman, who had been kneeling all the while, crept to his feet.

"My lord will give his children to me," she said in a low voice.

"You!" he cried, drawing back from her. "You! What could you do for them?"

"I could die for them," she said simply, "and for my lord."

"For me! Ha!" His voice carried unutterable scorn.

She cowered back to the floor.

"My children I can slay, but I will leave them in no house of lust."

"Oh!" she cried, clasping her hands upon her breast and swaying backwards and forwards upon her knees, "I will be a good woman. I will sin no more. Rosenblatt I shall send—"

"Rosenblatt!" cried the man with a fierce laugh. "After two days Rosenblatt will not be here."

"You will—?" gasped the woman.

"He will die," said the man quietly.

"Oh, my lord! Let me kill him! It would be easy for me at night when he sleeps. But you they will take and hang. In this country no one escapes. Oh! Do not you kill him. Let me."

Breathlessly she pleaded, holding him by the feet. He spurned her with contempt.

"Peace, fool! He is for none other than me. It is an old score. Ah, yes," he continued between his teeth, "it is an old score. It will be sweet to feel him slowly die with my fingers in his throat."

"But they will take you," cried the woman.

"Bah! They could not hold me in Siberia, and think you they can in this land? But the children," he mused. "Rosenblatt away." With a sudden resolve he turned to the woman. "Woman," he said, in a voice stern and low, "could you—"

She threw herself once more at his feet in a passion of entreaty. "Oh, my lord! Let me live for them, for them—and—for you!"

"For me?" he said coldly. "No. You have dishonoured my name. You are wife of mine no longer. Do you hear this?"

"Yes, yes," she panted, "I hear. I know. I ask nothing for myself. But the children, your children. I would live for them, would die for them!"

He turned from her and gazed through the window, pondering. That she would be faithful to the children he well knew. That she would gladly die for him, he was equally certain. With Rosenblatt removed, the house would be rid of the cause of her fall and her shame. There was no one else in this strange land to whom he could trust his children. Should death or exile take him in his work—and these were always his companions—his children would be quite alone. Once more he turned and looked down upon the kneeling woman. He had no love for her. He had never loved her. Simply as a matter of convenience he had married her, that she might care for the children of his dead wife whom he had loved with undying and passionate love.

"Paulina," he said solemnly, but the contempt was gone from his voice, "you are henceforth no wife of mine; but my children I give into your care."

Hitherto, during the whole interview, she had shed no tear, but at these words of his she flung her arms about his knees and burst into a passion of weeping.

"Oh, my lord! My dear lord! Oh, my lord! my lord!" she sobbed, wildly kissing his very boots.

He drew away from her and sat down upon a bench.

"Listen," he said. "I will send you money. You will require to take no man into your house for your support. Is there any one to whom I could send the money for you?"

She thought for a few moments.

"There is one," she said, "but she does not love me. She will come no longer into my house. She thinks me a bad woman." Her voice sank low. Her face flamed a dark red.

"Aha," said the man, "I would see that woman. To-morrow you will bring me to her. At dusk to-morrow I will pass your house. You will meet me. Now go."

She remained kneeling in her place. Then she crawled nearer his feet.

"Oh, my lord!" she sobbed, "I have done wrong. Will you not beat me? Beat me till the blood runs down. He was too strong for me. I was afraid for the children. I had no place to go. I did a great wrong. If my lord would but beat me till the blood runs down, it would be a joy to me."

It was the cry of justice making itself heard through her dull soul. It was the instinctive demand for atonement. It was the unconscious appeal for reinstatement to the privileges of wifehood.

"Woman," he said sternly, "a man may beat his wife. He will not strike a woman that is nothing to him. Go."

Once more she clutched his feet, kissing them. Then she rose and without a word went out into the dusky night. She had entered upon the rugged path of penitence, the only path to peace for the sinner.

After she had gone, the man stepped to the door and looked after her as if meditating her recall.

"Bah!" he said at length, "she is nothing to me. Let her go."

He put out the light, closed the door and passing through the crowd of revellers, went off to Simon's house.

Chapter V

The Patriot's Heart

The inside of Paulina's house was a wreck. The remains of benches and chairs and tables mingled with fragments of vessels of different sorts strewn upon the filth-littered floor, the windows broken, the door between the outer and inner rooms torn from its hinges, all this débris, together with the battered, bruised and bloody human shapes lying amidst their filth, gave eloquent testimony to the tempestuous character of the proceedings of the previous night.

The scene that greeted Paulina's eyes in the early grey of the morning might well have struck a stouter heart than hers with dismay; for her house had the look of having been swept by a tornado, and Paulina's heart was anything but stout that morning. The sudden appearance of her husband had at first stricken her with horrible fear, the fear of death; but this fear had passed into a more dreadful horror, that of repudiation.

Seven years ago, when Michael Kalmar had condescended to make her his wife, her whole soul had gone forth to him in a passion of adoring love that had invested him in a halo of glory. He became her god thenceforth to worship and to serve. Her infidelity meant no diminution of this passion. Withdrawn from her husband's influence, left without any sign of his existence for two years or more, subjected to the machinations of the subtle and unscrupulous Rosenblatt, the soul in her had died, the animal had lived and triumphed. The sound of her husband's voice last night had summoned into vivid life her dead soul. Her god had moved into the range of her vision, and immediately she was his again, soul and body. Hence her sudden fury at Rosenblatt; hence, too, the utter self-abandonment in her appeal to her husband. But now he had cast her off. The gates of Heaven, swinging open before her ravished eyes for a few brief moments, had closed to her forever. Small wonder that she brought a heavy heart to the righting of her disordered home, and well for her that Anka with her hearty, cheery courage stood at her side that morning.

Together they set themselves to clear away the filth and the wreckage, human and otherwise. Of the human wreckage Anka made short work. Stepping out into the frosty air, she returned with a pail of snow.

"Here, you sluggards," she cried, bestowing generous handfuls upon their sodden faces, "up with you, and out. The day is fine and dinner will soon be here."

Grunting, growling, cursing, the men rose, stretched themselves with prodigious yawning, and bundled out into the frosty air.

"Get yourselves ready for dinner," cried Anka after them. "The best is yet to come, and then the dance."

Down into the cellar they went, stiff and sore and still growling, dipped their hands and heads into icy water, and after a perfunctory toilet and a mug of beer or two all round, they were ready for a renewal of the festivities. There was no breakfast, but as the day wore on, from the shacks about came women with provisions for the renewal of the feast. For Anka, wise woman, had kept some of the more special dishes for the second day. But as for the beer, though there were still some kegs left, they were few enough to give Jacob Wassyl concern. It would be both a misfortune and a disgrace if the beer should fail before the marriage feast was over. The case was serious enough. Jacob Wassyl's own money was spent, the guests had all contributed their share,

Rosenblatt would sooner surrender blood than money, and Jacob was not yet sufficiently established as a husband to appeal to his wife for further help.

It was through Simon Ketzel that deliverance came, or rather through Simon's guest, who, learning that the beer was like to fail, passed Simon a bill saying, "It would be sad if disgrace should come to your friends. Let there be plenty of beer. Buy what is necessary and keep the rest in payment for my lodging. And of my part in this not a word to any man."

As a result, in the late afternoon a dray load of beer kegs appeared at Paulina's back door, to the unspeakable relief of Jacob and of his guests as well, who had begun to share his anxiety and to look forward to an evening of drouth and gloom.

As for Simon Ketzel, he found himself at once upon the very crest of a wave of popularity, for through the driver of the dray it became known that it was Simon that had come so splendidly to the rescue.

Relieved of anxiety, the revellers gave themselves with fresh and reckless zest to the duty of assuring beyond all shadow of doubt, the good health of the bride and the groom, and of every one in general in flowing mugs of beer. Throughout the afternoon, men and women, and even boys and girls, ate and drank, danced and sang to the limit of their ability.

As the evening darkened, and while this carouse was at its height, Paulina, with a shawl over her head, slipped out of the house and through the crowd, and so on to the outskirts of the colony, where she found her husband impatiently waiting her.

"You are late," he said harshly.

"I could not find Kalman."

"Kalman! My boy! And where would he be?" exclaimed her husband with a shade of anxiety in his voice.

"He was with me in the house. I could not keep him from the men, and they will give him beer."

"Beer to that child?" snarled her husband.

"Yes, they make him sing and dance, and they give him beer. He is wonderful," said Paulina.

Even as she spoke, a boy's voice rose clear and full in a Hungarian love song, to the wild accompaniment of the cymbal.

"Hush!" said the man holding up his hand.

At the first sound of that high, clear voice, the bacchanalian shoutings and roarings fell silent, and the wild weird song, throbbing with passion, rose and fell upon the still evening air. After each verse, the whole chorus of deep, harsh voices swelled high over the wailing violins and Arnud's clanging cymbal.

"Good," muttered the man when the song had ceased. "Now get him."

"I shall bring him to yonder house," said Paulina, pointing to the dwelling of Mrs. Fitzpatrick, whither in a few minutes she was seen half dragging, half carrying a boy of eight, who kept kicking and scratching vigorously, and pouring forth a torrent of English oaths.

"Hush, Kalman," said Paulina in Galician, vainly trying to quiet the child. "The gentleman will be ashamed of you."

"I do not care for any gentleman," screamed Kalman. "He is a black devil," glancing at the black bearded man who stood waiting them at the door of the Fitzpatrick dwelling.

"Hush, hush, you bad boy!" exclaimed Paulina, horrified, laying her hand over the boy's mouth.

The man turned his back upon them, pulled off his black beard, thrust it into his pocket, gave his mustaches a quick turn and faced about upon them. This transformation froze the boy's fury into silence. He shrank back to his mother's side.

"Is it the devil?" he whispered to his mother in Galician.

"Kalman," said the man quietly, in the Russian language, "come to me. I am your father."

The boy gazed at him fearful and perplexed.

"He does not understand," said Paulina in Russian.

"Kalman," repeated his father, using the Galician speech, "come to me. I am your father."

The boy hesitated, looking fixedly at his father. But three years had wiped out the memory of that face.

"Come, you little Cossack," said his father, smiling at him. "Come, have you forgotten all your rides?"

The boy suddenly started, as if waking from sleep. The words evidently set the grey matter moving along old brain tracks. He walked toward his father, took the hand outstretched to him, and kissed it again and again.

"Aha, my son, you remember me," said the father exultantly.

"Yes," said the boy in English, "I remember the ride on the black horse."

The man lifted the boy in his strong arms, kissed him again and again, then setting him down said to Paulina, "Let us go in."

Paulina stepped forward and knocked at the door. Mrs. Fitzpatrick answered the knock and, seeing Paulina, was about to shut the door upon her face, when Paulina put up her hand.

"Look," she cried, pointing to the man, who stood back in the shadow, "Irma fadder."

"What d'ye say?" enquired Mrs. Fitzpatrick.

"Irma fadder," repeated Paulina, pointing to Kalmar.

"Is my daughter Irma in your house?" said he, stepping forward.

"Yer daughter, is it?" said Mrs. Fitzpatrick, looking sharply into the foreigner's face. "An' if she's yer daughter it's yersilf that should be ashamed av it fer the way ye've deserted the lot o' thim."

"Is it permitted that I see my daughter Irma?" said the man quietly.

Mrs. Fitzpatrick scanned his face suspiciously, then called, "Irma darlin', come here an' tell me who this is. Give the babby to Tim there, an' come away."

A girl of between eleven and twelve, tall for her age, with pale face, two thick braids of yellow hair, and wonderful eyes "burnin' brown," as Mrs. Fitzpatrick said, came to the door and looked out upon the man. For some time they gazed steadily each into the other's face.

"Irma, my child," said Kalmar in English, "you know me?"

But the girl stood gazing in perplexity.

"Irma! Child of my soul!" cried the man, in the Russian tongue, "do you not remember your father?" He stepped from the shadow to where the light from the open door could fall upon his face and stood with arms outstretched.

At once the girl's face changed, and with a cry, "It is my fadder!" she threw herself at him.

Her father caught her and held her fast, saying not a word, but covering her face with kisses.

"Come in, come in to the warm," cried the kind-hearted Irish woman, wiping her eyes. "Come in out o' the cold." And with eager hospitality she hurried the father and children into the house.

As they passed in, Paulina turned away. Before Mrs. Fitzpatrick shut the door, Irma caught her arm and whispered in her ear.

"Paulina, is it? Let her shtop—" She paused, looking at the Russian. "Your pardon?" he enquired with a bow.

"It's Paulina," said Mrs. Fitzpatrick, her voice carrying the full measure of her contempt for the unhappy creature who stood half turning away from the door.

"Ah, let her go. It is no difference. She is a sow. Let her go."

"Thin she's not your wife at all?" said Mrs. Fitzpatrick, her wrath rising at this discovery of further deception in Paulina.

He shrugged his shoulders. "She was once. I married her. She is wife no longer. Let her go."

His contemptuous indifference turned Mrs. Fitzpatrick's wrath upon him.

"An' it's yersilf that ought to take shame to yersilf fer the way ye've treated her, an' so ye should!"

The man waved his hand as if to brush aside a matter of quite trifling moment.

"It matters not," he repeated. "She is only a cow."

"Let her come in," whispered Irma, laying her hand again on Mrs. Fitzpatrick's arm.

"Sure she will," cried the Irish woman; "come in here, you poor, spiritless craythur."

Irma sprang down the steps, spoke a few hurried words in Galician. Poor Paulina hesitated, her eyes upon her husband's face. He made a contemptuous motion with his hand as if calling a dog to heel. Immediately, like a dog, the woman crept in and sat far away from the fire in a corner of the room.

"Ye'll pardon me," said Mrs. Fitzpatrick to Kalmar, "fer not axin' ye in at the first; but indade, an' it's more your blame than mine, fer sorra a bit o' thim takes afther ye."

"They do not resemble me, you mean?" said the father. "No, they are the likeness of their mother." As he spoke he pulled out a leather case, opened it and passed it to Mrs. Fitzpatrick.

"Aw, will ye look at that now!" she cried, gazing at the beautiful miniature. "An' the purty face av her. Sure, it's a rale queen she was, an' that's no lie. An' the girl is goin' to be the very spit av her. An' the bye, he's got her blue eyes an' her bright hair. It's aisy seen where they git their looks," she added, glancing at him.

"Mind yer manners, now thin," growled Tim, who was very considerably impressed by the military carriage and the evident "quality" of their guest.

"Yes, the children have the likeness of their mother," said the father in a voice soft and reminiscent. "It is in their behalf I am here to-night, Madam—what shall I have the honour to name you?"

"Me name, is it?" cried Mrs. Fitzpatrick. "Mishtress Timothy Fitzpatrick, Monaghan that was, the Monaghans o' Ballinghalereen, an owld family, poor as Job's turkey, but proud as the divil, an' wance the glory o' Mayo. An' this," she added, indicating her spouse with a jerk of her thumb, "is Timothy Fitzpatrick, me husband, a dacent man in his way. Timothy, where's yer manners? Shtand up an' do yer duty."

Tim struggled to his feet, embarrassed with the burden of Paulina's baby, and pulled his forelock.

"And my name," said the Russian, answering Timothy's salutation with a profound bow, "is Michael Kalmar, with respect to you and Mr. Vichpatrick."

Mrs. Fitzpatrick was evidently impressed.

"An' proud I am to see ye in me house," she said, answering his bow with a curtsey. "Tim, ye owl ye! Why don't ye hand his honour a chair? Did ye niver git the air o' a gintleman before?"

It took some minutes to get the company settled, owing to the reluctance of the Russian to seat himself while the lady was standing, and the equal reluctance of Mrs. Fitzpatrick to take her seat until she had comfortably settled her guest.

"I come to you, Mrs. Vichpatrick, on behalf of my children."

"An' fine childer they are, barrin' the lad is a bit av a limb betimes."

In courteous and carefully studied English, Kalmar told his need. His affairs called him to Europe. He might be gone a year, perhaps more. He needed some one to care for his children. Paulina, though nothing to him now, would be faithful in caring for them, as far as food, clothing and shelter were concerned. She would dismiss her boarders. There had never been need of her taking boarders, but for the fraud of a wicked man. It was at this point that he needed help. Would Mrs. Fitzpatrick permit him to send her money from time to time which should be applied to the support of Paulina and the children. He would also pay her for her trouble.

At this Mrs. Fitzpatrick, who had been listening impatiently for some moments, broke forth upon him.

"Ye can kape yer money," she cried wrathfully. "What sort av a man are ye, at all, at all, that ye sind yer helpless childer to a strange land with a scut like that?"

"Paulina was an honest woman once," he interposed.

"An' what for," she continued wrathfully, "are ye lavin' thim now among a pack o' haythen? Look at that girl now, what'll come to her in that bloody pack o' thieves an' blackguards, d'ye think? Howly Joseph! It's mesilf that kapes wakin' benights to listen fer the screams av her. Why don't ye shtay like a man by yer childer an' tell me that?"

"My affairs—" began the Russian, with a touch of hauteur in his tone.

"An' what affairs have ye needin' ye more than yer childer? Tell me that, will ye?"

And truth to tell, Mrs. Fitzpatrick's indignation blazed forth not only on behalf of the children, but on behalf of the unfortunate Paulina as well, whom, in spite of herself, she pitied.

"What sort av a heart have ye, at all, at all?"

"A heart!" cried the Russian, rising from his chair. "Madam, my heart is for my country. But you would not understand. My country calls me."

"Yer counthry!" repeated Mrs. Fitzpatrick with scorn. "An' what counthry is that?"

"Russia," said the man with dignity, "my native land."

"Rooshia! An' a bloody country it is," answered Mrs. Fitzpatrick with scorn.

"Yes, Russia," he cried, "my bloody country! You are correct. Red with the blood of my countrymen, the blood of my kindred this hundred years and more." His voice was low but vibrant with passion. "You cannot understand. Why should I tell you?"

At this juncture Timothy sprang to his feet.

"Sit ye down, dear man, sit ye down! Shut yer clapper, Nora! Sure it's mesilf that knows a paythriot whin I sees 'im. Tear-an-ages! Give me yer hand, me boy. Sit ye down an' tell us about it. We're all the same kind here. Niver fear for the woman, she's the worst o' the lot. Tell us, dear man. Be the light that shines! it's mesilf that's thirsty to hear."

The Russian gazed at the shining eyes of the little Irishman as if he had gone mad. Then, as if the light had broken upon him, he cried, "Aha, you are of Ireland. You, too, are fighting the tyrant."

"Hooray, me boy!" shouted Tim, "an' it's the thrue word ye've shpoke, an' niver a lie in the skin av it. Oireland foriver! Be the howly St. Patrick an' all the saints, I am wid ye an' agin ivery government that's iver robbed an honest man. Go on, me boy, tell us yer tale."

Timothy was undoubtedly excited. The traditions of a hundred years of fierce rebellion against the oppression of the "bloody tyrant" were beating at his brain and in his heart. The Russian caught fire from him and launched forth upon his tale. For a full hour, now sitting in his chair, now raging up and down the room, now in a voice deep, calm and terrible, now broken and hoarse with sobs, he recounted deeds of blood and fire that made Ireland's struggle and Ireland's wrongs seem nursery rhymes.

Timothy listened to the terrible story in an ecstasy of alternating joy and fury, according to the nature of the episode related. It was like living again the glorious days of the moonlighters and the rackrenters in dear old Ireland. The tale came to an abrupt end.

"An' thin what happened?" cried Timothy.

"Then," said the Russian quietly, "then it was Siberia."

"Siberia! The Hivins be about us!" said Tim in an awed voice. "But ye got away?"

"I am here," he replied simply.

"Be the sowl of Moses, ye are! An' wud ye go back agin?" cried Tim in horror.

"Wud he!" said Nora, with ineffable scorn. "Wud a herrin' swim? By coorse he'll go back. An' what's more, ye can sind the money to me an' I'll see that the childer gets the good av it, if I've to wring the neck av that black haythen, Rosenblatt, like a chicken."

"You will take the money for my children?" enquired the Russian.

"I will that."

He stretched out his hand impulsively. She placed hers in it. He raised it to his lips, bending low as if it had been the lily white hand of the fairest lady in the land, instead of the fat, rough, red hand of an old Irish washer-woman.

"Sure, it's mighty bad taste ye have," said Tim with a sly laugh. "It's not her hand I'd be kissin'."

"Bad luck to ye! Have ye no manners?" said Nora, jerking away her hand in confusion.

"I thank you with all my heart," said Kalmar, gravely bowing with his hand upon his heart. "And will you now and then look over—over-look—oversee—ah yes, oversee this little girl?"

"Listen to me now," cried Mrs. Fitzpatrick. "Can she clear out thim men from her room?" nodding her head toward Paulina.

"There will be no men in her house."

"Can she kape thim out? She's only a wake craythur anyway."

"Paulina," said her husband.

She came forward and, taking his hand, kissed it, Mrs. Fitzpatrick looking on in disgust.

"This woman asks can you keep the men out of your room," he said in Galician.

"I will keep them out," she said simply.

"Aye, but can she?" said Mrs. Fitzpatrick, to whom her answer had been translated.

"I can kill them in the night," said Paulina, in a voice of quiet but concentrated passion.

"The saints in Hivin be above us! I belave her," said Mrs. Fitzpatrick, with a new respect for Paulina. "But fer the love o' Hivin, tell her there is no killin' in this counthry, an' more's the pity when ye see some men that's left to run about."

"She will keep the children safe with her life," said Kalmar. "She had no money before, and she was told I was dead. But it matters not. She is nothing to me. But she will keep my children with her life."

His trust in her, his contempt for her, awakened in Mrs. Fitzpatrick a kind of hostility toward him, and of pity for the wretched woman whom, while he trusted, he so despised.

"Come an' take an air o' the fire, Paulina," she said not unkindly. "It's cold forninst the door."

Paulina, while she understood not the words, caught the meaning of the gesture, but especially of the tone. She drew near, caught the Irish woman's hand in hers and kissed it.

"Hut!" said Mrs. Fitzpatrick, drawing away her hand. "Sit down, will ye?"

The Russian rose to his feet.

"I must now depart. I have still a little work to accomplish. To-morrow I leave the city. Permit me now to bid my children farewell."

He turned to the girl, who held Paulina's baby asleep in her arms. "Irma," he said in Russian, "I am going to leave you."

The girl rose, placed the sleeping baby on the bed, and coming to her father's side, stood looking up into his face, her wonderful brown eyes shining with tears she was too brave to shed.

He drew her to him.

"I am going to leave you," he repeated in Russian. "In one year, if all is well, at most in two, I shall return. You know I cannot stay with you, and you know why." He took the miniature from his pocket and opening it, held it before her face. "Your mother gave her life for her country." For some moments he gazed upon the beautiful face in the miniature. "She was a lady, and feared not death. Ah! ah! such a death!" He struggled fiercely with his emotions. "She was willing to die. Should not I? You do not grudge that I should leave you, that I should die, if need be?" An anxious, almost wistful tone crept into his voice.

Bravely the little girl looked up into the dark face.

"I remember my mother," she said; "I would be like her."

"Aha!" cried her father, catching her to his breast, "I judged you rightly. You are her daughter, and you will live worthy of her. Kalman, come hither. Irma, you will care for your brother. He is young. He is a boy. He will need care. Kalman, heart of my life!"

"He does not understand Russian," said Paulina. "Speak in Galician."

"Ha," cried the man, turning sharply upon her as if he had forgotten her existence. "Kalman, my son," he proceeded in Russian, "did you not understand what I said to your sister?"

"Not well, father," said the boy; "a little."

"Alas, that you should have forgotten your mother's speech!"

"I shall learn it again from Irma," said the boy.

"Good," replied the father in Galician. "Listen then. Never forget you are a Russian. This," putting the miniature before him, "was your mother. She was a lady. For her country she gave up rank, wealth, home and at last life. For her country, too, I go back again. When my work is done I shall return."

Through the window came sounds of revelry from the house near by.

"You are not of these cattle," he said, pointing through the window. "Your mother was a lady. Be worthy of her, boy. Now farewell."

The boy stood without word, without motion, without tear, his light blue eyes fixed upon his father's face, his fair skin white but for a faint spot of red on his cheek.

"Obey your sister, Kalman, and defend her. And listen, boy." His voice deepened into a harsh snarl, his fingers sank into the boy's shoulder, but the boy winced not. "If any man does her wrong, you will kill him. Say it, boy? What will you do?"

"Kill him," said the boy with fierce promptitude, speaking in the English tongue.

"Ha! yes," replied his father in English, "you bear your mother's face, her golden hair, her eyes of blue—they are not so beautiful—but you have your father's spirit. You would soon learn to kill in Russia, but in this land you will not kill unless to defend your sister from wrong."

His mood swiftly changed. He paused, looking sadly at his children; then turning to Mrs. Fitzpatrick he said, "They should go to the public school like Simon Ketzel's little girl. They speak not such good English as she. She is very clever."

"Sure, they must go to school," said she. "An' go they will."

"My gratitude will be with you forever. Good-by."

He shook hands with Timothy, then with Mrs. Fitzpatrick, kissing her hand as well. He motioned his children toward him.

"Heart of my heart," he murmured in a broken voice, straining his daughter to his breast. "God, if God there be, and all the saints, if saints there be, have you in their keeping. Kalman, my son," throwing one arm about him, "Farewell! farewell!" He was fast losing control of himself. The stormy Slavic passions were threatening to burst all restraint. "I give you to each other. But you will remember that it was not for my sake, but for Russia's sake, I leave you. My heart, my heart belongs to you, but my heart's heart is not for me, nor for you, but for Russia, for your mother's land and ours."

By this time tears were streaming down his cheek. Sobs shook his powerful frame. Irma was clinging to him in an abandonment of weeping. Kalman stood holding tight to his father, rigid, tearless, white. At length the father tore away their hands and once more crying "Farewell!" made toward the door.

At this the boy broke forth in a loud cry, "Father! My father! Take me with you! I would not fear! I would not fear to die. Take me to Russia!" The boy ran after his father and clutched him hard.

"Ah, my lad, you are your mother's son and mine. Some day you may go back. Who knows? But—no, no. Canada is your country. Go back." The lad still clutched him. "Boy," said his father, steadying his voice with great effort and speaking quietly, "with us, in our country, we learn first, obedience."

The lad dropped his hold.

"Good!" said the father. "You are my own son. You will yet be a man. And now farewell."

He kissed them again. The boy broke into passionate sobbing. Paulina came forward and, kneeling at the father's feet, put her face to the floor.

"I will care for the son of my lord," she murmured.

But with never a look at her, the father strode to the door and passed out into the night.

"Be the howly prophet!" cried Tim, wiping his eyes, "it's harrd, it's harrd! An' it's the heart av a paythriot the lad carries inside av him! An' may Hivin be about him!"

Chapter VI

The Grip of British Law

I t was night in Winnipeg, a night of such radiant moonlight as is
seen only in northern climates and in winter time. During the
early evening a light snow had fallen, not driving fiercely after the
Manitoba manner, but gently, and so lay like a fleecy, shimmering
mantle over all things.

Under this fleecy mantle, shimmering with myriad gems, lay Winnipeg asleep. Up from five thousand chimneys rose straight into the
still frosty air five thousand columns of smoke, in token that, though
frost was king outside, the good folk of Winnipeg lay snug and warm in
their virtuous beds. Everywhere the white streets lay in silence except
for the passing of a belated cab with creaking runners and jingling
bells, and of a sleighing party returning from Silver Heights, their four-
horse team smoking, their sleigh bells ringing out, carrying with them
hoarse laughter and hoarser songs, for the frosty air works mischief
with the vocal chords, and leaving behind them silence again.

All through Fort Rouge, lying among its snow-laden trees, across
the frost-bound Assiniboine, all through the Hudson's Bay Reserve,
there was no sign of life, for it was long past midnight. Even Main
Street, that most splendid of all Canadian thoroughfares, lay white
and spotless and, for the most part, in silence. Here and there men in
furs or in frieze coats with collars turned up high, their eyes peering

through frost-rimmed eyelashes and over frost-rimmed coat collars, paced comfortably along if in furs, or walked hurriedly if only in frieze, whither their business or their pleasure led.

Near the northern limits of the city the signs of life were more in evidence. At the Canadian Pacific Railway station an engine, hoary with frozen steam, puffed contentedly as if conscious of sufficient strength for the duty that lay before it, waiting to hook on to Number Two, nine hours late, and whirl it eastward in full contempt of frost and snow bank and blizzard.

Inside the station a railway porter or two drowsed on the benches. Behind the wicket where the telegraph instruments kept up an incessant clicking, the agent and his assistant sat alert, coming forward now and then to answer, with the unwearying courtesy which is part of their equipment and of their training, the oft repeated question from impatient and sleepy travellers, "How is she now?" "An hour," "half an hour," finally "fifteen minutes," then "any time now." At which cheering report the uninitiated brightened up and passed out to listen for the rumble of the approaching train. The more experienced, however, settled down for another half hour's sleep.

It was a wearisome business, and to none more wearisome than to Interpreter Elex Murchuk, part of whose duty it is to be in attendance on the arrival of all incoming trains in case that some pilgrim from Central and Southern Europe might be in need of direction. For Murchuk, a little borderland Russian, boasts the gift of tongues to an extraordinary degree. Russian, in which he was born, and French, and German, and Italian, of course, he knows, but Polish, Ruthenian, and all varieties of Ukranian speech are alike known to him.

"I spik all European language good, jus' same Angleesh," was his testimony in regard to himself.

As the whistle of the approaching train was heard, Sergeant Cameron strolled into the station house, carrying his six feet two and his two hundred pounds of bone and muscle with the light and easy movements of the winner of many a Caledonian Society medal. Cameron, at one time a full private in the 78th Highlanders, is now Sergeant in the Winnipeg City Police, and not ashamed of his job. Big, calm, good-tempered, devoted to his duty, keen for the honour of the force as he had been for the honour of his regiment in other days, Sergeant Cameron was known to all good citizens as an officer to be trusted and to all others as a man to be feared.

Just at present he was finishing up his round of inspection. After the train had pulled in he would go on duty as patrolman, in the place of Officer Donnelly, who was down with pneumonia. The Winnipeg Police Force was woefully inadequate in point of strength, there being no spare men for emergencies, and hence Sergeant Cameron found it necessary to do double duty that night, and he was prepared to do it without grumbling, too. Long watches and weary marches were nothing new to him, and furthermore, to-night there was especial reason why he was not unwilling to take a walk through the north end. Headquarters had been kept fully informed of the progress of a wedding feast of more than ordinary hilarity in the foreign colony. This was the second night, and on second nights the general joyousness of the festivities was more than likely to become unduly exuberant. Indeed, the reports of the early evening had been somewhat disquieting, and hence, Sergeant Cameron was rather pleased than not that Officer Donnelly's beat lay in the direction of the foreign colony.

At length Number Two rolled in, a double header, one engine alive and one dead, but both swathed in snow and frozen steam from cowcatcher to tender, the first puffing its proud triumph over the opposing elements, the second silent, cold and lifeless like a warrior borne from the field of battle.

The passengers, weary and full of the mild excitement of their long struggle with storm and drift across half a continent, emerged from their snow-clad but very comfortable coaches and were eagerly taken in charge by waiting friends and watchful hotel runners.

Sergeant Cameron waited till the crowd had gone, and then turning to Murchuk, he said, "You will be coming along with me, Murchuk. I am going to look after some of your friends."

"My friends?" enquired Murchuk.

"Yes, over at the colony yonder."

"My friends!" repeated Murchuk with some indignation. "Not motch!" Murchuk was proud of his official position as Dominion Government Interpreter. "But I will go wit' you. It is my way."

Away from the noise of the puffing engines and the creaking car wheels, the ears of Sergeant Cameron and his friend were assailed by other and less cheerful sounds.

"Will you listen to that now?" said the Sergeant to his polyglot companion. "What do you think of that for a civilised city? The Indians are not in it with that bunch," continued the Sergeant, who was diligently endeavouring to shed his Highland accent and to take on the colloquialisms of the country.

From a house a block and a half away, a confused clamour rose up into the still night air.

"Oh, dat noting," cheerfully said the little Russian, shrugging his shoulders, "dey mak like dat when dey having a good time."

"They do, eh? And how do you think their neighbours will be liking that sort of thing?"

The Sergeant stood still to analyse this confused clamour. Above the thumping and the singing of the dancers could be heard the sound of breaking boards, mingled with yells and curses.

"Murchuk, there is fighting going on."

"Suppose," agreed the Interpreter, "when Galician man get married, he want much joy. He get much beer, much fight."

"I will just be taking a walk round there," said the Sergeant. "These people have got to learn to get married with less fuss about it. I am not going to stand this much longer. What do they want to fight for anyway?"

"Oh," replied Murchuk lightly, "Polak not like Slovak, Slovak not like Galician. Dey drink plenty beer, tink of someting in Old Country, get mad, make noise, fight some."

"Come along with me," replied the Sergeant, and he squared his big shoulders and set off down the street with the quick, light stride that suggested the springing step of his Highland ancestors on the heather hills of Scotland.

Just as they arrived at the house of feasting, a cry, wild, weird and horrible, pierced through the uproar. The Interpreter stopped as if struck with a bullet.

"My God!" he cried in an undertone, clutching the Sergeant by the arm, "My God! Dat terrible!"

"What is it? What is the matter with you, Murchuk?"

"You know not dat cry? No?" He was all trembling. "Dat cry I hear long ago in Russland. Russian man mak dat cry when he kill. Dat Nihilist cry."

"Go back and get Dr. Wright. He will be needed, sure. You know where he lives, second corner down on Main Street. Get a move on! Quick!"

Meantime, while respectable Winnipeg lay snugly asleep under snow-covered roofs and smoking chimneys, while belated revellers and travellers were making their way through white, silent streets and under avenues of snow-laden trees to homes where reigned love and peace and virtue, in the north end and in the foreign colony the festivities in connection with Anka's wedding were drawing to a close in sordid drunken dance and song and in sanguinary fighting.

In the main room dance and song reeled on in uproarious hilarity. In the basement below, foul and fetid, men stood packed close, drinking while they could. It was for the foreigner an hour of rare opportunity. The beer kegs stood open and there were plenty of tin mugs about. In the dim light of a smoky lantern, the swaying crowd, here singing in maudlin chorus, there fighting savagely to pay off old scores or to avenge new insults, presented a nauseating spectacle.

In the farthest corner of the room, unmoved by all this din, about a table consisting of a plank laid across two beer kegs, one empty, the other for the convenience of the players half full, sat four men deep in a game of cards. Rosenblatt with a big Dalmatian sailor as partner, against a little Polak and a dark-bearded man. This man was apparently very drunk, as was evident by his reckless playing and his jibing, jeering manner. He was losing money, but with perfect good cheer. Not so his partner, the Polak. Every loss made him more savage and quarrelsome. With great difficulty Rosenblatt was able to keep the game going and preserve peace. The singing, swaying, yelling, cursing crowd beside them also gave him concern, and over and again he would shout, "Keep quiet, you fools. The police will be on us, and that will be the end of your beer, for they will put you in prison!"

"Yes," jeered the black-bearded man, who seemed to be set on making a row, "all fools, Russian fools, Polak fools, Galician fools, Slovak fools, all fools together."

Angry voices replied from all sides, and the noise rose higher.

"Keep quiet!" cried Rosenblatt, rising to his feet, "the police will surely be here!"

"That is true," cried the black-bearded man, "keep them quiet or the police will herd them in like sheep, like little sheep, baa, baa, baa, baa!"

"The police!" shouted a voice in reply, "who cares for the police?"

A yell of derisive assent rose in response.

"Be quiet!" besought Rosenblatt again. He was at his wits' end. The police might at any time appear and that would end what was for him a very profitable game, and besides might involve him in serious trouble. "Here you, Joseph!" he cried, addressing a man near him, "another keg of beer!"

Between them they hoisted up a keg of beer on an empty cask, knocked in the head, and set them drinking with renewed eagerness.

"Swine!" he said, seating himself again at the table. "Come, let us play."

But the very devil of strife seemed to be in the black-bearded man. He gibed at the good-natured Dalmatian, setting the Polak at him, suggested crooked dealing, playing recklessly and losing his own and his partner's money. At length the inevitable clash came. As the Dalmatian reached for a trick, the Polak cried out, "Hold! It is mine!"

"Yes, certainly it is his!" shouted the black-bearded man.

"Liar! It is mine," said the Dalmatian, with perfect good temper, and held on to his cards.

"Liar yourself!" hissed the little Polak, thrusting his face toward the Dalmatian.

"Go away," said the Dalmatian. His huge open hand appeared to rest a moment on the Polak's grinning face, and somehow the little man was swept from his seat to the floor.

"Ho, ho," laughed the Dalmatian, "so I brush away a fly."

With a face like a demon's, the Polak sprang at his big antagonist, an open knife in his hand, and jabbed him in the arm. For a moment the big man sat looking at his assailant as if amazed at his audacity. Then as he saw the blood running down his fingers he went mad, seized the Polak by the hair, lifted him clear out of his seat, carrying the plank table with him, and thereupon taking him by the back of the neck, proceeded to shake him till his teeth rattled in his head.

At almost the same instant the black-bearded man leaped across the fallen table like a tiger, at Rosenblatt's throat, and bore him down to the earthen floor in the dark corner. Sitting astride his chest, his knees on Rosenblatt's arms, and gripping him by the throat, he held him voiceless and helpless. Soon his victim lay still, looking up into his assailant's face in surprise, fear and rage unspeakable.

"Rosenblatt," said the bearded man in a soft voice, "you know me—me?"

"No," gasped Rosenblatt in terrible fury, "what do you—"

"Look," said the man. With his free hand he swept off the black beard which he stuffed into his pocket.

Rosenblatt looked. "Kalmar!" he gasped, terror in his eyes.

"Yes, Kalmar," replied the man.

"Help!—" The cry died at his teeth.

"No, no," said Kalmar, shutting his fingers upon his windpipe. "No noise. We are to have a quiet moment here. They are all too busy to notice us. Listen." He leaned far down over the ghastly face of the wretched man beneath him. "Shall I tell you why I am here? Shall I remind you of your crimes? No, I need not. You remember them well, and in a few minutes you will be in hell for them. Five years I froze and burned in Siberia, through you." As he said the word "you" he leaned a little closer. His voice remained low and soft, but his eyes were blazing with a light as of madness. "For this moment," he continued gently, "I have hungered, thirsted, panted. Now it has come. I regret I must hurry a little. I should like to drink this sweet cup slowly, oh so slowly, drop by drop. But—ah, do not struggle, nor cry. It will only add to your pain. Do you see this?" He drew from his pocket what seemed a knife handle, pressed a spring, and from this handle there shot out a blade, long, thin, murderous looking. "It has a sharp point, oh, a very sharp point." He pricked Rosenblatt in the cheek, and as Rosenblatt squirmed, laughed a laugh of singular sweetness. "With this beautiful instrument I mean to pick out your eyes, and then I shall drive it down through your heart, and you will be dead. It will not hurt so very much," he continued in a tone of regret. "No no, not so very much; not so much as when you put out the light of my life, when you murdered my wife; not so much as when you pierced my heart in betraying my cause. See, it will not hurt so very much." He put the sharp blade against Rosenblatt's breast high up above the heart, and drove it slowly down through the soft flesh till he came to bone. Like a mad thing, his unhappy victim threw himself wildly about in a furious struggle. But he was like a babe in the hands that gripped him. Kalmar laughed gleefully. "Aha! Aha! Good! Good! You give me much joy. Alas! it is so short-lived, and I must hurry. Now for your right eye. Or would you prefer the left first?"

As he released the pressure upon Rosenblatt's throat, the wretched man gurgled forth, "Mercy! Mercy! God's name, mercy!"

Piteous abject terror showed in his staring eyes. His voice was to Kalmar like blood to a tiger.

"Mercy!" he hissed, thrusting his face still nearer, his smile now all gone. "Mercy? God's name! Hear him! I, too, cried for mercy for father, brother, wife, but found none. Now though God Himself should plead, you will have only such mercy from me." He seemed to lose hold of himself. His breath came in thick sharp sobs, foam fell from his lips. "Ha," he gasped. "I cannot wait even to pick your eyes. There is some one at the door. I must drink your heart's blood now! Now! A-h-h-h!" His voice rose in a wild cry, weird and terrible. He raised his knife high, but as it fell the Dalmatian, who had been amusing himself battering the Polak about during these moments, suddenly heaved the little man at Kalmar, and knocked him into the corner. The knife fell, buried not in the heart of Rosenblatt, but in the Polak's neck.

There was no time to strike again. There was a loud battering, then a crash as the door was kicked open.

"Hello! What is all this row here?"

It was Sergeant Cameron, pushing his big body through the crowd as a man bursts through a thicket. An awed silence had fallen upon all, arrested, sobered by that weird cry. Some of them knew that cry of old. They had heard it in the Old Land in circumstances of heart-chilling terror, but never in this land till this moment.

"What is all this?" cried the Sergeant again. His glance swept the room and rested upon the huddled heap of men in the furthest corner. He seized the topmost and hauled him roughly from the heap.

"Hello! What's this? Why, God bless my soul! The man is dying!"

From a wound in the neck the blood was still spouting. Quickly the Sergeant was on his knees beside the wounded man, his thumb pressed hard upon the gaping wound. But still the blood continued to bubble up and squirt from under his thumb. All around, the earthen floor was muddy with blood.

"Run, some of you," commanded the Sergeant, "and hurry up that Dr. Wright, Main Street, two corners down!"

Jacob Wassyl, who had come in from the room above, understood, and sent a man off with all speed.

"Good Lord! What a pig sticking!" said the Sergeant. "There is a barrel of blood around here. And here is another man! Here you!" addressing Jacob, "put your thumb here and press so. It is not much good, but we cannot do anything else just now." The Sergeant straightened himself up. Evidently this was no ordinary "scrap." "Let no man leave this room," he cried aloud. "Tell them," he said, addressing Jacob, "you speak English; and two of you, you and you, stand by the door and let no man out except as I give the word."

The two men took their places.

"Now then, let us see what else there is here. Do you know these men?" he enquired of Jacob.

"Dis man," replied Jacob, "I not know. Him Polak man."

The men standing about began to jabber.

"What do they say?"

"Him Polak. Kravicz his name. He no bad man. He fight quick, but not a bad man."

"Well, he won't fight much more, I am thinking," replied the Sergeant.

A second man lay on his back in a pool of blood, insensible. His face showed ghastly beneath its horrible smear of blood and filth.

"Bring me that lantern," commanded the Sergeant.

"My God!" cried Jacob, "it is Rosenblatt!"

"Rosenblatt? Who is he?"

"De man dat live here, dis house. He run store. Lots mon'. My God! He dead!"

"Looks like it," said the Sergeant, opening his coat. "He's got a bad hole in him here," he continued, pointing to a wound in the chest. "Looks deep, and he is bleeding, too."

There was a knocking at the door.

"Let him in," cried the Sergeant, "it is the doctor. Hello, Doctor! Here is something for you all right."

The doctor, a tall, athletic young fellow with a keen, intellectual face, pushed his way through the crowd to the corner and dropped on his knees beside the Polak.

"Why, the man is dead!" said the doctor, putting his hand over the Polak's heart.

Even as he spoke, a shudder passed through the man's frame, and he lay still. The doctor examined the hole in his neck.

"Yes, he's dead, sure enough. The jugular vein is severed."

"Well, here is another, Doctor, who will be dead in a few minutes, if I am not mistaken," said the Sergeant.

"Let me see," said the doctor, turning to Rosenblatt. "Heavens above!" he cried, as his knees sank in the bloody mud, "it's blood!"

He passed round the other side of the unconscious man, got out his syringe and gave him a hypodermic. In a few minutes Rosenblatt showed signs of life. He began to breathe heavily, then to cough and spit mouthfuls of blood.

"Ha, lung, I guess," said the doctor, examining a small clean wound high up in the left breast. "Better send for an ambulance, Sergeant, and hurry them up. The sooner we get him to the hospital, the better. And here is another man. What's wrong with him?"

Beyond Rosenblatt lay a black-bearded man upon his face, breathing heavily. The doctor turned him over.

"He's alive anyway, and," after examination, "I can't find any wound. Heart all right, nothing wrong with him, I guess, except that he's got a bad jag on."

A cursory examination of the crowd revealed wounds in plenty, but nothing serious enough to demand the doctor's attention.

"Now then," said the Sergeant briskly, "I want to get your names and addresses. You can let me have them?" he continued, turning to Jacob.

"Me not know all mens."

"Go on," said the Sergeant curtly.

"Dis man Rosenblatt. Dis man Polak, Kravicz. Not know where he live."

"It would be difficult, I am thinking, for any one to tell where he lives now," said the Sergeant grimly, "and it does not much matter for my purpose."

"Poor chap," said the doctor, "it's too bad."

"What?" said the Sergeant, glancing at him, "well, it is too bad, that is true. But they are a bad lot, these Galicians."

"Poor chap," continued the doctor, looking down upon him, "perhaps he has got a wife and children."

A murmur rose among the men.

"No, he got no wife," said Jacob.

"Thank goodness for that!" said the doctor. "These fellows are a bit rough," he continued, "but they have never had a chance, nor even half a chance. A beastly tyrannical government at home has put the fear of death on them for this world, and an ignorant and superstitious Church has kept them in fear of purgatory and hell fire for the next. They have never had a chance in their own land, and so far, they have got no better chance here, except that they do not live in the fear of Siberia." The doctor had his own views upon the foreign peoples in the West.

"That is all right, Doctor," said the Sergeant, despite the Calvinism of generations beating in his heart, "it is hard on them, but there is nobody compelling them here to drink and fight like a lot of brutes."

"But who is to teach them any better?" said the doctor.

"Come on," said the Sergeant, "who is this?" pointing to the dark-bearded man lying in the corner.

"Dis man," said Jacob, "strange man."

"Any of you know him here?" asked the Sergeant.

There was a murmur of voices.

"What do they say?"

"No one know him. He drink much beer. He very drunk. He play cards wit' Rosenblatt," said Jacob.

"Playing cards, eh? I think we will be finding something now. Who else was in the card game?"

Again a murmur of voices arose.

"Dis Polak man," said Jacob, "and Rosenblatt, and dat man dere, and—"

Half a dozen voices rose in explanation, and half a dozen hands eagerly pointed out the big Dalmatian, who stood back among the crowd pale with terror.

"Come up here, you," said the Sergeant to him.

Instead of responding, with one bound the Dalmatian was at the door, and hurled the two men aside as if they were wooden pegs. But before he could tear open the door, the Sergeant was on him. At once the Dalmatian grappled with him in a fierce struggle. There was a quick angry growl from the crowd. They all felt themselves to be in an awkward position. Once out of the room, it would be difficult for any police officer to associate them in any way with the crime. The odds were forty to one. Why not make a break for liberty? A rush was made for the struggling pair at the door.

"Get back there!" roared the Sergeant, swinging his baton and holding off his man with the other hand.

At the same instant the doctor, springing up from his patient, and taking in the situation, put down his head and bored through the crowd in the manner which at one time had been the admiration and envy of his fellow-students in Manitoba College, till he found himself side by side with the Sergeant.

"Well done!" cried the Sergeant in cheerful approval, "you are the lad! We will just be teaching these chaps a fery good lesson, whateffer," continued the Sergeant, lapsing in his excitement into his native dialect. "Here you," he cried to the big Dalmatian who was struggling and kicking in a frenzy of fear and rage, "will you not keep quiet? Take that then." And he laid no gentle tap with his baton across the head of his captive.

The Dalmatian staggered to the wall and collapsed. There was a flash of steel and a click, and he lay handcuffed and senseless at the Sergeant's side.

"I hate to do that," said the Sergeant apologetically, "but on this occasion it cannot be helped. That was a good one, Doctor," he continued, as the doctor planted his left upon an opposing Galician chin, thereby causing a sudden subsidence of its owner. "These men have not got used to us yet, and we will just have to be patient with them," said the Sergeant, laying about with his baton as opportunity offered, not in any slashing wholesale manner, but making selection, and delivering his blows with the eye and hand of an artist. He was handling the situation gently and with discretion. Still the crowd kept pressing hard upon the two men at the door.

"We must put a stop to this," said the Sergeant seriously. "Here you!" he called to Jacob above the uproar.

Jacob pushed nearer to him.

"Tell these fellows that I am not wanting to hurt any of them, but if they do not get quiet soon, I will attack them and will not spare them, and that if they quit their fighting, none of them will be hurt except the guilty party."

At once Jacob sprang upon a beer keg and waving his arms wildly, he secured a partial silence, and translated for them the Sergeant's words.

"And tell them, too," said the doctor in a high, clear voice, "there is a man dying over there that I have got to attend to right now, and I haven't time for this foolishness."

As he spoke, he once more bored his way through the crowd to the side of Rosenblatt, who was continuing to gasp painfully and spit blood. The moment of danger was past. The excited crowd settled down again into an appearance of stupid anxiety, awaiting they knew not what.

"Now then," said the Sergeant, turning to the Dalmatian who had recovered consciousness and was standing sullen and passive. He had made his attempt for liberty, he had failed, and now he was ready to accept his fate. "Ask him what is his name," said the Sergeant.

"He say his name John Jarema."

"And what has he got to say for himself?"

At this the Dalmatian began to speak with eager gesticulation.

"What is he saying?" enquired the Sergeant.

"Dis man say he no hurt no man. Dis man," pointing to the dead Polak, "play cards, fight, stab knife into his arm," said Jacob, pulling up the Dalmatian's coat sleeve to show an ugly gash in the forearm. "Jarema hit him on head, shake him bad, and trow him in corner on noder man."

Again the Dalmatian broke forth.

"He say he got no knife at all. He cannot make hole like dat wit' his finger."

"Well, we shall see about that," said the Sergeant. "Now where is that other man?" He turned toward the corner. The corner was empty. "Where has he gone?" said the Sergeant, peering through the crowd for a black-whiskered face.

The man was nowhere to be seen. The Sergeant was puzzled and angered. He lined the men up around the walls, but the man was not to be found. As each man uttered his name, there were always some to recognize and to corroborate the information. One man alone seemed a stranger to all in the company. He was clean shaven, but for a moustache with ends turned up in military manner, and with an appearance of higher intelligence than the average Galician.

"Ask him his name," said the Sergeant.

The man replied volubly, and Jacob interpreted.

"His name, Rudolph Polkoff, Polak man. Stranger, come to dis town soon. Know no man here. Some man bring him here to dance."

The Sergeant kept his keen eye fastened on the man while he talked.

"Well, he looks like a smart one. Come here," he said, beckoning the stranger forward into the better light.

The man came and stood with his back to Rosenblatt.

"Hold up your hands."

The man stared blankly. Jacob interpreted. He hesitated a moment, then held up his hands above his head. The Sergeant turned him about.

"You will not be having any weepons on you?" said the Sergeant, searching his pockets. "Hello! What's this?" He pulled out the false beard.

The same instant there was a gasping cry from Rosenblatt. All turned in his direction. Into his dim eyes and pallid face suddenly sprang life; fear and hate struggling to find expression in the look he fixed upon the stranger. With a tremendous effort he raised his hand, and pointing to the stranger with a long, dirty finger, he gasped, "Arrest—he murder—" and fell back again unconscious.

Even as he spoke there was a quick movement. The lantern was dashed to the ground, the room plunged into darkness and before the

Sergeant knew what had happened, the stranger had shaken himself free from his grasp, torn open the door and fled.

With a mighty oath, the Sergeant was after him, but the darkness and the crowd interfered with his progress, and by the time he had reached the door, the man had completely vanished. At the door stood Murchuk with the ambulance.

"See a man run out here?" demanded the Sergeant.

"You bet! He run like buck deer."

"Why didn't you stop him?" cried the Sergeant.

"Stop him!" replied the astonished Murchuk, "would you stop a mad crazy bull? No, no, not me."

"Get that man inside to the hospital then. He won't hurt you," exclaimed the Sergeant in wrathful contempt. "I'll catch that man if I have to arrest every Galician in this city!"

It was an unspeakable humiliation to the Sergeant, but with such vigour did he act, that before the morning dawned, he had every exit from the city by rail and by trail under surveillance, and before a week was past, by adopting the very simple policy of arresting every foreigner who attempted to leave the town, he had secured his man.

It was a notable arrest. From all the evidence, it seemed that the prisoner was a most dangerous criminal. The principal source of evidence, however, was Rosenblatt, whose deposition was taken down by the Sergeant and the doctor.

The man, it appeared, was known by many names, Koval, Kolowski, Polkoff and others, but his real name was Michael Kalmar. He was a determined and desperate Nihilist, was wanted for many crimes by the Russian police, and had spent some years as a convict in Siberia where, if justice had its due, he would be at the present time. He had cast off his wife and children, whom he had shipped to Canada. Incidentally it came out that it was only Rosenblatt's generosity that had intervened between them and starvation. Balked in one of his desperate Nihilist schemes by Rosenblatt, who held a position of trust under the Russian Government, he had sworn vengeance, and escaping from Siberia, he had come to Canada to make good his oath. And but for the timely appearance of the police, he would have succeeded.

Meantime, Sergeant Cameron was receiving congratulations on all hands for his cleverness in making the arrest of a man who had escaped the vigilance of the Russian Police and Secret Service, said to be the finest in all Europe. In his cell, the man, as good as condemned, waited his trial, a stranger far from help and kindred, an object of terror and of horror to many, of compassion to a few. But however men thought of him, he had sinned against British civilisation, and would now have to taste of British justice.

Chapter VII

Condemned

The two months preceding the trial were months of restless agony to the prisoner, Kalmar. Day and night he paced his cell like a tiger in a cage, taking little food and sleeping only when overcome with exhaustion. It was not the confinement that fretted him. The Winnipeg jail, with all its defects and limitations, was a palace to some that he had known. It was not the fear of the issue to his trial that drove sleep and hunger from him. Death, exile, imprisonment, had been too long at his heels to be strangers to him or to cause him fear. In his heart a fire burned. Rosenblatt still lived, and vengeance had halted in its pursuit.

But deep as was the passion in his heart for vengeance, that for his country and his cause burned deeper. He had been able to establish lines of communication between his fatherland and the new world by means of which the oppressed, the hunted, might reach freedom and safety. The final touches to his plans were still to be given. Furthermore, it was necessary that he should make his report in person, else much of his labour would be fruitless. It was this that brought him "white nights" and black days.

Every day Paulina called at the jail and waited long hours with uncomplaining patience in the winter cold, till she could be admitted.

Her husband showed no sign of interest, much less of gratitude. One question alone, he asked day by day.

"The children are well?"

"They are well," Paulina would answer. "They ask to see you every day."

"They may not see me here," he would reply, after which she would turn away, her dull face full of patient suffering.

One item of news she brought him that gave him a moment's cheer.

"Kalman," she said, one day, "will speak nothing but Russian."

"Ha!" he exclaimed. "He is my son indeed. But," he added gloomily, "of what use now?"

Others sought admission,—visitors from the Jail Mission, philanthropic ladies, a priest from St. Boniface, a Methodist minister,—but all were alike denied. Simon Ketzel he sent for, and with him held long converse, with the result that he was able to secure for his defence the services of O'Hara, the leading criminal lawyer of Western Canada. There appeared to be no lack of money, and all that money could do was done.

The case began to excite considerable interest, not only in the city, but throughout the whole country. Public opinion was strongly against the prisoner. Never in the history of the new country had a crime been committed of such horrible and bloodthirsty deliberation. It is true that this opinion was based largely upon Rosenblatt's deposition, taken by Sergeant Cameron and Dr. Wright when he was supposed to be *in extremis*, and upon various newspaper interviews with him that appeared from time to time. *The Morning News* in a trenchant leader pointed out the danger to which Western Canada was exposed from the presence of these semibarbarous peoples from Central and Southern Europe, and expressed the hope that the authorities would deal with the present case in such a manner as would give a severe but necessary lesson to the lawless among our foreign population.

There was, indeed, from the first, no hope of acquittal. Staunton, who was acting for the Crown, was convinced that the prisoner would receive the maximum sentence allowed by law. And even O'Hara acknowledged privately to his solicitor that the best he could hope for was a life sentence. "And, by gad! he ought to get it! It is the most damnable case of bloody murder that I have come across in all my practice!" But this was before Mr. O'Hara had interviewed Mrs. Fitzpatrick.

In his hunt for evidence Mr. O'Hara had come upon his fellow countrywoman in the foreign colony. At first from sheer delight in her rich brogue and her shrewd native wit, and afterward from the conviction that her testimony might be turned to good account on behalf of his client, Mr. O'Hara diligently cultivated Mrs. Fitzpatrick's acquaintance. It helped their mutual admiration and their friendship not a little to discover their common devotion to "the cause o' the paythriot in dear owld Ireland," and their mutual interest in the prisoner Kalmar, as a fellow "paythriot."

Immediately upon his discovery of the rich possibilities in Mrs. Fitzpatrick Mr. O'Hara got himself invited to drink a "cup o' tay," which, being made in the little black teapot brought all the way from Ireland, he pronounced to be the finest he had had since coming to Canada fifteen years ago. Indeed, he declared that he had serious doubts as to the possibilities of producing on this side of the water and by people of this country just such tea as he had been accustomed to drink in the dear old land. It was over this cup of tea, and as he drew from Mrs. Fitzpatrick the description of the scene between the Nihilist and his children, that Mr. O'Hara came to realise the vast productivity of the mine he had uncovered. He determined that Mrs. Fitzpatrick should tell this tale in court.

"We'll bate that divil yet!" he exclaimed to his new-found friend, his brogue taking a richer flavour from his environment. "They would be having the life of the poor man for letting a little of the black blood out of the black heart of that traitor and blackguard, and may the divil fly away with him! But we'll bate them yet, and it's yersilf is the one to do it!" he exclaimed in growing excitement and admiration.

At first Mrs. Fitzpatrick was most reluctant to appear in court.

"Sure, what would I do or say in the face av His 'Anner an' the joorymin, with niver a word on the tongue av me?"

"And would you let the poor man go to his death?" cried O'Hara, proceeding to draw a lurid picture of the deadly machinations of the lawyer for the Crown, Rosenblatt and their associates against this unfortunate patriot who, for love of his country and for the honour of his name, had sought to wreak a well-merited vengeance upon the abject traitor.

Under his vehement eloquence Mrs. Fitzpatrick's Celtic nature kindled into flame. She would go to the court, and in the face of Judge and jury and all the rest of them, she would tell them the kind of man they were about to do to death. Over and over again O'Hara had her repeat her story, emphasising with adjurations, oaths and even tears, those passages that his experience told him would be most effective for his purpose, till he felt sure she would do full credit to her part.

During the trial the court room was crowded, not only with the ordinary morbid sensation seekers, but with some of Winnipeg's most respectable citizens. In one corner of the court room there was grouped day after day a small company of foreigners. Every man of Russian blood in the city who could attend, was there. It was against the prisoner's will and desire, but in accordance with O'Hara's plan of defence that Paulina and the children should be present at every session of the court. The proceedings were conducted through an interpreter where it was necessary, Kalmar pleading ignorance of the niceties of the English language.

The prisoner was arraigned on the double charge of attempted murder in the case of Rosenblatt, and of manslaughter in that of the dead Polak. The evidence of Dr. Wright and of Sergeant Cameron, corroborated by that of many eyewitnesses, established beyond a doubt that the wound in Rosenblatt's breast and in the dead Polak's neck was done by the same instrument, and that instrument the spring knife discovered in the basement of Paulina's house.

Kalmar, arrayed in his false black beard, was identified by the Dalmatian and by others as the Polak's partner in the fatal game of cards. Staunton had little difficulty in establishing the identity of the black-bearded man who had appeared here and there during the wedding festivities with Kalmar himself. From the stupid Paulina he skilfully drew evidence substantiating this fact, and though this evidence was ruled out on the ground that she was the prisoner's wife, the effect upon the jury was not lost.

The most damaging testimony was, of course, that offered by Rosenblatt himself, and this evidence Staunton was clever enough to use with dramatic effect. Pale, wasted, and still weak, Rosenblatt told his story to the court in a manner that held the crowd breathless with horror. Never had such a tale been told to Canadian ears. The only man unmoved was the prisoner. Throughout the narrative he maintained an attitude of bored indifference.

It was not in vain, however, that O'Hara sought to weaken the effect of Rosenblatt's testimony by turning the light upon some shady spots in his career. In his ruthless "sweating" of the witness, the lawyer forced the admission that he had once been the friend of the prisoner; that he had been the unsuccessful suitor of the prisoner's first wife; that he had been a member of the same Secret Society in Russia; that he had joined the Secret Service of the Russian Government and had given evidence leading to the breaking up of that Society; that he had furnished the information that led to the prisoner's transportation to Siberia. At this point O'Hara swiftly changed his ground.

"You have befriended this woman, Paulina Koval?"

"Yes."

"You have, in fact, acted as her financial agent?"

"I have assisted her in her financial arrangements. She cannot speak English."

"Whose house does she live in?"

Rosenblatt hesitated. "I am not sure."

"Whose house does she live in?" roared O'Hara, stepping toward him.

"Her own, I think."

"You think!" shouted the lawyer. "You know, don't you? You bought it for her. You made the first payment upon it, did you not?"

"Yes, I did."

"And since that time you have cashed money orders for her that have come month by month?"

Again Rosenblatt hesitated. "I have sometimes—"

"Tell the truth!" shouted O'Hara again; "a lie here can be easily traced. I have the evidence. Did you not cash the money orders that came month by month addressed to Paulina Koval?"

"I did, with her permission. She made her mark."

"Where did the money go?"

"I gave it to her."

"And what did she do with it?"

"I don't know."

"Did she not give you money from time to time to make payments upon the house?"

"No."

"Be careful. Let me remind you that there is a law against perjury. I give you another chance. Did you not receive certain money to make payments on this house?" O'Hara spoke with terrible and deliberate emphasis.

"I did, some."

"And did you make these payments?"

"Yes."

"Would you be surprised to know, as I now tell the court, that since the first payment, made soon after the arrival in the country, not a dollar further had been paid?"

Rosenblatt was silent.

"Answer me!" roared the lawyer. "Would you be surprised to know this?"

"Yes."

"This surprise is waiting you. Now then, who runs this house?"

"Paulina Koval."

"Tell me the truth. Who lets the rooms in this house, and who is responsible for the domestic arrangements of the house? Tell me," said O'Hara, bearing down upon the wretched Rosenblatt.

"I—assist—her—sometimes."

"Then you are responsible for the conditions under which Paulina Koval has been forced to live during these three years?"

Rosenblatt was silent.

"That will do," said O'Hara with contempt unspeakable.

He could easily have made more out of his sweating process had not the prisoner resolutely forbidden any reference to Rosenblatt's treatment of and relation to the unfortunate Paulina or the domestic arrangements that he had introduced into that unfortunate woman's household. Kalmar was rigid in his determination that no stain should come to his honour in this regard.

With the testimony of each succeeding witness the cloud overhanging the prisoner grew steadily blacker. The first ray of light came from an unexpected quarter. It was during the examination of Mrs. Fitzpatrick that O'Hara got his first opening. It was a master stroke of strategy on his part that Mrs. Fitzpatrick was made to appear as a witness for the Crown, for the purpose of establishing the deplorable and culpable indifference to and neglect of his family on the part of the prisoner.

Day after day Mrs. Fitzpatrick had appeared in the court, following the evidence with rising wrath against the Crown, its witnesses, and all the machinery of prosecution. All unwitting of this surging tide of indignation in the heart of his witness the Crown Counsel summoned her to the stand. Mr. Staunton's manner was exceedingly affable.

"Your name, Madam?" he enquired.

"Me name is it?" replied the witness. "An' don't ye know me name as well as I do mesilf?"

Mr. Staunton smiled pleasantly. "But the court desires to share that privilege with me, so perhaps you will be good enough to inform the court of your name."

"If the court wants me name let the court ask it. An' if you want to tell the court me name ye can plaze yersilf, fer it's little I think av a man that'll sit in me house by the hour forninst mesilf an' me husband there, and then let on before the court that he doesn't know the name av me."

"Why, my dear Madam," said the lawyer soothingly, "it is a mere matter of form that you should tell the court your name."

"A matter o' form, is it? Indade, an' it's mighty poor form it is, if ye ask my opinion, which ye don't, an' it's mighty poor manners."

At this point the judge interposed.

"Come, come," he said, "what is your name? I suppose you are not ashamed of it?"

"Ashamed av it, Yer 'Anner!" said Mrs. Fitzpatrick, with an elaborate bow to the judge, "ashamed av it! There's niver a shame goes with the name av Fitzpatrick!"

"Your name is Fitzpatrick?"

"It is, Yer 'Anner. Mistress Timothy Fitzpatrick, Monaghan that was, the Monaghans o' Ballinghalereen, which I'm sure Yer 'Anner'll have heard of, fer the intilligent man ye are."

"Mrs. Timothy Fitzpatrick," said the judge, with the suspicion of a smile, writing the name down. "And your first name?"

"Me Christian name is it? Ah, thin, Judge dear, wud ye be wantin' that too?" smiling at him in quite a coquettish manner. "Sure, if ye had

had the good taste an' good fortune to be born in the County Mayo ye wudn't nade to be askin' the name av Nora Monaghan o' Ballinghalcreen."

The judge's face was now in a broad smile.

"Nora Fitzpatrick," he said, writing the name down. "Let us proceed."

"Well, Mrs. Fitzpatrick," said the counsel for the Crown, "will you kindly look at the prisoner?"

Mrs. Fitzpatrick turned square about and let her eyes rest upon the prisoner's pale face.

"I will that," said she, "an' there's many another I'd like to see in his place."

"Do you know him?"

"I do that. An' a finer gintleman I niver saw, savin' Yer 'Anner's prisence," bowing to the judge.

"Oh, indeed! A fine gentleman? And how do you know that, Mrs. Fitzpatrick?"

"How do I know a gintleman, is it? Sure, it's by the way he trates a lady."

"Ah," said the lawyer with a most courteous bow, "that is a most excellent test. And what do you know of this—ah—this gentleman's manners with ladies?"

"An' don't I know how he trates mesilf? He's not wan to fergit a lady's name, you may lay to that."

"Oh, indeed, he has treated you in a gentlemanly manner?"

"He has."

"And do you think this is his usual manner with ladies?"

"I do," said Mrs. Fitzpatrick with great emphasis. "A gintleman, a rale gintleman, is the same to a lady wheriver he mates her, an' the same to ladies whativer they be."

"Mrs. Fitzpatrick," said Mr. Staunton, "you have evidently a most excellent taste in gentlemen."

"I have that same," she replied. "An' I know thim that are no gintlemen," she continued with meaning emphasis, "whativer their clothes may be."

A titter ran through the court room.

"Silence in the court!" shouted the crier.

"Now, Mrs. Fitzpatrick," proceeded Mr. Staunton, taking a firmer tone, "you say the prisoner is a gentleman."

"I do. An' I can tell ye—"

"Wait, Mrs. Fitzpatrick. Wait a moment. Do you happen to know his wife?"

"I don't know."

"You don't know his wife?"

"Perhaps I do if you say so."

"But, my good woman, I don't say so. Do you know his wife, or do you not know his wife?"

"I don't know."

"What do you mean?" said Mr. Staunton impatiently. "Do you mean that you have no acquaintance with the wife of the prisoner?"

"I might."

"What do you mean by might?"

"Aw now," remonstrated Mrs. Fitzpatrick, "sure, ye wouldn't be askin' a poor woman like me the manin' av a word like that."

"Now, Mrs. Fitzpatrick, let us get done with this fooling. Tell me whether you know the prisoner's wife or not."

"Indade, an' the sooner yer done the better I'd like it."

"Well, then, tell me. You either know the prisoner's wife or you don't know her?"

"That's as may be," said Mrs. Fitzpatrick.

"Then tell me," thundered Staunton, losing all patience, "do you know this woman or not?" pointing to Paulina.

"That woman is it?" said Mrs. Fitzpatrick. "An' why didn't ye save yer breath an' His 'Anner's time, not to shpake av me own that has to work fer me daily bread, by askin' me long ago if I know this woman?"

"Well, do you know her?"

"I do."

"Then why did you not say so before when I asked you?" said the exasperated lawyer.

"I did," said Mrs. Fitzpatrick calmly.

"Did you not say that you did not know the wife of the prisoner?"

"I did not," said Mrs. Fitzpatrick.

By this time the whole audience, including the judge, were indulging themselves in a wide open smile.

"Well, Mrs. Fitzpatrick," at length said the lawyer, "I must be decidedly stupid, for I fail to understand you."

"Indade, I'll not be contradictin' ye, fer it's yersilf ought to know best about that," replied Mrs. Fitzpatrick pleasantly.

A roar of laughter filled the court room.

"Silence in the court! We must have order," said the judge, recovering his gravity with such celerity as he could. "Go on, Mr. Staunton."

"Well, Mrs. Fitzpatrick, I understand that you know this woman, Paulina Koval."

"It's mesilf that's plazed to hear it."

"And I suppose you know that she is the prisoner's wife?"

"An' why wud ye be afther supposin' such a thing?"

"Well! well! Do you know it?"

"Do I know what?"

"Do you know that this woman, Paulina Koval, is the wife of the prisoner?"

"She might be."

"Oh, come now, Mrs. Fitzpatrick, we are not splitting hairs. You know perfectly well that this woman is the prisoner's wife."

"Indade, an' it's the cliver man ye are to know what I know better than I know mesilf."

"Well, well," said Mr. Staunton impatiently, "will you say that you do not consider this woman the prisoner's wife?"

"I will not," replied Mrs. Fitzpatrick emphatically, "any more than I won't say she's yer own."

"Well, well, let us get on. Let us suppose that this woman is his wife. How did the prisoner treat this woman?"

"An' how should he trate her?"

"Did he support her?"

"An' why should he, with her havin' two hands av her own?"

"Well now, Mrs. Fitzpatrick, surely you will say that it was a case of cruel neglect on the part of the prisoner that he should leave her to care for herself and her children, a stranger in a strange land."

"Indade, it's not fer me to be runnin' down the counthry," exclaimed Mrs. Fitzpatrick. "Sure, it's a good land, an' a foine counthry it is to make a livin' in," she continued with a glow of enthusiasm, "an' it's mesilf that knows it."

"Oh, the country is all right," said Mr. Staunton impatiently; "but did not this man abandon his wife?"

"An' if he's the man ye think he is wudn't she be the better quit av him?"

The lawyer had reached the limit of his patience.

"Well, well, Mrs. Fitzpatrick, we will leave the wife alone. But what of his treatment of the children?"

"The childer?" exclaimed Mrs. Fitzpatrick,—"the childer, is it? Man dear, but he's the thrue gintleman an' the tinder-hearted father fer his childer, an' so he is."

"Oh, indeed, Mrs. Fitzpatrick. I am sure we shall all be delighted to hear this. But you certainly have strange views of a father's duty toward his children. Now will you tell the court upon what ground you would extol his parental virtues?"

"Faix, it's niver a word I've said about his parental virtues, or any other kind o' virtues. I was talkin' about his childer."

"Well, then, perhaps you would be kind enough to tell the court what reason you have for approving his treatment of his children?"

Mrs. Fitzpatrick's opportunity had arrived. She heaved a great sigh, and with some deliberation began.

"Och! thin, an' it's just terrible heart-rendin' an' so it is. An' it's mesilf that can shpake, havin' tin av me own, forby three that's dead an' gone, God rest their sowls! an' four that's married, an' the rest all doin' well fer thimsilves. Indade, it's mesilf that has the harrt fer the childer. You will be havin' childer av yer own," she added confidentially to the lawyer.

A shout of laughter filled the court room, for Staunton was a confirmed and notorious old bachelor.

"I have the bad fortune, Mrs. Fitzpatrick, to be a bachelor," he replied, red to the ears.

"Man dear, but it's hard upon yez, but it's Hivin's mercy fer yer wife."

The laughter that followed could with difficulty be suppressed by the court crier.

"Go on, Mrs. Fitzpatrick, go on with your tale," said Staunton, who had frankly joined in the laugh against himself.

"I will that," said Mrs. Fitzpatrick with emphasis. "Where was I? The man an' his childer. Sure, I'll tell Yer 'Anner." Here she turned to the judge. "Fer he," with a jerk of her thumb towards the lawyer, "knows nothin' about the business at all, at all. It was wan night he came to me house askin' to see his childer. The night o' the dance, Yer 'Anner. As I was sayin', he came to me house where the childer was, askin' to see thim, an' him without a look o' thim fer years. An' did they know him?" Mrs. Fitzpatrick's voice took a tragic tone. "Not a hair av thim. Not at the first. Ah, but it was the harrt-rendin' scene, with not a house nor a home fer him to come till, an' him sendin' the money ivery month to pay fer it. But where it's gone, it's not fer me to say. There's some in this room" (here she regarded Rosenblatt with a steady eye) "might know more about that money an' what happened till it, than they know about Hivin. Ah, but as I was sayin', it wud melt the harrt av a Kerry steer, that's first cousin to the goats on the hills fer wildness, to see the way he tuk thim an' held thim, an' wailed over thim, the tinder harrt av him! Fer only wan small hour or two could he shtay wid thim, an' then aff to that haythen counthry agin that gave him birth. An' the way he suffered fer that same, poor dear! An' the beautiful wife he lost! Hivin be kind to her! Not her," following the judge's glance toward Paulina, "but an angel that need niver feel shame to shtand befure the blissid Payther himsilf, wid the blue eyes an' the golden hair in the picter he carries nixt his harrt, the saints have pity on him! An' how he suffered fer the good cause! Och hone! it breaks me harrt!" Here Mrs. Fitzpatrick paused to wipe away her tears.

"But, Mrs. Fitzpatrick," interrupted Mr. Staunton, "this is all very fine, but what has this to do—"

"Tut! man, isn't it that same I'm tellin' ye?" And on she went, going back to the scene she had witnessed in her own room between Kalmar and his children, and describing the various *dramatis personæ* and the torrential emotions that had swept their hearts in that scene of final parting between father and children.

Again and again Staunton sought to stay her eloquence, but with a majestic wave of her hand she swept him aside, and with a wealth of metaphor and an unbroken flow of passionate, tear-bedewed rhetoric that Staunton himself might well envy, she held the court under her sway. Many of the women present were overcome with emotion. O'Hara openly wiped away his tears, keeping an anxious eye the while upon the witness and waiting the psychological moment for the arresting of her tale.

The moment came when Mrs. Fitzpatrick's emotions rendered her speechless. With a great show of sympathy, Mr. O'Hara approached the witness, and offering her a glass of water, found opportunity to whisper, "Not another word, on your soul."

"Surely," he said, appealing to the judge in a voice trembling with indignant feeling, "my learned friend will not further harass this witness."

"Let her go, in Heaven's name," said Staunton testily; "we want no more of her."

"So I should suppose," replied O'Hara drily.

With Mrs. Fitzpatrick, the case for the Crown was closed. To the surprise of all, and especially of the Counsel for the Crown, O'Hara called no witnesses and offered no evidence in rebuttal of that before the court. This made it necessary for Staunton to go on at once with his final address to the jury.

Seldom in all his experience had he appeared to such poor advantage as on that day. The court was still breathing the atmosphere of Mrs. Fitzpatrick's rude and impassioned appeal. The lawyer was still feeling the sting of his humiliating failure with his star witness, and O'Hara's unexpected move surprised and flustered him, old hand as he was. With halting words and without his usual assurance, he reviewed the evidence and asked for a conviction on both charges.

With O'Hara it was quite otherwise. It was in just such a desperate situation that he was at his best. The plight of the prisoner, lonely, beaten and defenceless, appealed to his chivalry. Then, too, O'Hara, by blood and tradition, was a revolutionist. In every "rising" during the last two hundred years of Ireland's struggles, some of his ancestors had carried a pike or trailed a musket, and the rebel blood in him cried sympathy with the Nihilist in his devotion to a hopeless cause. And hence the passion and the almost tearful vehemence that he threw into his final address were something more than professional.

With great skill he took his cue from the evidence of the last witness. He drew a picture of the Russian Nihilist hunted like "a partridge on the mountains," seeking for himself and his compatriots a home and safety in this land of liberty. With vehement scorn he told the story of the base treachery of Rosenblatt, "a Government spy, a thief, a debaucher of women, and were I permitted, gentlemen, I could unfold a tale in this connection such as would wring your hearts with grief and indignation. But my client will not permit that the veil be drawn from scenes that would bring shame to the honoured name he wears."

With consummate art the lawyer turned the minds of the jury from the element of personal vengeance in the crime committed to that of retribution for political infidelity, till under his manipulation the prisoner was made to appear in the rôle of patriot and martyr doomed to suffer for his devotion to his cause.

"But, gentlemen, though I might appeal to your passions, I scorn to do so. I urge you to weigh calmly, deliberately, as cool, level-headed Canadians, the evidence produced by the prosecution. A crime has been committed, a most revolting crime,—one man killed, another seriously wounded. But what is the nature of this crime? Has it been shown either to be murder or attempted murder? You must have noticed, gentlemen, how utterly the prosecution has failed to establish any such charge. The suggestion of murder comes solely from the man who has so deeply wronged and has pursued with such deadly venom the unfortunate prisoner at the bar. This man, after betraying the cause of freedom, after wrecking the prisoner's home and family, after proving traitor to every trust imposed in him, now seeks to fasten upon his victim this horrid crime of murder. His is the sole evidence. What sort of man is this upon whose unsupported testimony you are asked to send a fellow human being to the scaffold? Think calmly, gentlemen, is he such a man as you can readily believe? Is his highly coloured story credible? Are you so gullible as to be taken in with this melodrama? Gentlemen, I know you, I know my fellow citizens too well to think that you will be so deceived.

"Now what are the facts, the bare facts, the cold facts, gentlemen? And we are here to deal with facts. Here they are. There is a wedding. My learned friend is not interested in weddings, not perhaps as much interested as he should be, and as such, apparently, he excites the pity of his friends."

This sally turned all eyes towards Mrs. Fitzpatrick, and a broad smile spread over the court.

"There is a wedding, as I was saying. Unhappily the wedding feast, as is too often the case with our foreign citizens, degenerates into a drunken brawl. It is a convenient occasion for paying off old scores. There is general melee, a scrap, in short. Suddenly these two men come face to face, their passions inflamed. On the one hand there is a burning sense of wrong, on the other an unquenchable hate. For, gentlemen, remember, the man that hates you most venomously is the man who has wronged you most deeply. These two meet. There is a fight. When all is over, one man is found dead, another with a wound in his breast. But who struck the first blow? None can tell. We are absolutely without evidence upon this point. In regard to the Polak, all that can be said is this, that it was a most unfortunate occurrence. The attempt to connect the prisoner with this man's death has utterly failed. In regard to the man Rosenblatt, dismissing his absurdly tragic story, what evidence has been brought before this court that there was any deliberate attempt at murder? A blow was struck, but by whom? No one knows. What was the motive? Was it in self-defence warding off some murderous attack? No one can say. I have as much right to believe that this was the case, as any man to believe the contrary. Indeed, from what we know of the character of this wretched traitor and thief, it is not hard to believe that the attack upon this stranger would come from him."

And so O'Hara proceeded with his most extraordinary defence. Theory after theory he advanced, quoting instance after instance of extraordinary killings that were discovered to be accidental or in self-defence, till with the bewildered jury no theory explanatory of the crime committed in the basement of Paulina's house was too fantastic to be considered possible.

In his closing appeal O'Hara carried the jury back to the point from which he had set out. With tears in his voice he recounted the scene of the parting between the prisoner and his children. He drew a harrowing picture of the unhappy fate of wife and children left defenceless and in poverty to become the prey of such men as Rosenblatt. He drew a vivid picture of that age-long struggle for freedom carried on by the down-trodden peasantry of Russia, and closed with a tremendous appeal to them as fathers, as lovers of liberty, as fair-minded, reasonable men to allow the prisoner the full benefit of the many doubts gathering round the case for the prosecution, and set him free.

It was a magnificent effort. Never in all his career as a criminal lawyer had O'Hara made so brilliant an attempt to lift a desperate case from the region of despair into that of hope. The effect of his address was plainly visible upon the jury and, indeed, upon the whole audience in the court room.

The judge's charge did much to clear the atmosphere, and to bring the jury back to the cold, calm air of Canadian life and feeling; but in the jury room the emotions and passions aroused by O'Hara's address were kindled again, and the result reflected in no small degree their influence.

The verdict acquitted the prisoner of the charge of manslaughter, but found him guilty on the count of attempted murder. The verdict, however, was tempered with a strong recommendation to mercy.

"Have you anything to say?" asked the judge before pronouncing sentence.

Kalmar, who had been deeply impressed by the judge's manner during his charge to the jury, searched his face a moment and then, as if abandoning all hope of mercy, drew himself erect and in his stilted English said: "Your Excellency, I make no petition for mercy. Let the criminal make such a plea. I stand convicted of crime, but I am no criminal. The traitor, the thief, the liar, the murderer, the criminal, sits there." As he spoke the word, he swung sharply about and stood with outstretched arm and finger pointing to Rosenblatt. "I stand here the officer of vengeance. I have failed. Vengeance will not fail. The day is coming when it will strike." Then turning his face toward the group of foreigners at the back of the room he raised his voice and in a high monotone chanted a few sentences in the Russian tongue.

The effect was tremendous. Every Russian could be picked out by his staring eyes and pallid face. There was a moment's silence, then a hissing sound as of the breath drawn sharply inward, followed by a murmur hoarse and inhuman, not good to hear. Rosenblatt trembled, started to his feet, vainly tried to speak. His lips refused to frame words, and he sank back speechless.

"What the deuce was he saying?" enquired O'Hara of the Interpreter after the judge had pronounced his solemn sentence.

"He was putting to them," said the Interpreter in an awed whisper, "the Nihilist oath of death."

"By Jove! Good thing the judge didn't understand. The bloody fool would have spoiled all my fine work. He would have got a life term instead of fourteen years. He's got enough, though, poor chap. I wish to Heaven the other fellow had got it."

As the prisoner turned with the officer to leave the dock, a wild sobbing fell upon his ear. It was Paulina. Kalmar turned to the judge.

"Is it permitted that I see my children before—before I depart?"

"Certainly," said the judge quickly. "Your wife and children and your friends may visit you at a convenient hour to-morrow."

Kalmar bowed with grave courtesy and walked away.

Beside the sobbing Paulina sat the children, pale and bewildered.

"Where is my father going?" asked the boy in Russian.

"Alas! alas! We shall see him no more!" sobbed Paulina.

Quickly the boy's voice rang out, shrill with grief and terror, "Father! father! Come back!"

The prisoner, who was just disappearing through the door, stopped, turned about, his pale face convulsed with a sudden agony. He took a step toward his son, who had run toward the bar after him.

"My son, be brave," he said in a voice audible throughout the room. "Be brave. I shall see you to-morrow."

He waved his hand toward his son, turned again and passed out with the officer.

Through the staring crowd came a little lady with white hair and a face pale and chastened into sweetness.

"Let me come with you," she said to Paulina, while the tears coursed down her cheeks.

The Galician woman understood not a word, but the touch upon her arm, the tone in the voice, the flowing tears were a language she could understand. Paulina raised her dull, tear-dimmed eyes, and for a brief moment gazed into the pale face above her, then without further word rose and, followed by her children, accompanied the little lady from the room, the crowd making respectful way before the pathetic group.

"Say, O'Hara, there are still angels going about," said young Dr. Wright, following the group with his eyes.

"Be Hivin!" replied the tender-hearted Irishman, his eyes suddenly dim, "there's wan annyway, and Margaret French is the first two letters of her name."

Chapter VIII

The Price of Vengeance

D r. Wright's telephone rang early next morning. The doctor was prompt to respond. His practice had not yet reached the stage that rendered the telephone a burden. His young wife stood beside him, listening with eager hope in her wide-open brown eyes.

"Yes," said the doctor. "Oh, it's you. Delighted to hear your ring." "No, not so terribly. The rush doesn't begin till later in the day." "Not at all. What can I do for you?" "Certainly, delighted." "What? Right away?" "Well, say within an hour."

"Who is it?" asked his wife, as the doctor hung up the phone. "A new family?"

"No such luck," replied the doctor. "This has been a frightfully healthy season. But the spring promises a very satisfactory typhoid epidemic."

"Who is it?" said his wife again, impatiently.

"Your friend Mrs. French, inviting me to an expedition into the foreign colony."

"Oh!" She could not keep the disappointment out of her tone. "I think Mrs. French might call some of the other doctors."

"So she does, lots of them. And most of them stand ready to obey her call."

"Well," said the little woman at his side, "I think you are going too much among those awful people."

"Awful people?" exclaimed the doctor. "It's awfully good practice, I know. That is, in certain lines. I can't say there is very much variety. When a really good thing occurs, it is whisked off to the hospital and the big guns get it."

"Well, I don't like your going so much," persisted his wife. "Some day you will get hurt."

"Hurt?" exclaimed the doctor. "Me?"

"Oh, I know you think nothing can hurt you. But a bullet or a knife can do for you as well as for any one else. Supposing that terrible man—what's his name?—Kalmar—had struck you instead of the Polak, where would you be?"

"The question is, where would he be?" said the doctor with a smile. "As for Kalmar, he's not too bad a sort; at least there are others a little worse. I shouldn't be surprised if that fellow Rosenblatt got only a little less than he deserved. Certainly O'Hara let in some light upon his moral ulcers."

"Well, I wish you would drop them, anyway," continued his wife.

"No, you don't," said the doctor. "You know quite well that you would root me out of bed any hour of the night to see any of their kiddies that happened to have a pain in their little tumtums. Between you and Mrs. French I haven't a moment to devote to my large and growing practice."

"What does she want now?" It must be confessed that her tone was slightly impatient.

"Mrs. French has succeeded in getting the excellent Mrs. Blazowski to promise for the tenth time, I believe, to allow some one, preferably myself, to take her eczematic children to the hospital."

"Well, she won't."

"I think it is altogether likely. But why do you think so?"

"Because you have tried before."

"Never."

"Well, Mrs. French has, and you were with her."

"That is correct. But to-day I shall adopt new tactics. Mrs. French's flank movements have broken down. I shall carry the position with a straight frontal attack. And I shall succeed. If not, my dear, that little fur tippet thing which you have so resolutely refused to let your eyes rest upon as we pass the Hudson's Bay, is yours."

"I don't want it a bit," said his wife. "And you know we can't afford it."

"Don't you worry, little girl," said the doctor cheerfully, "practice is looking up. My name is getting into the papers. A few more foreign weddings with attendant killings and I shall be famous."

At the Blazowski shack Mrs. French was waiting the doctor, and in despair. A crowd of children appeared to fill the shack and overflow through the door into the sunny space outside, on the sheltered side of the house.

The doctor made his way through them and passed into the evil-smelling, filthy room. For Mrs. Blazowski found it a task beyond her ability to perform the domestic duties attaching to the care of seven children and a like number of boarders in her single room. Mrs. French was seated on a stool with a little child of three years upon her knee.

"Doctor, don't you think that these children ought to go to the hospital to-day?" she said, as the doctor entered.

"Why, sure thing; they must go. Let's look at them."

He tried to take the little child from Mrs. French's knee, but the little one vehemently objected.

"Well, let's look at you, anyway," said the doctor, proceeding to unwind some filthy rags from the little one's head. "Great Scott!" he exclaimed in a low voice, "this is truly awful!"

The hair was matted with festering scabs. The ears, the eyes, the fingers were full of running sores.

"I had no idea this thing had gone so far," he said in a horrified voice.

"What is it?" said Mrs. French. "Is it—"

"No, not itch. It is the industrious and persevering *eczema pusculosum*, known to the laity as salt rheum of the domestic variety."

"It has certainly got worse this last week," said Mrs. French.

"Well, this can't go on another day, and I can't treat her here. She must go. Tell your mother," said the doctor in a decided tone to a little girl of thirteen who stood near.

Mrs. Blazowski threw up her hands with voluble protestation. "She says they will not go. She put grease on and make them all right."

"Grease!" exclaimed the doctor. "I should say so, and a good many other things too! Why, the girl's head is alive with them! Heavens above!" said the doctor, turning to Mrs. French, "she's running over with vermin! Let's see the other."

He turned to a girl of five, whose head and face were even more seriously affected with the dread disease.

"Why, bless my soul! This girl will lose her eyesight! Now look here, these children must go to the hospital, and must go now. Tell your mother what I say."

Again the little girl translated, and again the mother made emphatic reply.

"What does she say?"

"She say she not let them go. She fix them herself. Fix them all right."

"Perhaps we better wait, Doctor," interposed Mrs. French. "I'll talk to her and we'll try another day."

"No," said the doctor, catching up a shawl and wrapping around the little girl, "she's going with me now. There will be a scrap, and you will have to get in. I'll back you up."

As the doctor caught up the little child, the mother shouted, "No, no! Not go!"

"I say yes," said the doctor; "I'll get a policeman and put you all in prison. Tell her."

The threat made no impression upon the mother. On the contrary, as the doctor moved toward the door she seized a large carving-knife and threw herself before him. For a moment or two they stood facing each other, the doctor uncertain what his next move should be, but determined that his plan should not fail this time. It was Mrs. French who interposed. With a smile she laid her hand upon the mother's arm.

"Tell her," she said to the little girl, "that I will go with the children, and I promise that no hurt shall come to them. And I will bring them back again safe. Your mother can come and see them to-morrow— to-day. The hospital is a lovely place. They will have nice toys, dolls, and nice things to eat, and we'll make them better."

Rapidly, almost breathlessly, and with an eager smile on her sweet face, Mrs. French went on to describe the advantages and attractions of the hospital, pausing only to allow the little girl to translate.

At length the mother relented, her face softened. She stepped from the door, laying down her knife upon the table, moved not by the glowing picture of Mrs. French's words, but by the touch upon her arm and the face that smiled into hers. Once more the mother spoke.

"Will you go too?" interpreted the little girl.

"Yes, surely. I go too," she replied.

This brought the mother's final surrender. She seized Mrs. French's hand, and bursting into loud weeping, kissed it again and again. Mrs. French put her arms around the weeping woman, and unshrinking, kissed the tear-stained, dirty face. Dr. Wright looked on in admiring silence.

"You are a dead sport," he said. "I can't play up to that; but you excite my ambition. Get a shawl around the other kiddie and come along, or I'll find myself kissing the bunch."

Once more he started toward the door, but the mother was before him, talking and gesticulating.

"What's the row now?" said the doctor, turning to the little interpreter.

"She says she must dress them, make them clean."

"It's a big order," said the doctor, "but I submit."

With great energy Mrs. Blazowski proceeded to prepare her children for their momentous venture into the world. The washing process was simple enough. From the dish-pan which stood upon the hearth half full of dirty water and some of the breakfast dishes, she took a greasy dish-cloth, wrung it out carefully, and with it proceeded to wash, not untenderly, the festering heads, faces and fingers of her children, resorting from time to time to the dish-pan for a fresh supply of water. This done, she carefully dried the parts thus diligently washed with the handkerchief which she usually wore about her head. Then pinning shawls about their heads, she had her children ready for their departure, and gave them into Mrs. French's charge, sobbing aloud as if she might never see them more.

"Well," said the doctor, as he drove rapidly away, "we're well out of that. I was just figuring what sort of hold would be most fatal to the old lady when you interposed."

"Poor thing!" said Mrs. French. "They're very fond of their children, these Galicians, and they're so suspicious of us. They don't know any better."

As they passed Paulina's house, the little girl Irma ran out from the door.

"My mother want you very bad," she said to Mrs. French.

"Tell her I'll come in this afternoon," said Mrs. French.

"She want you now," replied Irma, with such a look of anxiety upon her face that Mrs. French was constrained to say, "Wait one moment, Doctor. I'll see what it is. I shall not keep you."

She ran into the house, followed by the little girl. The room was full of men who stood about in stolid but not unsympathetic silence, gazing upon Paulina, who appeared to be prostrated with grief. Beside her stood the lad Kalman, the picture of desolation.

"What is it?" cried Mrs. French, running to her. "Tell me what is the matter."

Irma told the story. Early that morning they had gone to the jail, but after waiting for hours they were refused admission by the guard.

"A very cross man send us away," said the girl. "He say he put us in jail too. We can see our fadder no more."

Her words were followed by a new outburst of grief on the part of Paulina and the two children.

"But the Judge said you were to see him," said Mrs. French in surprise. "Wait for me," she added.

She ran out and told the doctor in indignant words what had taken place, a red spot glowing in each white cheek.

"Isn't it a shame?" she cried when she had finished her story.

"Oh, it's something about prison rules and regulations, I guess," said the doctor.

"Prison rules!" exclaimed Mrs. French with wrath rare in her. "I'll go straight to the Judge myself."

"Get in," said the doctor, taking up the lines.

"Where are you going? We can't leave these poor things in this way," the tears gathering in her eyes and her voice beginning to break.

"Not much," said the doctor briskly; "we are evidently in for another scrap. I don't know where you will land me finally, but I'm game to follow your lead. We'll go to the jail."

Mrs. French considered a moment. "Let us first take these children to the hospital and then we shall meet Paulina at the jail."

"All right," said the doctor, "tell them so. I am at your service."

"You are awfully good, Doctor," said the little lady, her sweet smile once more finding its way to her pale face.

"Ain't I, though?" said the doctor. "If the spring were a little further advanced you'd see my wings sprouting. I enjoy this. I haven't had such fun since my last football match. I see the finish of that jail guard. Come on."

Within an hour the doctor and Mrs. French drove up to the jail. There, at the bleak north door, swept by the chill March wind, and away from the genial light of the shining sun, they found Paulina and her children, a shivering, timid, shrinking group, looking pathetically strange and forlorn in their quaint Galician garb.

The pathos of the picture appeared to strike both the doctor and his friend at the same time.

"Brute!" said the doctor, "it's some beast of an understrapper. He might have let them in, anyway. I'll see the head turnkey."

"Isn't it terribly sad?" replied Mrs. French.

The doctor rang the bell at the jail door, prepared for battle.

"I want to see Mr. Cowan."

The guard glanced past the doctor, saw the shrinking group behind him and gruffly announced, "This is not the hour for visitors."

"I want to see Mr. Cowan," repeated the doctor slowly, looking the guard steadily in the eye. "Is he in?"

"Come in," said the guard sullenly, allowing the doctor and his friend to enter, and shutting the door in the faces of the Galicians.

In a few moments Mr. Cowan appeared, a tall athletic man, kindly of face and of manner. He greeted Mrs. French and the doctor warmly.

"Come into the office," he said; "come in."

"Mr. Cowan," said Mrs. French, "there is a poor Galician woman and her children outside the door, the wife and children of the man who was condemned yesterday. The Judge told them they could see the prisoner to-day."

"The hour for visitors," said Mr. Cowan, "is three in the afternoon."

"Could you not let her in now? She has already waited for hours at the door this morning, and on being refused went home brokenhearted. She does not understand our ways and is very timid. I wish you could let her in now while I am here."

Mr. Cowan hesitated. "I should greatly like to oblige you, Mrs. French. You know that. Sit down, and I will see. Let that woman and her children in," he said to the guard.

The guard went sullenly to the door, followed by Mrs. French.

"Come in here," he said in a gruff voice.

Mrs. French hurried past him, took Paulina by the arm, and saying, "Come in and sit down," led her to a bench and sat beside her. "It's all right," she whispered. "I am sure you can see your husband. Tell her," she said to Irma.

In a short time Mr. Cowan came back.

"They may see him," he said. "It is against all discipline, but it is pretty hard to resist Mrs. French," he continued, turning to the doctor.

"It is quite useless trying," said the doctor; "I have long ago discovered that."

"Come," said that little lady, leading Paulina to the door of the cell.

The guard turned the lock, shot back the bolts, opened the door and motioning with his hand, said gruffly to Paulina, "Go in."

The woman looked into the cell in shrinking fear.

"Go on," said Mrs. French in an encouraging voice, patting her on the shoulder, "I will wait here."

Clinging to one another, the woman and children passed in through the door which the guard closed behind them with a reverberating clang. Mrs. French sat on the bench outside, her face cast down, her eyes closed. Now and then through the grating of the door rose and fell a sound of voices mingled with that of sobs and weeping, hearing which, Mrs. French covered her face with her hands, while the tears trickled down through her fingers.

As she sat there, the door-bell rang and two Galician men appeared, seeking admission.

"We come to see Kalmar," said one of them.

Mrs. French came eagerly forward. "Oh, let them come in, please. They are friends of the prisoner. I know them."

Without a word the guard turned from her, strode to the office where Mr. Cowan sat in conversation with the doctor, and in a few moments returned with permission for the men to enter.

"Sit down there," he said, pointing to a bench on the opposite side of the door from that on which Mrs. French was sitting.

Before many minutes had elapsed, the prisoner appeared at the door of his cell with Paulina and his children.

"Would you kindly open the door?" he said in a courteous tone to the guard. "They wish to depart."

The guard went toward the door, followed by Mrs. French, who stood waiting with hands outstretched toward the weeping Paulina. As the door swung open, the children came forth, but upon the threshold Paulina paused, glanced into the cell, ran back and throwing herself at the prisoner's feet, seized his hand and kissed it again and again with loud weeping.

For a single instant the man yielded her his hand, and then in a voice stern but not unkind, he said, "Go. My children are in your keeping. Be faithful."

At once the woman rose and came back to the door where Mrs. French stood waiting for her.

As they passed on, the guard turned to the men and said briefly, "Come."

As they were about to enter the cell, the boy suddenly left Paulina's side, ran to Simon Ketzel and clutching firm hold of his hand said, "Let me go with you."

"Go back," said the guard, but the boy still clung to Ketzel's hand.

"Oh, let him go," said Mrs. French. "He will do no harm." And the guard gave grudging permission.

With a respectful, almost reverential mien, the men entered the cell, knelt before the prisoner and kissed his hand. The moments were precious and there was much to say and do, so Kalmar lost no time.

"I have sent for you," he said, "first to give you my report which you will send back to headquarters."

Over and over again he repeated the words of his report, till he was certain that they had it in sure possession.

"This must go at once," he said.

"At once," replied Simon.

"In a few weeks or months," continued the prisoner in a low voice, "I expect to be free. Siberia could not hold me, and do you think that any prison in this country can? But this report must go immediately."

"Immediately," said Simon again.

"Now," said Kalmar solemnly, "there is one thing more. Our cause fails chiefly because of traitors. In this city is a traitor. My oath demands his death or mine. If I fail, I must pass the work on to another. It is for this I have called you here. You are members of our Brotherhood. What do you say?"

The men stood silent.

"Speak!" said Kalmar in a low stern voice. "Have you no words?"

But still they stood silent and distressed, looking at each other.

"Tell me," said Kalmar, "do you refuse the oath?"

"Master," said Joseph Pinkas sullenly, "this is a new country. All that we left behind. That is all well for Russia, but not for Canada. Here we do not take oath to kill."

"Swine!" hissed Kalmar with unutterable scorn. "Why are you here? Go from me!"

From his outstretched hand Joseph fell back in sudden fear. Kalmar strode to the door and rattled it in its lock.

"This man wishes to go," he said, as the guard appeared. "Let him go."

"What about the others?" said the guard.

"Permit them to remain for a few moments," said Kalmar, recovering the even tone of his voice with a tremendous effort.

"Now, Simon Ketzel," he said, turning back to the man who stood waiting him in fear, "what is your answer?"

Simon took his hand and kissed it. "I will serve you with my money, with my life. I am all Russian here," smiting on his breast, "I cannot forget my countrymen in bondage. I will help them to freedom."

"Ah," said Kalmar, "good. Now listen. This Rosenblatt betrayed us, brought death and exile to many of our brothers and sisters. He still lives. He ought to die. What do you say?"

"He ought to die," answered Simon.

"The oath is laid upon me. I sought the privilege of executing vengeance; it was granted me. I expect to fulfil my oath, but I may fail. If I fail," here he bent his face toward that of Simon Ketzel, his bloodshot eyes glowing in his white face like red coals, "if I fail," he repeated, "is he still to live?"

"Do you ask me to kill him?" said Simon in a low voice. "I have a wife and three children. If I kill this man I must leave them. There is no place for me in this country. There is no escape. I must lay upon my children that burden forever. Do you ask me to do this? Surely God will bring His sure vengeance upon him. Let him go into the hands of God."

"Let him go?" said Kalmar, his breath hissing through his shut teeth. "Listen, and tell me if I should let him go. Many years ago, when a student in the University, I fell under suspicion, and without trial was sent to prison by a tyrannical Government. Released, I found it difficult to make a living. I was under the curse of Government suspicion. In spite of that I succeeded. I married a noble lady and for a time prospered. I joined a Secret Society. I had a friend. He was the rejected suitor of my wife. He, too, was an enthusiast for the cause of freedom. He became a member of my Society and served so well that he was trusted with their most secret plans. He sold them to the Government, seeking my ruin. The Society was broken up and scattered, the members, my friend included, arrested and sent to prison, exile and death. Soon he was liberated. I escaped. In a distant border town I took up my residence, determined, when opportunity offered, to flee the country with my wife and two infant children, one a babe in his mother's arms. At this time my friend discovered me. I had no suspicion of him. I told him my plans. He offered to aid me. I gave him the money wherewith to bribe the patrol. Once more he betrayed me. Our road lay through a thick forest. As we drove along, a soldier hailed us. I killed him and we dashed forward, only to find another soldier waiting. We abandoned our sleigh and took to a woodcutter's track through the forest. We had only a mile to go. There were many tracks. The soldier pursued us through the deep snow, firing at random. A bullet found a place in my wife's heart. Ah! My God! She fell to the snow, her babe in her arms. I threw myself at her side. She looked up into my face and smiled. 'I am free at last,' she said. 'Farewell, dear heart. The children—leave me—carry them to freedom.' I closed her eyes, covered her with snow and fled on through the forest, and half frozen made my way across the border and was safe. My children I left with friends and went back to bring my wife. I found blood tracks on the snow, and bones." He put his hands over his face as if to shut out the horrid picture, then flinging them down, he turned fiercely upon Simon. "What do you say? Shall I let him go?"

"No," said Simon, reaching out both his hands. "By the Lord God Almighty! No! He shall die!"

Kalmar tore open his shirt, pulled out a crucifix.

"Will you swear by God and all the saints that if I fail you will take my place?"

Simon hesitated. The boy sprang forward, snatched the crucifix from his father's hand, pressed his lips against it and said in a loud voice, "I swear, by God and all the saints."

The father started back, and for a few moments silently contemplated his boy. "What, boy? You? You know not what you say."

"I do know, father. It was my mother you left there in the snow. Some day I will kill him."

"No, no, my boy," said the father, clasping him in his arms. "You are your father's son, your mother's son," he cried. "You have the heart, the spirit, but this oath I shall not lay upon you. No, by my hand he shall die, or let him go." He stood for some moments silent, his head leaning forward upon his breast. "No," he said again, "Simon is right. This is a new land, a new life. Let the past die with me. With this quarrel you have nothing to do. It is not yours."

"I will kill him," said the boy stubbornly, "I have sworn the oath. It was my mother you left in the snow. Some day I will kill him."

"Aha! boy," said the father, drawing him close to his side, "my quarrel is yours. Good! But first he is mine. When my hand lies still in death, you may take up the cause, but not till then. You hear me?"

"Yes, father," said the boy.

"And you promise?"

"I promise."

"Now farewell, my son. A bitter fate is ours. A bitter heritage I leave you!" He sank down upon the bench, drew his boy toward him and said brokenly, "Nay, nay, it shall not be yours. I shall free you from it. In this new land, let life be new with you. Let not the shadow of the old rest upon you." He gathered the boy up in his strong arms and strained him to his breast. "Now farewell, my son. Ah! God in Heaven!" he cried, his tears raining down upon the boy's face, "must I give up this too! Ah, those eyes are her eyes, that face her face! Is this the last? Is this all? How bitter is life!" He rocked back and forward on the bench, his boy's arms tight about his neck. "My boy, my boy! the last of life I give up here! Keep faith. This," pulling out the miniature, "I would give you now, but it is all I have left. When I die I will send it to you. Your sister I give to your charge. When you are a man guard her. Now go. Farewell."

The guard appeared at the door.

"Come, you must go. Time's up," he said roughly.

"Time is up," cried the father, "and all time henceforth is useless to me. Farewell, my son!" kissing him. "You must go from me. Don't be ashamed of your father, though he may die a prisoner or wander an exile."

The boy clung fast to his father's neck, drawing deep sobbing breaths.

"Boy, boy," said the father, mingling his sobs with those of his son, "help me to bear it!"

It was a piteous appeal, and it reached the boy's heart. At once he loosened one hand from its hold, put it up and stroked his father's face as his sobs grew quiet. At the touch upon his face, the father straightened himself up, gently removed his son's clinging arm from his neck.

"My son," he said quietly, "we must be men. The men of our blood meet not death so."

Immediately the boy slipped from his father's arms and stood erect and quiet, looking up into the dark face above him watchful for the next word or sign. The father waved his hand toward the door.

"We now say farewell," he said quietly. He stooped down, kissed his son gravely and tenderly first upon the lips, then upon the brow, walked with him to the barred door.

"We are ready," he said quietly to the guard who stood near by.

The boy passed out, and gave his hand to Paulina, who stood waiting for him.

"Simon Ketzel," said Kalmar, as he bade him farewell, "you will befriend my boy?"

"Master, brother," said Simon, "I will serve your children with my life." He knelt, kissed the prisoner's hand, and went out.

That afternoon, the name of Michael Kalmar was entered upon the roll of the Provincial Penitentiary, and he took up his burden of life, no longer a man, but a mere human animal driven at the will of some petty tyrant, doomed to toil without reward, to isolation from all that makes life dear, to deprivation of the freedom of God's sweet light and air, to degradation without hope of recovery. Before him stretched fourteen long years of slow agony, with cruel abundance of leisure to feed his soul with maddening memories of defeated vengeance, with fearful anxieties for the future of those dear as life, with feelings of despair over a cause for which he had sacrificed his all.

Chapter IX

Brother and Sister

Before summer had gone, Winnipeg was reminded of the existence of the foreign colony by the escape from the Provincial Penitentiary of the Russian prisoner Kalmar. The man who could not be held by Siberian bars and guards found escape from a Canadian prison easy. That he had accomplices was evident, but who they were could not be discovered. Suspicion naturally fell upon Simon Ketzel and Joseph Pinkas, but after the most searching investigation they were released and Winnipeg went back to its ways and forgot. The big business men rebuilding fortunes shattered by the boom, the little business men laying foundations for fortunes to be, the women within the charmed circle of Society bound to the whirling wheel of social functions, other women outside and striving to beg, or buy, or break their way into the circle, and still other women who cared not a pin's head whether they were within or without, being sufficient for themselves, the busy people of the churches with their philanthropies, their religious activities, striving to gather into their several folds the waifs and strays that came stumbling into their city from all lands—all alike, unaware of the growing danger area in their young city, forgot the foreign colony, its problems and its needs.

Meantime, summer followed winter, and winter summer, the months and years went on while the foreign colony grew in numbers and more slowly in wealth. More slowly in wealth, because as an individual member grew in wealth he departed from the colony and went out to make an independent home for himself in one of the farming colonies which the Government was establishing in some of the more barren and forbidding sections of the country; or it may be, loving the city and its ways of business, he rapidly sloughed off with his foreign clothes his foreign speech and manner of life, and his foreign ideals as well, and became a Canadian citizen, distinguished from his cosmopolitan fellow citizen only by the slight difficulty he displayed with some of the consonants of the language.

Such a man was Simon Ketzel. Simon was by trade a carpenter, but he had received in the old land a good educational foundation; he had, moreover, a shrewd head for affairs, and so he turned his energies to business, and with conspicuous success. For in addition to all his excellent qualities, Simon possessed as the most valuable part of his equipment a tidy, thrifty wife, who saved what her husband earned and kept guard over him on feast days, saved and kept guard so faithfully that before long Simon came to see the wisdom of her policy and became himself a shrewd and sober and well-doing Canadian, able to hold his own with the best of them.

His sobriety and steadiness Simon owed mostly to his thrifty wife, but his rapid transformation into Canadian citizenship he owed chiefly to his little daughter Margaret. It was Margaret that taught him his English, as she conned over her lessons with him in the evenings. It was Margaret who carried home from the little Methodist mission near by, the illustrated paper and the library book, and thus set him a-reading. It was Margaret that brought both Simon and Lena, his wife, to the social gathering of the Sunday School and of the church. It was thus to little Margaret that the Ketzels owed their introduction to Canadian life and manners, and to the finer sides of Canadian religion. And through little Margaret it was that those greatest of all Canadianising influences, the school and the mission, made their impact upon the hearts and the home of the Ketzel family. And as time went on it came to pass that from the Ketzel home, clean, orderly, and Canadian, there went out into the foul wastes about, streams of healing and cleansing that did their beneficent work where they went.

One of these streams reached the home of Paulina, to the great good of herself and her family. Here, again, it was chiefly little Margaret who became the channel of the new life; for with Paulina both Simon and Lena had utterly failed. She was too dull, too apathetic, too hopeless and too suspicious even of her own kind to allow the Ketzels an entrance to her heart. But even had she not been all this, she was too sorely oppressed with the burden of her daily toil to yield to such influence as they had to offer. For Rosenblatt was again in charge of her household. In a manner best known to himself, he had secured the mortgage on her home, and thus became her landlord, renting her the room in which she and her family dwelt, and for which they all paid in daily labour, and dearly enough. Rosenblatt, thus being her master, would not let her go. She was too valuable for that. Strong, patient, diligent, from early dawn till late at night she toiled and moiled with her baking and scrubbing, fighting out that ancient and primitive and endless fight against dirt and hunger, beaten by the one, but triumphing over the other. She carried in her heart a dull sense of injustice, a feeling that somehow wrong was being done her; but when Rosenblatt flourished before her a formidable legal document, and had the same interpreted to her by his smart young clerk, Samuel Sprink, she, with true Slavic and fatalistic passivity, accepted her lot and bent her strong back to her burden without complaint. What was the use of complaint? Who in all the city was there to care for a poor, stupid, Galician woman with none too savoury a reputation? Many and generous were the philanthropies of Winnipeg, but as yet there was none that had to do with the dirt, disease and degradation that were too often found in the environment of the foreign people. There were many churches in the city rich in good work, with many committees that met to confer and report, but there was not yet one whose special duty it was to confer and to report upon the unhappy and struggling and unsavoury foreigner within their city gate.

Yes, there was one. The little Methodist mission hard by the foreign colony had such a committee, a remarkable committee in a way, a committee with no fine-spun theories of wholesale reform, a committee with no delicate nostril to be buried in a perfumed handkerchief when pursuing an investigation (as a matter of fact, that committee had no sense of smell at all), a committee of one, namely, John James Parsons, the Methodist missionary, and he worked chiefly with committees of one, of which not the least important was little Margaret Ketzel.

It was through Margaret Ketzel that Parsons got his first hold of Paulina, by getting hold of her little girl Irma. For Margaret, though so much her junior in years and experience, was to Irma a continual source of wonder and admiration. Her facility with the English speech, her ability to read books, her fine manners, her clean and orderly home, her pretty Canadian dress, her beloved school, her cheery mission, all these were to Irma new, wonderful and fascinating. Gradually Irma was drawn to that new world of Margaret's, and away from the old, sordid, disorderly wretchedness of her own life and home.

After much secret conference with all the Ketzels, and much patient and skilful labour on the part of the motherly Lena, a great day at length arrived for Irma. It was the day on which she discarded the head shawl with the rest of the quaint Galician attire, and appeared dressed as a Canadian girl, discovering to her delighted friends and to all who knew her, though not yet to herself, a rare beauty hitherto unnoticed by any. Indeed, when Mr. Samuel Sprink, coming in from Rosenblatt's store to spend a few hurried minutes in gorging himself after his manner at the evening meal, allowed himself time to turn his eyes from his plate and to let them rest upon the little maid waiting upon his table, the transformation from the girl, slatternly, ragged and none too clean, that was wont to bring him his food, to this new being that flitted about from place to place, smote him as with a sudden blow. He laid down the instruments of his gluttony and for a full half minute forgot the steaming stew before him, whose garlic-laden odours had been assailing his nostrils some minutes previously with pungent delight. Others, too, of that hungry gorging company found themselves disturbed in their ordinary occupation by this vision of sweet and tender beauty that flitted about them, ministering to their voracity.

To none more than to Rosenblatt himself was the transformation of Irma a surprise and a mystery. It made him uneasy. He had an instinctive feeling that this was the beginning of an emancipation that would leave him one day without his slaves. Paulina, too, would learn the new ways; then she and the girl, who now spent long hours of hard labour in his service, would demand money for their toil. The thought grieved him sore. But there was another thought that stabbed him with a keener pain. Paulina and her family would learn that they need no longer fear him, that they could do without him, and then they would escape from his control. And this Rosenblatt dreaded above all things else. To lose the power to keep in degradation the wife and children of the man he hated with a quenchless hatred would be to lose much of the sweetness of life. Those few terrible moments when he had lain waiting for the uplifted knife of his foe to penetrate his shrinking eyeballs had taken years from him. He had come back to his life older, weaker, broken in nerve and more than ever consumed with a thirst for vengeance. Since Kalmar's escape he lived in daily, hourly fear that his enemy would strike again and this time without missing, and with feverish anxiety he planned to anticipate that hour with a vengeance which would rob death of much of its sting.

So far he had succeeded only partially. Paulina and Irma he held in domestic bondage. From the boy Kalman, too, he exacted day by day the full tale of his scanty profits made from selling newspapers on the street. But beyond this he could not go. By no sort of terror could he induce Paulina to return to the old conditions and rent floor space in her room to his boarders. At her door she stood on guard, refusing admittance. Once, indeed, when hard pressed by Rosenblatt demanding entrance, she had thrown herself before him with a butcher knife in her hand, and with a look of such transforming fierceness on her face as drove him from the house in fear of his life. She was no longer his patient drudge, but a woman defending, not so much her own, as her husband's honour, a tigress guarding her young.

Never again did Rosenblatt attempt to pass through that door, but schooled himself to wait a better time and a safer path to compass his vengeance. But from that moment, where there had been merely contempt for Paulina and her family, there sprang up bitter hatred. He hated them all—the woman who was his dupe and his slave, but who balked him of his revenge; the boy who brought him the cents for which he froze during the winter evenings at the corner of Portage and Main, but who with the cents gave him fierce and fearless looks; and this girl suddenly transformed from a timid, stupid, ill-dressed Galician child, into a being of grace and loveliness and conscious power. No wonder that as he followed her with his eye, noting all this new grace and beauty, he felt uneasy. Already she seemed to have soared far beyond his sordid world and far beyond his grasp. Deep in his heart he swore that he would find means to bring her down to the dirt again. The higher her flight, the farther her fall and the sweeter would be his revenge.

"What's the matter wit you, boss? Gone back on your grub, eh?"

It was his clerk, Samuel Sprink, whose sharp little eyes had not failed to note the gloomy glances of his employer.

"Pretty gay girl, our Irma has come to be," continued the cheerful Samuel, who prided himself on his fine selection of colloquial English. "She's a beaut now, ain't she? A regular bird!"

Rosenblatt started. At his words, but more at the admiration in Samuel's eyes, a new idea came to him. He knew his clerk well, knew his restless ambition, his insatiable greed, his intense selfishness, his indomitable will. And he had good reason to know. Three times during the past year his clerk had forced from him an increase of salary. Indeed, Samuel Sprink, young though he was and unlearned in the ways of the world, was the only man in the city that Rosenblatt feared. If by any means Samuel could obtain a hold over this young lady, he would soon bring her to the dust. Once in Samuel's power, she would soon sink to the level of the ordinary Galician wife. True, she was but a girl of fifteen, but in a year or so she would be ready for the altar in the Galician estimation.

As these thoughts swiftly flashed through his mind, Rosenblatt turned to Samuel Sprink and said, "Yes, she is a fine girl. I never noticed before. It is her new dress."

"Not a bit," said Samuel. "The dress helps out, but it is the girl herself. I have seen it for a long time. Look at her. Isn't she a bird, a bird of Paradise, eh?"

"She will look well in a cage some day, eh, Samuel?"

"You bet your sweet life!" said Samuel.

"Better get the cage ready then, Samuel," suggested Rosenblatt. "There are plenty bird fanciers in this town."

The suggestion seemed to anger Samuel, who swore an English oath and lapsed into silence.

Irma heard, but heeded little. Rosenblatt she feared, Samuel Sprink she despised. There had been a time when both she and Paulina regarded him with admiration mingled with awe. Samuel Sprink had many attractions. He had always plenty of money to jingle, and had a reputation for growing wealth. He was generous in his gifts to the little girl—gifts, it must be confessed, that cost him little, owing to his position as clerk in Rosenblatt's store. Then, too, he was so clever with his smart English and his Canadian manners, so magnificent with his curled and oily locks, his resplendent jewelry, his brilliant neckties. But that was before Irma had been brought to the little mission, and before she had learned through Margaret Ketzel and through Margaret's father and mother something of Canadian life, of Canadian people, of Canadian manners and dress. As her knowledge in this direction extended, her admiration and reverence for Samuel Sprink faded.

The day that Irma discarded her Galician garb and blossomed forth as a Canadian young lady was the day on which she was fully cured of her admiration for Rosenblatt's clerk. For such subtle influence does dress exercise over the mind that something of the spirit of the garb seems to pass into the spirit of the wearer. Self-respect is often born in the tailor shop or in the costumer's parlour. Be this as it may, it is certain that Irma's Canadian dress gave the final blow to her admiration of Samuel Sprink, and child though she was, she became conscious of a new power over not only Sprink, but over all the boarders, and instinctively she assumed a new attitude toward them. The old coarse and familiar horseplay which she had permitted without thought at their hands, was now distasteful to her. Indeed, with most of the men it ceased to be any longer possible. There were a few, however, and Samuel Sprink among them, who were either too dull-witted to recognise the change that had come to the young girl, or were unwilling to acknowledge it. Samuel was unwilling also to surrender his patronising and protective attitude, and when patronage became impossible and protection unnecessary, he assumed an air of bravado to cover the feeling of embarrassment he hated to acknowledge, and tried to bully the girl into her former submissive admiration.

This completed the revulsion in Irma's mind, and while outwardly she went about her work in the house with her usual cheerful and willing industry, she came to regard her admirer and would be patron with fear, loathing, and contempt. Of this, however, Samuel was quite unaware. The girl had changed in her manner as in her dress, but that might be because she was older, she was almost a woman, after the Galician standard of computation. Whatever the cause, to Samuel the change only made her more fascinating than ever, and he set himself seriously to consider whether on the whole, dowerless though she would be, it would not be wise for him to devote some of his time and energy to the winning of this fascinating young lady for himself.

The possibility of failure never entered Samuel's mind. He had an overpowering sense of his own attractions. The question was simply should he earnestly set himself to accomplish this end? Without definitely making up his mind on this point, much less committing himself to this object, Samuel allowed himself the pleasurable occupation of trifling with the situation. But alas for Samuel's peace of mind! and alas for his self-esteem! the daily presence of this fascinating maiden in her new Canadian dress and with her new Canadian manners, which appeared to go with the dress, quite swept him away from his ordinary moorings, and he found himself tossed upon a tempestuous sea, the helpless sport of gusts of passion that at once surprised and humiliated him. It was an intolerably painful experience for the self-centred and self-controlled Samuel; and after a few months of this acute and humiliating suffering he was prepared to accept help from almost any course.

At this point Rosenblatt, who had been keeping a watchful eye upon the course of events, intervened.

"Samuel, my boy," he said one winter night when the store was closed for the day, "you are acting the fool. You are letting a little Slovak girl make a game of you."

"I attend to my own business, all the same," growled Samuel.

"You do, Samuel, my boy, you do. But you make me sorry for you, and ashamed."

Samuel grunted, unwilling to acknowledge even partial defeat to the man whom he had beaten more than once in his own game.

"You desire to have that little girl, Samuel, and yet you are afraid of her."

But Samuel only snarled and swore.

"You forget she is a Galician girl."

"She is Russian," interposed Samuel, "and she is of good blood."

"Good blood!" said Rosenblatt, showing his teeth like a snarling dog, "good blood! The blood of a murdering Nihilist jail bird!"

"She is of good Russian blood," said Samuel with an ugly look in his face, "and he is a liar who says she is not."

"Well, well," said Rosenblatt, turning from the point, "she is a Galician in everything else. Her mother is a Galician, a low-bred Galician, and you treat the girl as if she were a lady. This is not the Galician manner of wooing. A bolder course is necessary. You are a young man of good ability, a rising young man. You will be rich some day. Who is this girl without family, without dower to make you fear or hesitate? What says the proverb? 'A bone for my dog, a stick for my wife.'"

"Yes, that is all right," muttered Samuel, "a stick for my wife, and if she were my wife I would soon bring her to time."

"Ho, ho," said Rosenblatt, "it is all the same, sweetheart and wife. They are both much the better for a stick now and then. You are not the kind of man to stand beggar before a portionless Slovak girl, a young man handsome, clever, well-to-do. You do not need thus to humble yourself. Go in, my son, with more courage and with bolder tactics. I will gladly help you."

As a first result of Rosenblatt's encouraging advice, Samuel recovered much of his self-assurance, which had been rudely shattered, and therefore much of his good humour. As a further result, he determined upon a more vigorous policy in his wooing. He would humble himself no more. He would find means to bring this girl to her place, namely, at his feet.

The arrival of a Saint's day brought Samuel an opportunity to inaugurate his new policy. The foreign colony was rigidly devoted to its religious duties. Nothing could induce a Galician to engage in his ordinary avocation upon any day set apart as sacred by his Church. In the morning such of the colony as adhered to the Greek Church, went *en masse* to the quaint little church which had come to be erected and which had been consecrated by a travelling Archbishop, and there with reverent devotion joined in worship, using the elaborate service of the Greek rite. The religious duties over, they proceeded still further to celebrate the day in a somewhat riotous manner.

With the growth of the colony new houses had been erected which far outshone Paulina's in magnificence, but Paulina's still continued to be a social centre chiefly through Rosenblatt's influence. For no man was more skilled than he in the art of promoting sociability as an investment. There was still the full complement of boarders filling the main room and the basement, and these formed a nucleus around which the social life of a large part of the colony loved to gather.

It was a cold evening in February. The mercury had run down till it had almost disappeared in the bulb and Winnipeg was having a taste of forty below. Through this exhilarating air Kalman was hurrying home as fast as his sturdy legs could take him. His fingers were numb handling the coins received from the sale of his papers, but the boy cared nothing for that. He had had a good afternoon and evening; for with the Winnipeg men the colder the night the warmer their hearts, and these fierce February days were harvest days for the hardy news-boys crying their wares upon the streets. So the sharp cold only made Kalman run the faster. Above him twinkled the stars, under his feet sparkled the snow, the keen air filled his lungs with ozone that sent his blood leaping through his veins. A new zest was added to his life to-night, for as he ran he remembered that it was a feast day and that at his home there would be good eating and dance and song. As he ran he planned how he would avoid Rosenblatt and get past him into Paulina's room, where he would be safe, and where, he knew, good things saved from the feast for him by his sister would be waiting him. To her he would entrust all his cents above what was due to Rosenblatt, and with her they would be safe. For by neither threatening nor wheedling could Rosenblatt extract from her what was entrusted to her care, as he could from the slow-witted Paulina.

Keenly sensitive to the radiant beauty of the sparkling night, filled with the pleasurable anticipation of the feast before him, vibrating in every nerve with the mere joy of living his vigorous young life, Kalman ran along at full speed, singing now and then in breathless snatches a wild song of the Hungarian plains. Turning a sharp corner near his home, he almost overran a little girl.

"Kalman!" she cried with a joyous note in her voice.

"Hello! Elizabeth Ketzel, what do you want?" answered the boy, pulling up panting.

"Will you be singing to-night?" asked the little girl timidly.

"Sure, I will," replied the lad, who had already mastered in the school of the streets the intricacies of the Canadian vernacular.

"I wish I could come and listen."

"It is no place for little girls," said Kalman brusquely; then noting the shadow upon the face of the child, he added, "Perhaps you can come to the back window and Irma will let you in."

"I'll be sure to come," said Elizabeth to herself, for Kalman was off again like the wind.

Paulina's house was overflowing with riotous festivity. Avoiding the front door, Kalman ran to the back of the house, and making entrance through the window, there waited for his sister. Soon she came in.

"Oh, Kalman!" she cried, throwing her arms about him and kissing him, "such a feast as I have saved for you! And you are cold. Your poor fingers are frozen."

"Not a bit of it, Irma," said the boy—they always spoke in Russian, these two, ever since the departure of their father—"but I am hungry, oh! so hungry!"

Already Irma was flying about the room, drawing from holes and corners the bits she had saved from the feast for her brother. She spread them on the bed before him.

"But first," she cried, "I shall bring to the window the hot stew. Paulina," the children always so spoke of her, "has kept it hot for you," and she darted through the door.

After what seemed to Kalman a very long time indeed, she appeared at the window with a covered dish of steaming stew.

"What kept you?" said her brother impatiently; "I am starved."

"That nasty, hateful, little Sprink," she said. "Here, help me through." She looked flushed and angry, her "burnin' brown eyes" shining like blazing coals.

"What is the matter?" said Kalman, when he had a moment's leisure to observe her.

"He is very rough and rude," said the girl, "and he is a little pig."

Kalman nodded and waited. He had no time for mere words.

"And he tried to kiss me just now," she continued indignantly.

"Well, that's nothing," said Kalman; "they all want to do that.".

"Not for months, Kalman," protested Irma, "and never again, and especially that little Sprink. Never! Never!"

As Kalman looked at her erect little figure and her flushed face, it dawned on him that a change had come to his little sister. He paused in his eating.

"Irma," he said, "what have you done to yourself? Is it your hair that you have been putting up on your head? No, it is not your hair. You are not the same. You are—" he paused to consider, "yes, that's it. You are a lady."

The anger died out of Irma's brown eyes and flushed face. A soft and tender and mysterious light suffused her countenance.

"No, I am not a lady," she said, "but you remember what father said. Our mother was a lady, and I am going to be one."

Almost never had the children spoken of their mother. The subject was at once too sacred and too terrible for common speech. Kalman laid down his spoon.

"I remember," he said after a few moments' silence. A shadow lay upon his face. "She was a lady, and she died in the snow." His voice sank to a whisper. "Wasn't it awful, Irma?"

"Yes, Kalman dear," said his sister, sitting down beside him and putting her arms about his neck, "but she had no pain, and she was not afraid."

"No," said the boy with a ring in his voice, "she was not afraid; nor was father afraid, either." He rose from his meal.

"Why, Kalman," exclaimed his sister, "you are not half done your feast. There are such lots of nice things yet."

"I can't eat, Irma, when I think of that—of that man. I choke here," pointing to his throat.

"Well, well, we won't think of him to-night. Some day very soon, we shall be free from him. Sit down and eat."

But the boy remained standing, his face overcast with a fierce frown.

"Some day," he muttered, more to himself than to his sister, "I shall kill him."

"Not to-day, at any rate, Kalman," said his sister, brightening up. "Let us forget it to-night. Look at this pie. It is from Mrs. Fitzpatrick, and this pudding."

The boy allowed his look to linger upon the dainties. He was a healthy boy and very hungry. As he looked his appetite returned. He shook himself as if throwing off a burden.

"No, not to-night," he said; "I am not going to stop my feast for him."

"No, indeed," cried Irma. "Come quick and finish your feast. Oh, what eating we have had, and then what dancing! And they all want to dance with me," she continued,—"Jacob and Henry and Nicholas, and they are all nice except that horrid little Sprink."

"Did you not dance with him?"

"Yes," replied his sister, making a little face, "I danced with him too, but he wants me to dance with no one else, and I don't like that. He makes me afraid, too, just like Rosenblatt."

"Afraid!" said her brother scornfully.

"No, not afraid," said Irma quickly. "But never mind, here is the pudding. I am sorry it is cold."

"All right," said the boy, mumbling with a full mouth, "it is fine. Don't you be afraid of that Sprink; I'll knock his head off if he harms you."

"Not yet, Kalman," said Irma, smiling at him. "Wait a year or two before you talk like that."

"A year or two! I shall be a man then."

"Oh, indeed!" mocked his sister, "a man of fifteen years."

"You are only fifteen yourself," said Kalman.

"And a half," she interrupted.

"And look at you with your dress and your hair up on your head, and —and I am a boy. But I am not afraid of Sprink. Only yesterday I—"

"Oh, I know you were fighting again. You are terrible, Kalman. I hear all the boys talking about you, and the girls too. Did you beat him? But of course you did."

"I don't know," said her brother doubtfully, "but I don't think he will bother me any more."

"Oh, Kalman," said his sister anxiously, "why do you fight so much?"

"They make me fight," said the boy. "They try to drive me off the corner, and he called me a greasy Dook. But I showed him I am no Doukhobor. Doukhobors won't fight."

"Tell me," cried his sister, her face aglow—"but no, I don't want to hear about it. Did you—how did you beat him? But you should not fight so, Kalman." In spite of herself she could not avoid showing her interest in the fight and her pride in her fighting brother.

"Why not?" said her brother; "it is right to fight for your rights, and if they bother me or try to crowd me off, I will fight till I die."

But Irma shook her head at him.

"Well, never mind just now," she cried. "Listen to the noise. That is Jacob singing; isn't it awful? Are you going in?"

"Yes, I am. Here is my money, Irma, and that is for—that brute. Give it to Paulina for him. I can hardly keep my knife out of him. Some day—" The boy closed his lips hard.

"No, no, Kalman," implored his sister, "that must not be, not now nor ever. This is not Russia, or Hungary, but Canada."

The boy made no reply.

"Hurry and wash yourself and come out. They will want you to sing. I shall wait for you."

"No, no, go on. I shall come after."

A shout greeted the girl as she entered the crowded room. There was no one like her in the dances of her people.

"It is my dance," cried one.

"Not so; she is promised to me."

"I tell you this mazurka is mine."

So they crowded about her in eager but good-natured contention.

"I cannot dance with you all," cried the girl, laughing, "and so I will dance by myself."

At this there was a shout of applause, and in a moment more she was whirling in the bewildering intricacies of a *pas seul* followed in every step by the admiring gaze and the enthusiastic plaudits of the whole company. As she finished, laughing and breathless, she caught sight of Kalman, who had just entered.

"There," she exclaimed, "I have lost my breath, and Kalman will sing now."

Immediately her suggestion was taken up on every hand.

"A song! A song!" they shouted. "Kalman Kalmar will sing! Come, Kalman, 'The Shepherd's Love.'" "No, 'The Soldier's Bride.'" "No, no, 'My Sword and my Cup.'"

"First my own cup," cried the boy, pressing toward the beer keg in the corner and catching up a mug.

"Give him another," shouted a voice.

"No, Kalman," said his sister in a low voice, "no more beer."

But the boy only laughed at her as he filled his mug again.

"I am too full to sing just now," he cried; "let us dance," and, seizing Irma, he carried her off under the nose of the disappointed Sprink, joining with the rest in one of the many fascinating dances of the Hungarian people.

But the song was only postponed. In every social function of the foreign colony, Kalman's singing was a feature. The boy loved to sing and was ever ready to respond to any request for a song. So when the cry for a song rose once more, Kalman was ready and eager. He sprang upon a beer keg and cried, "What shall it be?"

"My song," said Irma, who stood close to him.

The boy shook his head. "Not yet."

"'The Soldier's Bride,'" cried a voice, and Kalman began to sing. He had a beautiful face with regular clean-cut features, and the fair hair and blue grey eyes often seen in South Eastern Russia. As he sang, his face reflected the passing shades of feeling in his heart as a windless lake the cloud and sunlight of a summer sky. The song was a kind of Hungarian "Young Lochinvar." The soldier lover, young and handsome, is away in the wars; the beautiful maiden, forced into a hateful union with a wealthy land owner, old and ugly, stands before the priest at the altar. But hark! ere the fateful vows are spoken there is a clatter of galloping hoofs, a manly form rushes in, hurls the groom insensible to the ground, snatches away the bride and before any can interfere, is off on a coal-black steed, his bride before him. Let him follow who dares!

The boy had a voice of remarkable range and clearness, and he rendered the song with a verve and dramatic force remarkable in one of his age. The song was received with wild cheers and loud demands for more. The boy was about to refuse, when through the crowding faces, all aglow with enthusiastic delight, he saw the scowling face of Rosenblatt. A fierce rage seized him. He hesitated no longer.

"Yes, another song," he cried, and springing to the side of the musicians he hummed the air, and then took his place again upon the beer keg.

Before the musicians had finished the introductory bars, Irma came to his side and entreated, "Oh, Kalman, not that one! Not that one!"

But it was as though he did not hear her. His face was set and white, his blue eyes glowed black. He stood with lips parted, waiting for the cue to begin. His audience, to most of whom the song was known, caught by a mysterious telepathy the tense emotion of the boy, and stood silent and eager, all smiles gone from their faces. The song was in the Ruthenian tongue, but was the heart cry of a Russian exile, a cry for freedom for his native land, for death to the tyrant, for vengeance on the traitor. Nowhere in all the Czar's dominions dared any man sing that song.

As the boy's strong, clear voice rang out in the last cry for vengeance, there thrilled in his tones an intensity of passion that gripped hard the hearts of those who had known all their lives long the bitterness of tyranny unspeakable. In the last word the lad's voice broke in a sob. Most of that company knew the boy's story, and knew that he was singing out his heart's deepest passion.

When the song was finished, there was silence for a few brief moments; then a man, a Russian, caught the boy in his arms, lifted him on his shoulder and carried him round the room, the rest of the men madly cheering. All but one. Trembling with inarticulate rage, Rosenblatt strode to the musicians.

"Listen!" he hissed with an oath. "Do I pay you for this? No more of this folly! Play up a czardas, and at once!"

The musicians hastened to obey, and before the cheers had died, the strains of the czardas filled the room. With the quick reaction from the tragic to the gay, the company swung into this joyous and exciting dance. Samuel Sprink, seizing Irma, whirled her off into the crowd struggling and protesting, but all in vain. After the dance there was a general rush for the beer keg, with much noise and good-natured horse play. At the other end of the room, however, there was a fierce struggle going on. Samuel Sprink, excited by the dance and, it must be confessed, by an unusual devotion to the beer keg that evening, was still retaining his hold of Irma, and was making determined efforts to kiss her.

"Let me go!" cried the girl, struggling to free herself. "You must not touch me! Let me go!"

"Oh, come now, little one," said Samuel pleasantly, "don't be so mighty stiff about it. One kiss and I let you go."

"That's right, Samuel, my boy," shouted Rosenblatt; "she only wants coaxing just a little mucher."

Rosenblatt's words were followed by a chorus of encouraging cheers, for Samuel was not unpopular among the men, and none could see any good reason why a girl should object to be kissed, especially by such a man as Samuel, who was already so prosperous and who had such bright prospects for the future.

But Irma continued to struggle, till Kalman, running to her side, cried, "Let my sister go!"

"Go away, Kalman. I am not hurting your sister. It's only fun. Go away," said Sprink.

"She does not think it fun," said the boy quietly. "Let her go."

"Oh, go away, you leetle kid. Go away and sit down. You think yourself too much."

It was Rosenblatt's harsh voice. As he spoke, he seized the boy by the collar and with a quick jerk flung him back among the crowd. It was as if he had fired some secret magazine of passion in the boy's heart. Uttering the wild cry of a mad thing, Kalman sprang at him with such lightning swiftness that Rosenblatt was borne back and would have fallen, but for those behind. Recovering himself, he dealt the boy a heavy blow in the face that staggered him for a moment, but only for a moment. It seemed as if the boy had gone mad. With the same wild cry, and this time with a knife open in his hand, he sprang at his hated enemy, stabbing quick, fierce stabs. But this time Rosenblatt was ready. Taking the boy's stabs on his arm, he struck the boy a terrific blow on the neck. As Kalman fell, he clutched and hung to his foe, who, seizing him by the throat, dragged him swiftly toward the door.

"Hold this shut," he said to a friend of his who was following him close.

After they had passed through, the man shut the door and held it fast, keeping the crowd from getting out.

"Now," said Rosenblatt, dragging the half-insensible boy around to the back of the house, "the time is come. The chance is too good. You try to kill me, but there will be one less Kalmar in the world to-night. There will be a little pay back of my debt to your cursed father. Take that—and that." As he spoke the words, he struck the boy hard upon the head and face, and then flinging him down in the snow, proceeded deliberately to kick him to death.

But even as he threw the boy down, a shrill screaming pierced through the quiet of the night, and from the back of the house a little girl ran shrieking. "He is killing him! He is killing him!"

It was little Elizabeth Ketzel, who had been let in through the back window to hear Kalman sing, and who, at the first appearance of trouble, had fled by the way she had entered, meeting Rosenblatt as he appeared dragging the insensible boy through the snow. Her shrieks arrested the man in his murderous purpose. He turned and fled, leaving the boy bleeding and insensible in the snow.

As Rosenblatt disappeared, a cutter drove rapidly up.

"What's the row, kiddie?" said a man, springing out. It was Dr. Wright, returning from a midnight trip to one of his patients in the foreign colony. "Who's killing who?"

"It is Kalman!" cried Elizabeth, "and he is dead! Oh, he is dead!"

The doctor knelt beside the boy. "Great Cæsar! It surely is my friend Kalman, and in a bad way. Some more vendetta business, I have no doubt. Now what in thunder is that, do you suppose?" From the house came a continuous shrieking. "Some more killing, I guess. Here, throw this robe about the boy while I see about this."

He ran to the door and kicked it open. It seemed as if the whole company of twenty or thirty men were every man fighting. As the doctor paused to get his bearings, he saw across the room in the farthest corner, Irma screaming as she struggled in the grasp of Samuel Sprink, and in the midst of the room Paulina fighting like a demon and uttering strange weird cries. She was trying to force her way to the door.

As she caught sight of the doctor, she threw out her hands toward him with a loud cry. "Kalman—killing! Kalman—killing!" was all she could say.

The doctor thrust himself forward through the struggling men, crying in a loud voice, "Here, you, let that woman go! And you there, let that girl alone!"

Most of the men knew him, and at his words they immediately ceased fighting.

"What the deuce are you at, anyway, you men?" he continued, as Paulina and the girl sprang past him and out of the door. "Do you fight with women?"

"No," said one of the men. "Dis man," pointing to Sprink, "he mak fun wit de girl."

"Mighty poor fun," said the doctor, turning toward Sprink. "And who has been killing that boy outside?"

"It is that young devil Kalman, who has been trying to kill Mr. Rosenblatt," replied Sprink.

"Oh, indeed," said the doctor, "and what was the gentle Mr. Rosenblatt doing meantime?"

"Rosenblatt?" cried Jacob Wassyl, coming forward excitedly. "He mak for hurt dat boy. Dis man," pointing to Sprink, "he try for kiss dat girl. Boy he say stop. Rosenblatt he trow boy back. Boy he fight."

"Look here, Jacob," said Dr. Wright, "you get these men's names—this man," pointing to Sprink, "and a dozen more—and we'll make this interesting for Rosenblatt in the police court to-morrow morning."

Outside the house the doctor found Paulina sitting in the snow with Kalman's head in her lap, swaying to and fro muttering and groaning. Beside her stood Irma and Elizabeth Ketzel weeping wildly. The doctor raised the boy gently.

"Get into the cutter," he said to Paulina. Irma translated. The woman ran without a word, seated herself in the cutter and held out her arms for the boy.

"That will do," said the doctor, laying Kalman in her arms. "Now get some shawls, quilts or something for your mother and yourself, or you'll freeze to death, and come along."

The girl rushed away and returned in a few moments with a bundle of shawls.

"Get in," said the doctor, "and be quick."

The men were crowding about.

"Now, Jacob," said the doctor, turning to Wassyl, who stood near, "you get me those names and we'll get after that man, you bet! or I'm a Turk. This boy is going to die, sure."

As he spoke, he sprang into his cutter and sent his horse off at a gallop, for by the boy's breathing he felt that the chances of life were slipping swiftly away.

Chapter X

Jack French of the Night Hawk Ranch

A map of Western Canada showing the physical features of the country lying between the mountains on the one side and the Bay and the Lakes on the other, presents the appearance of a vast rolling plain scarred and seamed and pitted like an ancient face. These scars and seams and pits are great lazy rivers, meandering streams, lakes, sleughs and marshes which form one vast system of waters that wind and curve through the rolls of the prairie and nestle in its sunlit hollows, laving, draining, blessing where they go and where they stay.

By these, the countless herds of buffalo and deer quenched their thirst in the days when they, with their rival claimants for the land, the Black Feet and the Crees, roamed undisturbed over these mighty plains. These waterways in later days when The Honourable the Hudson's Bay Company ruled the West, formed the great highways of barter. By these teeming lakes and sleughs and marshes hunted and trapped Indians and half-breeds. Down these streams and rivers floated the great fur brigades in canoe and Hudson's Bay pointer with priceless bales of pelts to the Bay in the north or the Lakes in the south, on their way to that centre of the world's trade, old London. And up these streams and rivers went the great loads of supplies and merchandise for the far-away posts that were at once the seats of government and the emporiums of trade in this wide land.

Following the canoe and Hudson's Bay boat, came the river barge and side-wheeler, and with these, competing for trade, the overland freighter with ox train and pack pony, with Red River cart and shagginappi.

Still later, up these same waterways and along these trails came settlers singly or in groups, the daring vanguard of an advancing civilization, and planted themselves as pleased their fancy in choice spots, in sunny nooks sheltered by bluffs, by gem-like lakes or flowing streams, but mostly on the banks of the great rivers, the highways for their trade, the shining links that held them to their kind. Some there were among those hardy souls who, severing all bonds behind them, sought only escape from their fellow men and from their past. These left the great riverways and freighting trails, and pressing up the streams to distant head waters, there pitched their camp and there, in lonely, lordly independence, took rich toll of prairie, lake and stream as they needed for their living.

Such a man was Jack French, and such a spot was Night Hawk Lake, whose shining waters found a tortuous escape four miles away by Night Hawk Creek into the South Saskatchewan, king of rivers.

The two brothers, Jack and Herbert French, of good old English stock, finding life in the trim downs of Devon too confined and wearisome for their adventurous spirits, fell to walking seaward over the high head lands, and to listening and gazing, the soft spray dashing wet upon their faces, till they found eyes and ears filled with the sights and sounds of far, wide plains across the sea that called and beckoned, till in the middle seventies, with their mother's kiss trembling on their brows and on their lips, and their father's almost stern benediction stiffening their backs, they fared forth to the far West, and found themselves on the black trail that wound up the Red River of the North and reached the straggling hamlet of Winnipeg.

There, in one of Winnipeg's homes, they found generous welcome and a maiden, guarded by a stern old timer for a father and four stalwart plain-riding brothers, but guarded all in vain, for laughing at all such guarding, the two brothers with the hot selfishness of young love, each unaware of the other's intent, sought to rifle that house of its chief treasure.

To Herbert, the younger, that ardent pirate of her heart, the maiden struck her flaming flag, and on the same night, with fearful dismay, she sought pardon of the elder brother that she could not yield him like surrender. With pale appealing face and kind blue eyes, she sought forgiveness for her poverty.

"Oh, Mr. French," she cried, "if I only could! But I cannot give you what is Herbert's now."

"Herbert!" gasped Jack with parched lips.

"And oh, Jack," she cried again with sweet selfishness, "you will love Herbert still, and me?"

And Jack, having had a moment in which to summon up the reserves of his courage and his command, smiled into her appealing eyes, kissed her pale face, and still smiling, took his way, unseeing and unheeding all but those appealing, tearful eyes and that pleading voice asking with sweet selfishness only his life.

Three months he roamed the plains alone, finding at length one sunny day, Night Hawk Lake, whose fair and lonely wildness seemed to suit his mood, and there he pitched his camp. Thence back to Winnipeg a month later to his brother's wedding, and that over, still smiling, to take his way again to Night Hawk Lake, where ever since he spent his life.

He passed his days at first in building house and stables from the poplar bluffs at hand, and later in growing with little toil from the rich black land and taking from prairie, lake and creek with rifle and with net, what was necessary for himself and his man, the Scotch half-breed Mackenzie, all the while forgetting till he could forget no longer, and then with Mackenzie drinking deep and long till remembering and forgetting were the same.

After five years he returned to Winnipeg to stand by her side whose image lived ever in his heart, while they closed down the coffin lid upon the face dearest to her, dearest but one to him of all faces in the world. Then when he had comforted her with what comfort he had to give, he set face again toward Night Hawk Lake, leaving her, because she so desired it, alone but for her aged mother, bereft of all, husband, brothers, father, who might guard her from the world's harm.

"I am safe, dear Jack," she said, "God will let nothing harm me."

And Jack, smiling bravely still, went on his way and for a whole year lived for the monthly letter that advancing civilization had come to make possible to him.

The last letter of the year brought him the word that she was alone. That night Jack French packed his buckboard with grub for his six-hundred-mile journey, and at the end of the third week, for the trail was heavy on the Portage Plains, he drove his limping broncho up the muddy Main Street of Winnipeg.

When the barber had finished with him, he set forth to find his brother's wife, who, seeing him, turned deadly pale and stood looking sadly at him, her hand pressed hard upon her heart.

"Oh, Jack!" she said at length, with a great pity in her voice,—"poor Jack! why did you come?"

"To make you a home with me," said Jack, looking at her with eyes full of longing, "and wherever you choose, here or yonder at the Night Hawk Ranch, which is much better,"—at which her tears began to flow.

"Poor Jack! Dear Jack!" she cried, "why did you come?"

"You know why," he said. "Can you not learn to love me?"

"Love you, Jack? I could not love you more."

"Can you not come to me?"

"Dear Jack! Poor Jack!" she said again, and fell to sobbing bitterly till he forgot his own grief in hers. "I love my husband still."

"And I too," said Jack, looking pitifully at her.

"And I must keep my heart for him till I see him again." Her voice sank to a whisper, but she stood bravely looking into his eyes, her two hands holding down her fluttering heart as if in fear that it might escape.

"And is that the last word?" said Jack wearily.

"Yes, Jack, my brother, my dear, dear brother," she said, "it is the last. And oh, Jack, I have had much sorrow, but none more bitter than this!" And sobbing uncontrollably, she laid herself on his breast.

He held her to him, stroking her beautiful hair, his brown hand trembling and his strong face twisting strangely.

"Don't cry, dear Margaret. Don't cry like that. I won't make you weep. Never mind. You could not help it. And—I'll—get—over it—somehow. Only don't cry."

Then when she grew quiet again he kissed her and went out, smiling back at her as he went, and for fifteen years never saw her face again.

But month by month there came a letter telling him of her and her work, and this helped him to forget his pain. But more and more often as the years went on, Jack French and his man Mackenzie sat long nights in the bare ranch house with a bottle between them, till Mackenzie fell under the table and Jack with his hard head and his lonely heart was left by himself, staring at the fire if in winter, or out of the window at the lake if in summer, till the light on the water grew red, to his great hurt in body and in soul.

One spring day in the sixteenth year, in the middle of the month of May, when Jack had driven to the Crossing for supplies, an unexpected letter met him, which gave him much concern and changed forever the even current of his life. And this was the letter:

'MY DEAR JACK,—You have not yet answered my last, you bad boy, but you know I do not wait for answers, or you would seldom hear from me.' "And that's true enough," murmured Jack. 'But this is a special letter, and is to ask you to do a great thing for me, a very great thing. Indeed, you may not be able to do it at all.' "Indeed!" said Jack. 'And if you cannot do it, I trust you to tell me so.' "Trust me! well rather," said Jack again.

'You know something of my work among the Galicians, but you do not know just how sad it often is. They are poor ignorant creatures, but really they have kind hearts and have many nice things.' "By Jove! She'd find good points in the very devil himself!" 'And I know you would pity them if you knew them, especially the women and the children. The women have to work so hard, and the children are growing up wild, learning little of the good and much of the bad that Winnipeg streets can teach them.' "Heaven help them of their school!" cried Jack.

'Well, I must tell you what I want. You remember seeing in the papers that I sent you some years ago, the account of that terrible murder by a Russian Nihilist named Kalmar, and you remember perhaps how he nearly killed a horrid man who had treated him badly, very badly, named Rosenblatt. Well, perhaps you remember that Kalmar escaped from the penitentiary, and has not been heard of since. His wife and children have somehow come under the power of this Rosenblatt again. He has got a mortgage on her house and forces the woman to do his will. The woman is a poor stupid creature, and she has just slaved away for this man. The boy is different. He is a fine handsome little fellow, thirteen or fourteen years old, who makes his living selling newspapers and, I am afraid, is learning a great many things that he would be better without.' "Which is true of more than him," growled Jack. 'Of course, he does not like Rosenblatt. A little while ago there was a dance and, as always at the dances, that awful beer! The men got drunk and a good deal of fighting took place. Rosenblatt and a friend of his got abusing the girl. The boy flew at him and wounded him with a knife,' "And served him jolly well right," said Jack with an oath. 'and then Rosenblatt nearly killed him and threw him out in the snow. There he would have certainly died, had not Dr. Wright happened along and carried him to the hospital, where he has been ever since. The doctor had Rosenblatt up before the Court, but he brought a dozen men to swear that the boy was a bad and dangerous boy and that he was only defending himself. Fancy a great big man against a boy thirteen! Well, would you believe it, Rosenblatt escaped and laid a charge against the boy, and would actually have had him sent to jail, but I went to the magistrate and offered to take him and find a home for him outside of the city.' "Good brave little lady! I know you well," cried Jack.

'I thought of you, Jack,' "Bless your kind little heart," said Jack. 'and I knew that if you could get him you would make a man of him.' "Aha! You did!" exclaimed Jack. 'Here he is getting worse and worse every day. He is so quick and so clever, he has never been to school, but he reads and speaks English well. He is very popular with his own people, for he is a wonderful singer, and they like him at their feasts. And I have heard that he is as fond of beer as any of them. He was terribly battered, but he is all right again, and has been living with his sister and his step-mother in the house of a friend of his father's. But I have promised to get him out of the city, and if I do not, I know Rosenblatt will be after him. Besides this, I am afraid something will happen if he remains. The boy says quite quietly, but you can't help feeling that he means it, that he will kill Rosenblatt some day. It is terribly sad, for he is such a nice boy.' "Seems considerable of an angel," agreed Jack. 'I am afraid you will have to teach him a good many things, Jack, for he has some bad habits. But if he is with you and away from the bad people he meets with here, I am sure he will soon forget the bad things he has learned.' "Dear lady, God grant you may never know," said Jack ruefully.

'This is a long letter, dear Jack. How I should like to go up to Night Hawk Ranch and see you, for I know you will not come to Winnipeg, and we do not see enough of each other. We ought to, for my sake and for Herbert's too.' "Ah God! and what of me?" groaned Jack. 'I cannot begin to thank you for all your kindness. And, Jack, you must stop sending me money, for I do not need it and I will not use it, and I just keep putting what you send me in the bank for you. The Lord has given me many friends, and He never has allowed me to want.

'I shall wait two weeks, and then send you Kalman—that is his name, Kalman Kalmar, a nice name, isn't it? And he is a dear good boy; that is, he might be.' "Good heart, so might we all," cried Jack. 'But I love him just as he is.' "Happy boy." 'Wouldn't it be fine if you could make him a good man? How much he might do for his people! And if he stays here he will get to be terrible, for his father was terrible, although, poor man, it was hardly his fault.' "I surely believe in God's mercy," said poor Jack.

'This is a long rambling letter, dear Jack, but you will forgive me. I sometimes get pretty tired.' And Jack's brown lean hand closed swiftly. 'There is so much to do. But I am pretty well and I have many kind friends. So much to do, so many sick and poor and lonely. They need a friend. The Winnipeg people are very kind, but they are very busy.

'Now, my dear Jack, will you do for Kalman all you can? And—may I say it?—remember, he is just a boy. I do not want to preach to you, but he needs to be under the care of a good man, and that is why I send him to you.

'Your loving sister,

'MARGARET.'

There was a grim look on Jack French's face as he finished reading the letter the second time.

"You're a good one," he said, "and you have a wise little head as well as a tender heart. Don't want to preach to me, eh? But you get your work in all the same. Two weeks! Let's see, this letter has been four weeks on the way—up to Edmonton and back! By Jove! That boy ought to be along with Macmillan's outfit. I say, Jimmy," this to Jimmy Green, who, besides representing Her Majesty in the office of Postmaster, was general store keeper and trader to the community, "when will Macmillan be in?"

"Couple of days, Jack."

"Well, I guess I'll have to wait."

And this turned out an unhappy necessity for Jack French, for when the Macmillan outfit drove up to the Crossing he was lying incapable and dead to all around, in Jimmy Green's back store.

Chapter XI

The Edmonton Trail

Straight across the country, winding over plains, around sleughs, threading its way through bluffs, over prairie undulations, fording streams and crossing rivers, and so making its course northwest from Winnipeg for nine hundred miles, runs the Edmonton trail.

Macmillan was the last of that far-famed and adventurous body of men who were known all through the western country for their skill, their courage, their endurance in their profession of freighters from Winnipeg to the far outpost of Edmonton and beyond into the Peace River and Mackenzie River districts. The building of railroads cut largely into their work, and gradually the freighters faded from the trails. Old Sam Macmillan was among the last of his tribe left upon the Edmonton trail. He was a master in his profession. In the packing of his goods with their almost infinite variety, in the making up of his load, he was possessed of marvellous skill, while on the trail itself he was easily king of them all.

Macmillan was a big silent Irishman, raw boned, hardy, and with a highly developed genius for handling ox or horse teams of any size in a difficult bit of road, and possessing as well a unique command of picturesque and varied profanity. These gifts he considered as necessarily related, and the exercise of each was always in conjunction with the other, for no man ever heard Macmillan swear in ordinary conversation or on commonplace occasions. But when his team became involved in a sleugh, it was always a point of doubt whether he aroused more respect and admiration in his attendants by his rare ability to get the last ounce of hauling power out of his team or by the artistic vividness and force of the profanity expended in producing this desired result. It is related that on an occasion when he had as part of his load the worldly effects of an Anglican Bishop *en route* to his heroic mission to the far North, the good Bishop, much grieved at Macmillan's profanity, urged upon him the unnecessary character of this particular form of encouragement.

"Is it swearing Your Riverence objects to?" said Macmillan, whose vocabulary still retained a slight flavour of the Old Land. "I do assure you that they won't pull a pound without it."

But the Bishop could not be persuaded of this, and urged upon Macmillan the necessity of eliminating this part of his persuasion.

"Just as you say, Your Riverence. I ain't hurried this trip and we'll do our best."

The next bad sleugh brought opportunity to make experiment of the new system. The team stuck fast in the black muck, and every effort to extricate them served only to imbed them more hopelessly in the sticky gumbo. Time passed on. A dark and lowering night was imminent. The Bishop grew anxious. Macmillan, with whip and voice, encouraged his team, but all in vain. The Bishop's anxiety increased with the approach of a threatening storm.

"It is growing late, Mr. Macmillan, and it looks like rain. Something must be done."

"It does that, Your Lordship, but the brutes won't pull half their own weight without I speak to them in the way they are used to."

The good man was in a sore strait. Another half hour passed, and still with no result. It was imperative that his goods should be brought under cover before the storm should break. Again the good Bishop urged Macmillan to more strenuous effort.

"We can't stay here all night, sir," he said. "Surely something can be done."

"Well, I'll tell Your Lordship, it's one of two things, stick or swear, and there's nothing else for it."

"Well, well, Mr. Macmillan," said the Bishop resignedly, "we must get on. Do as you think best, but I take no responsibility in the matter." At which Pilate's counsel he retired from the scene, leaving Macmillan an untrammelled course.

Macmillan seized the reins from the ground, and walking up and down the length of his six-horse team, began to address them singly and in the mass in terms so sulphurously descriptive of their ancestry, their habits, and their physical and psychological characteristics, that when he gave the word in a mighty culminating roar of blasphemous excitation, each of the bemired beasts seemed to be inspired with a special demon, and so exerted itself to the utmost limit of its powers that in a single minute the load stood high and dry on solid ground.

One other characteristic made Macmillan one of the most trusted of the freighters upon the trail. While in charge of his caravan he was an absolute teetotaler, making up, however, for this abstinence at the end of the trip by a spree whose duration was limited only by the extent of his credit.

It was to Mr. Macmillan's care that Mrs. French had committed Kalman with many and anxious injunctions, and it is Macmillan's due to say that every moment of that four weeks' journey was one of undiluted delight to the boy, although it is to be feared that not the least enjoyable moments in that eventful journey were those when he stood lost in admiration while his host, with the free use of his sulphurously psychological lever, pried his team out of the frequent sleughs that harassed the trail. And before Macmillan had delivered up his charge, his pork and hard tack, aided by the ardent suns and sweeping winds of the prairie, had done their work, so that it was a brown and thoroughly hardy looking lad that was handed over to Jimmy Green at the Crossing.

"Here is Jack French's boy," said Macmillan. "And it's him that's got the ear for music. In another trip he'll dust them horses out of a hole with any of us. Swear! Well, I should smile! By the powers! he makes me feel queer."

"Swear," echoed a thick voice from behind the speaker, "who's swearing?"

"Hello! Jack," said Macmillan quietly. "Got a jag on, eh?"

"Attend to your own business, sir," said Jack French, whose dignity grew and whose temper shortened with every bottle. "Answer my question, sir. Who is swearing?"

"Oh, there's nothing to it, Jack," said Macmillan. "I was telling Jimmy here that that's a mighty smart boy of yours, and with a great tongue for language."

"I'll break his back," growled Jack French, his face distorted with a scowl. "Look here, boy," he continued, whirling fiercely upon the lad, "you are sent to me by the best woman on earth to make a man of you, and I'll have no swearing on my ranch," delivering himself of which sentiment punctuated by a *feu de joie* of muddled oaths, he lurched away into the back shop and fell into a drunken sleep, leaving the boy astonished and for some minutes speechless.

"Is that her brother?" he asked at length, when he had found voice.

"Whose brother?" said Jimmy Green.

"Yes, boy, that's her brother," said Macmillan. "But that is not himself any more than a mad dog. Jimmy here has been filling him up," shaking his finger at the culprit, "which he had no right to do, knowing Jack French as he does, by the same token."

"Oh, come on, Mac," said Jimmy apologetically. "You know Jack French, and when he gets a-goin' could I stop him? No, nor you."

Next morning when Kalman came forth from the loft which served Jimmy Green as store room for his marvellously varied merchandise, he found that Macmillan had long since taken the trail and was by this time miles on his journey toward Edmonton. The boy was lonely and sick at heart. Macmillan had been a friend to him, and had constituted the last link that held him to the life he had left behind in the city. It was to Macmillan that the little white-faced lady who was to the boy the symbol of all that was high and holy in character, had entrusted him for safe deliverance to her brother Jack French. Kalman had spent an unhappy night, his sleep being broken by the recurring vision of the fierce and bloated face of the man who had cursed him and threatened him on the previous evening. The boy had not yet recovered from the horror and surprise of his discovery that this drunken and brutalized creature was the noble-hearted brother into whose keeping his friend and benefactress had given him. That a man should drink himself drunk was nothing to his discredit in Kalman's eyes, but that Mrs. French's brother, the loved and honoured gentleman whom she had taught him to regard as the ideal of all manly excellence, should turn out to be this bloated and foul-mouthed bully, shocked him inexpressibly. From these depressing thoughts he was aroused by a cheery voice.

"Hello! my boy, had breakfast?"

He turned quickly and beheld a tall, strongly made and handsome man of middle age, clean shaven, neatly groomed, and with a fine open cheery face.

"No, sir," he stammered, with unusual politeness in his tone, and staring with all his eyes.

It was Jack French who addressed him, but this handsome, kindly, well groomed man was so different from the man who had reeled over him and poured forth upon him his abusive profanity the night before, that his mind refused to associate the one with the other.

"Well, boy," said Jack French, "you must be hungry. Jimmy, anything left for the boy?"

"Lots, Jack," said Jimmy eagerly, as if relieved to see him clothed again and in his right mind. "The very best. Here, boy, set in here." He opened a door which led into a side room where the remains of breakfast were disclosed upon the table. "Bacon and eggs, my boy, eggs! mind you, and Hudson's Bay biscuit and black strap. How's that?"

The boy, still lost in wonder, fell to with a great access of good cheer, and made a hearty meal, while outside he could hear Jack French's clear, cheery, commanding voice directing the packing of his buckboard.

The packing of the buckboard was a business calling for some skill. In the box seat were stowed away groceries and small parcels for the ranch and for settlers along the trail. Upon the boards behind the seat were loaded and roped securely, sides of pork, a sack of flour, and various articles for domestic use. Last of all, and with great care, French disposed a mysterious case packed with straw, the contents of which were perfectly well known to the boy.

The buckboard packed, there followed the process of hitching up,—a process at once spectacular and full of exciting incident, for the trip to the Crossing was to the bronchos, unbroken even to the halter, their first experience in the ways of civilized man. Wild, timid and fiercely vicious, they were brought in from their night pickets on a rope, holding back hard, plunging, snorting, in terror, and were tied up securely in an out shed. There was no time spent in gentle persuasion. French took a collar and without hesitation, but without haste, walked quietly to the side of one of the shuddering ponies, a buckskin, and paying no heed to its frantic plunging, slipped it over his neck, keeping close to the pony's side and crowding it hard against the wall. The rest of the harness offered more difficulty. The pony went wild at every approach of the trailing straps and buckles. Kalman looked on in admiration while French, without loss of temper, without oath or objurgation, went on quietly with his work.

"Have to put a hitch on him, Jimmy, I guess," said French after he had failed in repeated attempts.

Jimmy took a thin strong line of rope, put a running noose around the pony's jaw, threw the end over its neck and back through the noose again, thus making a most cruel bridle, and gave the rope a single sharp jerk. The broncho fell back upon its haunches, and before it had recovered from its pain and surprise, French had the harness on its back and buckled into place.

The second pony, a piebald or pinto, needed no "Commache hitch," but submitted to the harnessing process without any great protest.

"Bring him along, Jimmy," said French, leading out the pinto.

But this was easier said than done, for the buckskin after being faced toward the door, set his feet firmly in front of him and refused to budge an inch.

"Touch him up behind, boy," said Green to Kalman, who stood by eager to assist.

Kalman sprang forward with a stick in his hand, dodged under the poles which formed the sides of the stall, and laid a resounding whack upon the pony's flank. There was a flash of heels, a bang on the shed wall, a plunge forward, and the pony was found clear of the shed and Kalman senseless on the ground.

"Jimmy, you eternal fool!" cried French, "hold this rope!" He ran to the boy and picked him up in his arms. "The boy is killed, and there'll be the very deuce to pay."

He laid the insensible lad on the grass, ran for a pail of water and dashed a portion of it in his face. In a few moments the boy opened his eyes with a long deep sigh, and closed them again as if in contented slumber. French took a flask from his pocket, opened the boy's mouth, and poured some of its contents between his lips. At once Kalman began to cough, sat up, and gazed around in a stupid manner upon the ponies and the men.

"He's out," he said at length, with his eyes upon the pinto.

"Out? Who's out?" cried French.

"Judas priest!" exclaimed Jimmy, using his favourite oath. "He means the broncho."

"By Jove! he *is* out, boy," said French, "and you are as near out as you are likely to be for some time to come. What in great Cæsar's name were you trying to do?"

"He wouldn't move," said the boy simply, "and I hit him."

"Listen here, boy," said Jimmy Green solemnly, "when you go to hit a broncho again, don't take anything short of a ten-foot pole, unless you're on top of him."

The boy said nothing in reply, but got up and began to walk about, still pale and dazed.

"Good stuff, eh, Jimmy?" said French, watching him carefully.

"You bet!" said Jimmy, "genu*ine* clay."

"It is exceptionally lucky that you were standing so near the little beast," said French to the boy. "Get into the buckboard here, and sit down."

Kalman climbed in, and from that point of vantage watched the rest of the hitching process. By skillful manœuvring the two men led, backed, shoved the ponies into position, and while one held them by the heads, the other hitched the traces. Carefully French looked over all straps and buckles, drew the lines free, and then mounting the buckboard seat, said quietly, "Stand clear, Jimmy. Let them go." Which Jimmy promptly did.

For a few moments they stood surprised at their unexpected freedom, and uncertain what to do with it, then they moved off slowly a few steps till the push of the buckboard threw them into a sudden terror, and the fight was on. Plunging, backing, kicking, jibing, they finally bolted, fortunately choosing the trail that led in the right direction.

"Good-by, Jimmy. See you later," sang out French as, with cool head and steady hand, he directed the running ponies.

"Jumpin' cats!" replied Jimmy soberly, "don't look as if you would," as the bronchos tore up the river bank at a terrific gallop.

Before they reached the top French had them in hand, and going more smoothly, though still running at top speed. Kalman sat clinging to the rocking, pitching buckboard, his eyes alight and his face aglow with excitement. There was stirring in the boy's brain a dim and far-away memory of wild rides over the steppes of Southern Russia, and French, glancing now and then at his glowing face, nodded grim approval.

"Afraid, boy?" he shouted over the roar and rattle of the pitching buckboard.

Kalman looked up and smiled, and then with a great oath he cried, "Let them go!"

Jack French was startled. He hauled up the ponies sharply and turned to the boy at his side.

"Boy, where did you learn that?"

"What?" asked the boy in surprise.

"Where did you learn to swear like that?"

"Why," said Kalman, "they all do it."

"Who all?"

"Why, everybody in Winnipeg."

"Does Mrs. French?" said Jack quietly.

The boy's face flushed hotly.

"No, no," he said vehemently, "never her." Then after a pause and an evident struggle, "She wants me to stop, but all the men and the boys do it."

"Kalman," said French solemnly, "no one swears on my ranch."

Kalman was perplexed, remembering the scene of the previous night.

"But you—" he began, and then paused.

"Boy," repeated French with added solemnity, "swearing is a foolish and unnecessary evil. There is no swearing on my ranch. Promise me you will give up this habit."

"I will not," said the boy promptly, "for I would break my word. Don't you swear?"

French hesitated, and then as if forming a sudden resolution he replied, "When you hear me swear you can begin. And if you don't mean to quit, don't promise. A gentleman always keeps his word."

The boy looked him steadily in the eye and then said, as if pondering this remark, "I remember. I know. My father said so."

French forbore to press the matter further, but for both man and boy an attempt at a new habit of speech began that day.

Once clear of the Saskatchewan River, the trail led over rolling prairie, set out with numerous "bluffs" of western maple and poplar, and diversified with sleughs and lakes of varying size, a country as richly fertile and as fair to look upon as is given the eyes of man to behold anywhere in God's good world. In the dullest weather this rolling, tree-decked, sleugh-gemmed prairie presents a succession of scenes surpassingly beautiful, but with a westering sun upon it, and on a May day, it offers such a picture as at once entrances the soul and lives forever in the memory. The waving lines, the rounded hills, the changing colour, the chasing shadows on grass and bluff and shimmering water, all combine to make in the soul high music unto God.

For an hour and more the buckboard hummed along the trail smooth and winding, the bronchos pulling hard on the lines without a sign of weariness, till the bluffs began to grow thicker and gradually to close into a solid belt of timber. Beyond this belt of timber lay the Ruthenian Colony but newly placed. The first intimation of the proximity of this colony came in quite an unexpected way. Swinging down a sharp hill through a bluff, the bronchos came upon a man with a yoke of oxen hauling a load of hay. Before their course could be checked the ponies had pitched heavily into the slow moving and terrified oxen, and so disconcerted them that they swerved from the trail and upset the load. Immediately there rose a volley of shrill execrations in the Galician tongue.

"Whoa, buck! Steady there!" cried Jack French cheerily as he steered his team past the wreck. "Too bad that, we must go back and help to repair damages."

He tied the bronchos securely to a tree and went back to offer aid. The Galician, a heavily-built man, was standing on the trail with a stout stake in his hand, viewing the ruins of his load and expressing his emotions in voluble Galician profanity with a bad mixture of halting and broken English. Kalman stood beside French with wrath growing in his face.

"He is calling you very bad names!" he burst out at length.

French glanced down at the boy's angry face and smiled.

"Oh, well, it will do him good. He will feel better when he gets it all out. And besides, he has rather good reason to be angry."

"He says he is going to kill you," said Kalman in a low voice, keeping close to French's side.

"Oh! indeed," said French cheerfully, walking straight upon the man. "That is awkward. But perhaps he will change his mind."

This calm and cheerful front produced its impression upon the excited Galician.

"Too bad, neighbour," said French in a loud, cheerful tone as he drew near.

The Galician, who had recovered something of his fury, damped to a certain extent by French's calm and cheerful demeanour, began to gesticulate with his stake. French turned his back upon him and proceeded to ascertain the extent of the wreck, and to advise a plan for its repair. As he stooped to examine the wagon for breakages, the wrathful Galician suddenly swung his club in the air, but before the blow fell, Kalman shrieked out in the Galician tongue, "You villain! Stop!"

This unexpected cry in his own speech served at once to disconcert the Galician's aim, and to warn his intended victim. French, springing quickly aside, avoided the blow and with one stride he was upon the Galician, wrenched the stake from his grasp, and, taking him by the back of the neck, faced him toward the front wheels of the wagon, saying, as he did so, "Here, you idiot! take hold and pull."

The strength of that grip on his neck produced a salutary effect upon the excited Galician. He stood a few moments dazed, looking this way and that way, as if uncertain how to act.

"Tell the fool," said French to Kalman quietly, "to get hold of those front wheels and pull."

The boy stood amazed.

"Ain't you going to lick him?" he said.

"Haven't time just now," said French cheerfully.

"But he might have killed you."

"Would have if you hadn't yelled. I'll remember that too, my boy. But he didn't, and he won't get another chance. Tell him to take hold and pull."

Kalman turned to the subdued and uncertain Galician, and poured forth a volume of angry abuse while he directed him as to his present duty. Humbly enough the Galician took hold, and soon the wagon was put to rights, and after half an hour's work, was loaded again and ready for its further journey.

By this time the man had quite recovered his temper and stood for some time after all was ready, silent and embarrassed. Then he began to earnestly address French, with eager gesticulations.

"What is it?" said French.

"He says he is very sorry, and feels very bad here," said Kalman, pointing to his heart, "and he wants to do something for you."

"Tell him," said French cheerfully, "only a fool loses his temper, and only a cad uses a club or a knife when he fights."

Kalman looked puzzled.

"A cat?"

"No, a cad. Don't you know what a cad is? Well, a cad is—hanged if I know how to put it—you know what a gentleman is?"

Kalman nodded.

"Well, the other thing is a cad."

The Galician listened attentively while Kalman explained, and made humble and deprecating reply.

"He says," interpreted Kalman, "that he is very sorry, but he wants to know what you fight with. You can't hurt a man with your hands."

"Can't, eh?" said French. "Tell him to stand up here to me."

The Galician came up smiling, and French proceeded to give him his first lesson in the manly art, Kalman interpreting his directions.

"Put up your hands so. Now I am going to tap your forehead."

Tap, tap, went French's open knuckles upon the Galician's forehead.

"Look out, man."

Tap, tap, tap, the knuckles went rapping on the man's forehead, despite his flying arms.

"Now," said French, "hit me."

The Galician made a feeble attempt.

"Oh, don't be afraid. Hit me hard."

The Galician lunged forward, but met rigid arms.

"Come, come," said French, reaching him sharply on the cheek with his open hand, "try better than that."

Again the Galician struck heavily with his huge fists, and again French, easily parrying, tapped him once, twice, thrice, where he would, drawing tears to the man's eyes. The Galician paused with a scornful exclamation.

"He says that's nothing," interpreted Kalman. "You can't hurt a man that way."

"Can't, eh? Tell him to come on, but to look out."

Again the Galician came forward, evidently determined to land one blow at least. But French, taking the blow on his guard, replied with a heavy left-hander fair on the Galician's chest, lifted him clear off his feet and hurled him breathless against his load of hay. The man recovered himself, grinning sheepishly, nodding his head vigorously and talking rapidly.

"That is enough. He says he would like to learn how to do that. That is better than a club," interpreted Kalman.

"Tell him that his people must learn to fight without club or knife. We won't stand that in this country. It lands them in prison or on the gallows."

Kalman translated, his own face fiery red meanwhile, and his own appearance one of humiliation. He was wondering how much of his own history this man knew.

"Good-by," said French, holding out his hand to the Galician.

The man took it and raised it to his lips.

"He says he thanks you very much, and he wishes you to forget his badness."

"All right, old man," said French cheerfully. "See you again some day."

And so they parted, Kalman carrying with him an uncomfortable sense of having been at various times in his life something of a cad, and a fear lest this painful fact should be known to his new master and friend.

"Well, youngster," said French, noticing his glum face, "you did me a good turn that time. That beggar had me foul then, sure enough, and I won't forget it."

Kalman brightened up under his words, and without further speech, each busy with himself, they sped along the trail till the day faded toward the evening.

But the Edmonton trail that day set its mark on the lives of boy and man,—a mark that was never obliterated. To Kalman the day brought a new image of manhood. Of all the men whom he knew there was none who could command his loyalty and enthral his imagination. It is true, his father had been such a man, but now his father moved in dim shadow across the horizon of his memory. Here was a man within touch of his hand who illustrated in himself those qualities that to a boy's heart and mind combine to make a hero. With what ease and courage and patience and perfect self-command he had handled those plunging bronchos! The same qualities too, in a higher degree, had marked his interview with the wrathful and murderous Galician, and, in addition, all that day Kalman had been conscious of a consideration and a quickness of sympathy in his moods that revealed in this man of rugged strength and forceful courage a subtle something that marks the finer temper and nobler spirit, the temper and the spirit of the gentleman. Not that Kalman could name this thing, but to his sensitive soul it was this in the man that made appeal and that called forth his loyal homage.

To French, too, the day had brought thoughts and emotions that had not stirred within him since those days of younger manhood twenty years ago when the world was still a place of dreams and life a tourney where glory might be won. The boy's face, still with its spiritual remembrances in spite of all the sordidness of his past, the utter and obvious surrender of soul that shone from his eyes, made the man almost shudder with a new horror of the foulness that twenty years of wild license upon the plains had flung upon him. A fierce hate of what he had become, an appalling vision of what he was expected to be, grew upon him as the day drew to a close. Gladly would he have refused the awful charge of this young soul as yet unruined that so plainly exalted him to a place among the gods, but for a vision that he carried ever in his heart of a face sad and sweet and eloquent with trustful love.

"No, by Jove!" he said to himself between his shut teeth, "I can't funk it. I'd be a cad if I did."

And with these visions and these resolvings they, boy and man, swung off from the Edmonton trail black and well worn, and into the half-beaten track that led to Wakota, the centre of the Galician colony.

Chapter XII

The Making of a Man

Wakota, consisting of the mud-house of a Galician homesteader who owned a forge and did blacksmithing for the colony in a primitive way, they left behind half an hour before nightfall, with ten miles of bad going still before them. The trail wound through bluffs and around sleughs, dived into coulees and across black creeks, and only the most skilful handling could have piloted the bronchos through.

It was long after dark when they reached the ravine of the Night Hawk Creek, through which they must pass before arriving at the Lake. Down the sides of this ravine they zigzagged, dodging trees and boulders till they came to the last sharp pitch, at the foot of which ran the Creek. During this whole descent Kalman sat clinging to the back and side of the seat, expecting every moment to have the buckboard turn turtle over him, but when they reached the edge of the final pitch, were it not for sheer shame, he would have begged permission to scramble down on hands and knees rather than trust himself to the swaying, pitching vehicle. A moment French held his bronchos steady, poised on the brink of this rocky steep, and then reaching back, he seized the hind wheel and, holding it fast, used it as a drag, while the bronchos slid down on their haunches over the mass of gravel and rolling stones till they reached the bed of the Creek in safety. A splash through the water, a scramble up the other bank, a long climb, and they were out again on the prairie. A mile of good trail and they were at home, welcomed by the baying of two huge Russian wolf hounds.

Through the dim light Kalman could discover the outlines of what seemed a long heap of logs, but what he afterwards discovered to be a series of low log structures which did for house, stable and sheds of various kinds.

"Down! Bismark. Down! Blucher. Hello there, Mac! Where in the world are you?"

After some time Mackenzie appeared with a lantern, a short, grizzled, thick-set man, rubbing his eyes and yawning prodigiously.

"I nefer thought you would be coming home to-night," he said. "What brought ye at this time?"

"Never mind, Mac," said French. "Get the horses out, and Kalman and I will unload this stuff."

In what seemed to be an outer shed, they deposited the pork, flour, and other articles that composed the load. As Kalman seized the straw-packed case to carry it in, French interfered.

"Here, boy, I'll take that," he said quickly.

"I'll not break them," said Kalman, lifting the case with great care.

"You won't, eh?" replied French in rather a shamed tone. "Do you know what it is?"

"Why, sure," said Kalman. "Lots of that stuff used to come into our home in Winnipeg."

"Well, let me have the case," said French. "And you needn't say anything to Mac about it. Mac is all right, but a case of liquor in the house makes him unhappy."

"Unhappy? Doesn't he drink any?"

"That's just it, my boy. He is unhappy while it's outside of him. He's got Indian blood in him, you see, and he'd die for whiskey." So saying, French took up the case and carried it to the inner room and stowed it away under his bed.

But as he rose up from making this disposition of the dangerous stuff Mac himself appeared in the room.

"What are you standing there looking at?" said French with unusual impatience.

"Oh, nothing at all," said Mackenzie, whose strong Highland accent went strangely with his soft Indian voice and his dark Indian face. "It iss a good place for it, whatefer."

French stood for a moment in disgusted silence, and then breaking into a laugh he said: "All right, Mac. There's no use trying to keep it from you. But, mind you, it's fair play in this thing. Last time, you remember, you got into trouble. I won't stand that sort of thing again."

"Oh, well, well," said Mackenzie cheerfully, "it will not be for long anyway, more's the peety."

"Now then, get us a bite of supper, Mackenzie," said French sharply, "and let us to bed."

Some wild duck and some bannock with black molasses, together with strong black tea, made a palatable supper after a long day on the breezy prairie. After supper the men sat smoking.

"The oats in, Mac?"

"They are sowed, but not harrowed yet. I will be doing that to-morrow in the morning."

"Potato ground ready?"

"Yes, the ground is ready, and the seed is over at Garneau's."

"What in thunder were you waiting for? Those potatoes should have been in ten days ago. It's hardly worth while putting them in now."

"Garneau promised to bring them ofer," said Mackenzie, "but you cannot tell anything at all about that man."

"Well, we must get them in at once. We must not lose another day. And now let's get to bed. The boy here will sleep in the bunk," pointing to a large-sized box which did for a couch. "Get some blankets for him, Mac."

The top of the box folded back, revealing a bed inside.

"There, Kalman," said French, while Mackenzie arranged the blankets, "will that do?"

"Fine," said the boy, who could hardly keep his eyes open and who in five minutes after he had tumbled in was sound asleep.

It seemed as if he had been asleep but a few moments when he was wakened by a rude shock. He started up to find Mackenzie fallen drunk and helpless across his bunk.

"Here, you pig!" French was saying in a stern undertone, "can't you tell when you have had enough? Come out of that!"

With an oath he dragged Mackenzie to his feet.

"Come, get to your bed!"

"Oh, yes, yes," grumbled Mackenzie, "and I know well what you will be doing after I am in bed, and never a drop will you be leaving in that bottle." Mackenzie was on the verge of tears.

"Get on, you beast!" said French in tones of disgusted dignity, pushing the man before him into the next room.

Kalman was wide awake, but, feigning sleep, watched French as he sat with gloomy face, drinking steadily till even his hard head could stand no more, and he swayed into the inner room and fell heavily on the bed. Kalman waited till French was fast asleep, then rising quietly, pulled off his boots, threw a blanket over him, put out the lamp and went back to the bunk. The spectre of the previous night which had been laid by the events of the day came back to haunt his broken slumber. For hours he tossed, and not till morning began to dawn did he quite lose consciousness.

Broad morning wakened him to unpleasant memories, and more unpleasant realities. French was still sleeping heavily. Mackenzie was eating breakfast, with a bottle beside him on the table.

"You will find a basin on the bench outside," observed Mackenzie, pointing to the open door.

When Kalman returned from his ablutions, the bottle had vanished, and Mackenzie, with breath redolent of its contents, had ready for him a plate of porridge, to which he added black molasses. This, with toasted bannock, the remains of the cold duck of the night before, and strong black tea, constituted his breakfast.

Kalman hurried through his meal, for he hated to meet French as he woke from his sleep.

"Will he not take breakfast?" said the boy as he rose from the table.

"No, not him, nor denner either, like as not. It iss a good thing he has a man to look after the place," said Mackenzie with the pride of conscious fidelity. "We will just be going on with the oats and the pitaties. You will be taking the harrows."

"The what?" said Kalman.

"The harrows."

Kalman looked blank.

"Can you not harrow?"

"I don't know," said Kalman. "What is that?"

"Can you drop pitaties, then?"

"I don't know," repeated Kalman, shrinking very considerably in his own estimation.

"Man," said Mackenzie pityingly, "where did ye come from anyway?"

"Winnipeg."

"Winnipeg? I know it well. I used to. But that was long ago. But did ye nefer drive a team?"

"Never," said Kalman. "But I want to learn."

"Och! then, and what will he be wanting with you here?"

"I don't know," said Kalman.

"Well, well," said Mackenzie. "He iss a quare man at times, and does quare things."

"He is not," said Kalman hotly. "He is just a splendid man."

Mackenzie gazed in mild surprise at the angry face.

"Hoot! toot!" he said. "Who was denyin' ye? He iss all that, but he iss mighty quare, as you will find out. But come away and we will get the horses. It iss a peety you cannot do nothing."

"You show me what to do," said Kalman confidently, "and I'll do it."

The stable was a tumble-down affair, and sorely needing attention, as, indeed, was the case with the ranch and all its belongings. A team of horses showing signs of hard work and poor care, with harness patched with rope and rawhide thongs, were waiting in the stable. Even to Kalman's inexperienced eyes it was a deplorable outfit.

There was little done in the way of cultivation of the soil upon the Night Hawk Ranch. The market was far away, and it was almost impossible to secure farm labour. The wants of French and his household were few. A couple of fields of oats and barley for his horses and pigs and poultry, another for potatoes, for which he found ready market at the Crossing and in the lumber camps up among the hills, exhausted the agricultural pursuits of the ranch.

Kalman concentrated his attention upon the process of hitching the team to the harrows, and then followed Mackenzie up and down the field as he harrowed in the oats. It seemed a simple enough matter to guide the team across the ploughed furrows, and Kalman, as he observed, grew ambitious.

"Let me drive," he said at length.

"Hoot! toot! boy, you would be letting them run away with you."

"Aw, cut it out!" said Kalman scornfully.

"What are you saying? Cut what?"

"Oh, give us a rest!"

"A rest, iss it? You will be getting tired early. And who is keeping you from a rest?" said Mackenzie, whose knowledge of contemporary slang was decidedly meagre.

"Let me drive once," pleaded the boy.

"Well, try it, and I will walk along side of you," said Mackenzie, with apparent reluctance.

The attempt was eminently successful, but Kalman was quick both with hands and head. After the second round Mackenzie allowed the boy to go alone, remaining in the shade and calling out directions across the field. The result was to both a matter of unmixed delight. With Kalman there was the gratification of the boy's passion for the handling of horses, and as for Mackenzie, while on the trail or on the river, he was indefatigable, in the field he had the Indian hatred of steady work. To lie and smoke on the grass in the shade of a poplar bluff on this warm shiny spring day was to him sheer bliss.

But after a time Mackenzie grew restless. His cup of bliss still lacked a drop to fill it.

"Just keep them moving," he cried to Kalman. "I will need to go to the house a meenit."

"All right. Don't hurry for me," said Kalman, proud of his new responsibility and delighted with his new achievement.

"Keep them straight, mind. And watch your turning," warned Mackenzie. "I will be coming back soon."

In less than half an hour he returned in a most gracious frame of mind.

"Man, but you are the smart lad," he said as Kalman swung his team around. "You will be making a great rancher, Tommy."

"My name is Kalman."

"Well, well, Callum. It iss a fery good name, whatefer."

"Kalman!" shouted the boy.

Mackenzie nodded grave rebuke.

"There is no occasion for shouting. I am not deaf, Callum, my boy. Go on. Go on with your harrows," he continued as Kalman began to remonstrate.

Kalman drew near and regarded him narrowly. The truth was clear to his experienced eyes.

"You're drunk," he exclaimed disgustedly.

"Hoot, toot! Callum man," said Mackenzie in tones of grieved remonstrance, "how would you be saying that now? Come away, or I will be taking the team myself."

"Aw, go on!" replied Kalman contemptuously. "Let me alone!"

"Good boy," said Mackenzie with a paternal smile, waving the boy on his way while he betook himself to the bluff side and there supine, continued at intervals to direct the operation of harrowing.

The sun grew hot. The cool morning breeze dropped flat, and as the hours passed the boy grew weary and footsore, travelling the soft furrows. Mackenzie had long ceased issuing his directions, and had subsided into smiling silence, contenting himself with a friendly wave of the hand as Kalman made the turn. The poor spiritless horses moved more and more slowly, and at length, coming to the end of the field, refused to move farther.

"Let them stand a bit, Callum boy," said Mackenzie kindly. "Come and have a rest. You are the fine driver. Come and sit down."

"Will the horses stand here?" asked Kalman, whose sense of responsibility deepened as he became aware of Mackenzie's growing incapacity.

Mackenzie laughed pleasantly. "Will they stand? Yes, and that they will, unless they will lie down."

Kalman approached and regarded him with the eye of an expert.

"Look here, where's your stuff?" said the boy at length.

Mackenzie gazed at him with the innocence of childhood.

"What iss it?"

"Oh, come off your perch! you blamed old rooster! Where's your bottle?"

"What iss this?" said Mackenzie, much affronted. "You will be calling me names?"

As he rose in his indignation a bottle fell from his pocket. Kalman made a dash toward it, but Mackenzie was too quick for him. With a savage curse he snatched up the bottle, and at the same time made a fierce but unsuccessful lunge at the boy.

"You little deevil!" he said fiercely, "I will be knocking your head off!"

Kalman jibed at him. "You are a nice sort of fellow to be on a job. What will your boss say?"

Mackenzie's face changed instantly.

"The boss?" he said, glancing in the direction of the house. "The boss? What iss the harm of a drop when you are not well?"

"You not well!" exclaimed Kalman scornfully.

Mackenzie shook his head sadly, sinking back upon the grass. "It iss many years now since I have suffered with an indisposeetion of the bowels. It iss a coalic, I am thinking, and it iss hard on me. But, Callum, man, it will soon be denner time. Just put your horses in and I will be following you."

But Kalman knew better than that.

"I don't know how to put in your horses. Come and put them in yourself, or show me how to do it." He was indignant with the man on his master's behalf.

Mackenzie struggled to his feet, holding the bottle carefully in his outside coat pocket. Kalman made up his mind to possess himself of that bottle at all costs. The opportunity occurred when Mackenzie, stooping to unhitch the last trace, allowed the bottle to slip from his pocket. Like a cat on a mouse, Kalman pounced on the bottle and fled.

The change in Mackenzie was immediate and appalling. His smiling face became transformed with fury, his black eyes gleamed with the cunning malignity of the savage, he shed his soft Scotch voice with his genial manner, the very movements of his body became those of his Cree progenitors. Uttering hoarse guttural cries, with the quick crouching run of the Indian on the trail of his foe, he chased Kalman through the bluffs. There was something so fiendishly terrifying in the glimpses that Kalman caught of his face now and then that the boy was seized with an overpowering dread, and ceasing to tantalize his pursuing enemy, he left the bluffs and fled toward the house, with Mackenzie hard upon his track. Through the shed the boy flew and into the outer room, banging the door hard after him. But there was no lock upon the door, and he could not hope to hold it shut against his pursuer. He glanced wildly into the inner room. French was nowhere to be seen. As he stood in unspeakable terror, the door opened slowly and stealthily, showing Mackenzie's face, distorted with rage and cunning hate. With a silent swift movement he glided into the room, and without a sound rushed at the boy. Once, twice around the table they circled, Kalman having the advantage in quickness of foot. Suddenly, with a grunt of satisfaction, Mackenzie's eye fell upon a gun hanging upon the wall. In a moment he had it in his hand. As he reached for it, however, Kalman, with a loud cry, plunged headlong through the open window and fled again toward the bluffs. Mackenzie followed swiftly through the door, gun in hand. He ran a few short steps after the flying boy, and was about to throw his gun to his shoulder when a voice arrested him.

"Here, Mackenzie, what are you doing with that gun?"

It was French, standing between the stable and the house, dishevelled, bloated, but master of himself. Mackenzie stopped as if gripped by an unseen arm.

"What are you doing with that gun?" repeated French sternly. "Bring it to me."

Mackenzie stood in sullen, defiant silence, his gun thrown into the hollow of his arm. French walked deliberately toward him.

"Give me that gun, you dog!" he said with an oath, "or I'll kill you where you stand."

Mackenzie hesitated but only for a moment, and without a word surrendered the gun, the fiendish rage fading out of his face, the aboriginal blood lust dying in his eyes like the snuffing out of a candle. In a few brief moments he became once more a civilized man, subject to the restraint of a thousand years of life ordered by law.

"Kalman, come here," French called to the boy, who stood far off.

"Mackenzie," said French with great dignity as Kalman drew near, "I want you to know that this boy is a ward of a dear friend, and is to me like my own son. Remember that. Kalman, Mackenzie is my friend, and you are to treat him as such. Where did you get that?" he continued, pointing to the bottle which Kalman had kept clutched in his hand through all the exciting pursuit.

The boy stood silent, looking at Mackenzie.

"Speak, boy," said French sharply.

Kalman remained still silent, his eyes on Mackenzie.

"It iss a bottle myself had," said Mackenzie.

"Ah, I understand. All right, Kalman, it's none of your business what Mackenzie drinks. Now, Mackenzie, get dinner, and no more of this nonsense."

Without a word of parley or remonstrance Mackenzie shuffled off toward the field to bring in the team. French turned to the boy and, taking the bottle in his hand, said, "This is dangerous stuff, my boy. A man like Mackenzie is not to be trusted with it, and of course it is not for boys."

Kalman made no reply. His mind was in a whirl of perplexed remembrances of the sickening scenes of the past three days.

"Go now," said French, "and help Mackenzie. He won't hurt you any more. He never keeps a grudge. That is the Christian in him."

During the early part of the afternoon Mackenzie drove the harrows while French moved about the ranch doing up odds and ends. But neither of the men was quite at ease. At length French disappeared into the house, and almost immediately afterwards Mackenzie left his team in Kalman's hands and followed his boss. Hour after hour passed. The sun sank in the western sky, but neither master nor man appeared, while Kalman kept the team steadily on the move, till at length the field was finished. Weary and filled with foreboding, the boy drove the horses to the stable, pulled off the harness as best he could, gave the horses food and drink and went into the house. There a ghastly scene met his eye. On the floor hard by the table lay Mackenzie on his face, snoring heavily in a drunken sleep, and at the table, with three empty bottles beside him and a fourth in his hand, sat French, staring hard before him with eyes bloodshot and sunken, and face of a livid hue. He neither moved nor spoke when Kalman entered, but continued staring steadily before him.

The boy was faint with hunger. He was too heartsick to attempt to prepare food. He found a piece of bannock and, washing this down with a mug of water, he crept into his bunk, and there, utterly miserable, waited till his master should sink into sleep. Slowly the light faded from the room and the shadows crept longer and deeper over the floor till all was dark. But still the boy could see the outline of the silent man, who sat without sound or motion except for the filling and emptying of his glass from time to time. At length the shadowy figure bowed slowly toward the table and there remained.

Sick with grief and fear, the boy sprang from his bunk and sought to rouse the man from his stupor, but without avail, till at last, wearied with his ineffectual attempts and sobbing in the bitterness of his grief, he threw a blanket over the bowed form and retreated to his bunk again. But sleep to him was impossible, for often throughout the night he was brought to his feet with horrid dreams, to be driven shivering again to his bunk with the more horrid realities of his surroundings.

At length as day began to dawn he fell into a dead, dreamless slumber, waking, when it was broad day, to find Mackenzie sitting at the table eating breakfast, and with a bottle beside him. French was not to be seen, but Kalman could hear his heavy breathing from the inner room. To Kalman it seemed as if he were still in the grip of some ghastly nightmare. He rubbed his eyes and looked again at Mackenzie in stupid amazement.

"What are you glowering at yonder, Callum, man?" said Mackenzie, pleasantly ignoring the events of the previous day. "Your breakfast iss ready for you. You will be hungry after your day's work. Oh, yes, I haf been seeing it, and it iss well done, Callum, mannie."

Somehow his smiling face and his kindly tone filled Kalman with rage. He sprang out of his bunk and ran out of the house. He hated the sight of the smiling, pleasant-voiced Mackenzie. But his boy's hunger drove him in to breakfast.

"Well, Callum, man," began Mackenzie in pleasant salutation.

"My name is Kalman," snapped the boy.

"Never mind, it iss a good name, whatefer. But I am saying we will be getting into the pitaties after breakfast. Can ye drop pitaties?"

"Show me how," said Kalman shortly.

"And that I will," said Mackenzie affably, helping himself to the bottle.

"How many bottles of that stuff are there left?" asked Kalman disgustedly.

"And why would you be wanting to know?" enquired Mackenzie cautiously. "You would not be taking any of the whiskey yourself?" he added in grave reproof.

"Oh, go on! you old fool!" replied the boy angrily. "You will never be any good till it is all done, I know."

Kalman spoke out of full and varied experience of the ways of men with the lust of drink in them.

"Well, well, maybe so. But the more there iss for me, the less there iss for him," said Mackenzie, jerking his head toward the inner door.

"Why not empty it out?" said Kalman in an eager undertone.

"Hoot! toot! man, and would you be guilty of sinful waste like yon? No, no, never with Malcolm Mackenzie's consent. And you would not be doing such a deed yourself?" Mackenzie enquired somewhat anxiously.

Kalman shook his head.

"No," he said, "he might be angry. But," continued the boy, "those potatoes must be finished to-day. I heard him speaking about them yesterday."

"And that iss true enough. They are two weeks late now."

"Come on, then," cried Kalman, as Mackenzie reached for the bottle. "Come and show me how."

"There iss no hurry," said the deliberate Mackenzie, drinking his glass with slow relish. "But first the pitaties are to be got over from Garneau's."

Again and again, and with increasing rage, Kalman sought to drag Mackenzie away from his bottle and to his work. By the time the bottle was done Mackenzie was once more helpless.

Three days later French came forth from his room, haggard and trembling, to find every bottle empty, Mackenzie making ineffective attempts to prepare a meal, and Kalman nowhere to be seen.

"Where is the boy?" he enquired of Mackenzie in an uncertain voice.

"I know not," said Mackenzie.

"Go and look for him, then, you idiot!"

In a short time French was summoned by Mackenzie's voice.

"Come here, will you?" he was crying. "Come here and see this thing."

With a dread of some nameless horror in his heart, French hurried toward the little knoll upon which Mackenzie stood. From this vantage ground could be seen far off in the potato field the figure of the boy with two or three women, all busy with the potatoes.

"What do you make that out to be?" enquired French. "Who in the mischief are they? Go and see."

It was not long before Mackenzie stood before his master with Kalman by his side.

"As sure as death," said Mackenzie, "he has a tribe of Galician women yonder, and the pitaties iss all in."

"What do you say?" stammered French.

"It iss what I am telling you. The pitaties iss all in, and this lad iss bossing the job, and the Galician women working like naygurs."

"What does this mean?" said French, turning his eyes slowly upon Kalman. The boy looked older by years. He was worn and haggard.

"I saw a woman passing, she was a Galician, she brought the others, and the potatoes are done. They have come here two days. But," said the boy slowly, "there is nothing to eat."

With a mighty oath French sprang to his feet.

"Do you tell me you are hungry, boy?" he roared.

"I could not find much," said Kalman, his lip trembling in spite of himself.

"What are you standing there for, Mackenzie?" roared French. "Confound you for a drunken dog! Confound us both for two drunken fools! Get something to eat!"

There was something so terrible in his look and in his voice that Mackenzie fairly ran to obey his order. Kalman stood before his master pale and shaking. He was weak from lack of food, but more from anxiety and grief.

"I did the best I could," he said, struggling manfully to keep his voice steady, "and—I am—awful glad—you're—better." His command was all gone. He threw himself upon the grass while sobs shook his frame.

French stood a moment looking down upon him, his face revealing thoughts and feelings none too pleasant.

"Kalman, you're a good sort," he said in a hoarse voice. "You're a man, by Jove! and," in an undertone, "I'm hanged, if I don't think you'll make a man of me yet." Then kneeling by his side, he raised him in his arms. "Kalman," he said, "you are a brick and a gentleman. I have been a brute and a cad."

"Oh, no, no, no!" sobbed the boy. "You are a good man. But I wish—you would—leave—it—alone."

"In God's name," said French bitterly, "I wish it too."

Chapter XIII

Brown

Two weeks of life in the open, roaming the prairie alone with the wolf hounds, or with French after the cattle, did much to obliterate the mark which those five days left upon Kalman's body and soul. From the very first the boy had no difficulty in mastering the art of sticking on a broncho's back, partly because he was entirely without fear, but largely because he had an ear and an eye for rhythm in sound and in motion. He conceived clearly the idea by watching French as he loped along on his big iron grey, and after that it was merely a matter of translating the idea into action. Every successful rider must first conceive himself as a rider. In two weeks' time Kalman could sit the buckskin and send him across the prairie, swinging him by the neck guide around badger holes and gopher holes, up and down the steep sides of the Night Hawk ravine, without ever touching leather. The fearless ease he displayed in mastering the equestrian art did more than anything else to win him his place in the old half-breed Mackenzie's affection.

The pride of the ranch was Black Joe, a Percheron stallion that French a year before had purchased, with the idea of improving his horse stock to anticipate the market for heavy horses, which he foresaw the building of railroads would be sure to provide. Black Joe was kept in a small field that took in a bit of the bluff and ran down to the lake, affording shelter, drink, and good feeding.

Dismay, therefore, smote the ranch, when Mackenzie announced one morning that Black Joe had broken out and was gone.

"He can't be far away," said French; "take a circle round towards the east. He has likely gone off with Garneau's bunch."

But at noon Mackenzie rode back to report that nowhere could the stallion be seen, that he had rounded up Garneau's ponies without coming across any sign of the stallion.

"I am afraid he has got across the Eagle," said French, "and if he has once got on to those plains, there will be the very deuce to pay. Well, get a move on, and try the country across the creek first. No, hold on. I'll go myself. Throw the saddle on Roanoke; I'll put some grub together, for there's no time to be lost."

Kalman started up and stood eagerly expectant. French glanced at him.

"It will be a hard ride, Kalman; I am a little afraid."

"Try me, sir," said the boy, who had unconsciously in conversation with French dropped much of his street vernacular, and had adopted to a large extent his master's forms of speech.

"All right, boy. Get ready and come along."

While the horses were being saddled, French rolled up into two neat packs a couple of double blankets, grub consisting of Hudson's Bay biscuits, pork, tea and sugar, a camp outfit comprising a pan, a tea-pail, and two cups.

"So long, Mackenzie," said French, as they rode away. "Hold down the ranch till we get back. We'll strike out north from here, then swing round across the Night Hawk toward the hills and back by the Eagle and Wakota, and come up the creek."

To hunt up a stray beast on the wide open prairie seems to the uninitiated a hopeless business, but it is a simple matter, after all. One has to know the favourite feeding-grounds, the trails that run to these grounds, and have an idea of the limits within which cattle and horses will range. As a rule, each band has its own feeding-grounds and its own spots for taking shelter. The difficulties of search are enormously increased by the broken character of a rolling bluffy prairie. The bluffs intercept the view, and the rolls on the prairie can hide successfully a large bunch of cattle or horses, and it may take a week to beat up a country thickly strewn with bluffs, and diversified with coulees that might easily be searched in a single afternoon.

The close of the third day found the travellers on Wakota trail.

"We'll camp right here, Kalman," said French, as they reached a level tongue of open prairie, around three sides of which flowed the Eagle River.

Of all their camps during the three days' search none was so beautiful, and none lived so long in Kalman's memory, as the camp by the Eagle River near Wakota. The firm green sward, cropped short by a succession of campers' horses,—for this was a choice spot for travellers,—the flowing river with its soft gurgling undertone, the upstanding walls of the poplar bluffs in all the fresh and ample beauty of the early summer drapery, the over-arching sky, deep and blue, through which peeped the shy stars, and the air, so sweet and kindly, breathing about them. It was all so clean, so fresh, so unspoiled to the boy that it seemed as if he had dropped into a new world, remote from and unrelated to any other world he had hitherto known.

They picketed their horses, and with supper over, they sat down before their fire, for the evening air was chill, in weary, dreamy delight. They spoke few words. Like all men who have lived close to Nature, whether in woods or in plains, French had developed a habit of silence, and this habit, as all others, Kalman was rapidly taking on.

As they reclined thus dreamily watching the leaping fire, a canoe came down the river, in the stern of which sat a man whose easy grace proclaimed long practice in the canoeman's art. As his eyes fell upon the fire, he paused in his paddling, and with two or three swift flips he turned his canoe toward the bank, and landing, pulled it up on the shore.

He was a young man of middle height, stoutly built, and with a strong, good-natured face.

"Good evening," he said in a cheery voice, "camped for the night?"

"Yes, camped for the night," replied French.

"I have a tent up stream a little way. I should be glad to have you camp with me. It is going to be a little chilly."

"Oh, we're all right, aren't we, Kalman?" said French.

The boy turned and gave him a quick look of perfect satisfaction. "First rate! You bet!"

"The dew is going to be heavy, though," said the stranger, "and it will be cold before the night is over. I have not much to offer you, only shelter, but I'd like awfully to have you come. A visitor is a rare thing here."

"Well," said French, "since you put it that way we'll go, and I am sure it is very decent of you."

"Not at all. The favour will be to me. My name is Brown."

"And mine is French, Jack French throughout this country, as perhaps you have heard."

"I have been here only a few days, and have heard very little," said Brown.

"And this," continued French, "is Kalman Kalmar, a friend of mine from Winnipeg, and more remotely from Russia, but now a good Canadian."

Brown gave each a strong cordial grasp of his hand.

"You can't think," he said, "how glad I am to see you."

"Is there a trail?" asked French.

"Yes, a trail of a sort. Follow the winding of the river and you will come to my camp at the next bend. You can't miss it. I'll go up in the canoe and come down to meet you."

"Don't trouble," said French; "we know our way about this country."

Following a faint trail for a quarter of a mile through the bluffs, they came upon an open space on the river bank similar to the one they had left, in the midst of which stood Brown's tent. That tent was a wonder to behold, not only to Kalman, but also to French, who had a large experience in tents of various kinds. Ten by twelve, and with a four-foot wall, every inch was in use. The ground which made the floor was covered with fresh, sweet-smelling swamp hay; in one corner was a bed, neat as a soldier's; in the opposite corner a series of cupboards made out of packing cases, filled, one with books, one with drugs and surgical instruments, another with provisions. Hanging from the ridge-pole was a double shelf, and attached to the back upright were a series of pigeon-hole receptacles. It was a wonder of convenience and comfort, and albeit it was so packed with various impedimenta, such was the orderly neatness of it that there seemed to be abundance of room.

At the edge of the clearing Brown met them.

"Here you are," he cried. "Come along and make yourselves at home."

His every movement was full of brisk energy, and his voice carried with it a note of cheery frankness that bespoke the simplicity and kindliness of the good and honest heart.

In a few moments Brown had a fire blazing in front of the tent, for the night air was chill, and a heavy dew was falling.

"Here you are," he cried, throwing down a couple of rugs before the fire. "Make yourselves comfortable. I believe in comfort myself."

"Well," said French, glancing into the tent, throwing himself down before the fire, "you apparently do, and you have attained an unqualified success in exemplifying your belief. You certainly do yourself well."

"Oh, I am a lazy dog," said Brown cheerfully, "and can't do without my comforts. But you don't know how glad I am to see you. I can't stand being alone. I get most awfully blue and funky, naturally nervous and timid, you know."

"You do, eh?" said French, pleasantly. "Well, if you ask me, I believe you're lying, or your face is."

"Not a bit, not a bit. Good thing a fellow has a skin to draw over his insides. I'd hate the world to see all the funk that there is in my heart."

French pulled out his pipe, stirred up its contents with his knife, struck a match, and proceeded to draw what comfort he could from the remnants of his last smoke. The result was evidently not entirely satisfactory. He began searching his pockets with elaborate care, but all in vain, and with a sigh of disappointment he sank back on the rug.

"Hello!" said Brown, whose eyes nothing seemed to escape, "I know what you're after. You have left your pouch. Well, let that be a lesson to you. You ought not to indulge habits that are liable any moment to involve you in such distress. Now look at you, a big, healthy, able-bodied man, on a night like this too, with all the splendour and glory of sky and woods and river about you, with decent company too, and a good fire, and yet you are incapable of enjoyment. You are an abnormality, and you have made yourself so. You need treatment; I am going to administer it forthwith."

He disappeared into his tent, leaving Kalman in a fury of rage, and French with an amused smile upon his face. After a few moments' rummaging Brown appeared with a package in his hand.

"In cases like yours," he said gravely, "I prescribe *vapores nicoti-nenses*. I hope you have forgotten your Latin. Here is a brand, a very special brand, which I keep for decoy purposes. Having once used this, you will be sure to come back again. Try that," he cried in a threatening tone, "and look me in the eye."

The anger fled from Kalman's face, and he began to understand that their new friend had been simply jollying them, and he sincerely hoped that neither he nor French had noticed his recent rage.

French filled his pipe with the mixture, lit it, and took one or two experimental draws, then with a great sigh he threw himself back upon the rug, his arms under his head, and puffed away with every symptom of delight.

"See here, Brown," he said, sitting up again after a few moments of blissful silence, "this is 'Old London,' isn't it?"

"See here, French, don't you get off any of your high British nonsense. 'Old London,' indeed! No, sir, that is 'Young Canada'; that is, I have a friend in Cuba who sends me the Prince of Wales brand."

French smoked on for some moments.

"Without being rude, how much of this have you in stock?"

"How much? Enough to fill your pipe whenever you come round."

"My word!" exclaimed French. "You don't dispense this to the general public, do you?"

"Not much, I don't," said Brown. "I select my patients."

"Thank you," said French. "I take this as a mark of extreme hospitality. By the way, where is your own pipe?"

"I have abjured."

"What?"

"Abjured."

"And yet you have many of the marks of sanity."

"Sanity! You just note it, and the most striking is that I don't have a pipe."

"Expound me the riddle, please."

"The exposition is simple enough. I am constitutionally lazy and self-indulgent, and almost destitute of self-control—"

"And permit me to interject without offence, an awful liar," said French pleasantly. "Go on."

"I came out here to work. With a pipe and a few pounds of that mixture—"

"Pounds! Ah!" ejaculated French.

"I would find myself immersed in dreamy seas of vaporous and idle bliss—do you catch that combination?—and fancy myself, mark you, busy all the time. It is the smoker's dementia accentuated by such a mixture as this, that while he is blowing rings he imagines he is doing something—"

"The deuce he does! And he is jolly well right."

"So, having something other to do than blow rings, I have abjured the pipe. There are other reasons, but that will suffice."

"Abundantly," said French with emphasis, "and permit me to remark that you have been talking rot."

Brown shook his head with a smile.

"Now tell me," continued French, "what is your idea? What have you in view in planting yourself down here? In short, to put it bluntly, what are you doing?"

"Doing nothing, as yet," said Brown cheerfully, "but I want to do a lot. I have got this Galician colony in my eye."

"I beg your pardon," said French, "are you by any chance a preacher?"

"Well, I may be, though I can't preach much. But my main line is the kiddies. I can teach them English, and then I am going to doctor them, and, if they'll let me, teach them some of the elements of domestic science; in short, do anything to make them good Christians and good Canadians, which is the same thing."

"That is a pretty large order. Look here, now," said French, sitting up, "you look like a sensible fellow, and open to advice. Don't be an ass and throw yourself away. I know these people well. In a generation or two something may be done with them. You can't make a silk purse out of a sow's ear, you know. Give it up. Take up a ranch and go cattle raising. That is my advice. I know them. You can't undo in your lifetime the results of three centuries. It's a hopeless business. I tried myself to give them some pointers when they came in first, and worried a good deal about it. I got myself disliked for my pains and suffered considerable annoyance. Now I leave them beautifully alone. Their suspicions have vanished and they no longer look at me as if I were a thief."

Brown's face grew serious. "It's a fact, they are suspicious, frightfully. I have been talking school to them, but they won't have a school as a gift. My Church, the Presbyterian, you know, offers to put up a school for them, since the Government won't do anything, but they are mightily afraid that this is some subtle scheme for extracting money from them. But what can you expect? The only church they know has bled them dry, and they fear and hate the very name of church."

"By Jove! I don't wonder," said French.

"Nor do I."

"But look here, Brown," said French, "you don't mean to tell me,—I assure you I don't wish to be rude,—but you don't mean to tell me that you have come here, a man of your education and snap—"

"Thank you," said Brown.

"To teach a lot of Galician children."

"Well," said Brown, "I admit I have come partially for my health. You see, I am constitutionally inclined—"

"Oh, come now," said French, "as my friend Kalman would remark, cut it out."

"Partially for my health, and partially for the good of the country. These people here exist as an undigested foreign mass. They must be digested and absorbed into the body politic. They must be taught our ways of thinking and living, or it will be a mighty bad thing for us in Western Canada. Do you know, there are over twenty-five thousand of them already in this country?"

"Oh, that's all right," said French, "but they'll learn our ways fast enough. And as for teaching their children, pardon me, but it seems to me you are too good a man to waste in that sort of thing. Why, bless my soul, you can get a girl for fifty dollars a month who would teach them fast enough. But you—now you could do big things in this country, and there are going to be big things doing here in a year or two."

"What things?" said Brown with evident interest.

"Oh, well, ranching, farming on a big scale, building railroads, lumber up on the hills, then, later, public life. We will be a province, you know, one of these days, and the men who are in at the foundation making will stand at the top later on."

"You're all right," cried Brown, his eyes alight with enthusiasm. "There will be big things doing, and, believe me, this is one of them."

"What? Teaching a score of dirty little Galicians? The chances are you'll spoil them. They are good workers as they are. None better. They are easy to handle. You go in and give them some of our Canadian ideas of living and all that, and before you know they are striking for higher wages and giving no end of trouble."

"You would suppress the school, then, in Western Canada?" said Brown.

"No, not exactly. But if you educate these fellows, you hear me, they'll run your country, by Jove! in half a dozen years, and you wouldn't like that much."

"That's exactly it," replied Brown; "they'll run your country anyhow you put it, school or no school, and, therefore, you had better fit them for the job. You have got to make them Canadian."

"A big business that," said French.

"Yes," replied Brown, "there are two agencies that will do it."

"Namely."

"The school and the Church."

"Oh, yes, that's all right, I guess," losing interest in the discussion.

"That's my game too," said Brown with increasing eagerness. "That's my idea,—the school and the Church. You say the big things are ranches, railroads, and mills. So they are. But the really big things are the things that give us our ideas and our ideals, and those are the school and the Church. But, I say, you will be wanting to turn in. You wait a minute and I'll make your bed."

"Bed? Nonsense!" said French. "Your tent floor is all right. I've been twenty years in this country, and Kalman is already an old timer, so don't you start anything."

"Might as well be comfortable," said Brown cheerfully. "I have a great weakness for comfort. In fact, I can't bear to be uncomfortable. I live luxuriously. I'll be back in a few minutes."

He disappeared behind a bluff and came back in a short time with a large bundle of swamp-grass, which he speedily made into a very comfortable bed.

"Now then," he said cheerfully, "there you are. Have you any objection to prayers? It is a rule of this camp to have prayers night and morning, especially if any strangers happen along. I like to practise on them, you know."

French nodded gravely. "Good idea. I can't say it is common in this country."

Brown brought out two hymn books and passed one to French, stirred up the fire to a bright blaze, and proceeded to select a hymn. Suddenly he turned to Kalman. "I say, my boy, do you read?"

"Sure thing! You bet!" said Kalman indignantly.

"Educated, you see," said French apologetically. "Street University, Winnipeg."

"That's all right, boy. I'll get you a book for yourself. We have lots of them. Now, French, you select."

"Oh, me? You better go on. I don't know your book."

"No, sir," said Brown emphatically. "You have got to select, and you have got to read too. Rule of the camp. True, I didn't feed you, but then—I hesitate to speak of it—perhaps you remember that mixture."

"Do I? Oh, well, certainly, if you put it that way," said French. "Let's see, all the old ones are here. Suppose we make it a good old-fashioned one. How will this do?" He passed the book to Brown.

"Just the thing," said Brown. "'Nearer, my God, to Thee.' Can you find it, Kalman?"

"Why, cert," said Kalman.

French glanced apologetically at Brown.

"Recently caught," he explained, "but means no harm."

Brown nodded.

"Proceed with the reading," he said.

French laid down his pipe, took off his hat, Kalman following his example, and began to read. Instinctively, as he read, his voice took a softer modulation than in ordinary speech. His manner, too, became touched with reverent dignity. His very face seemed to grow finer. Brown sat listening, with his face glowing with pleasure and surprise.

"Fine old hymn that! Great hymn! And finely read, if I might say so. Now we'll sing."

His voice was strong, true, and not unmusical, and what he lacked of finer qualities he made up in volume and force. His visitors joined in the singing, Kalman following the air in a low sweet tone, French singing bass.

"Can't you sing any louder?" said Brown to Kalman. "There's nobody to disturb but the fish and the Galicians up yonder. Pipe up, my boy, if you can. I couldn't sing softly if I tried. Can he sing?" he enquired of French.

"Don't know. Sing up, Kalman, if you can," said French.

Then Kalman sat up and sang. Strong, pure, clear, his voice rose upon the night until it seemed to fill the whole space of clearing and to soar away off into the sky. As the boy sang, French laid down the book and in silence gazed upon the singer's face. Through verse after verse the others sang to the end.

"I say, boy," said Brown, "you're great! I'd like to hear you sing that last verse alone. Get up and try it. What do you say?"

Without hesitation the boy rose up. His spirit had caught the inspiration of the hymn and began,

> "Or if on joyful wing
>   Cleaving the sky,
> Sun, moon, and stars forgot,
>   Upward I fly,
> Still all my song shall be,
> Nearer, my God, to Thee,
>   Nearer to Thee!"

The warm soft light from the glow still left in the western sky fell on his face and touched his yellow hair with glory. A silence followed, so deep and full that it seemed to overflow the space so recently filled with song, and to hold and prolong the melody of that exquisite voice. Brown reached across and put his hand on the boy's shoulder.

"Boy, boy," he said solemnly, "keep that voice for God. It surely belongs to Him."

French neither spoke nor moved. He could not. Deep floods were surging through him. For one brief moment he saw in vision a little ivy-coloured church in its environment of quiet country lanes in far-away England, and in the church, the family pew, where sat a man stern and strong, a woman beside him and two little boys, one, the younger, holding her hand as they sat. Then with swift change of scene he saw a queer, rude, wooden church in the raw frontier town in the new land, and in the church himself, his brother, and between them, a fair, slim girl, whose face and voice as she sang made him forget all else in heaven and on earth. The tides of memory rolled in upon his soul, and with them strangely mingled the swelling springs rising from this scene before him, with its marvellous setting of sky and woods and river. No wonder he sat voiceless and without power to move.

All this Brown could not know, but he had that instinct born of keen sympathy that is so much better than knowing. He sat silent and waited. French turned to the index, found a hymn, and passed it over to Brown.

"Know that?" he asked, clearing his throat.

"'For all thy saints'? Well, rather," said Brown. "Here, Kalman," passing it to the boy, "can you sing this?"

"I have heard it," said Kalman.

"This is a favourite of yours, French?" enquired Brown.

"Yes—but—it was my brother's hymn. Fifteen years ago I heard him sing it."

Brown waited, evidently wishing but unwilling to ask a question.

"He died," said French softly, "fifteen years ago."

"Try it, Kalman," said French.

"Let me hear it," said the boy.

"Oh, never mind," said French hastily. "I don't care about having it rehearsed now."

"Sing it to me," said Kalman.

Brown sang the first verse. The boy listened intently. "Yes, I can sing it," he said eagerly. In the second verse he joined, and with more confidence in the third.

"There now," said Brown, "I only spoil it. You sing the rest. Can you?"

"I'll try."

Without pause or faltering Kalman sang the next two verses. But there was not the same subtle spiritual interpretation. He was occupied with the music. French was evidently disappointed.

"Thank you, Kalman," he said; "let it go at that."

"No," said Brown, "let me read it to you, Kalman. You are not singing the words, you are singing the notes. Now listen,

'The golden evening brightens in the west;
Soon, soon, to faithful warriors comes their rest;
Sweet is the calm of Paradise the blest.
Hallelujah!'

There it is. Do you see it?"

The boy nodded.

"Now then, sing," said Brown.

With face aglow and uplifted to the western sky the boy sang, gaining confidence with every word, till he himself caught and pictured to the others the vision of that "golden evening." When he came to the last verse, Brown stopped him.

"Wait, Kalman," he said. "Let me read that for you. Or better, you read it," he said, passing French the book.

French took the book, paused, made as if to give it back, then, as if ashamed of his hesitation, began to read in a voice quiet and thrilling the words of immortal vision.

> "From earth's wide bounds, from ocean's farthest coast,
> Through gates of pearl streams in the countless host."

But before the close his voice shook, and ended in a husky whisper. Touched by the strong man's emotion, the boy began the verse in tones that faltered. But as he went on his voice came to him again, and with a deeper, fuller note he sang the great words,

> "Singing to Father, Son, and Holy Ghost,
> Hallelujah!"

With the spell of the song still upon them Brown prayed in words simple, reverent, and honest, with a child's confidence, as if speaking to one he knew well. Around the open glade with its three worshippers breathed the silent night, above it shone the stars, the mysterious stars, but nearer than night, and nearer than the stars, seemed God, listening and aware.

Through all his after years Kalman would look back to that night as the night on which God first became to him something other than a name. And to French that evening song and prayer were an echo from those dim and sacred shrines of memory where dwelt his holiest and tenderest thoughts.

Next day, Black Joe, tired of freedom, wandered home, to the great joy of the household.

Chapter XIV

The Break

O pen your letter, Irma. From the postmark, it is surely from Kalman. And what good writing it is! I have just had one from Jack."

Mrs. French was standing in the cosy kitchen of Simon Ketzel's house, where, ever since the tragic night when Kalman had been so nearly done to death, Irma, with Paulina and her child, had found a refuge and a home. Simon had not forgotten his oath to his brother, Michael Kalmar.

Irma stood, letter in hand, her heart in a tumult of joy, not because it was the first letter she had ever received in her life, but because the letter was from Kalman. She had one passion, love for her brother. For him she held a strangely mingled affection of mother, sister, lover, all in one. By day she thought of him, at night he filled her dreams. She had learned to pray by praying for Kalman.

"Aren't you going to open your letter?" said her friend, rejoicing in her joy.

"Yes," cried the girl, and ran into the little room which she shared with Paulina and her child.

Once in that retreat, she threw herself on her knees by the bed, put the letter before her, and pressed her lips hard upon it, her tears wetting it as she prayed in sheer joy. It was just sixteen months, one week, three days, and nine hours since she had watched, through a mist of tears, the train carrying him away to join the Macmillan outfit at Portage la Prairie. Through Jack French's letters to his sister she had been kept in close touch with her brother, but this was his first letter to herself.

How she laughed and wept at the rude construction and the quaint spelling, for the letter was written in her native tongue.

"My sister, my Irma, my beloved," the letter ran. Irma kissed the words as she read them. "How shall I ever write this letter, for it must be in our own beloved tongue? I could have written long ago in English, but with you I must write as I speak, only in our dear mother's and father's tongue. It is so hard to remember it, for everything and every one about me is English, English, English. The hounds, the horses, the cattle call in English, the very wind sounds English, and I am beginning not only to speak, but to think and feel in English, except when I think of you and of our dear mother and father, and when I speak with old Portnoff, an old Russian nihilist, in the colony near here, and when I hear him tell of the bad old days, then I feel and breathe Russian again. But Russia and all that old Portnoff talks about is far away and seems like a dream of a year ago. It is old Portnoff who taught me how to write in Russian.

"I like this place, and oh! I like Jack, that is, Mr. French, my master. He told me to call him Jack. He is so big and strong, so kind too, never loses his temper, that is, never loses hold of himself like me, but even when he is angry, speaks quietly and always smiles. One day Elluck, the Galician man that works here sometimes, struck Blucher with a heavy stick and made him howl. Jack heard him. 'Bring me that stick, Elluck,' he said quietly. 'Now, Elluck, who strikes my dog, strikes me.' He caught him by the collar and beat him until Elluck howled louder than the dog, and all the while Jack never stopped smiling. He is teaching me to box, as he says that no gentleman ever uses a knife or a club, as the Galicians do, in fighting; and you know that when they get beer they are sure to fight, and if they use a knife they will kill some one, and then they are sorry.

"You know about my school. Jack has told Mrs. French. I like Mr. Brown, well, next to Jack. He is a good man. I wish I could just tell you how good and how clever he is. He makes people to work for him in a wonderful way. He got the Galicians to build his house for him, and his school and his store. He got Jack to help him too. He got me to help with the singing in the school every day, and in the afternoon on Sundays when we go down to meeting. He is a Protestant, but, although he can marry the people and baptise and say prayers when they desire it, I do not think he is a priest, for he will take no money for what he does. Some of the Galicians say he will make them all pay some day, but Jack just laughs at this and says they are a suspicious lot of fools. Mr. Brown is going to build a mill to grind flour and meal. He brought the stones from an old Hudson's Bay Company mill up the river, and he is fixing up an old engine from a sawmill in the hills. I think he wants to keep the people from going to the Crossing, where they get beer and whiskey and get drunk. He is teaching me everything that they learn in the English schools, and he gives me books to read. One book he gave me, I read all night. I could not stop. It is called 'Ivanhoe.' It is a splendid book. Perhaps Mrs. French may get it for you. But I like it best on Sunday afternoons, for then we sing, Brown and Jack and the Galician children, and then Brown reads the Bible and prays. It is not like church at all. There is no crucifix, no candles, no pictures. It is too much like every day to be like church, but Brown says that is the best kind, a religion for every day; and Jack, too, says that Brown is right, but he won't talk much about it.

"I am going to be a rancher. Jack says I am a good cattle man already. He gave me a pony and saddle and a couple of heifers for myself, that I saved last winter out of a snow-drift, and he says that when I grow a little bigger, he will take me for his partner. Of course, he smiles when he says this, but I think he means it. Would not that be splendid? I do not care to be a partner, but just to live with Jack always. He makes every one do what he likes because they love him and they are afraid of him too. Old Mackenzie would let him walk over his body. There is only one thing, and I don't like to speak of it, and I would not to any one else, but it makes me sore in my heart. When Jack and Old Mackenzie go to the Crossing, they bring back whiskey, and until it is done they have a terrible time. You know, I don't mind seeing the Galicians drink whiskey and beer. I drink it myself now and then. But Jack and old Mackenzie just sit down and drink and drink, and afterwards I know Jack feels very bad. Once we went here to a Galician wedding, and you know what that means. They all got drinking whiskey and beer, and then we had a terrible time. The whole roomful got fighting. They were all against Jack and Mackenzie. The Galicians had clubs and knives, but Jack just had his hands. It was fine to see him stand up and knock those Galicians back, and smiling all the time. Mackenzie had a hand-spike. Of course, I helped a little with a club. I thought they were going to kill Jack. We got away alive, but Jack was badly hurt, and for a week afterwards he did not look at me. Mackenzie said he was ashamed, but I don't know why. He made a big fight. Mackenzie says he did not like to fight with 'them dogs.' Brown heard all about it and came to see Jack, and he too looked ashamed and sorry. But Brown never fights; no matter what they do to him, he won't fight; and he is a strong man, too, and does not look afraid.

"Have you heard any word at all of father? I sometimes get so lonely for him and you. I used to dream I was back with you again, and then I would wake up and find myself alone and far away. It will not be so long now till I'm a man, and then you will come and live with me. Oh! I cannot write fast enough to put down the words to say how glad I am to think of that. But some day that will be.

"I send my love to Simon Ketzel and Lena and Margaret, and you tell Mrs. French I do not forget that I owe all I have here to her. Tell her I wish I could do something for her. Nothing would be too hard.

"I kiss this paper for you, my dear sister, my beloved Irma.

"Your loving and faithful brother,

"KALMAN."

Proud of her brother, Irma read parts of her letter to her friend, leaving out, with a quick sense of what was fitting, every unhappy reference to Jack French; but the little lady was keen of ear and quick of instinct where Jack French was concerned, and Irma's pauses left a deepening shadow upon her face. When the letter was done, she said: "Is it not good to hear of Kalman doing so well? Tell him he can do something for me. He can grow up a good man, and he can help Jack to be—" But here her loyal soul held her back. "No, don't say that," she said; "just tell him I am glad to know he is going to be a good man. There is nothing I want more for those I love than that. Tell him too," she added, "that I would like him and Jack to help Mr. Brown all they can," and this message Irma wrote to Kalman with religious care, telling him too how sad the dear sweet face had grown in sending the message.

But when Mrs. French reached her home, she read again parts out of the letter which the same mail had brought her from the Night Hawk Ranch, read them in the light of Kalman's letter, while the shadows deepened on her face.

"He is a strange little beggar," she read, "though, by Jove, he is little no longer. He is somewhere about sixteen, is away past my shoulder, and nearly as strong as I am, rides like a cowboy, and is as good after the cattle as I am, is afraid of nothing, and dearly loves a fight, and, I regret to say, he gets lots of it, for the Galicians are always after him for their feasts. He is a great singer, you know, and dances much too well; and at the feasts, as I suppose you know quite well, there are always fights. And here I want to consult you. I very nearly sent him back to you a little while ago, not for his fault, but, I regret to say, for mine. We went to a fool show among the Galicians, and, I am ashamed to say, played the fool. There was the deuce of a row, and Mackenzie and I were in a tight box, for a dozen or so of our Galician friends were determined upon blood. They got some of mine too, for they were using their knives, and, I am bound to say, it looked rather serious. At this juncture that young beggar, forgetting all my good training in the manly art, and reverting to his Slavic barbaric methods of defence, went in with a hand-spike, yelling, and, I regret to say, cursing, till I thought he had gone drunk or mad. Drunk, he was not, but mad,— well, he was possessed of some kind of demon none too gentle that night. I must acknowledge it was a good thing for us, and though I hate to think of the whole ghastly business, it was something fine, though, to see him raging up and down that room, taunting them for cowards, hurling defiance, and, by Jove, looking all the while like some Greek god In cowboy outfit, if your imagination can get that. I am telling you the whole sickening story, because I must treat you with perfect sincerity. I assure you next morning I was sick enough of myself and my useless life, sick enough to have done with the unhappy and disgraceful farce of living, but for your sake and for the boy's too, I couldn't play the cad, and so I continue to live.

"But I have come to the opinion that he ought not to stay with me. As I said before, he is a splendid chap in many ways, but I am afraid in these surroundings he will go bad. He is clean as yet, I firmly believe, thank God, but with this Colony near us with their low standard of morality, and to be quite sincere, in the care of such a man as I am, the boy stands a poor chance. I know this will grieve you, but it is best to be honest. I think he ought to go to you. I must refuse responsibility for his remaining here. I feel like a beast in saying this, but whatever shred of honour is left me forces me to say it."

In the postscript there was a word that brought not a little hope and comfort. "One thing in addition. No more Galician festivals for me." It was a miserably cruel letter, and it did its miserably cruel work on the heart of the little white-faced lady. She laid the letter down, drew from a box upon her table a photo, and laid it before her. It was of two young men in football garb, in all the glorious pride of their young manhood. Long she gazed upon it till she could see no more, and then went to pray.

It took Irma some days of thought and effort to prepare the answer to her letter, for to her, as to Kalman, English had become easier than her native Russian. To Jack French a reply went by return mail. It was not long, but, as Jack French read, the easy smile vanished, and for days he carried in his face the signs of the remorse and grief that gnawed at his heart. Then he rode alone to Wakota to take counsel with his friend Brown.

As he read, one phrase kept repeating itself in his mind: "The responsibility of leaving Kalman with you, I must take. What else can I do? I have no other to help me. But the responsibility for what you make him, you must take. God puts it on you, not I."

"The responsibility for making him is not mine," he said to himself impatiently. "I can teach him a lot of things, but I can't teach him morals. That is Brown's business. He is a preacher. If he can't do this, what's he good for?"

And so he argued the matter with himself with great diligence, and even with considerable heat of mind. He made no pretence to goodness. He was no saint, nor would he set up for one. All who knew him knew this, and none better than Kalman.

"I may not be a saint, but I am no hypocrite, neither will I play the part for any one." In this thought his mind took eager refuge, and he turned it over in various phrases with increasing satisfaction. He remembered with some anxiety that Brown's mental processes were to a degree lacking in subtlety. Brown had a disconcertingly simple and direct method of dealing with the most complex problems. If a thing was right, it was right; if wrong, it was wrong, and that settled the matter with Brown. There was little room for argument, and none for compromise. "He has a deucedly awkward conscience too," said Jack French, "and it is apt to get working long shifts." Would he show his sister-in-law's letter? It might be good tactics, but that last page would not help him much, and besides he shrank from introducing her name into the argument.

As he approached Wakota, he was impatient with himself that he was so keenly conscious of the need of arguments to support his appeal. He rode straight to the school, and was surprised to find Brown sitting there alone, with a shadow on his usually cheery face.

"Hello, Brown!" he cried, as he entered the building, "another holiday, eh! Seems to me you get more than your share."

"No," said Brown, "it is not holidays at all. It is a breaking up."

"What's the row, epidemic of measles or something?"

"I only wish it were," said Brown; "small-pox would not be too bad." Brown's good-natured face was smiling, but his tone told of gloom in his heart.

"What's up, Brown?" asked French.

"I'm blue, I'm depressed, I'm in a funk. It is my constitutional weakness that I cannot stand—"

"Oh, let it go at that, Brown, and get on with the facts. But come out into the light. That's the thing that makes me fear that something has really happened that you are moping here inside. Nothing wrong in the home I hope, Brown; wife and baby well?" said French, his tone becoming more kind and gentle.

"No, not a thing, thank God! both fine and fit," said Brown, as they walked out of the school and down the river path. "My school has folded itself up, and, like the Arab, has stolen away."

"Go on with your yarn. What has struck your school?"

"A Polish priest, small and dark and dirty; he can't help the first two, but with the Eagle River running through the country, he might avoid the last."

"What is he up to?"

"I wish I knew. He introduced himself by ordering, upon pain of hell fire, that no child attend my school; consequently, not a Galician child has shown up."

"What are you going to do—quit?"

"Quit?" shouted Brown, springing to his feet.

"I apologize," said French hastily; "I ought to have known better."

"No, I am not going to quit," said Brown, recovering his quiet manner. "If he wants the school, and will undertake to run it, why, I'll give him the building and the outfit."

"But," said French, "isn't that rather funking it?"

"Not a bit," said Brown emphatically. "I am not sent here to proselytize. My church is not in that business. We are doing business, but we are in the business of making good citizens. We tried to get the Government to establish schools among the Galicians. The Government declined. We took it up, and hence this school. We tried to get Greek Catholic priests from Europe to look after the religion and morals of these people. We absolutely failed to get a decent man to offer. Remember, I say decent man. We had offers, plenty of them, but we could not lay our hands on a single, clean, honest-minded man with the fear of God in his heart, and the desire to help these people. So, as I say, we will give this man a fair chance, and if he makes good, I will back him up and say, 'God bless you.' But he won't make good," added Brown gloomily, "from the way he starts out."

French waited, and Brown went on. "He was called to marry a couple the other day, got hopelessly drunk, charged them ten dollars, and they are not sure whether they are married or not. Last Sunday he drummed the people up to confession. It was a long time since they had had a chance, and they were glad to come. He charged them two dollars apiece, tried to make it five, but failed, and now he introduces himself to me by closing my school. He may mean well, but his methods would bear improvement. However, as I have said, we will give him a chance."

"And meantime?" enquired French.

"Meantime? Oh! I shall stick to my pills and plasters,—we have ten patients in the hospital now,—run the store and the mill, and try to help generally. If this priest gets at his work and makes good, I promise you I'll not bother him."

"And if not?" enquired French.

"If not? Well, then," said Brown, sinking back into his easy, good-natured manner, "you see, I am constitutionally indolent. I would rather he'd move out than I, and so while the colony stays here, it will be much easier for me to stay than to go. And," he added, "I shall get back my school, too."

French looked at him admiringly. Brown's lips had come together in a straight line.

"By George! I believe you," exclaimed French, "and I think I see the finish of the Polish gentleman. Can I help you out?"

"I do not know," said Brown, "but Kalman can. I want him to do some interpreting for me some of these days. By the way, where is he to-day? He is not with you."

French's face changed. "That reminds me," he said, "but I hate to unload my burden on you to-day when you have got your own."

"Do not hesitate," said Brown, with a return of his cheery manner; "another fellow's burden helps to balance one's own. You know I am constitutionally selfish and get thinking far too much of myself,—habit of mine, bad habit."

"You go to thunder, Brown, with your various and many constitutional weaknesses. When I look at you and your work for this thankless horde I feel something of a useless brute."

"Hold up there, now, don't you abuse my parishioners. They are a perfectly good lot if left alone. They are awfully grateful, and, yes, in many ways they are a good lot."

"Yes, a jolly lot of quitters they are. They have quit you dead."

Brown winced. "Let us up on that spot, French," he said. "It is a little raw yet. What's your trouble?"

"Well," said French, "I hardly know how to begin. It is Kalman." At once Brown was alert.

"Sick?"

"Oh! no, not he. Fit as a fiddle; but the fact is he is not doing just as well as he ought." `

"How do you mean?" said Brown anxiously.

"Well, he is growing up into a big chap, you know, getting towards sixteen, and pretty much of a man in many ways, and while he is a fine, clean, straight boy and all that, he is not just what I would like."

"None of us are," said Brown quietly.

"True, as far as I am concerned," replied French. "I do not know about you. But to go on. The boy has got a fiendish temper and, on slight provocation, he is into a fight like a demon."

"With you?" said Brown.

"Oh, come," said French, "you know better than that. No, he gets with those Galicians, and then there is a row. The other week, now— well—" French was finding it difficult to get on.

"I heard about it," said Brown; "they told me the boy was half drunk, and you more." Brown's tone was not encouraging.

"You've hit it, Brown, and that's the sort of thing that makes me anxious. The boy is getting into bad ways, and I thought you might take him in hand. I cannot help him much in these matters, and you can."

French's arguments had all deserted him.

"Look here," he said at length desperately, "here is a letter which I got a few days ago. I want you to read that last page. It will show you my difficulty. It is from my sister-in-law, and, of course, her position is quite preposterous; but you know a woman finds it difficult to understand some things in a man's life. You know what I mean, but read. I think you know who she is. It was she who sent Kalman out here to save him from going wrong. God save the mark!"

Brown took the letter and read it carefully, read it a second time, and then said simply:

"That seems straight enough. That woman sees her way through things. But what's the trouble?"

"Well, of course, it is quite absurd."

"What's absurd?" asked Brown shortly. "Your responsibility?"

"Hold on, now, Brown," he said. "I do not want you to miss my point of view."

"All right, let's have it," said Brown; and French plunged at once at his main argument, adopting with great effort the judicial tone of a man determined to examine dispassionately on the data at command.

"You see, she does not know me, has not seen me for fifteen years, and I am afraid she thinks I am a kind of saint. Now, you know better," Brown nodded his assent with his eyes steadily on the other's face, "and I know better, and I am not going to play the hypocrite for any man."

"Quite right," said Brown; "she does not ask you to."

"So it is there I want you to help me out."

"Certainly," said Brown, "count on me for all I can do. But that does not touch the question so far as I can see it, even remotely."

"What do you mean?"

"It is not a question of what I am to do in the matter."

"What can I do?" cried French, losing his judicial tone. "Do you think I am going to accept the rôle of moral preceptor to that youth and play the hypocrite?"

"Who asks you to?" said Brown, with a touch of scorn. "Be honest in the matter."

"Oh, come now, Brown, let us not chop words. Look at the thing reasonably. I came for help and not—"

"Count on me for all the help I can give," said Brown promptly, "but let's look at your part."

"Well," said French, "we will divide up on this thing. I will undertake to look after the boy's physical and—well—secular interests, if you like. I will teach him to ride, shoot, box, and handle the work on the ranch, in short, educate him in things practical, while you take charge of his moral training."

"In other words, when it comes to morals, you want to shirk."

French flushed quickly, but controlled himself.

"Excuse me, Brown," he said, in a quiet tone. "I came to talk this over with you as a friend, but if you do not want to—"

"Old man, I apologize for the tone I used just now, but I foresee that this is going to be serious. I can see as clearly as light what I ought to say to you now. There is something in my heart that I have been wanting to say for months, but I hate to say it, and I won't say it now unless you tell me to."

The two men were standing face to face as if measuring each other's strength.

"Go on," said French at length; "what are you afraid of?" His tone was unfortunate.

"Afraid," said Brown quickly, "not of you, but of myself." He paused a few moments, as if taking counsel with himself, then, with a sudden resolve, he spoke in tones quiet, deliberate, and almost stern. "First, be clear about this," he said; "I stand ready to help you with Kalman to the limit of my power, and to assure you to the full my share of responsibility for his moral training. Now then, what of your part in this?"

"Why, I—"

"But wait, hear me out. For good or for evil, you have that boy's life in your hands. Did you ever notice how he rides,—his style, I mean? It is yours. How he walks? Like you. His very tricks of speech are yours. And how else could it be? He adores you, you know that. He models himself after you. And so, mark me, without either of you knowing it, *you will make him in spite of yourself and in spite of him.* And it is your fate to make him after your own type. Wait, French, let me finish." Brown's easy good nature was gone, his face was set and stern. "You ask me to teach him morals. The fact is, we are both teaching him. From whom, do you think, will he take his lesson? What a ghastly farce the thing is! Listen, while the teaching goes on. 'Kalman,' I say, 'don't drink whiskey; it is a beastly and degrading habit.' 'Fudge!' he says, 'Jack drinks whiskey, and so will I.' 'Kalman,' I urge, 'don't swear.' 'Rot,' says he, 'Jack swears.' 'Kalman, be a man, straight, self-controlled, honourable, unselfish.' The answer is,—but no! the answer never will be,—'Jack is a drunken, swearing, selfish, reckless man!' No, for he loves you. But like you he will be, in spite of all I can say or do. That is your curse for the life you are leading. Responsibility? God help you. Read your letter again. That woman sees clearly. It is God's truth. Listen, 'The responsibility for what you make him you must take. God puts it there, not I.' You may refuse this responsibility, you may be too weak, too wilful, too selfish to set upon your own wicked indulgence of a foolish appetite, but the responsibility is there, and no living man or woman can take it from you."

French stood silent for some moments. "Thank you," he said, "you have set my sins before me, and I will not try to hide them; but by the Eternal, not for you or for any man, will I be anything but myself."

"What kind of self?" enquired Brown. "Beast or man?"

"That is not the question," said French hotly. "I will be no hypo-crite, as you would have me be."

"Jack French," said Brown, "you know you are speaking a lie before God and man."

French stepped quickly towards him.

"Brown, you will have to apologize," he said in a low, tense voice, "and quick."

"French, I will apologize if what I have said is not true."

"I cannot discuss it with you, Brown," said French, his voice thick with rage. "I allow no man to call me a liar; put up your hands."

"If you are a man, French," said Brown with equal calm, "give me a minute. Read your letter again. Does she ask you to be a hypocrite? Does she not, do I not, only ask you to be a man, and to act like a man?"

"It won't do, Brown. It is past argument. You gave me the lie."

"French, I wish to apologize for what I said just now," said Brown. "I said you knew you were speaking a lie. I take that back, and apologize. I cannot believe you knew. All the same, what you said was not the truth. No one asks you, nor does that letter ask you, to be a hypocrite. You said I did. That was not true. Now, if you wish to slap my face, go on."

French stood motionless. His rage well-nigh overpowered him, but he knew this man was speaking the truth. For some moments they stood face to face. Then, impulsively offering his hand, and with a quick change of voice, Brown said, "I am awfully sorry, French; let's forget it."

But ignoring the outstretched hand, French turned from him without a word, mounted his horse, and rode away.

Brown stood watching him until he was out of sight. "My God, forgive me," he cried, "what a mess I made of that! I have lost him and the boy too;" and with that he passed into the woods, coming home to his wife and baby late at night, weary, spent, and too sad for speech or sleep.

Chapter XV

The Maiden of the Brown Hair

Rumours of the westward march of civilization had floated from time to time up the country from the main line as far as the Crossing, and had penetrated even to the Night Hawk ranch, only to be allayed by succeeding rumours of postponement of the advance for another year.

It was Mackenzie who brought word of the appearance of the first *bôna fide* scout of the advancing host.

"There was a man with a bit flag over the Creek yonder," he announced one spring evening, while the snow was still lying in the hollows, "and another man with a stick or something, and two or three behind him."

"Ah, ha!" exclaimed French, "surveyors, no doubt; they have come at last."

"And what will that be?" said Mackenzie anxiously.

"The men who lay out the route for the railroad," replied French.

Mackenzie looked glum. "And will they be putting a railroad across our ranch?" he asked indignantly.

"Right across," said French, "and just where it suits them."

"Indeed, and it wouldn't be my land they would be putting that railroad over, I'll warrant ye."

"You could not stop them, Mack," said French; "they have got the whole Government behind them."

"I would be putting some slugs into them, whateffer," said Mackenzie. "There will be no room in the country any more, and no sleeping at night for the noise of them injins."

Mackenzie was right. That surveyor's flag was the signal that waved out the old order and waved in the new. The old free life, the only life Mackenzie knew, where each man's will was his law, and where law was enforced by the strength of a man's right hand, was gone forever from the plains. Those great empty spaces of rolling prairie, swept by viewless winds, were to be filled up now with the abodes of men. Mackenzie and his world must now disappear in the wake of the red man and the buffalo before the railroad and the settler. To Jack French the invasion brought mingled feelings. He hated to surrender the untrammelled, unconventional mode of life, for which twenty years ago he had left an ancient and, as it seemed to his adventurous spirit, a worn-out civilization, but he was quick to recognize, and in his heart was glad to welcome, a change that would mean new life and assured prosperity to Kalman, whom he had come to love as a son. To Kalman that surveyor's flag meant the opening up of a new world, a new life, rich in promise of adventure and achievement. French noticed his glowing face and eyes.

"Yes, Kalman, boy," he said, "it will be a great thing for you, great for the country. It means towns and settlements, markets and money, and all the rest."

"We will have no trouble selling our potatoes and our oats now," said the boy.

"Not a bit," said French; "we could sell ten times what we have to sell."

"And why not get ten times the stuff?" cried the boy.

French shrugged his shoulders. It was hard to throw off the old laissez faire of the pioneer.

"All right, Kalman, you go on. I will give you a free hand. Mackenzie and I will back you up; only don't ask too much of us. There will be hundreds of teams at work here next year."

"One hundred teams!" exclaimed Kalman. "How much oats do you think they will need? One thousand bushels?"

"One thousand! yes, ten thousand, twenty thousand."

Kalman made a rapid calculation.

"Why, that would mean three hundred acres of oats at least, and we have only twenty acres in our field. Oh! Jack!" he continued, "let us get every horse and every man we can, and make ready for the oats. Just think! one hundred acres of oats, five or six thousand bushels, perhaps more, besides the potatoes."

"Oh, well, they won't be along to-day, Kalman, so keep cool."

"But we will have to break this year for next," said the boy, "and it will take us a long time to break one hundred acres."

"That's so," said Jack; "it will take all our forces hard at it all summer to get one hundred acres ready."

Eagerly the boy's mind sprang forward into plans for the summer's campaign. His enthusiasm stirred French to something like vigorous action, and even waked old Mackenzie out of his aboriginal lethargy. That very day Kalman rode down to Wakota to consult his friend Brown, upon whose guidance in all matters he had come more and more to depend. Brown's Canadian training on an Ontario farm before he entered college had greatly enriched his experience, and his equipment for the battle of life. He knew all about farming operations, and to him, rather than to French or to Mackenzie, Kalman had come to look for advice on all practical details connected with cattle, horses, and crops. The breach between the two men was an unspeakable grief to the lad, and all the greater because he had an instinctive feeling that the fault lay with the man to whom from the first he had given the complete and unswerving devotion of his heart. Without explaining to Kalman, French had suddenly ceased his visits to Wakota, but he had taken care to indicate his desire that Kalman continue his studies with Brown, and that he should assist him in every way possible with the work he was seeking to carry on among the Galicians. This desire both Brown and Kalman were only too eager to gratify, for the two had grown into a friendship that became a large part of the lives of both. Every Sunday Kalman was to be found at Wakota. There, in the hospitable home of the Browns, he came into contact with a phase of life new and delightful to him. Brown's wife, and Brown's baby, and Brown's home were to him never-ending sources of wonder and joy. That French was shut out from all this was the abiding grief of Kalman's life, and this grief was emphasized by the all-too-evident effect of this exclusion. For with growing frequency French would ride off on Sunday afternoon to the Crossing, and often stay for three or four days at a time. On such occasions life would be to Kalman one long agony of anxiety. Through the summer he bore his grief in silence, never speaking of it even to Brown; but on one occasion, when French's absence had been extended from one Sunday to the next, his anxiety and grief became unsupportable, and he poured it forth to Brown.

"He has not been home for a week, Mr. Brown, and oh! I can't stand it any longer," cried the distracted boy. "I can't stay here while Jack is over there in such a terrible way. I must go to him."

"He won't like it, Kalman," said Brown; "he won't stand it, I am afraid. I would go, but I know it would only offend him."

"I am going down to the Crossing to-day," said Kalman. "I don't care if he kills me, I must go."

But his experience was such that he never went again, for Jack French in his madness nearly killed the boy, who was brought sadly battered to Brown's hospital, where he lay for a week or more. Every day, French, penetrated with penitence, visited him, lavishing on the boy a new tenderness. But when Kalman was on his feet again, French laid it upon him, and bound him by a solemn promise that he should never again follow him to the Crossing, or interfere when he was not master of himself. It was a hard promise to give, but once given, that settled the matter for both. With Brown he never discussed Jack French's weakness, but every Sunday afternoon, when in his own home Brown prayed for friends near and dear, committing them into the Heavenly Father's keeping, in their minds, chiefly and before all others was the man whom they had all come to love as an elder brother, and for whose redemption they were ready to lay down their lives. And this was the strongest strand in the bond that bound Kalman and his friend together. So to Brown Kalman went with his plans for the coming summer, and with most happy results. For through the spring and summer, following Brown's advice and under Kalman's immediate directions, a strong force of Galicians with horse teams and ox teams were kept hard at work, breaking and back-setting, in anticipation of an early sowing in the following spring. In the meantime Brown himself was full of work. The addition to his hospital was almost always full of patients; his school had begun to come back to him again, for the gratitude of his warm-hearted Galician people, in return for his many services to their sick and suffering, sufficed to overcome their fear of the Polish priest, whose unpriestly habits and whose mercenary spirit were fast turning against him even the most loyal of his people. In the expressive words of old Portnoff, who, it is to be feared, had little religion in his soul, was summed up the general opinion: "Dat Klazowski bad man. He drink, drink all time, take money, money for everyting. He damn school, send doctor man hell fire," the meaning of which was abundantly obvious to both Brown and his wife.

So full of work were they all, both at the ranch and at Wakota, that almost without their knowing it the summer had gone, and autumn, with its golden glorious days, nippy evenings, and brilliant starry nights, Canada's most delightful season, was upon them. Through-out the summer the construction gangs had steadily worked their way north and west, and had crossed the Saskatchewan, and were approaching the Eagle Hill country. Preceding the construction army, and following it, were camp followers and attendants of various kinds. On the one hand the unlicensed trader and whiskey pedlar, the bane of the contractor and engineer; on the other hand the tourist, the capitalist, and the speculator, whom engineers and contractors received with welcome or with scant tolerance, according to the letters of introduction they brought from the great men in the East.

Attached to the camp of Engineer Harris was a small and influential party, consisting of Mr. Robert Menzies of Glasgow, capitalist, and, therefore, possible investor in Canadian lands, mines, and railroads,— consequently, a man to be considered; with him, his daughter Marjorie, a brown-haired maid of seventeen, out for the good of her health and much the better of her outing, and Aunt Janet, maiden sister to Mr. Menzies, and guardian to both brother and niece. With this party travelled Mr. Edgar Penny, a young English gentleman of considerable means, who, having been a year in the country, felt himself eminently qualified to act as adviser and guide to the party. At present, however, Mr. Penny was far more deeply interested in the study of the lights that lurked in Miss Marjorie's brown eyes, and the bronze tints of her abundant hair, than in the opportunities for investments offered by Canadian lands, railroads, and mines.

With an elaborate equipment, this party had spent three months travelling as far as Edmonton, and now, on their way back, were attached to the camp of Engineer Harris, in order that the Scotch capitalist might personally investigate methods of railway construction as practised in Western Canada. At present, the party were encamped at a little distance from the Wakota trail, and upon the sunny side of a poplar bluff, for it was growing late in the year.

It was on a rare October morning that Kalman, rising before the sun, set out upon his broncho to round up the horses for their morning feed in preparation for the day's back-setting. With his dogs at his horse's heels, he rode down to the Night Hawk, and crossed to the opposite side of the ravine. As he came out upon the open prairie, Captain, the noble and worthy son of Blucher, caught sight of a prairie wolf not more than one hundred yards distant, and was off after him like the wind.

"Aha! my boy," cried Kalman, getting between the coyote and the bluff, and turning him towards the open country, "you have got your last chicken, I guess. It is our turn now."

Headed off from the woods that marked the banks of the Night Hawk Creek, the coyote in desperation took to the open prairie, with Captain and Queen, a noble fox-hound bitch, closing fast upon him. Two miles across the open country could be seen the poplar bluff, behind which lay the camp of the Engineer and his travelling companions. Steadily the gap between the wolf and the pursuing hounds grew less, till at length, fearing the inevitable, the hunted beast turned towards the little bluff, and entered it with the dogs only a few yards behind. Alas! for him, the bluff afforded no shelter. Right through the little belt of timber dashed the wolf with the dogs and Kalman hard upon his trail. At the very instant that the wolf came opposite the door of Aunt Janet's tent, Captain reached for the extreme point of the beast's extended tail. Like a flash, the brute doubled upon his pursuer, snapping fiercely as the hound dashed past. With a howl of rage and pain, Captain clawed the ground in his effort to recover himself, but before he could renew his attack, and just as the wolf was setting forth again, like a cyclone Queen was upon them. So terrific was her impact, that dogs and wolf rolled under the tent door in one snarling, fighting, snapping mass of legs and tails and squirming bodies. Immediately from within rose a wild shriek of terror.

"Mercy sakes alive! What, what is this? Help! Help! Help! Where are you all? Will some one not come to my help?" Kalman sprang from his horse, rushed forward, and lifted the tent door. A new outcry greeted his ear.

"Get out, get out, you man!" He dropped the flap, fled aghast before the appalling vision of Aunt Janet in night attire, with a ring of curl-papers round her head, driven back into the corner of the tent, and crouched upon a box, her gown drawn tight about her, while she gazed in unspeakable horror at the whirling, fighting mass upon the tent floor at her feet. Higher and higher rose her shrieks above the din of the fight. From a neighbouring tent there rushed forth a portly, middle-aged gentleman in pyjamas, gun in hand.

"What is it, Katharine? Where are you, Katharine?"

"Where am I? Where but here, ye gowk! Oh, Robert! Robert! I shall be devoured alive."

The stout gentleman ran to the door of the tent, lifted the flap, and plunged in. With equal celerity he plunged back again, shouting, "Whatever is all yon?"

"Robert! Robert!" screamed the voice, "come back and save me."

"What is this, sir?" indignantly turning upon Kalman, who stood in bewildered uncertainty.

"It is a wolf, sir, that my dogs—"

"A wolf!" screamed the portly gentleman, springing back from the door.

"Go in, sir; go in at once and save my sister! What are you looking at, sir? She will be devoured alive. I beseech you. I am in no state to attack a savage beast."

From another tent appeared a young man, rotund of form and with a chubby face. He was partly dressed, his night-robe being stuffed hastily into his trousers, and he held the camp axe in his hand.

"What the deuce is the row?" he exclaimed. "By Jove! sounds like a beastly dog fight."

"Aunt Janet! Aunt Janet! What is the matter?" A girl in a dressing-gown, with her hair streaming behind her, came rushing from another tent, and sprang towards the door of the tent, from which came the mingled clamour of the fighting dogs and the terror-stricken woman.

Kalman stepped quickly in front of her, caught her round the waist, and swung her behind him.

"Go back!" he cried. "Get away, all of you." There was an immediate clearance of the space in front of the tent. Seizing a club, he sprang among the fighting beasts.

"Oh! you good man! Come here and save me," cried Aunt Janet in a frenzy of relief. But Kalman was too busy for the moment to give heed to her cries. As he entered, a fiercer howl arose above the din. The wolf had seized hold of Captain's upper lip and was grimly hanging on, while Queen was gripping savagely for the beast's throat. With his club Kalman struck the wolf a heavy blow, stunning it so that it released its hold on the dog. Then, catching it by the hind leg, he hauled wolf and hounds out of the tent in one squirming mass.

"God help us!" cried the stout gentleman, darting into his own tent and poking his head out through the door. "Keep the brute off. There's my gun."

The girl screamed and ran behind Kalman. The young man with the chubby face dropped his axe and jumped hastily into a convenient wagon.

"Shoot the bloomin' brutes," he cried. "Some one bring me my gun."

But the wolf's days were numbered. Queen's powerful jaws were tearing at his throat, while Captain, having gripped him by the small of the back, was shaking him with savage fury.

"Oh! the poor thing! Call off the dogs!" cried the girl, turning to Kalman.

"No! No! Don't you think of it!" cried the man from the tent door. "He will attack us."

Kalman stepped forward, and beating the dogs from their quarry, drew his pistol and shot the beast through the head.

"Get back, Captain! Back! Back! I say. Down!"

With difficulty he drew the wolf from the jaws of the eager hounds, and swung it into the wagon out of the dogs' reach.

"My word!" exclaimed the young man, leaping from the wagon with precipitate haste. "What are you doing?"

"He won't hurt you, sir. He is dead."

The young man's red, chubby face, out of which peered his little round eyes, his red hair standing in a disordered halo about his head, his strange attire, with trailing braces and tag-ends of his night-robe hanging about his person, made a picture so weirdly funny that the girl went off into peals of laughter.

"Marjorie! Marjorie!" cried an indignant voice, "what are ye daein' there? Tak' shame to yersel', ye hizzie."

Marjorie turned in the direction of the voice, and again her peals of laughter burst forth. "Oh! Aunt Janet, you do look so funny." But at once the head with its aureole of curl-papers was whipped inside the tent.

"Ye're no that fine to look at yersel', ye shameless lassie," cried Aunt Janet.

With a swift motion the girl put her hand to her head, gathered her garments about her, and fled to the cover of her tent, leaving Kalman and the young man together, the latter in a state of indignant wrath, for no man can bear with equanimity the ridicule of a maiden whom he is especially anxious to please.

"By Jove, sir!" he exclaimed. "What the deuce did you mean, running your confounded dogs into a camp like that?"

Kalman heard not a word. He was standing as in a dream, gazing upon the tent into which the girl had vanished. Ignoring the young man, he got his horse and mounted, and calling his dogs, rode off up the trail.

"Hello there!" cried Harris, the engineer, after him. Kalman reined up. "Do you know where I can get any oats?"

"Yes," said Kalman, "up at our ranch."

"And where is that?"

"Ten miles from here, across the Night Hawk Creek." Then, as if taking a sudden resolve, "I'll bring them down to you this afternoon. How much do you want?"

"Twenty-five bushels would do us till we reach the construction camp."

"I'll bring them to-day," said Kalman, riding away, his dogs limping after him.

In a few moments the girl came out of the tent. "Oh!" she cried to the engineer, "is he gone?"

"Yes," said Harris, "but he'll be back this afternoon. He is going to bring me some oats." His smile brought a quick flush to the girl's cheeks.

"Oh! has he?" she said, with elaborate indifference. "What a lovely morning! It's wonderful for so late in the year. You have a splendid country here, Mr. Harris."

"That's right," he said; "and the longer you stay in it, the better you like it. You'll be going to settle in it yourself some day."

"I'm not so sure about that," cried the girl, with a deeper blush, and a saucy toss of her head. "It is a fine country, but it's no' Scotland, ye ken, as my Aunt would say. My! but I'm fair starving."

It happened that the ride to the Galician colony, planned for that afternoon by Mr. Penny the day before, had to be postponed. Miss Marjorie was hardly up to it. "It must be the excitement of the country," she explained carefully to Mr. Penny, "so I'll just bide in the camp."

"Indeed, you are wise for once in your life," said her Aunt Janet. "As for me, I'm fair dune out. With this hurly-burly of such terrible excitement I wonder I did not faint right off."

"Hoots awa', Aunt Janet," said her niece, "it was no time for fainting, I'm thinking, with yon wolf in the tent beside ye."

"Aye, lassie, you may well say so," said Aunt Janet, lapsing into her native tongue, into which in unguarded moments she was rather apt to fall, and which her niece truly loved to use, much to her Aunt's disgust, who considered it a form of vulgarity to be avoided with all care.

As the afternoon was wearing away, a wagon appeared in the distance. The gentlemen were away from camp inspecting the progress of the work down the line.

"There's something coming yonder," said Miss Marjorie, whose eyes had often wandered down the trail that afternoon.

"Mercy on us! What can it be, and them all away," said her Aunt in distress. "Put your saddle on and fly for your father or Mr. Harris. I am terrified. It is this awful country. If ever I get out alive!"

"Hoots awa', Aunt, it's just a wagon."

"Marjorie, why will you use such vulgar expressions? Of course, it's a wagon. Wha's—who's in it?"

"Indeed, I'm not caring," said her niece; "they'll no' eat us."

"Marjorie, behave yourself, I'm saying, and speak as you are taught. Run away for your father."

"Indeed, Aunt, how could I do this and leave you here by yourself? A wild Indian might run off with you."

"Mercy me! What a lassie! I'm fair distracted."

"Oh, Auntie dear," said Marjorie, with a change of voice, "it is just a man bringing some oats. Mr. Harris told me he was to get a load this afternoon. We will need to take them from him. Have you any money? We must pay him, I suppose."

"Money?" cried her Aunt. "What is the use of money in this country? No, your father has it all."

"Why," suddenly exclaimed her niece, "it's not the man after all."

"What man are you talking about?" enquired her Aunt. "What man is it not?"

"It's a stranger. I mean—it's—another man," said Marjorie, distinct disappointment in her tone.

"Here, who is it, or who is it no'?"

"Oh," said Marjorie innocently. "Mr. Harris is expecting that young man who was here this morning,—the one who saved us from that awful wolf, you know."

"That man! The impudent thing that he was," cried her Aunt. "Wait till I set my eyes on him. Indeed, I will not look at any one belonging to him." Aunt Janet flounced into the tent, leaving her niece to meet the stranger alone.

"Good afternoon! Am I right in thinking that this is the engineer's camp, for which a load of oats was ordered this morning?" Jack French was standing, hat in hand, looking his admiration and perplexity, for Kalman had not told him anything of this girl.

"Yes, this is the camp. At least, I heard Mr. Harris say he expected a load of oats; but," she added in slight confusion, "it was from another man, a young man, the man, I mean, who was here this morning."

"Confusion, indeed!" came a muffled voice from the closed tent.

Jack French glanced quickly around, but saw no one.

"Oh," said Miss Marjorie, struggling with her laughter, "it's my Aunt; she was much alarmed this morning. You see, the wolf and the dogs ran right into her tent. It was terrible."

"Terrible, indeed," said Jack French, with grave politeness. "I could only get the most incoherent account of the whole matter. I hope your Aunt was not hurt."

"Hurt, indeed!" ejaculated a muffled voice. "It was nearer killed, I was."

Upon this, Miss Marjorie ran to the tent door. "Aunt," she cried, lifting up the flap, "you might as well come out and meet Mr.—"

"French, Jack French, as I am known in this free country."

"My Aunt, Miss Menzies."

"Very happy to meet you, madam." Jack's bow was so inexpressibly elegant that Aunt Janet found herself adopting her most gracious, Glasgow society manner.

French was profuse in his apologies and sympathetic regrets, as he gravely listened to Aunt Janet's excited account of her warm adventure. The perfect gravity and the profuse sympathy with which he heard the tale won Aunt Janet's heart, and she privately decided that here, at last, she had found in this wild and terrible country a man in whom she could entirely confide.

Under Miss Marjorie's direction, French unloaded his oats, the girl pouring forth the while a stream of observations, exclamations, and interrogations upon all subjects imaginable, and with such an abandonment of good fellowship that French, for the first time in twenty years, found himself offering hospitality to a party in which ladies were to be found. Miss Menzies accepted the invitation with eager alacrity.

"Oh! it will be lovely, won't it, Aunt Janet? We have not yet seen a real ranch, and besides," she added, "we have no money to pay for our oats."

"That matters not at all," said French; "but if your Aunt will condescend to grace with her presence my poor bachelor's hall, we shall be most grateful."

Aunt Janet was quite captivated, and before she knew it, she had accepted the invitation for the party.

"Oh, good!" cried Miss Marjorie in ecstasy; "we shall come to-morrow, Mr. French."

And with this news French drove back to the ranch, to the disgust of old Mackenzie, who dreaded "women folks," and to Kalman's alternating delight and dismay. That short visit had established between the young girl and Jack French a warm and abiding friendship that in a more conventional atmosphere it would have taken years to develop. To her French realized at once all her ideals of what a Western rancher should be, and to French the frank, fresh innocence of her unspoiled heart appealed with irresistible force. They had discovered each other in that single hour.

Chapter XVI

How Kalman Found His Mine

The girl's enthusiasm for her new-found friend was such that the whole party decided to accept his invitation. And so they did, spending a full day and night on the ranch, exploring, under French's guidance, the beauty spots, and investigating with the greatest interest, especially on Miss Marjorie's part, the farming operations, over which Kalman was presiding.

That young man, in dumb and abashed confusion of face, strictly avoided the party, appearing only at meals. There, while he made a brave show, he was torn between the conflicting emotions of admiration of the easy nonchalance and self-possession with which Jack played the host, and of furious rage at the air of proprietorship which Mr. Edgar Penny showed towards Miss Marjorie. Gladly would he have crushed into a shapeless pulp the ruddy, chubby face of that young man. Kalman found himself at times with his eyes fixed upon the very spot where his fingers itched to grip that thick-set neck, but in spite of these passing moments of fury, the whole world was new to him. The blue of the sky, the shimmer of the lake, the golden yellow of the poplars, all things in earth and heaven, were shining with a new glory. For him the day's work had no weariness. He no longer trod the solid ground, but through paths of airy bliss his soul marched to the strains of celestial music.

Poor Kalman! When on that fateful morning upon his virgin soul there dawned the vision of the maid, the hour of fate struck for him. That most ancient and most divine of frenzies smote him. He was deliciously, madly in love, though he knew it not. It is something to his credit, however, that he allowed the maiden to depart without giving visible token of this divine frenzy raging within his breast, unless it were that in the blue of his eyes there came a deeper blue, and that under the tan of his cheek a pallor crept. But when on their going the girl suddenly turned in her saddle and, waving her hand, cried, "Good-by, Kalman," the pallor fled, chased from his cheek by a hot rush of Slavic blood as he turned to answer, "Good-by." He held his hat high in a farewell salutation, as he had seen Jack do, and then in another moment she was gone, and with her all the glory of that golden autumn day.

To Kalman it seemed as if months or years must have passed since he first saw her by her Aunt's tent on that eventful morning. To take up the ordinary routine was impossible to him. That very night, rolling up his blankets and grub for three days, and strapping on to his saddle an axe and a shovel, Kalman rode off down the Night Hawk Creek, telling Mackenzie gruffly, as he called his dogs to follow, that he purposed digging out a coyote's den that he knew lay somewhere between the lake and the Creek mouth.

The afternoon of the second day found him far down the Creek, where it plunged headlong into the black ravine below, not having discovered his wolf den and not much caring whether he should or not; for as he rode through the thick scrub he seemed to see dancing before him in the glancing beams that rained down through the yellow poplar leaves a maiden's face with saucy brown eyes that laughed at him and lured him and flouted him all at once.

At the edge of the steep descent he held up his broncho. He had never been down this way before. The sides of the ravine pitched sharply into a narrow gorge through which the Night Hawk brawled its way to the Saskatchewan two miles farther down.

"We'll scramble down here, Jacob," he said to his broncho,—so named by Brown, for that he had "supplanted" in Kalman's affection his first pony, the pinto.

He dismounted, drew the reins over the broncho's head, and began the descent, followed by his horse, slipping, sliding, hanging on now by trees and now by jutting rocks. By the edge of what had once been a small landslip, he clutched a poplar tree to save himself from going over; but the tree came away with him, and horse and man slid and rolled down the slope, bringing with them a great mass of earth and stone. Unhappily, Jacob in his descent rolled over upon the boy's leg. There was a snap, a twinge of sharp pain, and boy and horse lay half imbedded in the loose earth. Kalman seized a stick that lay near at hand.

"Get up, Jacob, you brute!" he cried, giving him a sharp blow.

Jacob responded with a mighty plunge and struggled free, making it possible for Kalman to extricate himself. He was relieved to discover that he could stand on his feet and could walk, but only with extreme pain. Upon examination he could find no sign of broken bones. He took a large handkerchief from his neck, bound it tightly about his foot and ankle.

"I say, Jacob, we're well out of that," he said, looking up at the great cave that had been excavated by the landslip. "Quite a hole, eh? A great place to sleep in. Lots of spruce about, too. We'll just camp here for the night. I guess I'll have to let those coyotes go this trip. This beastly foot of mine won't let me dig much. Hello!" he continued, "that's a mighty queer rock. I'll just take a look at that hole."

He struggled up over the debris and entered the cave. Through the earth there showed a glistening seam slanting across one side and ending in a broken ledge.

"By Jove!" he cried, copying Jack French in his habit of speech as in other habits, "that looks like the coal we used to find along the Winnipeg tracks."

He broke off a piece of the black seam. It crumbled in his hands.

"I guess not," he said; "but we'll get the shovel at it."

Forgetting for the time the pain of his foot, he scrambled down over the soft earth, got his shovel, and was soon hard at work excavating the seam. Soon he had a very considerable pile lying at the front of the cave.

"Now we'll soon see," he cried.

He hurriedly gathered some dry wood, heaped the black stuff upon it, lighted it, and sat down to wait the issue. Wild hopes were throbbing at his heart. He knew enough of the value of coal to realize the importance of the discovery. If it should prove to be coal, what a splendid thing it would be for Jack and for him! How much they would be able to do for Mrs. French and for his sister Irma! Amid his dreams a new face mingled, a face with saucy brown eyes, but on that face he refused to allow himself the rapture of looking. He dared not, at least not yet. Keenly he watched the fire. Was it taking hold of the black lumps? The flames were dying down. The wood had nearly burned itself out. The black lumps were charred and dead, and with their dying died his hopes.

He glanced out upon the ravine. Large soft flakes of snow were falling lazily through the trees.

"I'll get my blankets and grub under cover, and get some more wood for the night. It's going to be cold."

He heaped the remains of the wood he had gathered upon the fire, and with great difficulty, for his foot was growing more and more painful with every move, he set about gathering wood, of which there was abundance near at hand, and making himself snug for the night. He brought up a pail of water from the Creek, and tethered his broncho where there was a bunch of grass at the bottom of the ravine. Before he had finished these operations the ground was white with snow, and the wind was beginning to sigh ominously through the trees.

"Going to be a blizzard, sure," he said. "But let her blow. We're all right in here. Hello! where are those dogs? After the wolves, I'll be bound. They'll come back when they're ready."

With every moment the snow came down more thickly, and the wind grew toward a gale.

"If it's going to be a storm, I'd better lay in some more wood."

At the cost of great pain and labour, he dragged within reach of the cave a number of dead trees. He was disgusted to find his stock of provisions rather low.

"I wish I'd eaten less," he grumbled. "If I'm in for a three days' storm, and it looks like that, my grub will run out. I'll have a cup of tea to-night and save the grub for to-morrow."

As he was busy with these preparations, a sudden darkness fell on the valley. A strange sound like a muffled roaring came up the ravine. In a single minute everything was blotted out before him. There hung down before his eyes a white, whirling, blinding, choking mass of driving snow.

"By Jove! that's a corker of a blizzard, sure enough! I'll draw my fire further in."

He seized his shovel and began to scrape the embers of his fire together. With a shout he dropped his shovel, fell on his knees, and gazed into the fire. Under the heap of burning wood there was a mass of glowing coal.

"Coal!" he shouted, rushing to the front of the cave. "Coal! Coal! Oh, Jack! Dear old Jack! It's coal!"

Trembling between fear and hope, he broke in pieces the glowing lumps, rushed back to the seam, gathered more of the black stuff, and heaped it around the fire. Soon his doubts were all at rest. The black lumps were soon on fire and blazed up with a blue flame. But for his foot, he would have mounted Jacob and ridden straight off for the ranch through all the storm.

"Let her snow!" he cried, gazing into the whirling mist before his eyes. "I've got the stuff that beats blizzards!"

He turned to his tea making, now pausing to examine the great black seam, and again going to the cave entrance to whistle for his dogs. As he stood listening to the soft whishing roar of the storm, he thought he heard the deep bay of Queen's voice. Holding his breath, he listened again. In the pause of the storm he heard, and distinctly this time, that deep musical note.

"They're digging out a wolf," he said. "They'll get tired and come back soon."

He drank his tea, struggled down the steep slope, the descent made more difficult by the covering of soft snow upon it, and drew another pail of water for evening use. Still the dogs did not appear. He went to the cave's mouth again, and whistled loud and long. This time quite distinctly he caught Queen's long, deep bay, and following that, a call as of a human voice.

"What?" he said, "some one out in that storm?"

He dropped upon his knees, put his hands up to his ears, and listened intently again. Once more, in a lull of the gale, he heard a long, clear call.

"Heavens above!" he cried, "a woman's voice! And I can't make a hundred yards with this foot of mine."

He knew enough of blizzards to realize the extreme danger to any one caught in those blinding, whirling snow clouds.

"I can't stay here, and I can't make it with this foot, but—yes— By Jove! Jacob can, though."

He seized his saddle and struggled out into the storm. Three paces from the door he fell headlong into a soft drift, wrenching his foot anew. Choking, blinded, and almost fainting with the pain, he got to his feet once more and fought his way down the slope to where he knew his horse must be.

"Jacob!" he called, "where are you?"

The faithful broncho answered with a glad whinny.

"All right, old boy, I'll get you."

In a few minutes he was on the broncho's back and off down the valley, feeling his way carefully among the trees and over stones and logs. As he went on, he caught now and then Queen's ringing bugle-note, and as often as he caught it he answered with a loud "Halloo!" It was with the utmost difficulty that he could keep Jacob's head toward the storm. Yard by yard he pressed his way against the gale, holding his direction by means of the flowing stream. Nearer and nearer sounded the cry of the hound, till in answer to his shouting he heard a voice call loud and clear. The valley grew wider, the timber more open, and his progress became more rapid. Soon, through the drifting mass, he caught sight of two white moving figures. The dogs bounded toward him.

"Hello there!" he called. "Here you are; come this way."

He urged forward his horse till he was nearly upon them.

"Oh, Kalman! Kalman! I knew it was you!"

In an instant he was off his horse and at her side.

"You! You!" he shouted aloud above the howling gale. "Marjorie! Marjorie!" He had her in his arms, kissing her face madly, while sobbing, panting, laughing, she sank upon his breast.

"Oh, Kalman! Kalman!" she gasped. "You must stop! You must stop! Oh! I am so glad! You must stop!"

"God in Heaven!" shouted the man, boy no longer. "Who can stop me? How can I stop? You might have died here in the snow!"

At a little distance the other figure was hanging to a tree, evidently near to exhaustion.

"Oh, Kalman, we were fair done when the dogs came, and then I wouldn't stop, for I knew you were near. But my! my! you were so long!"

The boy still held her in his arms.

"I say, young man, what the deuce are we going to do? I'm played out. I cawn't move a blawsted foot."

The voice recalled Kalman from heaven to earth. He turned to the speaker and made out Mr. Edgar Penny.

"Do!" cried Kalman. "Why, make for my camp. Come along. It's up stream a little distance, and we can feel our way. Climb up, Marjorie."

"Can I?"

"Yes, at once," said Kalman, taking full command of her. "Now, hold on tight, and we'll soon be at camp."

With the gale in their backs, they set off up stream, the men holding by the stirrups. For some minutes they battled on through the blizzard. Well for them that they had the brawling Creek to guide them that night, for through this swaying, choking curtain of snow it was impossible to see more than a horse length.

In a few minutes Mr. Penny called out, "I say, I cawn't go a step further. Let's rest a bit." He sat down in the snow. Every moment the wind was blowing colder.

"Come on!" shouted Kalman through the storm. "We must keep going or we'll freeze."

But there was no answer.

"Mr. Penny! Mr. Penny!" cried Marjorie, "get up! We must go on!"

Still there was no answer. Kalman made his way round to the man's side. He was fast asleep.

"Get up! Get up, you fool, or you will be smothered!" said Kalman, roughly shaking him. "Get up, I say!"

He pulled the man to his feet and they started on once more, Mr. Penny stumbling along like a drunken man.

"Let me walk, Kalman," entreated Marjorie. "I feel fresh and strong. He can't go on, and he will only keep us back."

"You walk!" cried Kalman. "Never! If he can't keep up let him stay and die."

"No, Kalman, I am quite strong."

She slipped off the horse, Kalman growling his wrath and disgust, and together they assisted Mr. Penny to mount. By this time they had reached the thickest part of the woods. The trees broke to some extent the force of the wind, but the cold was growing more intense.

"Single file here!" shouted Kalman to Marjorie. "You follow me."

Slowly, painfully, through the darkness and drifted snow, with teeth clenched to keep back the groans which the pain of his foot was forcing from him, Kalman stumbled along. At length a misstep turned his foot. He sank with a groan into the snow. With a cry Marjorie was beside him.

"Oh, Kalman, you have hurt yourself!"

"It is this cursed foot of mine," he groaned. "I twisted it and something's broken, I am afraid, and it *is* rather sore."

"Hello there! what's up?" cried Mr. Penny from his saddle. "I'm getting beastly cold up here."

Marjorie turned wrathfully upon him.

"Here, you great lazy thing, come down!" she cried. "Kalman, you must ride."

But Kalman was up and once more leading the way.

"We're almost there," he cried. "Come along; he couldn't find the path."

"It's just a great shame!" cried Marjorie, half sobbing, keeping by his side. "Can't I help you? Let me try."

Her arm around him put new life into him.

"By Jove! I see a fire," shouted Mr. Penny.

"That's camp," said Kalman, pausing for breath while Marjorie held him up. "We're just there."

And so, staggering and stumbling, they reached the foot of the landslip. Here Kalman took the saddle off Jacob, turned him loose, and clambered up to the cave, followed by the others. Mr. Penny sank to the ground and lay upon the cave floor like one dead.

"Well, here we are at last," said Kalman, "thank God!"

"Yes, thank God!" said Marjorie softly, "and—you, Kalman."

She sank to her knees on the ground, and putting her face in her hands, burst into tears.

"What is it, Marjorie?" said Kalman, taking her hands down from her face. "Are you hurt? What is it? I can't bear to see you cry like that." But he didn't kiss her. The conventionalities were seizing upon him again. His old shyness was stealing over his spirit. "Tell me what to do," he said.

"Do!" cried Marjorie through her sobs. "What more can you do? Oh, Kalman, you have saved me from an awful death!"

"Don't speak of it," said the boy with a shudder. "Don't I know it? I can't bear to think of it. But are you all right?"

"Right?" said Marjorie briskly, wiping away her tears. "Of course I'm all right, an' sair hungry, tae."

"Why, of course. What a fool I am!" said Kalman. "I'll make you tea in a minute."

"No, let me," cried Marjorie. "Your poor foot must be awful. Where's your teapot? I'm a gran' tea maker, ye ken." She was in one of her daft moods, as Aunt Janet would say.

Never was such tea as that which they had from the tin tea pail and from the one tin cup. What though the blizzard howled its loudest in front of their cave? What though the swirling snow threatened now and then to douse their fire? What though the tea boiled over and the pork burned to a crisp? What though a single bannock stood alone between them and starvation? What cared they? Heaven was about them, and its music was ringing in their hearts.

Refreshed by their tea, they sat before the blazing fire, all three, drying their soaked garments, while Mr. Penny and Marjorie recounted their experiences. They had intended to make Wakota, but missed the trail. The day was fine, however, and that gave them no concern till the storm came up, when suddenly they had lost all sense of direction and

allowed their ponies to take them where they would. With the instinct
bred on the plains, the ponies had made for the shelter of the Night
Hawk ravine. Up the ravine they had struggled till the darkness and
the thick woods had forced them to abandon the ponies.

"I wonder what the poor things will do?" interjected Marjorie.

"They'll look after themselves, never fear," said Kalman. "They live
out all winter here."

Then through the drifts they had fought their way, till in the
moment of their despair the dogs came upon them.

"We thought they were wolves," cried Marjorie, "till one began to
bay, and I knew it was the fox-hound. And then I was sure that you
would not be far away. We followed the dogs for a while, and I kept
calling and calling,—poor Mr. Penny had lost his voice entirely,—till
you came and found us."

A sweet confusion checked her speech. The heat of the fire became
suddenly insupportable, and putting up her hand to protect her face,
she drew back into the shadow.

Mr. Penny, under the influence of a strong cup of boiling tea and
a moderate portion of the bannock and pork,—for Kalman would not
allow him full rations,—became more and more confident that they
"would have made it."

"Why, Mr. Penny," cried Marjorie, "you couldn't move a foot further. Don't you remember how often you sat down, and I had just to
pull you up?"

"Oh," said Mr. Penny, "it was the beastly drift getting into my eyes
and mouth, don't you know. But I would have pulled up again in a
minute. I was just getting my second wind. By Jove! I'm strong on my
second wind, don't you know."

But Marjorie was quite unconvinced, while Kalman said nothing.
Over and over again they recounted the tale of their terrors and their
struggle, each time with some new incident; but ever and anon there
would flame up in Marjorie's cheek the flag of distress, as if some

memory smote her with a sudden blow, and her hand would cover her cheek as if to ward off those other and too ardent kisses of the dancing flames. But at such times about her lips a fitful smile proclaimed her distress to be not quite unendurable.

At length Mr. Penny felt sleepy, and stretching himself upon the dry earth before the fire, passed into unconsciousness, leaving the others to themselves. Over the bed of spruce boughs in the corner Kalman spread his blankets, moving about with painful difficulty at his task, his groans growing more frequent as they called forth from his companion exclamations of tender commiseration.

The story of those vigil hours could not be told. How they sat now in long silences, gazing into the glowing coals, and again conversing in low voices lest Mr. Penny's vocal slumbers should be disturbed; how Marjorie told the short and simple story of her life, to Kalman all wonderful; how Kalman told the story of his life, omitting parts, and how Marjorie's tender eyes overflowed and her rosy cheeks grew pale and her hand crept toward his arm as he told the tragedy of his mother's death; how she described with suppressed laughter the alarms of her dear Aunt Janet that morning—was it a month ago?—how he told of Jack French, what a man he was and how good; how she spoke of her father and his strength and his tenderness, and of how he spoiled her, against which Kalman vehemently protested; how he told of Brown and his work for the poor ignorant Galicians, and of the songs they sang together; how she made him sing, at first in undertones soft and low, lest poor Mr. Penny's sleep should be broken, and then in tones clear and full, the hymns in which Brown and French used to join, and then, in obedience to her peremptory commands, his own favourite Hungarian love-song, of which he shyly told her; how her eyes shone like stars, her cheeks paled, and her hands held fast to each other in the ecstasy of her rapture while he told her what it all meant, at first with averted looks, and then boldly pouring the passion of his soul into her eyes, till they fell before the flame in his as he sang the refrain,

> "While the flower blooms in the meadow,
>   And fishes swim the sea,
> Heart of my heart, soul of my soul,
>   I'll love and live for thee";

how then shyness fell on her and she moved ever so little to her own
side of the fire; how he, sensitive to her every emotion, rose at once
to build the fire, telling her for the first time then of his wonderful
discovery, which he had clean forgot; how together on tiptoe they
examined, with heads in close proximity and voices lowered to a
whisper, the black seam that ran down a side of the cave; how they
discussed the possible value of it and what it might mean to Kalman;
and then how they fell silent again till Kalman commanded her to
bed, to which she agreed only upon condition that he should rouse
Mr. Penny when his watch should be over; how she woke in broad
daylight to find him with breakfast ready, the blizzard nearly done, and
the sun breaking through upon a wonderful world, white and fairylike;
how they vainly strove to simulate an ease of manner, to forget some of
the things that happened the night before, and that neither could ever
forget till the heart should cease to beat.

   All this might be told, had one the art. But no art or skill of man
could tell how, as they talked, there flew from eye to eye, hers brown
and his blue-grey, those swift, fluttering signals of the heart; how he
watched to see on her cheek the red flush glow and pale again, not
sure whether it was from the fire upon the cave floor or from the fire
that burns eternal in the heart of man and maid; how, as he talked and
sang, she feared and loved to see the bold leap of passion in his eyes;
and how she speedily learned what words or looks of hers could call up
that flash; how, as she slept, he piled high the fire, not that she might
be warm, but that the light might fall upon her face and he might
drink and drink till his heart could hold no more, of her sweet loveliness; how, when first waking, her eyes fell on him moving softly about

the cave, and then closed again till she could dream again her dream and drink in slow sips its rapture; how he feared to meet her waking glance, lest it should rebuke his madness of the night; how, as her eyes noted the haggard look of sleepless watching and of pain, her heart flowed over as with a mother's pity for her child, and how she longed to comfort him but dared not; how he thought of the coming days and feared to think of them, because in them she would have no place or part; how she looked into the future and wondered what like would be a life in this new and wonderful land—all this, no matter what his skill or art, no man could tell.

It was still morning when Jack French and Brown rode up the Night Hawk ravine, driving two saddled ponies before them. Their common anxiety had furnished the occasion for the healing of the breach that for a year and more had held these friends apart.

With voluble enthusiasm Mr. Penny welcomed them, plunging into a graphic account of their struggle with the storm till happily they came upon the dogs, who led them to Kalman and his camp. But French, brushing him aside, strode past to where, trembling and speechless, Marjorie stood, and then, taking her in his arms, he whispered many times in her ears, "Thank God, little girl, you are safe."

And Marjorie, putting her arms around Jack's neck, whispered through radiant tears, "It was Kalman, Jack. Don't listen to yon gommeril. It was Kalman saved us; and oh, Jack, he is just lovely!"

And Jack, patting her cheek, said, "I know all about him."

"Do you, indeed?" she answered, with a knowing smile. "I doubt. But oh! he has broken his foot or something. And oh, Jack, he has got a mine!"

And Jack, not knowing what she meant, looked curiously into her face and wondered, till Brown, examining Kalman's foot and finding a broken bone, exclaimed wrathfully, "Say, boy, you don't tell me you have been walking on this foot?"

But Kalman answered nothing.

"He came for me—for us, Mr. Brown, through that awful storm," cried Marjorie penitently; "and is it broken? Oh, Kalman, how could you?"

But Kalman still answered nothing. His dream was passing from him. She was restored to her world and was no longer in his care.

"And here's his mine," cried Marjorie, turning Jack toward the black seam.

"By Jove!" cried Mr. Penny, "and I never saw it. You never showed it to me."

But during those hours spent in the cave Kalman and Marjorie had something other to occupy their minds than mines. Jack French examined the seam closely and in growing excitement.

"By the Lord Harry! Kalman, did you find this?"

Kalman nodded indifferently. Mines were nothing to him now.

"How did you light upon it?"

And Kalman told him how.

"He's just half dead and starved," said Marjorie in a voice that broke with pity. "He watched all last night while we slept away like a pair o' stirks."

At the tone in her voice, Jack French turned and gave her a searching look. The quick, hot blood flamed into her cheeks, and in her eyes dawned a frank shyness as she gave him back his look.

"I don't care," she said at length; "he's fair dune oot."

But Jack only nodded his head sagely while he whispered to her, "Happy boy, happy boy! Two mines in one night!"

At which the red flamed up again and she fell to examining with greater diligence the seam of black running athwart the cave side.

In a few minutes they were mounted and away, Brown riding hard to bring the great news to the engineer's camp and recall the hunting parties; the rest to make the ranch, Marjorie in front in happy sparkling converse with Jack French, and Kalman, haggard and gloomy, bringing up the rear. A new man was being brought to birth within him, and sore were the parturition pangs. For one brief night she had been his; now back to her world, she was his no more.

It was quite two days before the shining sun and the eager air had licked up from earth the drifts of snow, and two days before Marjorie felt quite sure she was able to bear again the rigours of camp life, and two days before Aunt Janet woke up to the fact that that foreign young man was altogether too handsome to be riding from morning till night with her niece. For Jack, meanwhile, was attending with assiduous courtesy the Aunt and receiving radiant looks of gratitude from the niece. Two days of Heaven, when Kalman forgot all but that she was beside him; two days of hell when he remembered that he was but a poor foreign boy and she a great English lady. Two days and they said farewell. Marjorie was the last, turning first to French, who kissed her, saying, "Come back again, little girl," and then to Kalman, sitting on his broncho, for he hated to go lame before them all.

"Good-by, Kalman," she said, smiling bravely, while her lips quivered. "I'll no forget yon awful and," leaning slightly toward him as he took her hand, "yon happy night. Good-by for now. I'll no forget."

And Kalman, looking straight into her eyes, held her hand without a word till, withdrawing it from his hold, she turned away, leaving the smile with him and carrying with her the quivering lips.

"I shall ride a bit with you, little girl," said Jack French, who was ever quick with his eyes.

She tried to smile at him, but failed piteously. But Jack rode close to her, talking bright nothings till she could smile again.

"Oh, Jack, but you are the dear!" she said to him as they galloped together up the trail, Mr. Penny following behind. "I'll mind this to you."

But before they took the descent to the Night Hawk ravine, they heard a thunder of hoofs, and wheeling, found Kalman bearing down upon them.

"Mercy me!" cried Aunt Janet, "what's wrang wi' the lad?"

"I have come to say good-by," he shouted, his broncho tearing up the earth by Marjorie's side.

Reaching out his hands, he drew her toward him and kissed her before them all, once, again, and yet again, with Aunt Janet screaming, "Mercy sakes alive! The lad is daft! He'll do her a hurt!"

"Hoots! woman, let the bairns be," cried Marjorie's father. "He saved her for us."

But having said his farewell, Kalman rode away, waving his hand and singing at the top of his voice his Hungarian love-song,

> "While the flower blooms in the meadow,
>   And fishes swim the sea,
> Heart of my heart, soul of my soul,
>   I'll love and live for thee,"

which none but Marjorie could understand, but they all stood watching as he rode away, and listening,

> "With my lances at my back,
>   My good sword at my knee,
> Light of my life, joy of my soul,
>   I'll fight, I'll die for thee!"

And as the song ceased she rode away, and as she rode she smiled.

Chapter XVII

The Fight for the Mine

The early approach of winter checked the railroad construction proper, but with the snow came good roads, and contractors were quick to take advantage of the easier methods of transportation furnished by winter roads to establish supply depots along the line, and to open tie camps up in the hills. And so the old Edmonton Trail was once more humming with life and activity far exceeding that of its palmiest days.

As for Kalman, however, it was the mine that absorbed his attention and his energies. By day and by night he planned and dreamed and toiled for the development of his mine. With equal enthusiasm Brown and French joined in this enterprise. It was French that undertook to deal with all matters pertaining to the organization of a company by which the mine should be operated. Registration of claim, the securing of capital, the obtaining of charter, all these matters were left in his hands. A few weeks' correspondence, however, revealed the fact that for Western enterprises money was exceedingly difficult to secure. French was eager to raise money by mortgaging his ranch and all his possessions, but this proposal Kalman absolutely refused to consider. Brown, too, was opposed to this scheme. Determined that something should be done, French then entered into contracts with the Railroad Company for the supply of ties. But though he and Mackenzie took a large force into the woods, and spent their three months in arduous toil, when the traders and the whiskey runners had taken their full toll little was left for the development of the mine.

The actual working of the mine fell to Kalman, aided by Brown. There was an immediate market for coal among the Galicians of the colony, who much preferred it to wood as a fuel for the clay ovens with which they heated their houses. But they had little money to spare, and hence, at the beginning of the work, Kalman hit upon the device of bartering coal for labour, two days' work in the mine entitling a labourer to a load of coal. Brown, too, needed coal for his mill. At the Crossing there was large demand for coal, while correspondence with the Railroad Company discovered to Kalman a limitless market for the product of his mine. By outside sales Kalman came to have control of a little ready money, and with this he engaged a small force of Galicians, who, following lines suggested by Brown, pushed in the tunnel, ran cross drifts, laid down a small tramway, and accomplished exploration and development work that appeared to Kalman's uninstructed eyes wonderful indeed. The interest of the whole colony centred in the mine and in its development, and the confidence of the people in Kalman's integrity and efficiency became more and more firmly established.

But Brown was too fully occupied with his own mission to give much of his time to the mine. The work along the line of construction and in the camps meant sickness and accident, and consequently his hospital accommodation had once more to be increased, and this entailed upon himself and his wife, who acted as matron, a heavy burden of responsibility and of toil.

It was a happy inspiration of Jack French's that led Brown to invoke the aid of Mrs. French in securing the services of a nurse, and Mrs. French's proposal that Irma, who for two years had been in regular training, should relieve Mrs. Brown of her duties as matron, was received by all concerned with enthusiastic approval. And so, to the great relief of Mrs. Brown and to the unspeakable joy of both Kalman and his sister, Irma and Paulina with her child were installed in the Wakota institution, Irma taking charge of the hospital and Paulina of the kitchen.

It was not by Brown's request or even desire that Paulina decided to make her home in the Wakota colony. She was there because nothing could prevent her coming. Her life was bound up with the children of her lord, and for their sakes she toiled in the kitchen with a devotion that never flagged and never sought reward.

The school, too, came back to Brown and in larger numbers than before. Through the autumn and early winter, by his drunkenness and greed, Klazowski had fallen deeper and deeper into the contempt of his parishioners. It was Kalman, however, that gave the final touch to the tottering edifice of his influence and laid it in ruins. It was the custom of the priest to gather his congregation for public worship on Sunday afternoon in the schoolhouse which Brown placed at his disposal, and of which he assumed possession as his right, by virtue of the fact that it was his people who had erected the building. On a Sunday afternoon, as the winter was nearing an end, Klazowski, under the influence of a too complete devotion to the beer barrel that stood in his host's kitchen, spent an hour in a furious denunciation of the opponents of his holy religion, and especially of the heretic Brown and all his works, threatening with excommunication those who in any degree would dare after this date to countenance him. His character was impugned, his motives declared to be of the basest. This was too much for his congregation. Deep murmurs rose among the people, but unwarned, the priest continued his execrations of the hated heretic.

At length Kalman, unable any longer to contain his indignation, sprang to his feet, gave the priest the lie direct and appealed to the people.

"You all know Mr. Brown," he cried, "what sort of man is he? And what sort of man is this priest who has spoken to you? You, Simon

Simbolik, when your child lay dead and you sought help of this Klazowski, what answer did he give you?"

"He asked me for ten dollars," said Simon promptly, "and when I could not give it he cursed me from him. Yes," continued Simbolik, "and Mr. Brown made the coffin and paid for it, and would take no money. My daughter is in his school, and is learning English and sewing, beautiful sewing, and she will stay there."

"You, Bogarz," cried Kalman, "when your children were down with scarlet fever and you went to the priest for help, what was his reply?"

"He drove me from his house. He was afraid to death."

"Yes," continued Kalman, "and Mr. Brown came and took the children to his hospital, and they are well to-day."

"Yes," cried Bogarz, "and he would take nothing for it all, but I paid him all I could, and I will gladly pay him more."

And so from one to another went the word. The friends of Klazowski, for he still had a following, were beaten into silence. Then rose more ominous murmurs.

"I would not have Klazowski in my house with my family," cried one, "a single day. It would not be safe. I need say no more."

Others were found with similar distrust of Klazowski's morals. Klazowski was furious, and sought with loud denunciations and curses to quell the storm of indignation that had been roused against him. Then Kalman executed a flank movement.

"This man," he cried, his loud, clear voice gaining him a hearing, "This man is promising to build us a church. He has been collecting money. How much money do you think he has by this time? I, myself, gave him ten dollars; Mr. French gave him twenty-five."

At once cries came from all parts of the building. "I gave him twenty-five." "And I ten." "And I five." And so on, Kalman keeping count.

"I make it nearly two hundred dollars," he cried. "Has any one seen the books? Does any one know where the money is?".

"No, no," cried the crowd.

"Then," cried Kalman, "let us enquire. We are not sheep. This is a free country, and we are free men. The days of the old tyranny are gone." The house rocked with the wild cheers of the excited crowd. "Let us examine into this. Let us appoint a committee to find out how much money has been paid and where it is."

With enthusiasm Kalman's suggestion was carried into effect. A committee was appointed and instructed to secure the information with all speed.

Next day Klazowski was not to be found in the colony. He had shaken the Wakota snow from off his feet, and had departed, carrying with him the people's hard-earned money, their fervent curses, and a deep, deep grudge against the young man upon whom he laid the responsibility for the collapse of his influence among the faithful and long-suffering people of Wakota.

A few days later, to an interested and devout congregation in the city of Winnipeg, he gave an eloquent account of his labours as a missionary in the remote colony of Wakota, depicted in lurid colours the persecutions he had endured at the hands of the heretic Brown, reserving his most fervid periods for the denunciation of the unscrupulous machinations of an apostate and arch traitor, Kalman Kalmar, whose name would forever be remembered by his people with infamy.

Among those who remained to congratulate and sympathize with the orator, none was more cordial than Mr. Rosenblatt, with whom the preacher went home to dine, and to whom, under the mellowing influence of a third bottle, he imparted full and valuable information in regard to Wakota, its possibilities as a business centre, its railroad prospects, its land values, its timber limits, and especially in regard to the character and work of Kalman Kalmar, and the wonderful mine which the young man had discovered.

The information thus obtained Rosenblatt was careful to impart to his friend and partner, Samuel Sprink. As a result of further interviews with the priest and of much shrewd bargaining with railroad contractors and officials, in early spring, before the break up of the roads, Mr. Samuel Sprink had established himself along the line of construction as a vendor of "gents' furnishings," working men's supplies, tobaccos and cigars, and other useful and domestic articles. It was not announced, however, in the alluring posters distributed among the people in language suited to their comprehension, that among his stores might be found a brand of whiskey of whose virtues none could speak with more confidence than Mr. Sprink himself, for the sufficient reason that he was for the most part the sole manufacturer thereof.

Chief among Mr. Sprink's activities was that of "claim jumping,"— to wit, the securing for himself of homesteads for which patents had not been obtained, the homesteaders for one reason or another having not been able to complete the duties required by Government. In the prosecution of this business Mr. Sprink made a discovery, which he conveyed in a letter to Mr. Rosenblatt, who was still in charge of the Winnipeg end of the Company's business.

"You must come at once," wrote Mr. Sprink. "I have a great business on hand. I have discovered that no application has been made for the coal mine claimed by young Kalmar, and this means that the mine is still open. Had I the full description of the property, I should have jumped the claim at once, you bet. So get a move on and come. Get the description of the land on the quiet, and then do some work among the Galician people to prepare for the change of ownership, because there will be trouble, sure. So, come along. There is other big business too, so you must come."

Rosenblatt needed no further urging. In a week he was on the ground.

Meanwhile, Kalman was developing his mine, and dreaming great dreams as to what he should do when he had become a great mine owner. It was his custom, ever since Irma's coming, to spend the Sunday evening with her at the hospital. His way to the mine lay through scrub and sleugh, a heavy trail, and so he welcomed the breaking up of the ice on the Eagle River. For, taking Brown's canoe, he could paddle down to the Saskatchewan, and thence to the mouth of the Night Hawk Creek, from which point it was only a short walk to camp.

It was a most fortunate thing for old Père Garneau that Kalman had adopted this method of transportation on the very night the old priest had chosen for his trip down the Eagle. Père Garneau, a pioneer priest of the North Saskatchewan country, had ministered for twenty years, by river and by trail, to the spiritual and temporal needs of the half-breeds and the Indians under the care of his church. A heroic soul was the old Father, not to be daunted by dangers, simple as a child, and kindly. But the years had done their work with him on eye and hand. The running ice in the spring flood of the Eagle River got itself under the nose of the good Father's canoe, and the current did the rest. His feeble cry would have brought no aid, had not Kalman, at the very moment, been shoving out his canoe into the current of the Eagle. A few strong sweeps of the paddle, and Kalman had the old priest in tow, and in a few minutes, with Brown's aid, into the hospital and snugly in bed, with his canoe, and what of his stuff could be rescued, safe under cover. Two days of Irma's nursing and of Brown's treatment, and the ill effects of his chilly dip had disappeared sufficiently to allow the Father to proceed on his way.

"Eet will be to me a pleasant remembrance of your hospitalite," he said to Brown on the morning of the third day.

"And to us of your stay, Father Garneau," replied Brown. "But you need not go to-day. You are not strong enough, and, besides, I have some work for you. There is a poor Galician woman with us here who cannot see the morning. She could not bear the priest Klazowski. She had trouble with him, and I think you could comfort her."

"Ah, dat Klazowski!" exclaimed Père Garneau. "Eet ees not a good man. Many peep' tell me of dat man. He will be no more priest, for certainly. I would see dis woman, poor soul!"

"To-night Kalman will be here," said Brown, "and he will interpret for you."

"Ah, he ees a fine young man, Kalman. He mak' troub' for dat priest, ees eet not?"

"Well, I am afraid he did," said Brown, laughing. "But I fancy it was the priest made trouble for himself."

"Yes, dat ees so, and dat ees de worse troub' of all," said the wise old man.

The poor woman made her confession, received her Sacrament, and thus comforted and at peace, made exit from this troubled life.

"My son," said the priest to Kalman when the service was over, "I would be glad to confess you."

"Thank you, Father," said Kalman. "I make my confession to God."

"Ah, my son, you have been injured in your faith by dat bad priest Klazowski."

"No, I think not," said Kalman. "I have for some years been reading my Bible, and I have lived beside a good man who has taught me to know God and our Lord and Saviour Jesus Christ. I seek to follow him as Peter and the others did. But I am no longer of the Galician way of religion, neither Greek nor Roman."

"My son," exclaimed the old priest in horror, "you are not an apostate? You have not denied your faith?"

"No, I have not. I try to please Christ."

Long and painfully, and with tears, did the old priest labour with Kalman, to whom his soul went out in gratitude and affection, but without making any change in the young man's mind. The teaching, but more the life, of his friend had not been lost, and Kalman had come to see clearly his way.

Next morning the good Father was ready for his journey.

"I leave to you," he said to Brown, "my double blessing, of the stranger whom you received, and of the sick to whom you served. Ah!

what a peety you are in the darkness of error," he continued with a gentle smile; "but I will pray for you, for you both, my children, many times."

"Thank you, thank you," said Brown warmly. "The prayers of a good man bring blessing, and I love to remember the words of our Master, 'He that is not against us is on our part.'"

"Ah! dat ees true, dat ees true. Dat ees like Heem. Adieu."

For some days Rosenblatt had been at work quietly in the colony, obtaining information and making friends. Among the first who offered their services was old Portnoff and a friend of his,—an old man with ragged beard, and deep-set, piercing eyes looking out from under shaggy brows, to whom Portnoff gave the name of Malkarski. As Portnoff seemed to be a man of influence among his people, Rosenblatt made him foreman over one of the gangs of workmen in his employ. It was through Portnoff he obtained an accurate description of the mine property. But that same night Portnoff and Malkarski were found at Brown's house.

"There is a man," said Portnoff, "who wishes to know about the mine. Perhaps he desires to purchase."

"His name?" enquired Brown.

"Rosenblatt."

"Rosenblatt? That name has a familiar sound. It would be wise," he continued, "to carry your information to Kalman at once."

"It shall be done to-night," said Malkarski in a deep voice. "It is important. Portnoff will go." Portnoff agreed.

The following morning brought Kalman to Wakota. The arrival of Rosenblatt in the country had changed for him the face of heaven and earth. Before his eyes there rose and remained the vision of a spot in a Russian forest where the snow was tramped and bloody. With sobs and execrations he poured forth his tale to Brown.

"And my father has sworn to kill him, and if he fails I shall take it up."

"Kalman, my boy," said Brown, "I cannot wonder that you feel like this. Killing is too good for the brute. But this you cannot do. Vengeance is not ours, but God's."

"If my father fails," said Kalman quietly, "I shall kill him."

"You must not think like that, much less speak so," said Brown. "This is Canada, not Russia. You are a Christian man and no heathen."

"I can't help it," said Kalman; "I can only see that bloody snow." He put his hands over his eyes and shuddered violently. "I must kill him!"

"And would you ruin your own life? Would you shut yourself off forever from your best and holiest thoughts? And what of your sister, and Jack, and me? And what of—of—all your friends? For this one fierce and sinful passion—for it is sinful, Kalman—you would sacrifice yourself and all of us."

"I know all that. It would sacrifice all; but in here," smiting his breast, "there is a cry that will not cease till I see that man's blood."

"God pity you, Kalman. And you call yourself a follower of Him who for His murderers prayed, 'Father, forgive them.'" Then Brown's voice grew stern. "Kalman, you are not thinking clearly. You must face this as a Christian man. The issue is quite straight. It is no longer between you and your enemy; it is between you and your Lord. Are you prepared to-night to reject your Lord and cut yourself off from Him? Listen." Brown took his Bible, and turning over the leaves, found the words, "'If ye forgive not men their trespasses, neither will your Father forgive your trespasses'; and remember, these are the words of Him who forgave those who had done their worst on Him, blighting His dearest hopes, ruining His cause, breaking His heart. Kalman, you dare not."

And Kalman went his way to meet his Gethsemane in the Night Hawk ravine, till morning found him on his face under the trees, with his victory still in the balance. The hereditary instincts of Slavic blood cried out for vengeance. The passionate loyalty of his heart to the memory of his mother and to his father cried out for vengeance.

His own wrongs cried out for vengeance, and against these cries there stood that single word, "Father, forgive them, they know not what they do."

Before a week was gone old Portnoff came hot foot to Brown to report that early that morning Rosenblatt had ridden off in the direction of the Fort, where was the Government Land Office.

"It is something about the mine. He was in good spirits. He offered me something good on his return. If this were only Russia!" said the old Nihilist.

"Yes, yes," growled his friend Malkarski, in his deep voice, "we should soon do for him."

"Left this morning?" said Brown. "How long ago?"

"Two hours."

Brown thought quickly. What could it mean? Was it possible the registration had been neglected? Knowing French's easy-going methods of doing business, he knew it to be quite possible. French was still away in his tie camp. Kalman was ten miles off at the mine. It was too great a chance to take.

"Throw the saddle on my horse, Portnoff," he cried. "I must ride to the Fort."

"It would be good to kill this man," said old Malkarski quietly.

"What are you saying?" cried Brown in horror. "Be off with you."

He made a few hurried preparations, sent word to Kalman, and departed. He had forty miles before him, and his horse was none of the best. Rosenblatt had two hours' lead and was, doubtless, well mounted. There was a chance, however, that he would take the journey by easy stages. But a tail chase is a long chase, especially when cupidity and hate are spurring on the pursued. Five hours' hard riding brought Brown to the wide plain upon which stood the Fort. As he entered upon the plain, he discovered his man a few miles before him. At almost the same instant of his discovery, Rosenblatt became aware of his pursuer, and the last five miles were done at racing speed. But

Brown's horse was spent, and when he arrived at the Land Office, it was to find that application had been made for one hundred and sixty acres of mining land, including both sides of the Night Hawk ravine. Brown stared hard at the entry.

"Is there no record of this claim having been entered before?" said Brown.

"None," said the agent.

"This man," Brown said at length to the agent, "never saw the mine. He is not the discoverer."

"Who is?"

"A young friend of mine, Kalman Kalmar. To that I can swear." And he told the story of the discovery, adding such details as he thought necessary in regard to Rosenblatt's character.

The official was sympathetic and interested.

"And how long is it since the discovery was made?" he enquired.

"Six months or so."

"And why was there no application sent in?"

Brown was silent.

"The Government cannot be responsible for neglect," he said. "You have yourselves to blame for it. Nothing can be done now."

The door opened, and Brown turned to find Rosenblatt with a smile of triumph upon his face. Before he was aware, his open hand had swung hard upon the grinning face, and Rosenblatt fell in a huddled heap into the corner. He rose up sputtering and spitting.

"I will have the law on you!" he shouted. "I call you as witness," he continued to the agent.

"What's the matter with you?" said the agent. "I didn't see anything. If you trip yourself up and pitch into the corner, that is your own business. Get out of this office, you disorderly beast! Hurry up!" The agent put his hand upon the counter and leaped over.

Rosenblatt fled, terrified.

"Brute!" said the agent, "I can't stand these claim jumpers. You did that very neatly," he said to Brown, shaking him warmly by the hand. "I am awfully sorry, but the thing can't be helped now."

Brown was too sick at heart to reply. The mine was gone, and with it all the splendid castles he and Kalman had been building for the last six months. He feared to meet his friend. With what heart now could he ask that this brute, who had added another to the list of the wrongs he had done, should be forgiven? It was beyond all human strength to wipe out from one's mind such an accumulation of injuries. Well for Brown and well for his friend that forty miles lay before him. For forty miles of open country and of God's sun and air, to a man whose heart is open to God, work mighty results. When at last they came together, both men had won their victory.

Quietly Brown told his story. He was amazed to find that instead of rousing Kalman to an irrepressible fury, it seemed to make but little impression upon him that he had lost his mine. Kalman had faced his issue, and fought out his fight. At all costs he could not deny his Lord, and under this compulsion it was that he had surrendered his blood feud. The fierce lust for vengeance which had for centuries run mad in his Slavic blood, had died beneath the stroke of the Cross, and under the shock of that mighty stroke the loss of the mine had little effect upon him. Brown wondered at him.

The whole colony was thrown into a ferment of indignation by the news that Kalman had been robbed of his mine. But the agents of Rosenblatt and Sprink were busy among the people. Feast days were made hilarious through their lavish gifts of beer. Large promises in connection with the development of the mine awakened hopes of wealth in many hearts. After all, what could they hope from a young man without capital, without backing, without experience? True, it was a pity he should lose his mine, but men soon forget the losses and injuries of others under the exhilaration of their own ambitions and dreams of success. Kalman's claims and Kalman's wrongs were soon obliterated. He had been found guilty of the unpardonable crime of failure. The new firm went vigorously to work. Cabins were erected at the mine, a wagon road cut to the Saskatchewan. In three weeks the whole face of the ravine was changed.

It was in the end of April before French returned from his tie camp, with nothing for his three months' toil but battered teams and empty pockets, a worn and ill-favoured body, and with a heart sick with the sense of failure and of self-scorn. Kalman, reading at a glance the whole sordid and heart-breaking story, met him with warm and cheery welcome. It was for French, more than for himself, that he grieved over the loss of the mine. Kalman was busy with his preparations for the spring seeding. He was planning a large crop of everything the ranch would grow, for the coming market.

"And the mine, Kalman?" enquired French.

"I've quit mining. The ranch for me," exclaimed Kalman, with cheerful enthusiasm.

"But what's up?" said French, with a touch of impatience.

"Jack, we have lost the mine," said Kalman quietly. And he told the story.

As he concluded the tale, French's listlessness vanished. He was his own man again.

"We will ride down and see Brown," he said with decision.

"No use," said Kalman, wishing to save him further pain. "Brown saw the entry at the Land Office, and the agent plainly told him nothing could be done."

"Well, we won't just lie down yet, boy," said Jack. "Come along— or—well, perhaps I'd better go alone. You saddle my horse."

In half an hour French appeared clean shaven, dressed in his "civilization clothes," and looking his old self again.

"You're fine, Jack," said Kalman in admiration. "We have got each other yet."

"Yes, boy," said Jack, gripping his hand, "and that is the best. But we'll get the mine, too, or I'm a Dutchman." All the old, easy, lazy air was gone. In every line of his handsome face, in every movement of his body, there showed vigour and determination. The old English fighting spirit was roused, whose tradition it was to snatch victory from the jaws of defeat and despair.

Four weeks passed before Kalman saw him again. Those four weeks he spent in toil from early dawn till late at night at the oats and the potatoes, working to the limit of their endurance Mackenzie and the small force of Galicians he could secure, for the mine and the railroad offered greater attractions. At length the level black fields lay waiting the wooing of the sun and rain and genial air. Then Kalman rode down for a day at Wakota, for heart and body were exhausted of their vital forces. He wanted rest, but he wanted more the touch of a friend's hand.

At Wakota, the first sight that caught his eye was French's horse tethered on the grassy sward before Brown's house, and as he rode up, from within there came to his ear the sound of unusual and hilarious revelry.

"Hello there!" yelled Kalman, still sitting his horse. "What's happened to you all?"

The cry brought them all out,—Brown and his wife, French and Irma, with Paulina in the background. They crowded around him with vociferous welcome, Brown leading in a series of wild cheers. After the cheering was done, Brown rushed for him.

"Congratulations, old boy!" he cried, shaking him by the hand. "It's all right; we've won, after all! Hurrah! Hurrah! Hurrah!" Brown had clearly gone mad.

Then Irma came running toward him.

"Yes, it's all true, Kalman dear," she cried, pulling down his head to kiss him, her voice breaking in a sob and her eyes radiant with smiles and tears.

"Don't be alarmed, old man," said French, taking him by the hand when Irma had surrendered her place. "They are all quite sane. We've got it, right enough. We've won out."

Kalman sat still on his horse, looking from one to the other in utter bewilderment. Brown was still yelling at intervals, and wildly waving his hat. At length Kalman turned to Mrs. Brown.

"You seem to be sane, anyway," he said; "perhaps you will tell me what they all mean?"

"It means, Kalman," said the little woman, offering him both hands, "we are so glad that we don't know what to do. We have got back our mine."

"The mine!" gasped Kalman faintly. "Impossible! Why, Brown there—"

"Yes! Brown here," yelled that individual; "I know Brown. He's a corker! But he's sometimes wrong, and this is one of the times. A mine, and a company! And there's the man that did it! Jack French, to whom I take off my hat! He has just got home, and we have just heard his tale, and—school's out and the band's going to play and the game begin. And get down from your broncho, you graven image!" Here Brown pulled Kalman headlong from his horse. "And Jack will perform. I have not been mad like this for a thousand years. I have been in Hades for the last month, and now I'm out! I know I am quite mad, but it's fine while it lasts. Now, Jack, the curtain's up. Let the play proceed."

The story was simple enough. Immediately after the discovery of the mine French had arranged with Mr. Robert Menzies that he should make application with the Department of the Interior at Ottawa for the necessary mining rights. The application had been made, but the Department had failed to notify the local agent.

"So," said Jack, "the mine is yours again, Kalman."

"No," said Kalman, "not mine, ours; yours as much as mine, Jack, or not mine at all."

249

"And the Company!" yelled Brown. "Tell him about the Company. Let the play proceed."

"Oh," said French, with an air of indifference, "Mr. Menzies has a company all organized and in his pocket, waiting only approval of the owner of the mine."

"And the party will arrive in about three weeks, I think you said, French," remarked Brown, with a tone of elaborate carelessness.

Kalman's face flushed hot. The eyes of both men were upon him.

"Yes, in about three weeks," replied French.

"If it were not that I am constitutionally disinclined to an active life, I should like to join myself," said Brown; "for it will be a most remarkable mining company, if I know anything of the signs."

But Kalman could not speak. He put his arm around Jack's shoulder, saying, "You are a great man, Jack. I might have known better."

"All right, boy," said Jack. "From this time we shall play the man. Life is too good to lose for nothing. A mine is good, but there are better things than mines."

"Meaning?" said Brown.

"Men!" said Jack with emphasis.

"*And*," shouted Brown, slipping his arm round his wife, "women."

"Brown," said Jack solemnly, "as my friend Pierre Lamont would say, 'you have reason.'"

Chapter XVIII

For Freedom and for Love

The hut of the Nihilist Portnoff stood in a thick bluff about midway between Wakota and the mine, but lying off the direct line about two miles nearer the ranch. It was a poor enough shack, made of logs plastered over with mud, roofed with poplar poles, sod, and earth. The floor was of earth, the walls were whitewashed, and with certain adornments that spoke of some degree of culture. Near one side of the shack stood the clay oven stove, which served the double purpose of heating the room and of cooking Portnoff's food. Like many of the Galician cabins, Portnoff's stood in the midst of a garden, in which bloomed a great variety of brilliant and old-fashioned flowers and shrubs, while upon the walls and climbing over the roof, a honeysuckle softened the uncouthness of the clay plaster.

It was toward the end of the third week which followed French's return that Portnoff and Malkarski were sitting late over their pipes and beer. The shack was illumined with half a dozen candles placed here and there on shelves attached to the walls. The two men were deep in earnest conversation. At length Portnoff rose and began to pace the little room.

"Malkarski," he cried, "you are asking too much. This delay is becoming impossible to me."

"My brother," said Malkarski, "you have waited long. There must be no mistake in this matter. The work must be thoroughly done, so let us be patient. And meantime," he continued with a laugh, "he is having suffering enough. The loss of this mine is like a knife thrust in his heart. It is pleasant to see him squirm like a reptile pierced by a stick. He is seeking large compensation for the work he has done,—three thousand dollars, I believe. It is worth about one."

Portnoff continued pacing up and down the room.

"Curse him! Curse him! Curse him!" he cried, lifting his clenched hands above his head.

"Be patient, brother."

"Patient!" cried Portnoff. "I see blood. I hear cries of women and children. I fall asleep and feel my fingers in his throat. I wake and find them empty!"

"Aha! I too," growled Malkarski. "But patience, patience, brother!"

"Malkarski," cried Portnoff, pausing in his walk, "I have suffered through this man in my country, in my people, in my family, in my heart!"

"Aha!" ejaculated old Malkarski with fierce emphasis, "have you? Do you know what suffering is? But—yes, Portnoff, we must be patient yet." As he spoke he took on a dignity of manner and assumed an attitude of authority that Portnoff was quick to recognize.

"You speak truly," replied the latter gravely. "I heard a good thing to-day," he continued with a change of tone. "It seems that Sprink—"

"Sprink!" muttered Malkarski with infinite contempt, "a rat, a pig! Why speak of him?"

"It is a good story," replied Portnoff with a laugh, "but not pleasant for Sprink to tell. It appears he was negotiating with Mr. French, suggesting a partnership in the mine, but Mr. French kicked him out. It was amusing to hear Sprink tell the tale with many oaths and curses. He loves not French any more."

"Bah!" said Malkarski, "the rest of the tale I heard. He had the impudence to propose—the dog!—alliance with the young lady Irma. Bah!" he spat upon the ground. "And French very properly kicked him out of his house and gave him one minute to remove himself out of gun range. There was quick running," added old Malkarski with a grim smile. "But he is a cur. I wipe him out of my mind."

"We must keep close watch these days," said Portnoff. "They are both like mad dogs, and they will bite."

"Ha!" cried Malkarski with sudden vehemence, "if we could strike at once, now! To-night!" His voice rose in a cry, "Ah, if it were to-night! But patience," he muttered. "Ah, God! how long?"

"Not long, my brother, surely," said Portnoff.

"No, not long," answered Malkarski. "Let them go away from the mine, away from these people. On the railroad line many accidents occur. Let us not spoil all by undue haste."

"It is your day to watch to-morrow, Malkarski," said Portnoff.

"I shall keep watch to-morrow," said Malkarski. "After all, it is joy to look on his face and think how it will appear when we have done our work." He rose and paced the floor, his deep-set eyes gleaming like live coals in his haggard old face. "Ah," he continued in his deep undertone, "that will be joy."

Ever since the arrival of Rosenblatt in the country he had been under surveillance of one of these two old Nihilists, walking, though he knew it not, side by side with death. To Malkarski fell the task of keeping within sight and sound of Rosenblatt during the following day.

The negotiations in connection with the transfer of the mine property were practically completed. The money for the improvements effected had been paid. There remained only a few minor matters to be settled, and for that a meeting was arranged at the mine on the evening of the following day. At this meeting Kalman had with great reluctance agreed to be present. The place of meeting was the original cave, which had been enlarged to form a somewhat spacious room, from which there had been run back into the hill a tunnel. At the entrance to this tunnel a short cross-tunnel had been cut, with an exit on the side of the hill and at right angles to the mouth. Across the ravine from the cave stood a small log building which Messrs. Rosenblatt and Sprink had used as an office during the month of their régime. Further down the ravine were scattered the workmen's cabins, now deserted.

In the preparing of plans for this last meeting Rosenblatt and Sprink spent long hours that day. Indeed, it was late in the afternoon when their conference broke up.

An hour later found Malkarski, pale and breathless, at the door of Portnoff's cabin, unable to recover his speech till Portnoff had primed him with a mug of Sprink's best whiskey.

"What is it, my brother?" cried Portnoff, alarmed at his condition. "What is it?"

"A plot!" gasped Malkarski, "a most damnable plot! Give me another drink."

Under the stimulus of the potent liquid, Malkarski was able in a few minutes between his gasps to tell his story. Concealed by a lumber pile behind Rosenblatt's shack, with his ear close to a crack between the logs, he had heard the details of the plot. In the cross tunnel at the back of the cave bags of gunpowder and dynamite were to be hidden. To this mass a train was to be laid through the cross tunnel to a convenient distance. At a certain point during the conference Rosenblatt would leave the cave on the pretext of securing a paper left in his cabin. A pile of brushwood at some distance from the cave would be burning. On his way to his cabin Rosenblatt would fire the train and wait the explosion in his own shack, the accidental nature of which could easily be explained under the circumstances. In order to remove suspicion from him, Rosenblatt was to appear during the early evening in a railway camp some distance away. The plot was so conceived and the details so arranged that no suspicion could attach to the guilty parties.

"And now," said Malkarski, "rush to Wakota, where I know Mr. French and Kalman are to be to-day. I shall go back to the mine to warn them if by any chance you should miss them."

Old Portnoff was long past his best. Not for many years had he quickened his pace beyond a slow dog trot. The air was heavy with an impending storm, the blazed trail through the woods was rough, and at times difficult to find, so that it was late in the evening when the old man stumbled into the missionary's house and poured out his tale between his sobbing gasps to Brown and a Sergeant of the Mounted Police, who was present on the Queen's business. Before the tale was done the Sergeant was on his feet.

"Where are French and Kalman?" he said sharply.

"Gone hours ago," cried Brown. "They must be at the mine by now."

"Can this man be relied upon?" enquired the Sergeant.

"Absolutely," said Brown. "Fly! I'll follow."

Without further word the Sergeant was out of the house and on his horse.

"What trail?" he shouted.

"It is best by the river," cried Brown. "The cross trail you might lose. Go! Go, in God's name!" he added, rushing toward his stable, followed by Portnoff and his wife. "Where is Paulina?" he cried.

"Paulina," said his wife, "is gone. She is acting strangely these days,—goes and comes, I don't know where."

"Get a boy, then," said her husband, "and send him to the ranch. There is a bare chance we may stop them there. Portnoff, there is another pony here; saddle and follow me. We'll take the cross trail. And pray God," he added, "we may be in time!"

Great masses of liver-coloured clouds were piling up in the west, blotting out the light from the setting sun. Over all a heavy silence had settled down, so that in all the woods there was no sound of living thing. Lashing his pony into a gallop, heedless of the obstacles on the trail, or of the trees overhead, Brown crashed through scrub and sleugh, with old Portnoff following as best he could. Mile after mile they rode, now and then in the gathering darkness losing the trail, and with frantic furious haste searching it again, till at length, with their ponies foaming and trembling, and their own faces torn and bleeding with the brush, they emerged into the clearing above the ravine.

Meantime, the ghastly tragedy was being enacted. Impatiently at the cave mouth French and Kalman waited the coming of those they were to meet. At length, in the gathering gloom, Rosenblatt appeared, coming up the ravine. He was pale and distraught.

"I have ridden hard," he said, "and I am shaken with my ride. My papers are in my cabin. I shall get them."

In a few moments he returned, bringing with him a bottle and two cups.

"Drink!" he said. "No? Then I will." He poured out a cup full of raw whiskey and drank it off. "My partner is late," he said. "He will be here in a few moments. Meantime, we can look over the papers."

"It is too dark here," said French. "We can't see to read. You have in your cabin a light, let us go there."

"Oh," cried Rosenblatt hastily, "it is more comfortable here. I have a lantern."

He rummaged in the sides of the cave and produced a lantern.

"Here is a light," said French, striking a match.

Rosenblatt snatched the match from his hand, crushed it in his fingers and hurried out of the cave.

"Ah," he exclaimed, "I am shaking with my hurried ride."

With great care he lighted his lantern outside of the cave and set it upon a table that had been placed near the cave's mouth. French drew out his pipe, slowly filled it and proceeded to light it, when Rosenblatt in a horror-stricken voice arrested him.

"Don't smoke!" he cried. "I mean—it makes me very ill—when I am—in this—condition—the smell of tobacco smoke."

French looked at him with cool contempt.

"I am sorry for you," he said, lighting his pipe and throwing the match down.

Rosenblatt sprang to the cave mouth, came back again, furtively treading upon the match. The perspiration was standing out upon his forehead.

"It is a terrible night," he said. "Let us proceed. We can't wait for my partner. Read, read."

With fingers that trembled so that he could hardly hold the papers, he thrust the documents into Kalman's hand.

"Read," he cried, "I cannot see."

Opening the papers, Kalman proceeded to read them carefully, by the light of the lantern, French smoking calmly the while.

"Have you no better light than this, Rosenblatt?" said French at length. "Surely there are candles about here." He walked toward the back of the cave.

"Ah, my God!" cried Rosenblatt, seizing him and drawing him toward the table again. "Sit down, sit down. If you want candles, let me get them. I know where they are. But we need no candles here. Yes," he cried with a laugh, "young eyes are better than old eyes. The young man reads well. Read, read."

"There is another paper," said French after Kalman had finished. "There is a further agreement."

"Yes, truly," said Rosenblatt. "Is it not there? It must be there. No, I must have left it at my cabin. I will bring it."

"Well, hurry then," said French. "Meantime, my pipe is out."

He drew a match, struck it on the sole of his boot, lighted his pipe and threw the blazing remnant toward the back of the cave.

"Ah, my God!" cried Rosenblatt, his voice rising almost to a shriek. Both men looked curiously at him. "Ah," he said, with his hand over his heart, "I have pain here. But I will get the paper."

His face was livid, and the sweat was running down his beard. As he spoke he ran out and disappeared, leaving the two men poring over the papers together. Beside the burning heap of brushwood he stood a moment, torn in an agony of uncertainty and fear.

"Oh!" he said, wringing his hands, "I dare not do it! I dare not do it!"

He rushed past the blazing heap, paused. "Fool!" he said, "what is there to fear?"

He crept back to the pile of burning brush, seized a blazing ember, ran with it to the train he had prepared of rags soaked in kerosene, leading toward the mouth of the cross tunnel, dropped the blazing stick upon it, and fled. Looking back, he saw that in his haste he had dashed out the flame and that besides the saturated rags the stick lay smoking. With a curse he ran once more to the blazing brush heap, selected a blazing ember, carried it carefully to the train, and set the saturated rags on fire, waiting until they were fully alight. Then like a man pursued by demons, he fled down the ravine, splashed through the Creek and up the other side, not pausing to look behind until he had shut the door of his cabin.

As he closed the door, a dark figure appeared, slipped up to the door, there was a click, a second, and a third, and the door stood securely fastened with three stout padlocks. In another moment Rosenblatt's livid face appeared at the little square window which overlooked the ravine.

At the same instant, upon the opposite side of the ravine, appeared Brown, riding down the slope like a madman, and shouting at the top of his voice, "French! French! Kalman! For God's sake, come here!"

Out of the cave rushed the two men. As they appeared Brown stood waving his hands wildly. "Come here! Come, for God's sake! Come!" His eyes fell upon the blazing train. "Run! run!" he shouted, "for your lives! Run!"

He dashed toward the blazing rags and trampled them under his feet. But the fire had reached the powder. There was a quick hissing sound of a burning fuse, and then a great puff. Brown threw himself on his face and waited, but there was nothing more. His two friends rushed to him and lifted him up.

"What, in Heaven's name, is it, Brown?" cried French.

"Come away!" gasped Brown, stumbling down the ravine and dragging them with him.

Meantime, the whole hillside was in flames. In the clear light of the blazing trees the Sergeant was seen riding his splendid horse at a hard gallop. Soon after his appearing came Portnoff.

"What does all this mean?" said French, looking around from one to the other with a dazed face.

Before they could answer, a voice clear and sonorous drew their eyes across the ravine towards Rosenblatt's cabin. At a little distance from the cabin they could distinguish the figure of a man outlined in the lurid light of the leaping flames. He was speaking to Rosenblatt, whose head could be seen thrust far out of the window.

"Who is that man?" cried the Sergeant.

"Mother of God!" said old Portnoff in a low voice. "It is Malkarski. Listen."

"Rosenblatt," cried the old man in the Russian tongue, "I have something to say to you. Those bags of gunpowder, that dynamite with which you were to destroy two innocent men, are now piled under your cabin, and this train at my feet will fire them."

With a shriek Rosenblatt disappeared, and they could hear him battering at the door. Old Malkarski laughed a wild, unearthly laugh.

"Rosenblatt," he cried again, "the door is securely fastened! Three stout locks will hold it closed."

The wretched man thrust his head far out of the window, shrieking, "Help! Help! Murder! Help!"

"Listen, you dog!" cried Malkarski, his voice ringing down through the ravine, "your doom has come at last. All your crimes, your treacheries, your bloody cruelties are now to be visited upon you. Ha! scream! pray! but no power in earth can save you. Aha! for this joy I have waited long! See, I now light this train. In one moment you will be in hell."

He deliberately struck a match. A slight puff of wind blew it out. Once more he struck a match. A cry broke forth from Kalman.

"Stop! stop! Malkarski, do not commit this crime!"

"What is he doing?" said the Sergeant, pulling his pistol.

"He is going to blow the man up!" groaned Kalman.

The Sergeant levelled his pistol.

"Here, you man," he cried, "stir in your tracks and you are dead!"

Malkarski laughed scornfully at him and proceeded to strike his third match. Before the Sergeant could fire, old Portnoff sprang upon him with the cry, "Would you murder the man?"

Meantime, under the third match, the train was blazing, and slowly creeping toward the cabin. Shriek after shriek from the wretched victim seemed to pierce the ears of the listeners as with sharp stabs of pain.

"Rosenblatt," cried old Malkarski, putting up his hand, "you know me now?"

"No! no!" shrieked Rosenblatt. "Mercy! mercy! quick! quick! I know you not."

The old man drew himself up to a figure straight and tall. The years seemed to fall from him. He stepped nearer Rosenblatt and stood in the full light and in the attitude of a soldier at attention.

"Behold," he cried, "Michael Kalmar!"

"Ah-h-h-h!" Rosenblatt's voice was prolonged into a wail of despair as from a damned soul.

"My father!" cried Kalman from across the ravine. "My father! Don't commit this crime! For my sake, for Christ's dear sake!"

He rushed across the ravine and up the other slope. His father ran to meet him and grappled with him. Upon the slope they struggled,

Kalman fighting fiercely to free himself from those encircling arms, while like a fiery serpent the flame crept slowly toward the cabin.

With a heavy iron poker which he found in the cabin, Rosenblatt had battered off the sash and the frame of the window, enlarging the hole till he could get his head and one arm free; but there he stuck fast, watching the creeping flames, shrieking prayers, entreaties, curses, while down upon the slope swayed the two men in deadly struggle.

"Let me go! Let me go, my father!" entreated Kalman, tearing at his father's arms. "How can I strike you!"

"Never, boy. Rather would I die!" cried the old man, his arms wreathed about his son's neck.

At length, with his hand raised high above his head, Kalman cried, "Now God pardon me this!" and striking his father a heavy blow, he flung him off and leaped free. Before he could take a single step, another figure, that of a woman, glided from the trees, and with a cry as of a wild cat, threw herself upon him. At the same instant there was a dull, thick roar; they were hurled stunned to the ground, and in the silence that followed, through the trees came hurtling a rain of broken rock and splintered timbers.

Slowly recovering from the shock, the Sergeant staggered down the ravine, crying, "Come on!" to the others who followed him one by one as they recovered their senses. On the other side of the slope lay Kalman and the woman. It was Paulina. At a little distance was Malkarski, or Kalmar, as he must be called, and where the cabin had been a great hole, and at some distance from it a charred and blackened shape of a man writhing in agony, the clothes still burning upon him.

Brown rushed down to the Creek, and with a hatful of water extinguished the burning clothes.

"Water! water!" gasped the wretch faintly.

"Bring him some water, some one," said Brown, who was now giving his attention to Kalman. But no one heeded him.

Old Portnoff found a can, and filling it at the stream, brought it to the group on the slope. In a short time they began to revive, and before long were able to stand. Meantime, the wretched Rosenblatt was piteously crying for water.

"Oh, give him some water," said Kalman to Brown, who was anxiously taking his pulse.

Brown took the can over, gave the unhappy wretch a drink, pouring the rest over his burned and mangled limbs. The explosion had shattered the lower part and one side of Rosenblatt's body, leaving untouched his face and his right arm.

The Sergeant took charge of the situation.

"You I arrest," he said, taking old Kalmar by the shoulder.

"Very well; it matters not," said the old man, holding up his hands for the handcuffs.

"Can anything be done for this man?" asked the Sergeant, pointing to Rosenblatt.

"Nothing. He can only live a few minutes."

Rosenblatt looked up and beckoned the Sergeant toward him.

"I would speak with you," he said faintly.

The Sergeant approached, bringing Kalmar along with him.

"You need not fear, I shall not try to escape," said Kalmar. "I give you my honour."

"Very well," said the Sergeant, turning from him to Rosenblatt. "What do you wish?"

"Come nearer," said the dying man.

The Sergeant kneeled down and leaned over him to listen. With a quick movement Rosenblatt jerked the pistol from the Sergeant's belt and fired straight at old Kalmar, turned the pistol toward Kalman and fired again. But as he levelled his gun for the second time, Paulina, with a cry, flung herself upon Kalman, received the bullet, and fell to the ground. With a wild laugh, Rosenblatt turned the pistol on himself, but before he could fire the Sergeant had wrested it from his hand.

"Aha," he gasped, "I have my revenge!"

"Fool!" said old Kalmar, who was being supported by his son. "Fool! You have only done for me what I would have done for myself."

With a snarl as of a dog, Rosenblatt sank back upon the ground, and with a shudder lay still.

"He is dead," said Brown. "God's mercy meet him!"

"Ah," said old Kalmar, "I breathe freer now that his breath no longer taints the air. My work is done."

"Oh, my father," cried Kalman brokenly, "may God forgive you!"

"Boy," said the old man sternly, "mean you for the death of yon dog? You hang the murderer. He is many times a murderer. This very night he had willed to murder you and your friend. He was condemned to death by a righteous tribunal. He has met his just doom. God is just. I meet Him without fear for this. For my sins, which are many, I trust His mercy."

"My father," said Kalman, "you are right. I believe you. And God is merciful. Christ is merciful."

As he spoke, he leaned over, and wiping from his father's face the tears that fell upon it, he kissed him on the forehead. The old man's breath was growing short. He looked towards Brown. At once Brown came near.

"You are a good man. Your religion is good. It makes men just and kind. Ah, religion is a beautiful thing when it makes men just and kind."

He turned his eyes upon Jack French, who stood looking down sadly upon him.

"You have been friend to my son," he said. "You will guide him still?"

French dropped quickly on his knee, took him by the hand and said, "I will be to him a brother."

The old man turned his face and said, "Paulina."

"She is here," said old Portnoff, "but she can't move."

At the sound of his voice, the woman struggled up to her knees, crawled over to his side, the blood flowing from her wound, and taking his hand, held it to her lips.

"Paulina," he said, "you have done well—you are—my wife again—come near me."

The woman made an inarticulate moan like some dumb beast, and lifted her face toward him.

"Kiss me," he said.

"Ah, my lord," she cried, sobbing wildly, "my dear lord, I dare not."

"Kiss me," he said again.

"Now let me die," she cried, kissing him on the lips, and falling down in a faint beside him.

Brown lifted her and laid her in Portnoff's arms. The dying man lay silent, gathering his strength. He was breathing now with great difficulty.

"My son! I cannot see you—"

Brown came and took Kalman's place.

"Here I am, father," said Kalman, kneeling beside him and holding his two hands.

"Bid—my daughter Irma—farewell! She will be safe with you." Then after a pause he whispered, "In my pocket."

Kalman understood, found a packet, and from it drew the miniature of his mother.

"I give you this," said the father, lifting it with difficulty to his lips. "No curse with it now—only blessing—farewell—you have brought me joy—let me see her face—ah, dear heart—" he said, fastening his glazing eyes upon the beautiful face, "I come to you—ah! freedom!—sweet freedom at last!—and love—all love! My son—farewell!—my love!"

"Dear God!" cried Kalman, "Jesu, have pity and save!"

A smile as of an infant falling asleep played over the rugged face, while the poor lips whispered, "At last—freedom!—and—love!"

He breathed once, deep and long, and then no more. The long, long fight was done, the fight for freedom and for love.

Chapter XIX

My Foreigner

The Night Hawk Mining Company, after a period of doubt and struggle, was solidly on its feet at last. True, its dividends were not large, but at least it was paying its way, and it stood well among the financial institutions of the country. Its satisfactory condition was accounted for by its President, Sir Robert Menzies, at the last Annual Meeting of the Company, in the following words: "It is to the fidelity, diligence, good judgment, and ability to handle men, shown by our young Manager, Mr. Kalmar, during the past five years, that the Company owes its present excellent standing."

The Foreign Colony and the mine reacted upon each other, to their mutual advantage, the one furnishing labourers, the other work and cash. The colony had greatly prospered on this account, but perhaps more on account of the influence of Dr. Brown and his mission. The establishment of a Government school had relieved the missionary of an exacting and laborious department of his work, and allowed him to devote himself to his Hospital and his Training Home. The changes apparent in the colony, largely as the result of Dr. Brown's labours, were truly remarkable. The creating of a market for their produce by the advent of the railway, and for their labour by the development of the mine, brought the Galician people wealth, but the influence of

Dr. Brown himself, and of his Home, and of his Hospital, was apparent in the life and character of the people, and especially of the younger generation. The old mud-plastered cabins were giving place to neat frame houses, each surrounded by its garden of vegetables and flowers. In dress, the sheep skin and the shawl were being exchanged for the ready-made suit and the hat of latest style. The Hospital, with its staff of trained nurses under the direction of the young matron, the charming Miss Irma, by its ministrations to the sick, and more by the spirit that breathed through its whole service, wrought in the Galician mind a new temper and a new ideal. In the Training Home fifty Galician girls were being indoctrinated into that most noble of all sciences, the science of home-making, and were gaining practical experience in all the cognate sciences and arts.

At the Night Hawk ranch too were all the signs of the new order of things. Fenced fields and imported stock, a new ranch house with stables and granaries, were some of the indications that the coming of the market for the produce of the ranch had synchronized with the making of the man for its administration. The call of the New Time, and the appeal of the New Ideal, that came through the railroad, the mine, but, more than both, through the Mission and its founder, found a response in the heart of Jack French. The old *laissez faire* of the pioneer days gave place to a sense of responsibility for opportunity, and to habits of decisive and prompt attention to the business of the hour. Five years of intelligent study of conditions, of steady application to duty, had brought success not in wealth alone, but in character and in influence.

But upon Kalman, more than upon any other, these five years had left their mark. The hard grind of daily work, the daily burden of administration, had toughened the fibre of his character and hardened the temper of his spirit, and this hardening and toughening could be seen in every line of his face and in every motion of his body. Twice during the five years he had been sent by Jack French to the city for a three months' term in a Business College, where he learned to know, not only the books of his College curriculum, but, through Jack's introductions, the men who were doing big things for the country. He had returned to his place and to his work in the mine with vision enlarged, ideal exalted, and with the purpose strengthened to make the best out of life. In every sense the years had made a man of him. He was as tall as Jack, lithe and strong; in mind keen and quick, in action resolute. To those he met in the world of labour and of business he seemed hard. To his old friends on the ranch or at the Mission, up through all the hardness there welled those springs that come from a heart kind, loyal, and true. Among the Galicians of the colony, he was their acknowledged leader, because he did justly by them and because, although a Canadian among Canadians, he never forgot to own and to honour the Slav blood that flowed in his veins, and to labour for the advancement of his people.

But full of work and ambition as he was, yet there were times when Jack French read in his eyes the hunger of his heart. For after all, it is in the heart a man carries his life, it is through the heart come his finest ideals, from the heart his truest words and deeds.

At one such time, and the week before she came again, Jack French, looking through the window of his own heart and filled with a great pity for the young man who had come to be more than brother to him, had ventured to speak. But only once, for with such finality of tone and manner as made answer impossible, Kalman had made reply.

"No, Jack, I had my dream. It was great while it lasted, but it is past, and I shall dream no more."

"Kalman, my boy, don't make a mistake. Life is a long thing, and can be very dreary." There was no mistaking the pain in Jack's voice.

"Is it, Jack?" said Kalman. "I am afraid you are right. But I can never forget—my father was a foreigner, and I am one, and the tragedy of that awful night can never be wiped from her mind. The curse of it I must bear!"

"But, Kalman, you are not ashamed of your blood—of your father?"

Then Kalman lifted up his head and his voice rang out. "Of my blood? No. But it is not hers. Of my father? No. To me he was the just avenger of a great cause. But to her," his voice sank to a hoarse whisper, "he was a murderer! No, Jack, it may not be."

"But, Kalman, my boy," remonstrated Jack, "think of all—"

"Think? For these five years I have thought till my heart is sore with thinking! No, Jack, don't fret. I don't. Thank God there are other things. There is work, a people to help, a country to serve."

"Other things!" said French bitterly. "True, there are, and great things, but, Kalman, boy, I have tried them, and to-night after thirty years, as I speak to you—my God!—my heart is sick of hunger for something better than things! Love! my boy, love is the best!"

"Poor Jack!" said Kalman softly, "dear old boy!" and went out. But of that hunger of the heart they never spoke again.

And now at the end of five years' absence she was coming again. How vivid to Kalman was his remembrance of the last sight he had of her. It was at the Night Hawk ranch, and on the night succeeding that of the tragedy at the mine. In the inner room, beside his father's body, he was sitting, his mind busy with the tragic pathos of that grief-tortured, storm-beaten life. Step by step, as far as he knew it, he was tracing the tear-wet, blood-stained path that life had taken; its dreadful scenes of blood and heart agony were passing before his mind; when gradually he became aware that in the next room the Sergeant, with bluff and almost brutal straightforwardness, was telling her the story of Rosenblatt's dreadful end. "And then, begad! after grilling the wretch for all that time, didn't the infernal, bloodthirsty fiend in the most cheerful manner touch off the powder and blow the man into eternity." Then through the thin partition he heard her faint cry of horror. He remembered how, at the Sergeant's description of his father, something seemed to go wrong in his brain. He had a dim remembrance of how, dazed with rage, he had felt his way out to the next room, and cried,

"You defamer of the dead! you will lie no more!" He had a vivid picture of how in horror she had fled from him while he dragged out the Sergeant by the throat into the night, and how he had been torn from him by the united efforts of Brown and French together. He remembered how, after the funeral service, when he had grown master of himself again, he had offered the Sergeant his humble apology before them all. But most vivid of all was his memory of the look of fear and repulsion in her eyes when he came near her. And that was the last look he had had of her. Gladly would he have run away from meeting her again; but this he could not do, for Jack's sake and for his own. Carefully he rehearsed the scene, what he would say, and how he would carry himself; with what rigid self-control and with what easy indifference he would greet her.

But the meeting was quite other than he had planned. It was at the mine. One shiny September morning the heavy cars were just starting down the incline to the mine below, when through the carelessness of the operator the brake of the great drum slipped, and on being applied again with reckless force, broke, and the car was off, bringing destruction to half a dozen men at the bottom of the shaft. Quick as a flash of light, Kalman sprang to the racing cog wheels, threw in a heavy coat that happened to be lying near, and then, as the machinery slowed, thrust in a handspike and checked the descent of the runaway car. It took less than two seconds to see, to plan, to execute.

"Great work!" exclaimed a voice behind him.

He turned and saw Sir Robert Menzies, and between him and French, his daughter Marjorie.

"Glad to see you, Sir Robert," he exclaimed heartily.

"That was splendid!" said his daughter, pale and shaken by what she had seen.

One keen searching look he thrust in through her eyes, scanning her soul. Bravely, frankly, she gave him back his look. Kalman drew a deep breath. It was as if he had been on a long voyage of discovery, how long he could not tell. But what he had seen brought comfort to his heart. She had not shrunk from him.

"That was fine!" cried Marjorie again, offering him her hand.

"I am afraid," he said, holding back his, "that my hand is not clean enough to shake with you."

"Give it to me," she said almost imperiously. "It is the hand of a brave man and good."

Her tone was one of warm and genuine admiration. All Kalman's practised self-control deserted him. He felt the hot blood rising in his face. With a great effort he regained command of himself and began pointing out the features of interest in the mine.

"Great changes have taken place in the last five years," she said, looking down the ravine, disfigured by all the sordid accompaniments of a coal mine.

"Yes, great changes," said Kalman.

"At Wakota, too, there are great changes," she said, walking a little apart from the others. "That Mr. Brown has done wonderful things for those foreigners."

"Yes," said Kalman proudly, "he has done great things for my people."

"They are becoming good Canadians," replied Marjorie, her colour showing that she had noted his tone and meaning.

"Yes, they will be good Canadians," said Kalman. "They are good Canadians now. They are my best men. None can touch them in the mine, and they are good farmers too."

"I am sure they are," cried Marjorie heartily. "How wonderful the power of this country of yours to transform men! It is a wonderful country, Canada."

"That it is," cried Kalman with enthusiasm. "No man can tell, for no man knows the magnificence of its possibilities. We have only skirted round the edge and scratched its surface."

"It is a fine thing," said Marjorie, "to have a country to be made, and it is fine to be a man and have a part in the making of it."

"Yes," agreed Kalman, "it is fine."

"I envy you," cried Marjorie with enthusiasm.

A shadow fell on Kalman's face. "I don't know that you need to, after all."

Then she said good-by, leaving him with heart throbbing and nerves tingling to his finger tips. Ah, how dear she was! What mad folly to think he could forget her! Every glance of her eye, every tone in her soft Scotch voice, every motion of hand and body, how familiar they all were! Like the faint elusive perfume from the clover fields of child-hood, they smote upon his senses with intoxicating power. Standing there tingling and trembling, he made one firm resolve. Never would he see her again. To-morrow he would make a long-planned trip to the city. He dared not wait another day. To-morrow? No, that was Sunday. He would spend one full happy day in that ravine seeking to recatch the emotions that had thrilled his boy's heart on that great night five years ago, and having thus filled his heart, he would take his departure without seeing her again.

It was the custom of the people of the ranch to spend Sunday afternoon at the Mission. So without a word even to French, calling his dogs, Captain and Queen, Kalman rode down the trail that led past the lake and toward the Night Hawk ravine. By that same trail he had gone on that memorable afternoon, and though five years had passed, the thoughts, the imaginings of that day, were as freshly present with him as if it had been but yesterday. And though they were the thoughts and imaginings of a mere boy, yet to-day they seemed to him good and worthy of his manhood.

Down the trail, well beaten now, through the golden poplars he rode, his dogs behind him, till he reached the pitch of the ravine. There, where he had scrambled down, a bridle path led now. It was very different, and yet how much remained unchanged. There was the same glorious sun raining down his golden beams upon the yellow poplar leaves, the same air, sweet and genial, in him the same heart, and before him the same face, but sweeter it seemed, and eyes the same that danced with every sunbeam and lured him on. He was living again the rapture of his boyhood's first great passion.

At the mine's mouth he paused. Not a feature remained of the cave that he had discovered five years ago, but sitting there upon his horse, how readily he reconstructed the scene! Ah, how easy it was! Every line of that cave, the new fresh earth, the gleaming black seam, the very stones in the walls, he could replace. Carefully, deliberately, he recalled the incidents of the evening spent in the cave: the very words she spoke; how her lips moved as she spoke them; how her eyes glanced, now straight at him, now from under the drooping lids; how she smiled, how she wept, how she laughed aloud; how her face shone with the firelight playing on it, and the soul light radiating through it. He revelled in the memory of it all. There was the very spot where Mr. Penny had lain in vocal slumber. Here he had stood with the snowstorm beating on his face. He resolved to trace step by step the path he had taken that night, and to taste again the bliss of which he had drunk so deep. And all the while, as he rode down the gorge, underneath the rapture of remembering, he was conscious of an exquisite pain. But he would go through with it. He would not allow the pain to spoil his day, his last day near her. Down by the running water, as on that night, underneath and through the crowding trees, out to where the gorge widened into the valley, he rode. When hark! He paused. Was that Queen's bay? Surely it was. "A wolf?" he thought. "No, there are none left in the glen." He shrank from meeting any one that afternoon. He waited to hear again that deep, soft trumpet note, and strained his ear for voices. But all was still except for the falling of a ripe leaf now and then through the trees. He hated to give up the afternoon he had planned.

He rode on. He reached the more open timber. He remembered that it was here he had first caught the sound of voices behind that blinding drift. Through the poplars he pressed his horse. It was at this very spot that, through an opening in the storm, he had first caught sight—what! His heart stood still, and then leaped into his throat. There, on the very spot where he had seen her that night, she stood again to-day! Was it a vision of his fond imagination? He passed his hand over his eyes. No, she was there still! standing among the golden poplars, the sunlight falling all around her. With all his boyhood's frenzy in his heart, he gazed at her till she turned and looked toward him. A moment more, with his spurs into his horse's side, he crashed through the scrub and was at her side.

"You! you!" he cried, in the old cry. "Marjorie! Marjorie!"

Once more he had her in his arms. Once more he was kissing her face, her eyes, her lips. Once more she was crying, "Oh, Kalman! Stop! You must stop! You must stop!" And then, as before, she laid her head upon his breast, sobbing, "When I saw the dogs I feared you would come, but I could not run away. Oh, you must stop! Oh, I am so happy!" And then he put her from him and looked at her.

"Marjorie," he said, "tell me it is no dream, that it is you, that you are mine! Yes," he shouted aloud, "do you hear me? You are mine! Before Heaven I say it! No man, nothing shall take you from me!"

"Hush, Kalman!" she cried, coming to him and laying her hand upon his lips; "they are just down by the river there."

"Who are they? I care not who they are, now that you are mine!"

"And oh, how near I was to losing you!" she cried. "You were going away to-morrow, and I should have broken my heart."

"Ah, dear heart! How could I know?" he said. "How could I know you could ever love a foreigner, the son of a—"

"The son of a hero, who paid out his life for a great cause," she cried with a sob. "Oh, Kalman, I have been there. I have seen the people, your father's people."

Kalman's face was pale, his voice shaking. "You have seen? You understand? You do not shrink from me?" He felt his very soul trembling in the balance.

"Shrink from you!" she cried in scorn. "Were I Russian, I should be like your father!"

"Now God be thanked!" cried Kalman. "That fear is gone. I fear nothing else. Ah, how brave you are, sweetheart!"

"Stop, Kalman! Man, man, you are terrible. Let me go! They are coming!"

"Hello there! Steady all." It was Brown's voice. "Now, then, what's this?"

Awhile they stood side by side, then Marjorie came shyly to Sir Robert.

"I didn't mean to, father," she said penitently, "not a bit. But I couldn't help myself. He just made me."

Sir Robert kissed her.

Kalman stepped forward. "And I couldn't help it, Sir," he said. "I tried my best not to. Will you give her to me?"

"Listen to him, now, will you?" said Sir Robert, shaking him warmly by the hand. "It wasn't the fault of either of them."

"Quite true, Sir," said French gravely. "I'm afraid it was partly mine. I saw the dogs—I thought it would be good for us three to take the other trail."

"Blame me, Sir," said Brown penitently. "It was I who helped to conquer her aversion to the foreigner by showing her his many excellences. Yes," continued Brown in a reminiscent manner, "I seem to recall how a certain young lady into these ears made solemn declaration that never, never could she love one of those foreigners."

"Ah," said Marjorie with sweet and serious emphasis, "but not my foreigner, my Canadian foreigner."

Afterword

You could say that Ralph Connor attended the birth of Canadian literature as a field of serious study, and that he was almost immediately dismissed from it. When *The Foreigner* was first published in 1909, Reverend Charles William Gordon's *nom de plume* of "Ralph Connor" was a household name throughout the English-speaking world. He was the first Canadian to become an international literary star, selling millions of books in Canada, the USA, Britain, New Zealand, and Australia. Despite his enormous success and his serving as one of the early presidents of the Canadian Authors Association, however, Connor never found favour with the literary establishment. In 1922, J.D. Logan, the Acadia University professor who is credited with giving the first course of lectures in Canadian Literature at any university, wrote to Lorne Pierce, the editor at the Ryerson Press in Toronto who was compiling the field-defining Makers of Canadian Literature Series, that Connor's "work, both in substance and in artistry, is a concoction so vile that it ranks with literature in the same way that bootlegger booze ranks with real Scotch whiskey" (qtd. in Karr 191). Gordon himself admitted that he "had not the slightest ambition to be a writer [and] made little effort after polished literary style" (150–51). Scholars have largely agreed with these views. George Woodcock's

1988 assessment is representative: "Gordon's novels should be required reading for Canadian social historians, but his place in a serious critical work . . . is at best marginal, and justifiable only because he was present so long and so copiously in Canadian bookstores and on Canadian bookshelves" (17). Even his relevance for social history gets questioned when John Lennox concludes that Connor's books describe a "Canadian identity that had begun to pass away as he began to write about it" and that therefore "his books exist, with all their faults, as signposts of a Canada that no longer exists" (149). According to this line of thought, we acknowledge these signposts of a faded past but quickly insist that we moderns have moved beyond them. Connor is a sign of a past we would rather not connect in any direct way to the present.

With the recent turn to a cultural-studies-influenced approach to Canadian literature, in which the primary aim has not been so much to sort out "high" art from "low" but instead to study how literary works circulate in, articulate, and shape cultural formations, some critics have shown renewed interest in releasing Ralph Connor from historical quarantine and reconnecting him to the present. In *Authors and Audiences: Popular Canadian Fiction in the Early Twentieth Century* (2000), for example, Clarence Karr analyzes Connor's career in some detail to understand the rise in early-twentieth-century Canada of popular fiction, a form of writing and a book economy that has continued to increase in social influence. In *Dominion and Agency: Copyright and the Structuring of the Canadian Book Trade, 1867–1918* (2011), Eli MacLaren devotes a chapter to the publishing history of Connor's first novel, *Black Rock*, as a case study of how early Canadian authors negotiated conflicting and uneven copyright regulations between the United States, Britain, and Canada, once again an ongoing topic of concern. And in *White Civility: The Literary Project of English Canada* (2006), I discuss a range of Connor's novels in a study that traces the formulation of a specific form of whiteness based on a British model of civility that was naturalized between the late nineteenth and early twentieth centuries into a definitive norm for English Canadian cultural identity that remains entrenched to this day. Connor's works are getting renewed attention, not so much as markers of a society that either never existed or has faded away, but as ways we can track aesthetic tastes, literary forms, and social and economic conditions as well as cultural assumptions that remain influential today.

This renewed interest may suggest why Connor might be reissued now, but, among his thirty-two published volumes, why republish *The Foreigner*? Others of his novels, such as *The Man from Glengarry* (1901) and *Glengarry School Days* (1902), have been repeatedly reissued in the New Canadian Library series by McClelland & Stewart, but aside from a failed effort to reissue *The Foreigner* in the University of Toronto Press's Social History of Canada series in the 1970s, this novel has lain dormant. I submit that this particular novel is worthy of reissuing because there is a lot to learn from it. Among the Connor novels, *The Foreigner* stands out. Most of his novels grew out of Gordon's own biography, telling the story of a young Scottish Canadian male protagonist (usually from Ontario) who struggles against adversity to develop the kind of rugged, socially responsible character that makes him a natural leader in a resource-rich, expanding Canada (usually in the west). This story is pretty much Connor's standard formula. *The Foreigner*, by contrast, tracks the career of a different kind of character by featuring as its protagonist one of the non-English-speaking immigrants that Wilfrid Laurier's Minister of the Interior, Clifford Sifton, had aggressively recruited in the late 1890s and early 1900s to populate the territories the Canadian government had recently purchased from the Hudson's Bay Company in 1870. Among Connor's many novels, then, this one encourages us to read something different. It urges us to read *for* difference, which is to say that it turns our attention to how the formula that had made Connor into a household name encounters people and ideas that it marks as foreign to its own standard procedure.

With this aim of reading for an encounter with difference in mind, I would like to outline three vectors that I think would reward further analysis. First, there is a lot to learn from the career of the novel itself, as it offers a case study in which we can examine how the foreign figures in what was happening in the marketing and distribution of popular Canadian writing at the turn of the twentieth century. Second, there is a lot to learn from the role difference plays within the genre of the novel—that is, from the novel's form and structure—and what its method can tell us about its intended impact. Finally, there is a lot to learn about the context of the novel, which is to say, what its deployment of the foreign reveals about the world it assumed its audience would appreciate and recognize.

The Career of *The Foreigner*

Connor was at the height of his popularity when he wrote *The Foreigner*. He had sold 140,348 copies of his previous books in Canada, 1,695,696 in the USA, and 279,579 in Britain and the colonies (mostly New Zealand and Australia), for a total of 2,115,623 (Karr 53). *The Foreigner* itself was the second national bestseller the year it was published in 1909 and tenth in 1910 (Lennox 137). Connor went on to publish a total of twenty-three novels, each selling between 20,000 and 60,000 copies in Canada alone well into the 1920s (Karr 53). There are many other signs of his immense popularity. His first novel, *Black Rock* (1898), recorded eleven pirated editions (Watt 11), and by 1902 his British publisher wrote to say he was matching sales with Rudyard Kipling (Karr 68). The novel he published that year, *Glengarry School Days*, sold over 5 million copies before Gordon's death in 1937 (Waterston 186). Long after scholars say his popularity had waned in the 1920s, the Toronto Public Library could hardly keep its 700 copies of Connor's novels on the shelves (Karr 28). Six of his novels were made into movies in the 1920s, including *The Foreigner* retitled as *God's Crucible* (Karr 179–86). Mary Vipond's studies of Canadian bestsellers in the first thirty years of the twentieth century indicate that Connor was far and away Canada's most financially successful writer before the First World War, outstripping even Robert Service, L.M. Montgomery, Gilbert Parker, Nellie L. McClung, and Stephen Leacock. He appeared fifteen times in the top ten sales in Canada between 1899 and 1918, and he fell behind only Montgomery in the top ten listings between 1919 and 1928 (see Vipond's two articles). After his novel *The Doctor* (1906) passed 30,000 sales within weeks of publication, W.E. Robertson at the Westminster publishing company in Toronto wrote to Gordon: "Just think of it! One copy for every 100 English-speaking people in Canada" (qtd. in Karr 53). A leading contender for nomination as Canada's first celebrity author, Connor was feted and hosted not just by Canadians but by major figures around the world, including industrialists like Henry Ford (Ferré 60) and political leaders such as Teddy Roosevelt, Woodrow Wilson, Wilfrid Laurier, and Herbert Asquith (Thompson and Thompson 159). Seeing persuasive power in his enormous popularity, the Borden government in Ottawa commissioned him to tour the United States to urge their government to join the Great War of 1914–1918. So great was the press of crowds seeking his autograph that police were called to hold back the crush (Ferré 60).

Connor's remarkable career as an author was possible because he lived in what Karr has called the "golden age" of mass publishing. A concatenation of developments produced the conditions for this golden age. For one thing, new technologies made it possible to produce books much more cheaply and quickly than ever before. Whereas the printing press had existed since the 1450s, when Gutenberg converted a wine press into a machine that could press ink onto paper, the increasing availability of cheap electricity just as Connor began writing in the 1890s meant that presses now operated at a speed that could produce millions of pages in short order. These pages could be folded, the bindings sewn, and covers glued on in mass-production assembly-line-style factories undreamed of in a fair-copyist's scriptorium or a Grub Street print shop. Electricity also meant that readers could sit up late and read into the night hours without having to trim the wick or clean the soot from a lamp's glass chimney. The expansion of forest industries meant paper was getting cheaper and more abundant.

The plot of *The Foreigner* opens in the year 1884, precisely the period when Sir John A. Macdonald's national policy was pushing the "sea to sea" transcontinental railway towards completion. The timing is no happenstance, for a major contribution to Connor's career, let alone the career of books more generally, came from the growing network of railways in Canada and around the world. Railways made it cheap to bring large quantities of paper from the resource frontiers of the north and west to the big city presses. Central to turn-of-the-century processes of national economic and social consolidation, they made it possible to establish national postal services with their associated postage stamps, postal money orders, postcard advertising, bulk mail rates, free rural delivery, and mail order catalogues. Rail travellers no longer had to keep an eye on the horses or the carriage driver, and the smooth ride in a well-lighted railcar meant they could read to while away the journey. These developments, too, called for the production of cheap, lightweight reading material that people could tuck under their arms as they passed from platform to railcar to taxi. So newsagents established shops at train stations where they sold newspapers, popular magazines, and, of course, books (Karr 27–32; Manguel 141–42). In 1822, the British publisher Pickering had been the first to use cloth rather than expensive leather to bind books, and, because cloth can absorb ink, publishers soon realized they could catch the eyes of fellow railway passengers with advertisements printed there—or, better yet, on the paper slip covers in which they wrapped the new, travel-sized books. So books became advertisements for other books and products. Through the mid-nineteenth century, their illustrated covers became more colourful and the cardboard made of thinner and thinner stock until they become known as "paperbacks." As Alberto Manguel puts it in *A History of Reading* (1996), compared with the morocco-bound tomes of the great libraries, the new, portable "book was a less aristocratic object, less forbidding, less grand. It shared with the reader a certain middle-class elegance that was economical yet pleasing" (140).

As Manguel indicates, the new physical properties of the book appealed to a new kind of reading public. Participation in the modern world of railways, mass industrialization, and increasingly technical employment required a self-improving, practically educated populace. Literacy rates increased dramatically during Connor's writing career, rising to 90 per cent of Canadians by the end of the 1920s (Karr 32). And the hunger for books meant that the number of bookstores in Canada rose from 70 in 1871 to 309 in 1895, and from 892 in 1911 to 1,274 in 1921 (Karr 29). These new readers were not Eatonian or Oxonian elites, trained in the classics, who would inherit family fortunes. They were upwardly mobile workers who read for entertainment, as well as to improve their lot in life.

Charles William Gordon's Connor novels offered an appealing formula to these electric-lighted, railway-carriaged, modernizing readers. The world around them may be flying past their carriage window at previously unimaginable speeds, but a Ralph Connor novel guaranteed a number of things. It would serve up heart-pounding adventure that kept pace with the rapid movement of the wheels underneath them and hurry the hours to their destination. The high derring-do of the story would inspire and motivate them in the midst of struggle and change. It reassured them that decisive individual action could influence the course of history. Furthermore, readers would be assured that narrative excitement could serve a moral purpose. The story would move the heart and damp the eye with romance, whether that of love and marriage or of family, assuring readers that loyalty in these domains could endure the shocks of changing times. Furthermore, a

Connor novel would show how religious and ethnic traditions, drawn from Gordon's own Scottish Presbyterian roots, could provide the moral values to negotiate these changes, *if* those traditions evolved to face the challenges of a Canada that was expanding its influence in a quickly reconfiguring, transforming world. A Connor novel helped readers envision a heroic, religious encounter with the new conditions of techno-industrial expansion—the very conditions that made it possible for his novels to become bestsellers—and so to function as an instructive allegory for how to live in the modern world.

There are critics who have accused Connor of avoiding modernity, of writing anti-modern fictions (Lennox 149), and therefore of misfitting the emergence in his lifetime of "high" modernists such as James Joyce and T.S. Eliot or, in Canada, Frederick Philip Grove and Martha Ostenso. There is no mistaking the massive aesthetic and philosophical distance between, say, the heroic allegory of Connor's *The Gaspards of Pinecroft* (1923) and the existential bluntness of Grove's *Settlers of the Marsh* (1925) or the anti-patriarchal rebellion of Ostenso's *Wild Geese* (1925), even though all three novels were written by Manitoba authors within a couple of years of one another. But it makes little sense to prescribe a single response to the complex of conditions that we call modernity. The rarefied alienation of an art-for-art's-sake elite is a reasonable response to the crass commercialism and hustle of modernity, but so is a roll-up-your-sleeves formula for engagement.

Connor meant his novels to be a direct engagement with the modern world. One could say that *The Foreigner* addresses one of the most troubling questions of modernity: with the explosion of new technologies for mass production, mass transportation, and mass communication, what would happen to the logics of place, inheritance, and tradition? The mobility of people, products, and capital loosened the mutually enforcing ties of place, time, and natality. Why should not a burgeoning, ambitious nation like Canada purchase almost four million square miles of what had been called Rupert's Land and begin to pump it full of settlers who would turn the newly acquired lands into wheat, coal mines, and taxes? And, if the aspiring settlers could not be found in sufficient numbers from traditional sources in Great Britain and France, why not recruit them from regions such as the Ukraine, whose topography and climate was comparable to those of the newly purchased prairies? Canada's rapid expansion into the Great Plains threw a monkey wrench into the assumption of its founding elites that the new country would remain loyalist, white, and British, for expansion required what they perceived as "foreign" labour. The fact that British domination in the region was being established over Metis[1] and Indigenous contenders only through the use of force in 1870 and 1885, and that incoming British settlers themselves were mostly foreign to the area, did not deter the newly arrived elites from thinking of their new recruits as "foreigners." The railway had arrived in Winnipeg in 1884, the year Connor's novel opens, but it had not yet reached the segment being built from British Columbia through the Rockies. It was the railway that had brought General Middleton's troops to Saskatchewan in 1885 to crush Louis Riel, Gabriel Dumont, and the Metis who were trying to establish a locally responsible provincial government in the new province of Manitoba. It was the same railway that made Connor into a bestseller that also brought new immigrants from the port in Halifax across the continent to Winnipeg and transformed the city over the next twenty-five years into a massive immigrant encampment. And it was the encampment of "foreigners" in the 1890s that brought socially progressive Presbyterian church leaders, like Charles William Gordon and his friend J.S. Woodsworth, to Winnipeg to minister to what Woodsworth, in a book published the same year as Connor's, called *The Strangers within Our Gates, or Coming Canadians*.

"In Western Canada there is to be seen to-day that most fascinating of all human phenomena, the making of a nation," writes Connor in his preface to the novel *The Foreigner*. "Out of breeds diverse in traditions, in ideals, in speech, and in manner of life, Saxon and Slav, Teuton, Celt and Gaul, one people is being made. . . . It will be our wisdom to grip these peoples to us with living hooks of justice and charity till all lines of national cleavage disappear" (5). Here is Connor's direct encounter with messy modernity, his thesis for an encounter with strangers set within the standard formula of his hugely popular heroic allegories. How do "we" deal with difference, with the displacements of modernity? And who is "them"? Who has the right to claim citizenship and its rights? Who is foreign? How long does it take for those who are out of place to find themselves in place? And what kinds of accommodation are required for displaced peoples, thrown together by global economic and political forces, to form a workable political entity? These questions remain as urgent, and as fitfully addressed, today as they were in 1909.

The Genre of *The Foreigner*

I have called Connor's genre "heroic allegory," because his novels are generally *Bildungsromans* that trace a young man of obscure social origins whose inherent virtue is tried and tempered by familial adversity and the physical demands of a harsh and bracing landscape until, through a crisis requiring self-sacrifice and spiritual conversion that is usually inspired and guided by a strong female mentor, he emerges as a muscular Christian, a heroic model for a new, progressive social order. Connor's is a fiction of aspiration and inspiration narrated through a mixture of high-flown rhetoric and everyman vernacular that presents characters as types in a grand struggle to build a new society. Action, emotions, and gestures are all drawn broadly, theatrically, as if the novels were written to be made into the silent movies that were then the newest form of public entertainment.

It is important to see how this formula constitutes an engagement with, rather than a flight from, modernity. "Not far from the centre of the American Continent," writes Connor on the novel's opening page, midway between the Gulf and the Arctic Sea, on the rim of a plain, . . . beautiful in its sunlit glory, stands Winnipeg, the cosmopolitan capital of the last of the Anglo-Saxon Empires,—Winnipeg, City of the Plain, which from the eyes of the world cannot be hid. Miles away, secure in her sea-girt isle, is old London, port of all seas; miles away, breasting the beat of the Atlantic, sits New York, capital of the New World, and mart of the world Old and New; far away to the west lie the mighty cities of the Orient, Peking and Hong Kong, Tokio and Yokohama; and fair across the highway of the world's commerce sits Winnipeg, Empress of the Prairies. Her Trans-Continental railways thrust themselves in every direction,—south into the American Republic, east to the ports of the Atlantic, west to the Pacific, and north to the Great Inland Sea. (7)

Here is the heroic voice establishing its allegorical setting through an oratory of Biblical, globally confident, late-imperial cosmopolitanism, with its capital letters, its commanding geographical position within the world of international commerce shining like a beacon to the world, its unworried displacement of old London and penetration of American territory. This is the voice mass audiences of the 1910s consumed voraciously. A voice of confidence, of vision and possibility, a voice that could articulate, over the clatter of a vehicle's wheels, the roar of blast furnaces, and the babble of foreign languages, a collective mission. It is a heroic voice because it fights its way boldly through the collapse of old empires and the emergence of new ones to ultimate possibility. Paulina Kovac's boarding house, jammed with its forty-five garlic-eating, beer-swilling "Galician" workmen, may not seem to confirm Winnipeg as the "Empress of the Prairies," but when her rough little urchin of a stepson, Kalman Kalmar, grows into his coal mine and ranch in the resource-rich surrounding prairies, the potential of the western city will not be hid.

The heroic voice, however, must engage the grit of everyday life. And so it enters into dialogue with vernaculars of many kinds and types. "Y're wife will not be nadin' ye, I'm thinkin'," says the Irish washerwoman Mrs. Fitzpatrick (15). "Eet ees not my woman," replies the uncertainly ethnic and villainous Mr. Rosenblatt (15), who may be Ruthenian, Bukowinian, and/or Ukrainian, but is certainly the stereotype of the avaricious Jew. "It was the East meeting the West," explains the heroic orator, "the Slav facing the Anglo-Saxon. Between their points of view stretched generations of moral development. It was not a question of absolute moral character so much as a question of moral standards" (17). As with the opening orations about the new nation and the city of the plains, the vernaculars of difference here are deployed by the heroic voice into a grand allegory dramatizing the encounters of blood, race, and geocultural stereotype. It is a rhetoric of eugenic types that was, before Naziism showed the world the uses that could be made of the concept of race, perfectly consistent with progressive visions of the well-planned society (see Henderson; McLaren; Valverde). Note that for all the use of stereotypes, Connor's progressive narrator is careful to insist that "East" and "West" are not static, unchangeable categories. Difference is not determined by "absolute moral character" but by a time lag in "moral development" and the resulting differences in "moral standards."

We might say that, held up against the long and still lively debate between essentialists and constructionists (that is, between those who trace human differences to unchangeable biological features and those who trace differences to variation in social conditions), Connor's heroic allegory, though it leans heavily on the language of blood and essence, assumes that differences are the product of social circumstances and that they can therefore change. This assumption makes *The Foreigner*'s allegory an assimilationist fiction of social reform. Like other writers of the social gospel, such as the co-founder of the CCF party, J.S. Woodsworth, feminist politician Nellie L. McClung, and many others,

Connor stole from Marx to pay Jesus—which is to say that social reformers found Marx's teaching on the inequities of capital and the alienation of labour convincing, even as they rejected outright revolt as espoused by the Bolsheviks in 1917. Instead, they routed a more gradual path to liberation and a just social order through Christian concepts of personal and social conversion, being one's brother's keeper, and the forthright defence of the disadvantaged. The two most prominent characters in the social reform genre are the muscular Christian and the maternal feminist. These parts are played in *The Foreigner* by Mrs. Margaret French and Dr. Wright in the first half of the novel, when as a team or singly they invade Paulina's home to help the police break up a fight (65–74) or to apprehend her eczema-ridden children and take them to the hospital (97–99), and then go on to force bigoted prison guards to recognize prisoners' rights at the jail (101–03). The muscular-maternal role is picked up again by Reverend Brown in the second half of the novel as he builds a church, a school, and a hospital to serve the Galician colony and then punches Rosenblatt in the face when he tries to claim-jump the hero Kalman's coal mine (245). The novel of social reform presents social intervention as a class-reorganizing adventure. Indeed, much of the high derring-do in *The Foreigner* rises from the heroic acts of the agents of social change. The fight scenes, the drawn knives and bloodshed, the mysterious bearded-man disguises, the treacherous murder plots, and the strings of dynamite—these all arise when the courageous muscular Christian confronts the ignorance and folly of greed, dark oaths of revenge, and what Connor's narrator calls the gap in moral development.

The genre of social reform bolstered confidence in a kind of divinely ordained social Darwinism. Renowned theologian Henry Drummond of New College, Edinburgh, where Gordon had studied, influenced a whole generation of social progressives when he argued against the divide between science and religion in his *Natural Law in the Spiritual World* (1882) and *The Ascent of Man* (1894), suggesting

instead that, while the "Struggle for Life" had defined the first movement of evolution, its second phase turned to the "Struggle for the
Life of Others," which he said defined the mission of the Christian
era. According to Drummond, the "Mother Principle" was the catalyst
whereby male selfishness and egoism could be overcome by maternal
self-sacrifice for the lives of others, producing a society characterized
by cooperation instead of competition (Mack 142–45). Such a theology
contains and tempers the bloodless cruelty of the survival of the fittest,
as well as the bloody cruelty of political revolution, within the romance
of the family. Now that evolution has shifted beyond its initial phase
of fierce competition, the human family can, in the new era, evolve
together. But the muscular Christian and the maternal feminist need
an Other to struggle with and for. Enter the foreigner, the stranger at
the gates, perpetually at the gates, for whose life, over whose life, the
Christian parents must struggle. And the path of evolution within that
family is predetermined. There is no possibility that social reform can
go foreign. Instead, in the words of Brown, it will absorb this "undigested foreign mass" into the body politic (181): "I can teach them English, and then I am going to doctor them, and, if they'll let me, teach
them some of the elements of domestic science; in short, do anything
to make them good Christians and good Canadians, which is the same
thing" (180). Before the First World War and the Great Depression
kicked the stuffing out of optimistic assumptions of human progress
and social evolution, the genre of social reform was full of confidence
in the rightness of its own mission.

The Context of *The Foreigner*

In 1909, three influential books were published that focused on
Winnipeg and Manitoba: I have mentioned Connor's *The Foreigner*
and Woodsworth's *Strangers within Our Gates* but have not yet
referred to the historian George Bryce's *The Romantic Settlement*

of Lord Selkirk's Colonists. All three books represent a repositioning of Canadian self-understanding from Ontario and Quebec to the North West as the driving force of the expanding nation. Whereas Connor's and Woodsworth's books focused on the challenge of the foreign in a Winnipeg that represents the epicentre of Canada's rapidly changing demographics, Bryce's research into the history of a Red River colony that predated the War of 1812 promoted a history of British settlement in the region that did not take its origins exclusively from central Canada. In *Promise of Eden: The Canadian Expansionist Movement and the Idea of the West, 1856–1900* (1980), Doug Owram shows how the scientific expeditions led by Henry Youle Hind and John Palliser in 1857–1859 and by John Macoun in 1880 shifted the popular impression of the North West from that of a desert wasteland to a garden in waiting. Bryce and the "Manitoba school" built on this revised image of the North West to establish a historical narrative for understanding western Canada as fully capable of being self-sufficient. Contained within this narrative of British law and loyalty in the Selkirk colony, writes Owram,

> was a rejection of the eastern, and therefore derivative, nature of the contemporary western society. . . . In fact, it could be argued that the westerner, with his unique blend of experience, opportunity, and history, best epitomized the spirit of the young Dominion of Canada. The West had lifted British North America from provincialism to nationalism and only the westerner could completely understand the new role Canada had assumed in the Empire and the world. (216)

These three 1909 publications, then, present two major developments in emerging Canadian national consciousness: the concept of the North West as rising to the fore in Canada's self-understanding and the way in which that expansion into the North West introduced the necessity and the question of non-charter-group peoples in the emerging nation (for more on the myth of the north in Canada, see Berger, "True"; Hulan).

The North West signified Canada's future. Having been transformed from wasteland into a source of agricultural and mineral bounty, it fed Canada's ambitions of becoming the breadbasket and motherlode for a reconfigured British empire that would displace the tiny isles between the Atlantic and the North Sea as its centre (see Berger, *Sense* 259–61). "What say you, little puffing steam-fed industry of England, to the industry of Coming Canada," Stephen Leacock boasted about Canada's hydroelectric potential in 1907. "Think you, you can heave your coal hard enough, sweating and grunting with your shovel to keep pace with the snow-fed cataracts of the north?" (6–7). The North West functioned not only as a resource frontier but also as a crucible to smelt and test the mettle of the emerging nation (Lennox 113, 132). The rigours of its cold climate required thrift, industry, and endurance, the kind of initiative and persistence that Canadian imperialists believed people from southern climates could never muster. This is why Margaret French sends Kalman, a southeastern European youth at risk of juvenile detention, to Jack French out in Saskatchewan, where the demands and disciplines of hard work and fresh air will "make a man of him" (139). The demanding North West functions as "God's Crucible," the title the moviemaker Earnest Shipman gave to Kalman's story in 1922 (Karr 183–86). Connor is following here the line of thought advocated by Canadian leaders such as George Parkin, principal of Upper Canada College and world-travelling proponent of the Imperial Federation League, who

called the climate "one of our greatest blessings," because it functioned, in Darwinian terms, as "a persistent process of natural selection" by discouraging the immigration and successful settlement of tramps and lower races. . . . The stern climate, moreover, ensured that the Dominion would have no Negro problem "which weighs like a troublesome nightmare upon the civilization of the United States." (Berger, *Sense* 130–31)

The myth of the Canadian North West fed a racist Darwinist narrative of imperial expansion.

For this story of bold expansion to work, the region must be emptied of any vestige of legitimate prior habitation so that English immigrants such as Jack French can unproblematically possess a ranch in the Saskatchewan river country and "foreigners" like Kalman can prove their mettle by developing a coal mine in *terra nullius*. Bryce may have recognized the British–Metis skirmishes between the North-West and Hudson's Bay companies as significant in local history, but for the purposes of Connor's novel and imperialists such as Parkin, the traders and Indigenous dwellers of the North West were nomads and drifters who had no strong claim to the land. With their claims easily dismissed, the resource frontier can be subjected to the rule of "finders keepers" in favour of the newcomers. "It was all so clean, so fresh, so unspoiled to the boy" who has recently arrived at the Night Hawk Ranch "that it seemed as if he had dropped into a new world, remote from and unrelated to any other world he had hitherto known" (175). This fresh and bracing new world removes the incoming youth from the murky entanglements of his father's old-world loyalties and hereditary oaths of vengeance. It serves as a testing ground for his new energies, where he can step forth boldly into a world of progress, cooperative citizenship, and collective moral improvement.

The myth of newness also removes him from the murky ethics of the dispossession of the Cree, Metis, Salteaux, Assiniboine, and other Indigenous peoples who lived in the region. Significantly, for a novel that begins in 1884, Connor's book is resoundingly silent about the uprisings of 1870 and 1885—the *ê-mâyahkamikahk*, Cree for "where it went wrong" (McLeod 36). It does not mention the battles at Frog

Lake and Batoche that had been recently fought on the same river that flows by Jack's ranch and Kalman's mine. The novel's only allusion to these events illustrates how readily they can be disappeared. Kalman may breathe in fresh prairie air, but there is no such invigorating oxygen in this narrative for Malcolm Mackenzie, whose Scottish–Cree pedigree links him to the history of the Selkirk colony and the common-law marriages between fur traders and Indigenous women whose descendants participated in the uprisings of 1870 and 1885. We do not know how Jack French got his ranch. Could he have bought property that Mackenzie had given up for government-issued scrip, those pieces of paper that were supposed to compensate Metis and "halfbreeds" whose lands in the Red and Saskatchewan river watersheds had been confiscated? The novel does not speak to these details. Instead, we learn that when Mackenzie goes on a drinking binge, which is often, "his soft Scotch voice" and "genial manner" give way to the "guttural cries" and "quick crouching run" of "his Cree progenitors" (166). And when he is brought back to his senses by Jack's British authority, "the aboriginal blood lust" would give way to his better self as a "civilized man, subject to the restraint of a thousand years of life ordered by law" (167). Just as the arrival of Middleton's troops and Gatling guns on the railway signalled a dead end—literally—for Metis and Indigenous democracy, so too does the arrival of the railway in the environs of Night Hawk Ranch signal the Darwinist dismissal of Mackenzie from the heroic allegory of the emerging North West. "Mackenzie and his world must now disappear," the narrator explains, "in the wake of the red man and the buffalo before the railroad and the settler" (204). The onrush of progress, the unquestioned necessity of improvement and cultivation, explains his coming disappearance as simply a matter of natural evolution.

Behind Connor's naturalization of this Darwinist narrative of disappearance were much more deliberate actions of suppression, delay, and avoidance. Not only are the Metis uprisings suppressed in the narrative, so also is mention of the negotiations of Treaties One to Six, through which the government of Canada removed Cree, Anishinaabe (Ojibway), Metis, Salteaux, and Assiniboine peoples to reservations and believed that it had extinguished their claims to their traditional territories between northwestern Ontario and Alberta between 1871 and 1889. These critical developments in the annexation of the North West by the Dominion of Canada may be silenced in *The Foreigner*, but they have only grown more vociferous in the century since Connor's novel was published. Harold Cardinal and Walter Hildebrandt's interviews with Indigenous leaders throughout Saskatchewan collected in *Treaty Elders of Saskatchewan: Our Dream Is That Our Peoples Will One Day Be Clearly Recognized as Nations* (2000) make it clear that Indigenous oral histories do not accept the government record that the treaties extinguished their rights to the land and resources to the government (see esp. 62–63). Far from disappearing, the Metis have repeatedly campaigned over the past century for government recognition of their existence as a people and the promises that were made to them. The intensity and tenacity of this campaign has its most recent instance in *Manitoba Métis Federation Inc. v. Canada*, a Supreme Court decision of March 2013, in which the highest court in the country ruled that the federal government had reneged on its 1870 promises in the province-founding Manitoba Act to set aside 5,565 square kilometres of land for 7,000 children of the Red River Metis, land that includes what is now the city of Winnipeg. This ruling found that the government had deliberately delayed reserving this territory for the Metis in the precise period when immigrants were being sought to settle in the region—exactly when *The Foreigner* is set. By inaction, inattention, and foot-dragging, the government succeeded in displacing the Metis through inaction ("Métis"). More generally, current Canadian demographics indicate that the social Darwinist genocide failed utterly and devastatingly: in the first half of the twentieth century the Indigenous population in Canada grew by 29 per cent in comparison to the overall population, which grew by 161 per cent, but between 1951 and 2001 the Indigenous population grew sevenfold, almost three and a half times the growth rate of the overall population, which only doubled (Canada, "2001"). While at a conservative estimate more than three thousand Indigenous children died in the residential schools ("At Least") and many more were abused physically, emotionally, sexually, and spiritually, Indigenous and Metis peoples were emphatically not extinguished, nor were their understandings of the treaties or their claims upon land. Connor's narrator is right only in the immediate context: the railway did signal doom for Mackenzie and his generation in the North West. What that narrator did not foresee was how resilient Mackenzie's descendants would be, nor how the injustice hidden within that Darwinist narrative would refuse to disappear below the onrush of progress and development.

Connor's narrator may assume that Mackenzie and his ancestors could be extinguished, but the troubling genocidal afterlife of that assumption is if anything more rather than less alive today. How then do we understand Canada's treaties with First Nations, Metis, and Inuit now? What place do the Metis, who were included neither in the treaty process nor in the arrangements of the Indian Act, have in the national polity? More generally, how should Canadians understand the human relationship to land, nature, and resources, which were understood so differently by Indigenous peoples? How should flora and fauna, minerals, and running waters be understood and treated? If the North West can be imagined as a crucible in which the mettle of Canadian maturity and vision can be tested, how might we understand concepts such as "improvement," "progress," or "ethics" if prior inhabitants and their rights—human, animal, plant, and mineral—have not been extinguished? And how will we deal with our differences over these questions?

Despite its racist dismissal of Mackenzie from Canada's future, Connor's heroic allegory does intervene in the British-exclusive thinking that dominated Canadian expansionism of the early twentieth century. It does so by featuring a foreigner—to many readers of his time a suspicious figure indeed—in the story of Canada's expansion into the North West. Insofar as it challenges an Anglos-only immigration policy, it affirms a Canada that welcomes the strangers at the nation's gates; but insofar as it requires that strangers assimilate to mainstream British-Protestant whiteness, it anticipates and parallels the Multiculturalism Act's contradictory commitment to "preserve and enhance the use of languages other than English and French, while strengthening the status and use of the official languages of Canada" (Section 3.1.i). In both cases, we witness how the foreign other can be welcomed only if it does not threaten the primacy of Canada's charter groups. We can see the limits of this welcome by noting the characters in this allegory who, along with Mackenzie, are disqualified from the allegory's future: think of Kalman's father Michael Kalmar, the Russian zealot, whose patriotism may be honourable but whose vigilante vendetta disqualifies him from Canadian civility. His sometime wife, Paulina, is represented as unthinkingly loyal to his extremist cause, so she joins the rejected. Their nemesis and the novel's villain, Rosenblatt, whose avarice shows no awareness of justice or morality, places him too among the disappeared. Nor can Klazowski, the drunken Polish priest, be retained in the future community of the prairies. Each of these figures is an ethnically or racially laden stereotype. The "moral gap" is too wide for them to become Canadians. The novel makes much of how these figures represent old-world values and traditions that must be abandoned and defused so that the new world can get its new, progressive start. Kalman, for example, must go through a Gethsemane of the heart, wherein he must relinquish the "hereditary instincts of Slavic blood" that "cried out for vengeance" (243) until he can utter Christ's statement: "Father, forgive them, they know not what they do" (244). This conversion makes him a Christian and a Canadian, which according to Connor's Presbyterian missionary Brown is the same thing.

We can contrast these characters with others who *can* join the heroic allegory. And they are not all "foreigners." To make sure we do not interpret the allegory as entirely anti-Catholic, the virtuous and caring French-Canadian priest Père Garneau counterbalances the avarice and drunkenness of Klazowski. Nor is it just Kalman and his sister Irma, along with the colony of "Galicians," who must take up civil behaviour and the responsibility to build up a new country. The allegory of maturation and improvement also requires a conversion of the Englishman Jack French. French cannot rest upon Englishness alone to maintain his status in the emerging prairie community. He is an instance of the figure of the remittance man, a stock character in prairie fiction who, as a second son of an aristocratic family in England, will not inherit the family estate. He has therefore been sent to make his way in the colonies, where a monthly remittance is meant to establish him in his new enterprises. Like the aforementioned stock figure, French is in danger of drinking away his money and his ranch. Indeed, if Brown had not confronted him with his responsibility for Kalman's raising and welfare, and if it were not for the powerful corrective influence of Margaret French, he may easily have done so. French's story of conversion reminds the reader that even Englishness does not have an automatic entry into the allegory's future. The Englishman, too, must assimilate to the muscular Christian, progressive vision of social reform and improvement.

The theorist and social critic Sara Ahmed writes that the figure of the stranger does not pre-exist the moment in which she or he is recognized as stranger, but rather that the stranger is produced as alien or other by the mode of encounter itself (3). She explains: "Particularity does not belong to an-other, but names the meetings and encounters that produce or flesh out others, and hence *differentiates others from other others*" (144). Connor's allegorical formula, with its range of character "types," demonstrates how a particular stranger, the titular "foreigner," is created by means of its differentiation within and among a range of "other others." The desirable foreigner, the one Marjorie Menzies calls "my Canadian foreigner," is clearly differentiated from a variety of other rejected foreigners. He is also differentiated from figures like Jack French, who shores up his claim to Canadian citizenship by responding to the challenge of Kalman's assimilation, as well as from figures such as Margaret French and Reverend Brown, whose virtues allow them to assume their exemplary places in the temporal gap of moral development.

The allegorical formula that presents this differentiation between other others tips readily into the typology of race rhetoric. W.J. Mihaychuk, who reviewed *The Foreigner* in *The Canadian Magazine* in 1910, indicated that the novel's inaccuracies about "Galicians"—confusing Russians, Ruthenians, Bukovinians, Ukrainians, Hungarians, and more generally all those of "Slavic blood"—made him "sick at heart" (487). Humans are all one blood, Mihaychuk wrote, and we need less of the language of "breeds" and "bloods" (489). Almost seventy years later, in *Ukrainian Canadians: A Survey of Their Portrayal in English-Language Works* (1978), Frances Swyripa shows how confused Connor was about his characters: he marries Michael Kalmar, a Russian nobleman, to Paulina, a Galician peasant; he puts Rosenblatt, a Bukovinian, in cahoots with the Russian secret police; and he gives Kalman and Irma Hungarian names that misfit their description as Russians or Ukrainians (13–14). Indeed, Reverend Gordon himself came to regret his misrepresentations of "Galicians" in the novel. In his *Canadian Mosaic: The Making of a Northern Nation* (1938), John Murray Gibbon tells of how Winnipeggers who had read Connor's novel were inclined not to attend Gibbon's New Heritage Festival because it featured Polish and Ukrainian dancers. So he invited Gordon to meet one of the Polish dance troupes. After seeing these Eastern Europeans' finesse as dancers and talking with them, Gordon said, "I feel I have done them an injustice in my book" (Gibbon 277). We might see his regret as rising from the trap of the genre of heroic allegory, which had given him his career as a writer. For the genre itself assumes the hubris that was essential to the very elements that made it popular: its confident, heroic engagement in social reform from the unquestioned foundation of white, Protestant, Anglo-Celtic superiority, its progressive engagement with the complexities of modernity.

So, to return to my opening question: Why reissue a book like this? Connor regretted it, just as Woodsworth later regretted his *Strangers within Our Gates*. Many literary critics have regretted Connor's writing, too. It is not hard to scoff at its formulaic aesthetic, its racism, its naive ideas of romance and salvation. But it is important for Canadians in the twenty-first century to see what confidence looks like *from its other end*, from the perspectives of its rejected other others. For it is not only early-twentieth-century expansionism that lusts after confidence. Periods of massive and rapid change, like ours and Connor's, produce social and political complexities for which there are no easy and ready answers. It can become tiring in such circumstances to live with the ambiguities and compromises, the endless negotiations of difference, and to seek to regain the romance of certainty, the adventure of decisive action, the heroism in an allegory that has swagger. Whether that heroic allegory gets dramatized in the rapidly peopled North West or by NATO peacemakers in Afghanistan, whose guns and jets are more powerful and more expensive than those assigned the UN peacekeepers before them, the desire for confidence runs the risk of the same regrets. If the desire for confidence expresses itself in tough-on-crime bills or bellicose international invasions supposedly to protect veiled women from extremist patriarchs, the allegorical figures of the muscular Christian and the maternal feminist remain powerful in Canadian public awareness. *The Foreigner*'s engagement with modernity is not a sign of a past that has disappeared. Its project speaks directly to the present.

DANIEL COLEMAN, *McMaster University*

Note

1   For this afterword, I spell "Metis" without the accent in accordance with the
     preferred spelling of the *Canadian Oxford Dictionary*. In practice, however, both
     "Metis" and "Métis" continue to be used by scholars, organizations, and individuals,
     and both forms are acceptable in English. The Metis Council of Ontario, the Metis
     Association of the NWT, and the Manitoba Metis Federation use the unaccented
     spelling, whereas the Métis National Council uses the accented spelling. These
     different spellings reflect the diversity of heritages and histories referred to by this
     important term.

Works Cited

Ahmed, Sara. *Strange Encounters: Embodied Others in Post-Coloniality*. London:
     Routledge, 2000. Print.

"At Least 3,000 Died in Residential Schools, Research Shows." *CBC News Online*. CBC,
     18 Feb. 2013. Web. 10 Mar. 2013.

Berger, Carl. *The Sense of Power: Studies in the Ideas of Canadian Imperialism 1867–1914*.
     Toronto: U of Toronto P, 1970. Print.

———. "The True North Strong and Free." *Nationalism in Canada*. Ed. Peter Russell.
     Toronto: McGraw–Hill, 1966. 3–26. Print.

Bryce, George. *The Romantic Settlement of Lord Selkirk's Colonists: The Pioneers of
     Manitoba*. Winnipeg: Russell, Lang, 1909. Print.

Canada. "Canadian Multiculturalism Act." *Justice Laws Website*. Government of Canada,
     1988. Web. 19 Mar. 2013.

———. "2001 Census: Aboriginal Peoples of Canada." *Statistics Canada*. Government of
     Canada, n.d. Web. 10 Mar. 2013.

Cardinal, Harold, and Walter Hildebrandt, ed. and comp. *Treaty Elders of Saskatchewan:
     Our Dream Is That Our Peoples Will One Day Be Clearly Recognized as Nations*. Calgary:
     U of Calgary P, 2000. Print.

Coleman, Daniel. *White Civility: The Literary Project of English Canada*. Toronto: U of
     Toronto P, 2006. Print.

Ferré, John P. *A Social Gospel for the Millions: The Religious Bestsellers of Charles Sheldon,
     Charles Gordon, and Harold Bell Wright*. Bowling Green: Bowling Green State
     U Popular P, 1988. Print.

Gibbon, John Murray. *Canadian Mosaic: The Making of a Northern Nation*. Toronto: McClelland & Stewart, 1938. Print.

Gordon, Charles William. *Postscript to Adventure: The Autobiography of Ralph Connor*. 1938. Toronto: McClelland & Stewart, 1975. Print.

Henderson, Jennifer. *Settler Feminism and Race Making in Canada*. Toronto: U of Toronto P, 2003. Print.

Hulan, Renée. *Northern Experience and the Myths of Canadian Culture*. Montreal: McGill–Queen's UP, 2002. Print.

Karr, Clarence. *Authors and Audiences: Popular Canadian Fiction in the Early Twentieth Century*. Montreal: McGill–Queen's UP, 2000. Print.

Leacock, Stephen. "Greater Canada: An Appeal." 1907. *The Social Criticism of Stephen Leacock*. Ed. Alan Bowker. Toronto: U of Toronto P, 1973. 4–11. Print.

Lecker, Robert, Jack David, and Ellen Quigley, eds. *Canadian Writers and Their Works: Fiction Series*. Vol. 3. Toronto: ECW, 1988. Print.

Lennox, John. "Charles W. Gordon ['Ralph Connor'] (1860–1937)." Lecker, David, and Quigley 103–59.

Mack, D. Barry. "Modernity without Tears: The Mythic World of Ralph Connor." *The Burning Bush and a Few Acres of Snow: The Presbyterian Contribution to Canadian Life and Culture*. Ed. William Klempa. Ottawa: Carleton UP, 1994. 139–57. Print.

MacLaren, Eli. *Dominion and Agency: Copyright and the Structuring of the Canadian Book Trade, 1867–1918*. Toronto: U of Toronto P, 2011. Print.

Manguel, Alberto. *A History of Reading*. Toronto: Alfred A. Knopf Canada, 1996. Print.

McLaren, Angus. *Our Own Master Race: Eugenics in Canada, 1885–1945*. Toronto: McClelland & Stewart, 1990. Print.

McLeod, Neal. *Cree Narrative Memory: From Treaties to Contemporary Times*. Saskatoon: Purich, 2007. Print.

"Métis Celebrate Historic Supreme Court Land Ruling." *CBC News Online*. CBC, 8 Mar. 2013. Web. 19 Mar. 2013.

Mihaychuk, W.J. Review of *The Foreigner*, by Ralph Connor. *The Canadian Magazine* Mar. 1910: 487–89. Print.

Owram, Doug. *Promise of Eden: The Canadian Expansionist Movement and the Idea of the West, 1856–1900*. Toronto: U of Toronto P, 1980. Print.

Swyripa, Frances. *Ukrainian Canadians: A Survey of Their Portrayal in English-Language Works*. Edmonton: U of Alberta P, 1978. Print.

Thompson, J. Lee, and John H. Thompson. "Ralph Connor and the Canadian Identity." *Queen's Quarterly* 79.2 (1972): 159–70. Print.

Valverde, Mariana. *The Age of Light, Soap, and Water: Moral Reform in English Canada, 1885–1925*. Toronto: McClelland & Stewart, 1991. Print.

Vipond, Mary. "Best Sellers in English Canada, 1899–1918: An Overview." *Journal of Canadian Fiction* 24 (1979): 96–119. Print.

———. "Best Sellers in English Canada: 1919–1928." *Journal of Canadian Fiction* 35–36 (1986): 73–106. Print.

Waterston, Elizabeth. *Rapt in Plaid: Canadian Literature and Scottish Tradition*. Toronto: U of Toronto P, 2001. Print.

Watt, F.W. "Western Myth: The World of Ralph Connor." *Writers of the Prairies*. Ed. Donald G. Stephens. Vancouver: UBC P, 1973. 7–16. Print.

Woodcock, George. Introduction. Lecker, David, and Quigley 7–19.

Woodsworth, J.S. *Strangers within Our Gates, or Coming Canadians*. 1909. Toronto: U of Toronto P, 1972. Print.

Books in the Early Canadian Literature Series
Published by Wilfrid Laurier University Press

The Foreigner: A Tale of Saskatchewan / Ralph Connor / Afterword by Daniel Coleman / 2014 / x + 302 pp. / ISBN 978-1-55458-944-9

Painted Fires / Nellie L. McClung / Afterword by Cecily Devereux / forthcoming 2014 / ISBN 978-1-55458-979-1

The Traditional History and Characteristic Sketches of the Ojibway Nation / George Copway / Afterword by Shelley Hulan / forthcoming 2014 / ISBN 978-1-55458-976-0

The Seats of the Mighty / Gilbert Parker / Afterword by Andrea Cabajsky / forthcoming 2014 / ISBN 978-1-77112-044-9

The Forest of Bourg-Marie / S. Frances Harrison / Afterword by Cynthia Sugars / forthcoming 2014 / ISBN 978-1-77112-029-6